Snake in the City

Roy McLarty left school at fifteen and was glad to, worked on farms and in shops, sang in a band, married and had two children. Returned to education in his thirties, became a university lecturer and made frequent appearances on TV and radio.

In 1980 he moved to Norfolk where he taught and directed thousands of students, found time to write papers and sit on several Boards where he saw a lot of the City.

Roy likes cycling, meeting people, and finds something new every day in life.

Dr McLarty, PhD, MBA, MA, was awarded an Emeritus Professorship in 2005. He is also a visiting Professor at various international universities.

Roy McLarty

Snake in the City

A CIP catalogue record for this title is
available from the British Library.

ISBN 978 1 84963 220 1

www.austinmacauley.com

First Published (2012)
Austin & Macauley Publishers Ltd.
25 Canada Square
Canary Wharf
London
E14 5LB

Printed & Bound in Great Britain

Dedication

To my wife Mary, my family and friends for support.

Acknowledgements

Written in collaboration with my brother John.

Also, many thanks to Dexter Petley, Bill Napier and Clem Dane for encouragement and kind suggestions.

1

Time was moving on when the radio said there had been a fatal shooting at Great Square and that made me look up because I was due there in an hour. The report didn't elaborate, shootings are ten a penny in London and there were probably no details available anyway. Yet there was something unsettling about it. A shooting? Surely that had nothing to do with the Snake or the day's activities? Without doubt he was capable of murder but that would be a serious departure from type, risking a blaze of publicity that he of all people would not welcome. So it was probably nothing more than a coincidence, though that's something a lot of people don't believe in. That said, in the absence of any motive, it was likely to be just that, so I continued to glue my false beard.

Then I took out the letter and reread it.

The Snake will be at the Great Square Event. Be there.

The writer had omitted to sign the missive and seemed determined to say as little as possible, but that's only to be expected when the Snake's involved. For more than a year I had nursed a compulsive loathing of the man, the only person I had ever hated in my life and it was intriguing to know he would be at Great Square. But there were difficulties. Who knew enough to write the thing? I held it to the light and saw bog-standard office paper without telltale signs. It bore only its double spaced message, was undated and had been printed by a computer. The paper was creased exactly into two folds and the envelope was addressed to Mr Ron Miles and seemed to have come from the same device. But what about its message? That was something else. The writer would have to know about my preoccupation with the Snake and so far as I could see that limited the senders to the grand total of three: the Snake himself, Frank, and of course Wallace.

First I eliminated the Snake. What motive could he have for such a thing? I was one person he would wish to avoid and he was too conceited to refer to himself as the Snake. Then there was Frank and he had no motive either, nor had he access to a computer, this being the eighties. Third, there was Wallace, and he was a negative too. That very morning he'd phoned me and mentioned nothing. Why should he? There was no money in it and Wallace has no other interests.

Which raised the possibility of a fourth person: but that presented a difficulty. This individual would probably be on the Snake's side of the divide. Possibly he had told someone who had then written the letter after falling foul of him. Yet it was unlikely: the Snake was too cold a fish to confide in anyone and even if he did, it was questionable if he would pass on my details. You don't want your enemies uniting.

Of course there was a case for ignoring the whole thing but I wasn't tempted to do that. When you're on your way up, it's bad policy to ignore banana skins and he was an outstanding example of the genre. He had conned me once and though it was unlikely I'd ever recoup my money, it made sense to watch him from a distance. He knew too much about me while I knew nothing about him. And I had to admit to a fascination for a man who could flit between identities and somehow come out on top without once revealing his true self.

Unlikely that he was involved in the shooting, but there was no doubt he was dangerous and it would be best if he didn't spot me. Theoretically, he should have been avoiding me, but in the real world it doesn't work that way. His motives in attending the event were obscure, but quite possibly he'd have backup, so I elected to go incognito in old clothes and a false beard. And it wasn't bad either; I couldn't recognise myself in the mirror. Then I switched off the radio and left by the back stairs in case one of my fancy neighbours saw me in disguise.

Outside, the rain had ceased and the streets were almost dry, though the clouds were heavy and there was a damp wind that promised more rain. I had arranged to meet Frank on the way and found him waiting at the agreed corner where I amused myself by limping past him before he recognised me. He wasn't pleased, but then he seldom is.

"Oh it's you. You should be on the stage."

"Everything okay?"

"How could it be? Let's go."

And go we did, with Frank lighting a gasper as he plodded beside me, staring at the road and blowing smoke in my direction.

He was eight years older than me, thin as a matchstick, with a Wyatt Earp moustache that didn't work. Having done two years for burglary, he was resentful of life's little surprises. Today, things were bad: his wife – a blonde bombshell who should have known better – had made off with her current lover and taken their toddler with her. This had happened before and each time with a different man. It seemed the lady liked variety. He had agreed to come for thirty minutes only.

"You're better off without her," I said by way of comfort.

"You can be damn ignorant at times!"

At that point I had been thinking about the Snake and I may have seemed flippant – I've been accused of that before – but his reaction was over the top and I made an angry reply. For a moment it looked like he would walk away, but he lowered his head and continued. Now we were both irritated, walking too fast, not speaking or looking at each other. I am not without sympathy, but I don't see why I should get my head bitten off just because his wife wants a change.

Soon the traffic was jammed, with red tail lights as far as the eye could see, possibly because the roads had been sealed off at Great Square. In silence, we crossed to the other side and walked for half a mile before turning to a footpath that was strewn with broken bottles and dog turds and which brought us to an open-air market that was milling with people. I caught a glimpse of our sullen faces as we passed a shop window. Then we emerged onto a main road and my mood lightened. The prospect of seeing the Snake created all kinds of possibilities and I might need all the goodwill I could get.

"What was the shooting?" I said to break the silence. For years I'd nursed the suspicion that Frank was a police nark without having seen anything to support it. Certainly he knew a lot of things. Contact would be made by phone and his handler would ply him with police gossip to keep him talking. The cops are good at that kind of thing.

"No idea," he said, sounding grumpy, but he was going to come round. "The bloke was CID or something."

"Drugs?"

"Dunno… well, probably not. He'd be above that. What's today's plan?"

"Locate the Snake, that's all. I might follow him."

"Eh? I'd be careful on that one."

Yes, so would I.

"It don't sound his kinda thing. You're sure he'll be there?"

"Dunno."

Of course a hunch based on an anonymous letter was a poor basis for a decision and this was a dangerous man. At that point in my life, I was on a high – according to *The Times*, I was now the City's top investment manager – a position that could be destroyed by one set of bad figures, or one act of sheer stupidity and I was capable of both. When you're at the top the only way is down. Perhaps I should have ignored Great Square, it wasn't necessary to see the Snake and the stolen money was petty beside my Donald Fund. Yes, the man was dangerous and of course there had been a shooting. But we plodded on.

At 11.45, we arrived at our destination. All neighbouring streets had been closed to traffic and the area had been pedestrianised for the day. Across the Square, the great building had been revamped and was looking well, with a series of fluted columns rising to the roof and a huge array of flags on its first floor balcony. I think the owner wanted to create a store to rival Harrods, but the area was wrong and I had my doubts about his chances. On the Square itself, a colourful stage had been erected on which a band of twelve musicians was giving a good account of itself. There were a number of kiddies' entertainments and the area was congested with young couples and their broods.

"Too much happening," muttered Frank, shaking his head at the crowds and possibly upset to see so many happy families.

The carnival atmosphere gave the impression that everybody was having a good time and the noise was attracting still more. Pretty girls were distributing free sweets and silver balloons to the delight of the kids who were running amok. Frank jumped when there was a loud bang behind us.

"I thought that was mortar fire from the Snake," he said. "I take it I'm here for observation, I don't go near him?"

"That's right."

"Suits me. Okay we split. You stay here and I'll do the far side. At least he's easy to spot… If he's here… Now listen, if I see him I'll wave this rolled up paper like I'd spotted a long lost friend. You'll come and join me."

"Right. If I get lost meet me at the far corner."

"You don't get lost. I've only got thirty minutes, remember."

And he disappeared while I barged through the crowds for ten minutes seeing neither my quarry nor the rolled-up newspaper.

Perhaps the letter had been a hoax. I returned to my original position.

Come noon, the amusements ground to a standstill, the band played a fanfare and a team of executives came on to the stage with the boss at the front waving nervously at the crowd. Then Billy Bolde, the guest comedian, was at the rostrum to rapturous applause. He was shorter than he seemed on the box and wore a suit of near luminous blue.

Clutching a silver balloon, I felt some concern for the man. In church I have often had to listen to our vicar mess things up with a few words to a restless congregation, but this was no church, there were thousands of people present and most of them were young. The amusements were the attraction, not the platform party, and once you lose the sympathy of a big crowd you're in trouble. But the man was brilliant, with a witticism in every sentence that even the youngest seemed to appreciate. His secret was brevity. We applauded when he introduced us to the multimillionaire who had made it all possible, then after a good joke he declared the 'Emporium of Emporiums' open and it was over.

The band began to play as the senior men shook hands with each other and made their way back into the building followed by crowds of potential shoppers who were no doubt influenced by the Lucky Draw of a car.

A voice in my ear made me jump.

"Well, he ain't here."

"No... I didn't see him either."

"Hardly his thing... He'd be an alien here. More so than usual."

I let my balloon soar into the air. The visit had been enjoyable but there was little chance of finding him among that crowd.

"There he is!"

In the act of turning, my eye caught a tall figure among the dignitaries filing into the building. It was the Snake, and even at this distance I could see he was dressed in his trademark suit with maroon waistcoat. Curiously, his superciliousness seemed to be on the back burner, his head was down and his shoulders were slumped, perhaps he was indignant at having been at the back. He was carrying an attaché case.

"What's *he* doing on the platform?" said Frank.

A good question, but we had work to do: we began to push our way into the building and it took an age before we could get through the door. By that time it was all too likely my quarry had gone, clearly it was going to be difficult to find anyone among those hordes, even if he was six and a half feet tall.

"What's going on," said Frank, frowning at me, "what's he up to?"

"Dunno, but I'll bet there's money in it."

Although the entrance hall was big, the fire regulations must have been breached by the sheer size of the crowd. At the centre, there was a raised dais on which the owner entertained a number of visitors while Billy Bolde signed autographs on a lower plinth and a gorgeous girl handed free lollipops to all and sundry. Ahead, there were the bright lights of the women's department, while on the right and left two moving stairways carried people upwards. My gut feeling was that he was somewhere in the hall beside us.

"I'll try the escalator – There he is!"

He was a mere ten paces in front of us, stepping on to the crowded escalator and he didn't look pleased. Frank hesitated.

"Time's up, I'd better go."

"Frank, stay for two minutes. Please."

Annoyed, he fell in behind me and we began to move forward, pushing our way through the shoppers who were streaming in all directions. Ten paces is a lifetime in a crowd. Naturally he was gone when we reached the next floor.

"Lost him," muttered Frank, angry. He'd wanted to get away. "Put your head down. Try and look like a shopper. I'll do the watching."

This floor erred towards the functional rather than the grand, though it had the advantage of being less crowded. I adopted my lame walk and paused at a set of cutlery. I had a feeling he'd been in the company of another man or a group of men but now I saw only typical shoppers around me.

"There he is," said Frank in an undertone.

Then I saw him, mean-faced and seemingly angry, as he ascended the escalator to the next floor and, yes, he was with a Middle Eastern man who looked familiar and who was leaning over to make a point while the Snake leaned away. He too was carrying a parcel. They were totally unaware of us.

"Come on."

"Not too fast, something's going on."

"Right then, you lead."

Annoyed, he turned to the stairs and I followed him. At the next floor the Snake had disappeared again.

Here, another stairway rose upwards but he hadn't had time to use it. I browsed through a swatch of cloths and kept my head down for there were now relatively few people around us. Frank stood back and watched before giving me a slight nod.

In the background, a man approached talking in accented English and I heard the Snake answer him with one word at which point I caught their reflection in the glass. He was no more than twenty paces away and his companion was engaged in a long rant that was clearly annoying him. Was it possible that we had walked past them without noticing? John Masters, my old trainer, would have despaired of me.

"Where were they?" I muttered.

"Dunno... Better watch yourself. If I was you I'd hop it."

"They've spotted us?"

"No, don't think so. Can I go now?"

Clearly he was fed up with it all. I slipped him his money and he disappeared.

Behind, there was a change in their voices as the Snake and his companion took the stairs to the next level. After some indecision I followed to find myself on the top floor where a few shoppers were looking at fancy rugs. On the right, a door opened to Carpets which boasted an enormous range of floor coverings. Inside, the Snake and his companion could just be seen as they walked to the opposite side of the room. I saw him glance at his watch.

At this point I was tempted to leave. This floor was nearly deserted and if he looked around he wouldn't be fooled by my false beard for a minute, but why should I worry about that? Surely I was perfectly safe in the heart of London? So I followed them into a long rectangular room that could easily hold a hundred people. It was well lit with no windows and was festooned with carpets, some piled waist-high in great bundles in the middle of the floor. The

Snake was out of sight and I had to assume he had exited by a door on the far side. A salesman was displaying an Axminster to a middle-aged couple. Four people of Middle Eastern origin, a tall woman and three men, were standing at the back as though they were waiting for something. I didn't like the look of them.

Edging my way to the far door, I ignored the *private* sign and tried the handle to find it locked. Sensing a threat I looked up to find the four scowling at me. Curiously they didn't look like shoppers. All innocent, I paused to admire a Ship's Wilton that had a price tag to frighten an oil sheik. The locked door had surprised me. Meanwhile the couple decided the Axminster was too expensive and began to leave. This altered the attitude of the four, who straightened up and began moving towards the door while I, too, decided to leave. The man and wife, innocent of events, paused at the door as the woman wondered if she should have another look at the carpet while the man grumbled at the price. By this time the four were around me. The salesman, displeased at the lost sale, was frowning and shaking his head. Then the couple went through the door. I attempted to follow and was knocked to the floor by a blow to my shoulder while the door was closed with a bang. The salesman's mouth was opening and closing: neither of us could believe that this was happening.

"You are a hostage of the People's Republic of Unpronounceable," said the tall woman with some pride, as though I'd just won a coconut.

2

Throughout my life I have been involved in acts of stupidity, but all of these faded to zero beside the present debacle. What kind of grown man walks into a trap like this? I should have ignored the letter because the writer's motives were unknown. Frank had smelt a rat when I'd mooted attending it and had been careful to disappear long before things went belly up. I had blundered, wide-eyed, into a mess that promised to be the biggest mistake of my life.

Now it became bedlam. First, one of the men went to the telephone and after some shouting got connected to 'the chief of security', demanding that the entire building be evacuated immediately. He and his fellows meant business, they were heavily armed and if there was any violence the results would be catastrophic. Then they began to shout at one another in their own language. This may well have been their standard mode of communication, but it sounded like a furious bust-up and was unsettling to listen to. The carpet salesman complained in a nervous voice and suddenly a fattish woman of about fifty rushed in, bawling in an Irish accent, ordering the four out. At this, a young boy, obviously the department's junior, came out of a side room and looked at us with his mouth open. Someone outside began banging on the door with such force that it was in danger of being knocked down.

A kidnapper gestured us into the far corner while they worked among themselves, producing objects from a large carton in the opposite side of the room. Disconcertingly, these included handguns as well as a collection of grenades, knives and what looked like two AK-47s. The Snake's attaché case was on the top of the bundle, no doubt other things had been brought in by sympathisers.

Since their backs were to us, I tried the far door again to find it was still locked. "Where's the key?" I said to the fat woman, but she was in shock and didn't grasp my question. The salesman produced a bunch of keys but we found it was blocked by a key in the other side.

"Is this an exit?" I said, gesturing at the door.

"Yes, it's the backstairs."

I put my shoulder to the door, but it wouldn't budge. At this there was a bellow from the man who had struck me. Clutching a black handgun, he ran over and ordered us against the wall. It's a senior moment when a maniac comes at you with a gun. Then the tall woman said something at which he returned to his fellows.

Ten minutes, which seemed like twenty years, passed with the phone ringing continuously. The wail of sirens competed with the noise of a megaphone as they cleared the Square.

"We'd better do something," said the salesman to me.

"Don't let me stop you."

Across the room they were still arguing, every one of them shouting while we stood against the wall and looked at them with white faces. Easy to dismiss them as idiots, but somewhere in that chaos there was order. They were heavily armed and had some kind of objective. The woman said something and the tallest man went to the department's phone to announce that in thirty minutes he would read a statement to the press in the rug department next door. No policemen or soldiers would be allowed. Only one TV team would be permitted, the press could take all the photographs they wanted, but no weapons would be tolerated. If there was any funny stuff they would shoot to kill. His accent was almost unintelligible and he'd a tendency to shout.

"Is there another way out?" I said to the salesman, who looked at me without seeming to comprehend the question.

"The fire escape, through that corridor," said the boy.

But that meant crossing the room in full view of the maniacs. It might have been possible five minutes ago but now it was clearly too late.

By this time they were all holding guns and one had a breast belt from which the grenades were suspended. Not a pretty sight. The woman produced a padlock and passed it to a man who hurried off to seal the door in the corridor. Then they became silent as they looked at us with narrowed eyes. The woman uttered an order and they seized the whimpering salesman.

But it was nothing more than an airport-style search at which the thug who had hit me seemed accomplished. I stood back, all too aware that my false beard declared I was not quite an innocent shopper. At that time there had been a lot of terrorist activity, it was almost a ritual to shoot a hostage and a pain in my gut told me that they didn't shoot women or boys – I was the likely candidate. Meanwhile they removed a pen and keys from the salesman. Next it was the young chap's turn during which they found nothing and then the manageress was searched under her loud complaints which must have been audible in the street below. Madam Boss rebuked him for his clumsiness: the woman's protest might give the authorities all the excuse they needed for a shoot-out. Next it was my turn and I couldn't believe it, he failed to spot the beard and I had nothing of the remotest interest to him.

Then the smallest and youngest of the gang gestured for me to sit on a pile of carpets where he fastened a plastic tie around my ankles and tied my hands behind my back. This was repeated with my fellow hostages. He pushed me so that I was lying on my back, but I struggled back to a sitting position, the ceiling being an object of no great interest. The tie was strong and unbreakable and he had a carton of them.

Here the tall woman produced a mirror to examine her face, dabbing make-up on her nose and turning her head to take advantage of the light, brushing her long black hair, to tease a few difficult tresses. Then they donned black masks and walked to the door which was opened by the grenade carrier to the sounds of a crowd outside. The tall man read a statement in accented English that was inaudible to us, sounding both fierce and, at the same time, nervous, like a rookie sergeant at a royal parade. Flashes from cameras illuminated the carpet department with their own peculiar violence. The statement over, there was an eruption of questions in all kinds of voices which he declined to answer. Obviously there were scores of reporters next door and I envied them their freedom.

Madam Boss uttered an order and they stepped back. The door was closed, locked, and the key removed: a bad moment. We were now confined with the four scowling maniacs. The manageress uttered a half scream, while I wondered at my own sanity. All four removed their masks.

"What's going to happen?" said the boy, in a frightened voice.

"Terrorists," said the salesman, making the understatement of the year, watching the men carry a long table from a side room on which they placed their handguns, two AK-47s, and what looked like military walkie-talkies as well as the phone. There was also an array of knives that would have impressed a Glasgow gang. Chairs were brought so that each had a position at the table. Two had pale chins which indicated they'd recently shaved their beards. Soon Madam Boss was reading a foolscap document as though she was waiting for a plane, the tall man had a magazine about sports cars, while the man with the grenades cleaned his guns with relish.

"I want the toilet," said the fat woman.

This was ignored.

"I want the toilet."

The tall woman made a relaxed remark at which they untied her and she was escorted away by the smallest man.

"Could we rush them?" said the salesman.

"Are you off your head?" I said, sotto.

There was some shouting and a bit of scuffling before the manageress returned.

"Beast! He kept the door open."

"Do any of you wish – to toilet?" said the small man.

We all elected to go, which happened one at a time. This involved a walk of about twenty paces along a corridor that had several windows, all of them barred, overlooking the flat roof. From the terrorists' viewpoint, it was a poor position that could be rushed by any squad of soldiers, the SAS would consider it a doddle, though the last thing I wanted was a shoot-out.

In minutes we were returned to our places, trussed up again, with nothing to do except watch the gang and it wasn't a pretty sight. Then the tall man who had read the statement heaved himself to his feet and approached the manageress.

"What is name, plis?"

For this he got a mouthful of abuse.

"Name, plis," and a steely note had crept into his voice.

"Better tell him," I said, and she did. He wrote slowly in block capitals, his face screwed up in concentration.

"Address."

Why a terrorist, of all persons, needed our details was a surprise to me and there was no way I would co-operate. I too was on unlawful business of a sort and all of one's instincts are to avoid attention. He took the salesman's next and then the boy's, writing each on a separate page. Then he stepped in front of me with pen raised.

"John Smith, 18 Bakevan Drive," I muttered.

Yes, I'd done the right thing. For the moment, I'd hide my cards and hope for the best. There was no such address though there were certainly tens of thousands of Smiths. Of course there was a risk they'd get my identity when my absence was noticed in my work. Tomorrow I'd miss the organ and on Monday I'd fail to appear at Howardsons and they'd phone my flat immediately (I had several appointments). When there was no reply they would phone the vicar, my nominated next-of-kin, who would confirm my absence on Sunday. Then they'd call the police who, sooner or later, might note that the missing man resembled 'John Smith' with his false address and false beard. But did these things matter? The real question – the only one that mattered – was whether I would survive.

"We eat soon, what you want?" said the man.

I had no appetite and no doubt the others didn't feel like eating either, but I said: "Tea and a cheese roll."

Of course there would be no tea. John Masters had been firm on that one; a cup of tea, or any other hot beverage, is an excellent weapon and no doubt our kidnappers knew that too.

The others elected for something similar and yes, the drinks would be cold. The man at the phone barked out an order that took five minutes of which the lion's share was for themselves. The voice at the other end queried something.

"You knock at door in an hour. Only one person... pushing trolley... one only. I hand over list of hostages. No funny stuff. Or we all die, right."

He seemed proud of his status: the way he addressed the cop had to be heard to be believed. Maybe they owed him money.

"It's my girlfriend's birthday," said the salesman to me with a whine. "I was taking her to an Indian – An' it's the first day in my new job too."

Yes we were all experiencing an unwelcome interruption to our dull lives. I hoped that was all he had to worry about.

At this point my mouth went dry when I looked up to see the tall woman, one eye closed, frowning in concentration and aiming an AK-47 at me. Time came to a standstill and I was too paralysed to throw myself to the side, but it was all right, she was merely checking the sights. She handed it back to the grenade carrier for adjustment. Something in my gut told me I was expendable.

Suddenly Madam Boss put her papers down and came over. Rather unnerving to have this tall woman looking down at me when I was trussed like a chicken, but at least she wasn't wielding her gun. She'd a silk scarf around her neck that did little to soften her bitter mouth. I couldn't see her hurrying home to feed the kids.

"What is your occupation?"

"Um... wages clerk."

"Ah – It's not very nice being tied up, I'm sorry about that, but it will all work out in the end, it really will. Try and make yourself as comfortable as possible."

I looked at her to see if this was some kind of humour, but no, she was deadly serious. No doubt the trick is to keep the victims as compliant as possible. There was now no trace of a foreign accent, she wore expensive clothes, smelt of expensive perfume and her hands were cleaner than a surgeon's. Curiously, her fingers were trembling.

"How long have we got?" asked the fat woman, in a tone that implied she was ready to start screaming.

"Ah now, sadly I do not have the answer to that. Others are negotiating your release and I have no knowledge of their progress, but you will be well fed and as comfortable as possible. We will not harm you and neither will the local forces."

We hope. Despite these big noises, they looked like a bunch of maniacs to me and the idea that it was a jolly party that would end with a handshake seemed a bit lyrical. Mind you, I hoped the SAS would share her sentiments.

"Bully for her in her designer suit," muttered the manageress in her Irish accent, as Madam Boss turned away. "Costs a month's wages... Strutting her stuff like Lady Muck. An' her bum still looks big."

When under stress some people say provocative things. I'd a feeling John Masters would advise against the expression of such sentiments.

Suddenly I felt a jab, as though I'd been touched by a stiletto. Only now did a detail in my subconscious come to the fore and that was last night's shooting. What had happened? A man dead, and it happened at Great Square. Was it the work of this bunch of maniacs? If so, it gave the lie to Madam Boss's speech. Had the dead man learnt something of their plans? Granted, it would be unwise for terrorists to risk their project with an on-site killing, but given their mentality, it was doubtful if they'd let a man's life get in their way. At the very least, the shooting was a tremendous coincidence.

Madam Boss returned to her table to empower one of the walky-talkies and speaking in a foreign language uttered several carefully pronounced words, of which the opening was 'Ahmad'. This seemed to be important to her. That completed, they began to speak among themselves and suddenly they were arguing while she gestured for calm. In the midst of a volley of words there was also mention of Abdel and Elias. A memory stirred. This trio, Ahmad, Abdel and Elias – I had dealt with them at Howardsons several months ago. What a co-incidence!

"They're mad," said salesman under his breath. "Ravin'."

He might have been right though I was in no position to claim sanity, having allowed my hatred of the Snake to get me into the mess. Without doubt he was a dangerous man in league with the terrorists. His contacts would be useful for bringing money and equipment into the country. I recalled Ahmad, Abdel and Elias laughing when I asked who had recommended them to Howardsons. But I was overstating his interest in me. The Snake didn't know I'd followed him and besides why would he want me involved when I might – provided I survived – give evidence against him? Or did that mean I wouldn't survive? Also there was no sign the terrorists were remotely interested in Ron Miles, having accepted my alias of 'John Smith' without a query. So I had been right, the Snake was not the author of the letter.

"Will they let me go if I say I've got asthma?" said the boy. "I can prove it, my inhaler's in my jacket."

"No chance," said the woman. "Be a man. We're here for a while."

She was right. We hadn't heard their statement: but in the great tradition of kidnappers they were probably making demands that the government would ignore.

Lunch arrived on time and they loosed our hands so that we could eat. Most of the food went to our captors who spread it on their table and ate ravenously while we hostages ate sparingly.

Thirty minutes later the phone rang to be answered with some reluctance by the tall man who, after listening for a few moments, put his hand on the mouthpiece and addressed some remarks to Madam Boss. This brought a roar from the others, who started shouting. The phone was slammed down while the row continued for five minutes after which the tall woman had her way. Plainly, she was the commanding officer though she didn't seem to enjoy the respect of her troops. Eventually the phone was lifted and the conversation renewed. Then the tall man stood up and said to us:

"You will identify yourselves on phone, right? Say your names and that you are okay. Say nothing else or we cut, right?" His knife had a serrated blade. It wasn't clear whether he would cut the line or the hostage.

He approached me first and held the phone to my mouth.

"John Smith, I'm all right," I muttered.

The others did the same and then the phone was returned to the desk. Ten minutes later it rang again and after some words he said to me:

"You – they can't get your address."

"Tell them I'm fine."

"What address?"

"I forget."

"You hear him say it," he shouted into the mouthpiece. "He is okay. You no' trouble me, right." And the phone was slammed down.

Since few of us forget our address, it might be obvious that I had something to hide and I waited for him to take a knife to jog my memory, but he seemed to have other things on his mind.

"All's well," said Madam Boss. "It's going to plan."

Yes, the plan. So far the kidnap would be a minor item in the world news, front page stuff in the London papers for a couple of days and thereafter consigned to page five with no coverage in the foreign press. *Four people imprisoned in a Carpet Department* hardly makes for sensational reading, but the terrorists hadn't hired the Snake or smuggled weapons into the building just to blow a damp squib. There was sure to be something else. And it would probably involve bloodshed.

Now there was more activity. From her handbag, Madam Boss produced three envelopes which she passed to her henchmen, checking their names as she did so. Their attitude implied that this was important and they ripped the high-quality paper to reveal a booklet and a credit card which they each studied with care, not looking at one another. Something jabbed me. These booklets were passports, probably false ones. She was handing them new identities and that meant (unless the passports were nothing more than a sop to keep her troops loyal) they intended to escape. An incredible assumption, given that the place was surrounded by cops. Or was it? John Masters had always said the impossible became easier if you first immobilised your enemy and there were several ways to do that. One was an act of violence and here I found myself wondering about a bomb in Great Square – they were certainly capable of it. In the confusion it might be possible to get away – perhaps a copter could be landed on the flat roof outside, I didn't know. But it would make big headlines and that's what terrorism is all about.

But where would that leave the hostages? I'd a funny feeling that our lives were already forfeited. They wouldn't want us to talk. A grenade would do the trick nicely. No, it would be a knife. The brute would enjoy cutting our throats.

Time passed slowly and I found myself planning a miraculous escape. If they could do it, so could I. It was uncomfortable to lie on my back with my hands tied beneath me and to lie face down wasn't the solution either. We had fish and chips for dinner, the terrorists had many arguments, the phone rang often, and darkness fell.

3

It was the darkest hour of the night when I gave my keeper a light kick. Since my hands and feet were tied, this took some manoeuvring. My head was buzzing, my hands were shaking, and I could hardly breathe. This was the hour of action when armies launch surprise attacks, the hour when their enemies were most likely to be sound asleep, and in my case, the hour of sheer desperation since the opportunity would never come again. Later in the day the police and military would have the place under wraps, oodles of monitoring devices would be installed and the carpet department would be more secure than a prison.

Last night Madam Boss had protested when sounds had been heard next door and had obtained assurance that no one would be allowed on to the fourth floor without her authority. She had also refused to sanction any lights in the Carpet Department and we had retired early, with the terrorists making little dens for themselves among the carpets – all except our keeper, the smallest man, who had to sleep beside us, and sleep he did. I had to prod him three times before he opened his eyes.

"Toilet."

He sat up rubbing his eyes, not moving for an entire minute. In the dim light I saw the salesman and the boy were asleep behind him and in the background the manageress was snoring with her mouth open. Lucky them: I hadn't slept at all.

An escape would involve all kinds of difficulties, but that was a risk I'd have to take. A big building of this size would have a number of exits and would be linked to other properties. Once outside I could rely on my old expertise, provided it wasn't swarming with coppers and that was unlikely at this time in the morning.

But this was dicey. John Masters had said I was a weakling without talent for action. My mindset was wrong; my strong point was the sneaky deal rather than confrontation and my chances were worse than any student he'd ever seen. Yet there was no alternative. If I remained passive I was finished.

He uttered a weary sigh and cut my ties with his knife. I rubbed my wrists and ankles as though suffering pins and needles. From what I could see of them, the gang were sound asleep. Madam Boss was on the same carpet as one of the men and they made a lovely pair. There was some snoring. The room was in near darkness, the sole source of light being the street lamps. My keeper stood up, still insensible, wanting to get back to sleep and looking at the floor with an anxious expression as he began to walk across the room, his head down, a pathetic little man who didn't seem to believe in his cause. At the entrance to the corridor he stopped and gestured for me to lead, which I did with shoulders slumped as though I too was half asleep. I noted with some misgivings that he had a strong frame, a bull neck, and broad shoulders and he seemed to be fit. In the corridor there was a swing door at which someone had placed an object to jam it open. I kicked it away, accidental-like, and it swung shut, almost striking my follower. With a bit of luck it would muffle sounds. This was life or death and only one of us would go the distance. I tried to keep a cool head but an aura of unreality began to fog my mind. The door to the toilets was wide open, revealing a wash basin and two stalls.

Hesitate and you're lost, or so they say, but how does an incompetent fighter kill a man who has presumably been trained in a terrorist camp? To make it worse you should never doubt yourself when you launch an attack.

I had a moment's hesitation in which my every instinct urged me to forget it. Stick to the routine and hope for the best. Only psychos and oddities strike another human being. And anyway I would get the worst of the exchange.

But no, it was all systems go.

Inside the toilets, I took a deep breath and swung round to stare in horror at his feet, drawing a fierce breath and pointing in alarm. His head went down and I was close enough to make a fierce chop at his neck, hitting him with all my weight in a terrible blow that almost broke my arm. But my aim was wild, the blow fell on a point between his shoulder and neck. But I had the advantage of surprise and he fell with a solid thump that shook the floor. I waited for him to rise up and kill me, but he lay still. A miracle.

Not a moment to lose I closed the door, opened the window, and began to pull at the bar but it was rock solid and the blow had damaged my hand to the extent that I could barely grasp it. This was a small window and it was difficult to get leverage. Then with both hands clutching the metal I put my feet against the wall and pulled but it wouldn't budge and I had to give up. I'd assumed this would be the easy bit, too.

So far there had been blissful silence from the terrorists, but for how long? Sweat poured from me when I went back to the corridor and opened the nearest window. This was a triple-barred system and the middle bar bent by several inches but it came in my direction rather than laterally and the gap remained impossibly narrow. By this time I was gasping for breath. Then I shifted one of the side bars and, in utter desperation, got my head into the cold night at some cost to my ears. Provided you're not too fat, your shoulders and pelvis need less width than your head, or so they say, and I wriggled out of the window at which point, being unable to find support, I fell with a thump on to the flat roof outside.

Everything was silent in the light drizzle as I scurried away, dreading the rage of the terrorists. Sounds don't carry well in a carpet salesroom, but my victim's fall must have been clearly audible. Of course there was another side to the problem and that was their own attitude. There is a scuffle and someone is deemed dead, but they might hesitate to rush to the rescue. For a start they don't know what's happened. A supposed assassin, if that's what I was, might bring them down. And I might not be the assassin, it might be the SAS.

Or perhaps they'd slept through the whole thing.

Then there was the question of the police. It being a fair assumption that there were more cops in the building than at the last Police Convention, there would surely be a listening post with various devices – or had they yet to be installed? In the early hours of the morning there is a blow – a relatively quiet one, certainly, but fisticuffs nevertheless – followed by the sound of a body hitting the floor. Surely that would be deemed an emergency with the phone blazing with queries about the hostages, yet nothing had happened. Perhaps they were sleeping too.

I ran silently with my head down. Recent building work had left a lot of debris on the roof that promised to trip me and I had to be careful: fortunately there were also various housings to mask me from the terrorists' window.

The carpet department was a big dormer built on to the third floor. At my feet were several skylights that would need a jemmy to open. In another place I found builders' things including scaffolding poles, heavy batons of wood and an old aluminium ladder – few roofs in London don't have some builders' props and here the work was ongoing – then I found myself looking down at Great Square fifty feet below me, with three bored policemen standing beside a van. A convoy of army trucks was parked in the middle where some sad-looking dodgems and kiddies' entertainments still remained. I tried the next side, to find a narrow lane about fifteen feet wide with several police vehicles parked below. Opposite, the building soared upwards for six floors and the windows were dark.

The depressing truth was that there were no exterior fire-escapes, the building was detached and there was no exit for me. Staring through one of the skylights, I saw a staffroom with a table and a fridge. It offered security and possibly food, perhaps I could hide there until the emergency was over? But the window was sealed like a vault.

"Use your head," they say. "There's always a way out."

Only now did I start to analyse the situation. Having killed a man in cold blood in a building surrounded by police, I was now trapped. Plainly the roof was no hiding place. When daylight came any passing plane would spot me and already there was a faint glow in the east. There wasn't even cover from the rain. I crossed to the far side to find another narrow lane which probably dated back to the nineteenth century and was just wide enough for two carts to pass. Fifty feet below, there were more police cars.

Opposite, there was a building of the same height, or a mere three feet higher, and it looked like the Promised Land as it stretched into the darkness, offering freedom from both terrorists and police. If I could only reach it I would be free. Then I remembered the ladder.

Returning to the pile of builders' junk, I grabbed it, upsetting some planks which slithered rather then fell. Would nothing go right? It wasn't in good nick either, but at least it looked as though it would bear my weight.

When laid across the lane there was length enough to spare, or so it seemed, though it would certainly bend with my weight. By now the eastern sky was a lot lighter and but for the rain clouds it might well have been daylight. Presumably the ladder was visible on the street below though any policeman's view would be masked by the lighting.

Thus began my precarious journey, not letting myself be deflected by the bending of the ladder or the terrible drop below me. Ladders are designed for vertical use, the rungs bit into my knees and shins and it would be easy to put a foot into empty space with a risk of overbalancing. I crawled with my eyes closed, being seriously afraid of heights, and in a moment of utter stupidity opened them when barely halfway. The drop was breathtaking. But that was the least of it: what was infinitely worse was that the ladder was bent like a bow. At that point I panicked and had to cling to the rungs, unable to move.

Curiously, now that it was too late, I wondered at the problems my fall would create. Why should an investment manager of staid, old Howardsons plunge off a building at five in the morning? My death would be deemed less than honourable and only a minor official from the firm would attend the funeral. Why would a supposedly sane man who influenced the investment of billions of pounds, cross between two buildings in a false beard and old clothes? Sir James would send a wreath with an anodyne note and some of the choir and possibly a few old ladies from the church would come to the funeral, otherwise it would be badly attended and the vicar would go easy on the eulogies.

No, not quite. They'd link my death to the man's demise – because shortly Madam Boss would have his body removed and there'd be confirmation that a hostage had escaped. Yes, they'd know the truth in no time. Ron Miles was up to no good, having failed to go to the police when he escaped. Or did he escape? Perhaps he was in league with the terrorists. Sir James wouldn't send the wreath.

But this would never do. Sooner or later a passing policeman would look up and see me clinging to the ladder like an outsize sloth. With eyes closed I crawled to the next rung – paused – then the next, not daring to look down, while the huge drop seemed to pull at me. Several years later my hand touched the opposite side and I pulled myself on to the flat roof – a close call – there was, in fact, a mere six inches of ladder to spare. I had broken the rules of *Health & Safety*: the ladder should have been secured to prevent it drifting. Trembling like a leaf, I had to sit for a full minute before I could collect my thoughts.

But it was getting light. Clumsily, I pulled the ladder across – it dangled for a breathtaking moment over the side and placed it beside a dormer. Then I began to walk away from the Square. The roofline continued at the same level over private dwellings and I had to move carefully since people were sleeping below me. At least I had some experience of flat roofs when Frank and I had dabbled in the art of the burglar.

I had never felt more miserable in my life and the drizzle didn't help, I was still vulnerable and images of the dead man's face kept coming to mind. Possibly I had over-reacted, he'd been the least offensive of the gang and I hated myself.

Somewhere along the way I found a building with scaffolding down to the street. Nearby, a dog began to bark, but that wasn't going to stop me: I moved on to the top tier and descended as silently as possible over its creaking surfaces, dropping the last eight feet because the bottom ladder had been removed for security purposes.

Straightening my shoulders I began to walk at a workman's pace. Having killed a man, I'd squeezed through a barred window, crossed a road from a height of fifty feet, and was now on terra firma with bruised ears, a sore back, and a genuine limp only to discover there was yet another problem. The street was closed with a barrier at the junction from which a grim policeman was watching me. I kept walking.

"Anything happened yet?" I asked.

He seemed on the young side, little more than a trainee and bored out of his head.

"No sir. What are you doing?"

"Oh, I live here, number 31. I'm off to work," I said, suddenly aware that my wet clothes were clear evidence that I'd been in the rain for some time.

But he noticed nothing. He turned away and I moved on.

4

Church was well-attended that morning and the service went reasonably well, though the organist was off-colour with a number of errors on the pedals not to mention a difficulty in relating to the spirit of things. His right hand was swollen, his fingers had some trouble with the chords and he started playing the third hymn before the vicar had finished announcing it. But one of the things about church is that nobody listens too critically and most of the congregation can be depended on to take a charitable view of my failings. Like all churches, it has its share of old ladies and I have always been their darling, they even greet me in the street like a long-lost grandson and they're all proud of my status in the City. I'd even been on the telly! Had I been as attractive to seventeen-year-old girls my lifestyle would have been changed beyond recognition.

The organist is expected to be there one hour in advance of the service to check the tunes and to rehearse the choir (who might or might not, depending on their numbers, sing an introit). I was five minutes late and they were talking among themselves about the Siege – a world event that was less than two miles away.

"What'll happen now it's over?" I asked big Bill, a police sergeant who sang bass.

"Over?" he said in surprise. "It isn't over. At least it wasn't when I left the house."

"But it must be!"

"Eh? Why must it? Who said it was over?"

He was looking at me with narrowed eyes and suddenly I felt uncertain of myself.

"...A man... a taxi-driver."

"How did he know? It wasn't on the news ten minutes ago."

"So it's still on?"

"Of course it is. They'll drag it out for a while."

Bill didn't know about the body and naturally I wasn't going to tell him.

That morning I'd slept like the dead for three hours after staggering in the door at six. I'd taken my false beard, shoes, and every single piece of clothing and sent them down the garbage chute. I'd burnt the letter, scrubbed myself – my fingernails were cleaner than any surgeon's, washed my hair with an energy I've never known before and here I was with blood still on my hands. There was also blood, or at least contusions, on my head too, having bruised both ears in my escape and my back was sore.

The service over, I went home to watch the news on the telly. The purpose of the Siege was to demand the release of a lunatic who had hijacked a plane with the loss of several lives and who was now in custody awaiting trial. Since he was in a foreign jail, the UK government had no powers to order his release, so the whole charade was about nothing more than publicity.

There were, if you can believe it, four terrorists and four hostages in the Carpet Department, a TV clip even showed lunch for eight being carried into the building past a guard of grim policemen. How could this be? Wasn't I a hostage and wasn't I sitting in my flat three miles away? A bearded psychologist was wheeled in to explain that the biggest problem for hostages was sheer boredom, nothing happened until they were released. Oh yes? How were they going to release me and how were they going to find *four* kidnappers? I couldn't see how the authorities would gain from this kind of misrepresentation. There then followed some details of the three hostages, with their photos and brief biography as well as interviews with their anxious relatives.

"There is a fourth hostage," said the commentator, "a Mr John Smith. For unknown reasons the kidnappers have refused to give his details. Scotland Yard want to know more about him. If you know a Mr John Smith who failed to come home last night, please contact them immediately and help us to clear up the mystery."

Wait... What if they didn't know I'd escaped? – Perhaps the Terrorists wouldn't care to air their failures to the world. But since you can't leave bodies lying around, Madam Boss would have to get my victim removed – therefore the authorities knew of his death and had consciously withheld that information.

The news continued. There was a protest march in central London to demand the release of the same hijacker whose ugly face was inflicted on the screen.

I thought about the trio. Ahmad, Elias and Abdel were directing the terror and had probably organised the day's march as well. Having dealt with them in Howardsons, I had their address in my notebook and that gave me the opportunity to fire a shot across their bows. The longer the Siege continued, the more the cops would suss things out – they had little else to do. By this time they probably had my victim's body and would know the blow to his neck was from a hostage and the cop at the barrier would be able to describe me. Then they'd trace my route over the rooftop, find the ladder and get my prints. A diversion was essential. It took a lot of willpower to leave the house, there had been enough trouble already and so much could go wrong, yet it must be done.

I walked to Piccadilly Circus which had batteries of phones in use twenty-four hours a day, usually with a queue waiting at each one, a decently anonymous place, and today it was busier than I had ever seen it. The amount of people caused the queues to bend into each other. It took an age before it was my turn. Three phones away a man making a call to India was shouting so loudly they could almost have heard him acoustically. Eventually I got a phone and dialled.

It rang for some time.

"'Allo?" said a suspicious voice. I could tell he was having a bad day. A kidnapper had been killed and a hostage had escaped: this wasn't going to be the Kidnap of the Year, and his troubles were only just beginning.

"Is that you Ahmad?" I said in my best guttural, something I don't pretend to be good at but it was essential to hide my London accent.

He hesitated before saying: "No."

"I want to speak to Ahmad."

There was a lot of suspicion in his voice: "Who is that?"

"A friend – Are you Ahmad?"

"I tell you, no," he said with a waver.

"I must speak to Ahmad now," I said, trying to force him.

"He's out – What do you want?" It was just my luck to get an idiot on the line.

There were people all around me: I would have to hope that the local noise would mask me.

"Urgent, urgent! I need to speak to him."

"I tell you, he's no' here."

"I know he's there. He's been on the short-wave radio. I need to speak to him."

At this he switched to a foreign language, issuing a torrent of words.

"You have to give me Ahmad," I said, keeping calm.

"Who are you?"

"Not on an open line."

"Password?"

"Too late for that, I need Ahmad, now."

"He's out."

So I was stymied. Snorting in disbelief I said, speaking slowly: "Then here is the message. It is an emergency. The police are on to you, they know about Great Square. Get out quick."

"Wha' – Hold on."

A new voice and I recognised it from the past: "Who is that?" Ahmad was more alert than his henchman though just as suspicious.

"A brother, it's too late. They've got a van at the end of Fey Way. A squad of SAS paratroopers are on their way. Your calls to Great Square have been intercepted. Get out the back door, they're already at the front: you've still got a chance."

"Who…?"

And I rang off.

Then to the annoyance of the people behind I made another call, this time to the old Whitehall 1212 number which was answered immediately by a cop with a deep voice.

"Scotland Yard."

Again I adopted my best guttural,

"I want the officer in charge of the Great Square Siege."

No chance of that, of course, but it was necessary to get his undivided attention.

"Oh I can hardly do that, sir," he said in his not-another-nutter voice. "Perhaps I could take a message?"

"Could you give me your name, please?"

"Constable Blanche. What is your name?"

"I cannot tell you. Here is the message, Mr Blanche. I won't repeat it. The terrorists at Great Square have been given false passports..."

There was an incredulous pause of several seconds.

"Fascinating, sir, and how would you know that?"

"...And the Siege is being directed by three men, Ahmad, Elias, and Abdel. Their address is 14a Fey Way. They are heavily armed and they use short wave radio. Act on it now..."

Despite the line being bad, I caught a change in his attitude, he'd even drawn a breath at the mention of the names and now a cunning tone came into his voice.

"Was that Bray Road you said, sir?"

"No, Fey Way. F-E-Y."

"You really must tell me how you know this sir."

"Act now. They're getting ready to leave."

There was a click on the line as someone started to listen in.

I put the phone down and left the building to walk the twenty-minute journey home. Both phone calls had been an anticlimax and I suspected they'd be ignored. I'd mentioned the passports in the hope that they'd work out the implications for themselves. The rain came on in a drizzle that began to soak through my clothes. Odd that I'd spent the night in fear of my life and now that I was a free again, I was not one bit happier.

5

I loved my flat: it was an oasis of peace in the heart of a noisy city. The rooms were comfortable, well furnished, with nice carpets on the floor: my neighbours never caused me the slightest trouble and were sometimes even polite. I went to the kitchen and wondered what to eat and then decided to leave it till later. I was still light headed though my walk in the rain had eased my head. In other circumstances I'd have gone to bed but that would mean waking at two and being unable to sleep thereafter.

The phone rang.

"Are you all right?" asked an indignant voice.

"Oh, it's you Frank! Yes, I'm fine."

"What the hell happened? I couldn't get you last night. I thought they'd got you into that Siege, dammit. What happened?"

"Sorry, I meant to phone."

"Yeh, but what happened?"

"I had to go... out."

"I phoned umpteen times."

"Sorry about that."

"You could've phoned me."

"I know."

"That's some carry-on."

"Yes, I've only just put the TV on."

Frank hesitated and the anger went out of his voice.

"'Course, you don't watch the box. You're okay then? I didn't know what to do."

"I'm fine."

"Mind, there's not a lot I could have done if you'd got tangled."

"Good point."

"That's some business. If you ask me that's the Snake's doing... he's up to his neck in it... the most evil man in London. I'd have nothing to do with him."

Yes, it was difficult to disagree with his assessment and certainly I'd no intention of approaching the Snake if I lived to be a hundred. But I doubted if he'd anything to do with the Siege itself, though he was certainly co-operating with the kidnappers. It's not his style to worry about details: he grabs the money and runs.

"You're right."

"Did you get near him yesterday?"

"I'd to keep away. He was with another bloke."

Frank cleared his throat and changed his tone again:

"Listen, the wife came back last night."

"Oh... I'm glad for you."

"Things are back to normal again."

"I'm glad."

"She goes through stages... Likes a change... but she's all right in the end."

"...Of course she is."

Then he prattled on for ten minutes, oblivious of my sharp relies. I was tired and sore and anxious to relax. And I was also determined to tell him nothing: Frank might or might not have been a police nark but I was much safer if he knew nothing.

Still feeling sickly, I went out to the balcony and tried to relax.

"Isn't that Siege in Great Square quite dreadful?" said a cultured voice nearby and I looked up, with sinking heart, to see the retired judge, my nearest neighbour, sitting in his balcony with a glass in hand.

I agreed.

"This is going to be the pattern of the future, make no mistake. There will be more outrages and the politicians will only make things worse. When I was on the bench we didn't always get things right but crime was stamped on and I don't think we were unfair. It's the guns, you know: anybody with a loaded gun should feel the full weight of the law."

Despite having killed a man that morning, I agreed.

"Of course we're dealing with terrorists here, quasi-militaries. And they're always going to be armed. What's needed is the SAS: they'd sort it out in a jiffy."

I agreed, with the caveat that the hostages might get shot.

"Even so, young man, it would have the stamp of authority. It would discourage other adventurers. One thing breeds another. Just look at that shooting in Fey Way. We will soon be worse than the wild west."

"Shooting?"

"Yes... three men in a flat, they're supposed to be something to do with Great Square... there was a newsflash just before I came out."

"Has anyone been hurt?"

"I should say so. They've got a body."

"Not a policeman?"

"No, no, a foreigner. One of them, I assume, though I must say I never trust TV reports, they're sure to get the details wrong."

I had the box on in seconds to get an overhead view of the street from a helicopter. Come to think of it I had seen it from the balcony when the ex-judge was speaking. Fey Way seemed to be a smart address, a big wide street with fancy flats and underground parking. Thick black smoke was billowing from a first-floor flat where the windows had been blown out, frames and all. Police in flak jackets were ushering householders out, while a crowd watched from a hundred yards away. Then the camera panned to their man on the ground who was holding a mike and looking excited as the rain ran down his face.

"What seems to be happening, Cedric?"

"Well, Bob, the police are absolutely refusing to answer any questions. And of course the street is cordoned off. But apparently three men from the flat ran out the back door. Then there was the most tremendous bang and the flat went up. It may have been a gas explosion but the feeling here is that it was a bomb."

"What about the body, Cedric?"

"Ah, yes, the body. Neighbours dashing out after the explosion stumbled over a man's body. It seems he was shot in the head... the three occupants of the flat are missing There have been reports that two of them have been seen running along the canal... this of course is not confirmed."

"And all this is connected to the Siege?"

"Well, Bob, there have been reports that it is. It seems that the police were already on their way to Fey Way after a tip-off when the incident took place. Apparently there have been comments among the neighbours about the activities of these men and I understand that some suspicions had been aired to the authorities."

Was this the result of my two phone calls? Yes, it must have been, but who in hell had shot the man? – well one of the trio, obviously – but why? I could understand the bomb, there was probably enough evidence in the flat to damn them forever, but why the death? That was one thing I'd wanted to avoid. After the Siege this was too much! I went to the kitchen to make tea and toast. Not having eaten all day, my head was spinning and I was beginning to feel sick. I switched on the kettle and put a slice of bread in the toaster, noting as I did so that my hands were trembling. There had been two deaths and that meant a lot of enquiries. I was at risk. They'd get my fingerprints off the ladder and descriptions of me from the other hostages when it was over. And there was another problem too – the writer of the letter – someone was taking an unhealthy interest in my affairs and that person might drop a note to the authorities.

Something else was annoying me: the toast was burning.

Forget the food, I went to my study and spent thirty minutes tidying my affairs and shredding every redundant document I could find. I took a number of false beards and destroyed them. Then I opened my safe and checked that there was nothing to embarrass me. There were other papers, including title deeds for the apartment that must be kept.

By this time thirty minutes had passed and I returned to the lounge and made more tea and toast. With a bit of luck I'd get a chance to eat it. Then the TV was interrupted by another newsflash.

"Cedric, it seems that there have been developments?"

The camera focussed on Cedric who was now so wet it looked like he'd been pulled out of the Thames. He was still in Fey Way where the ruined building was now being hosed by a fire team.

"Yes, Bob, two more bodies have been found. I can't be sure if they're the men from the flat. I have to make that clear. But the police have confirmed that there are two bodies. I understand – and this is not confirmed either – that one man was shot in the head at the canal and that the gunman then leapt onto the railway where he fell on the live rails and was electrocuted. All lines to Waterloo are off by the way and likely to remain off until tomorrow. The whole area is covered by the police and everybody in this part of Fey Way has been ordered out of their homes."

I had taken only one bite from the toast and spilled my tea. What the hell was going on? They say you can't retire from Terror and if you do they shoot you. But if Ahmad and company were *directing* the Siege they must have been above these petty rules. Difficult to second guess a Terrorist's mindset but surely they wouldn't kill each other when things got awkward. Dead bodies are evidence and there are times when everybody's got to pull together. But possibly – just possibly – the motive was robbery: they had nearly a million in Howardsons (and perhaps more elsewhere). Did the gunner shoot his fellows with a view to claiming the loot? He should have known to keep clear of live rails, particularly in the rain, but who was I to comment? I'd been living dangerously myself.

I went out to the balcony.

"They've got another two bodies."

"Ah. I knew something was happening. Just look at those planes."

Yes, it looked like a helicopter jamboree. It was just possible to see the pall of smoke through the drizzle.

"Looks like three men are dead," I said. "These men must have had a lot of money. They'd need it to finance the Siege. Will the police investigate their finances?"

"You can never tell with the police."

"The flat's been bombed, there's smoke pouring out the windows. I'd imagine all records would be destroyed."

The ex-judge rubbed his Roman nose and shook his head. He must have been all of eighty and was, I hoped, still clear headed.

"Oh they'll only present the obvious. Unless there are clear records listing all – and I mean all – the trio's finances that angle will be ignored. Documents will have been destroyed by the fire."

"But surely the prosecutor needs financial evidence?"

"Only pertinent factors are considered. If the money and its whereabouts are unclear it'll be ignored. The Crown case is about terrorism not money. No one will think about bank accounts – But there won't be a case. The men are dead."

Yes, and they had left a million.

Returning to the lounge, I switched on the kettle, perhaps this time I could have a quiet snack. But no, the TV – which was still running in the background – was interrupted by another newsflash. The camera panned in on an excited Cedric who had been moved to Great Square with the departmental store as a backdrop. There were a lot of police about.

"Bob, the Siege is over. The terrorists have surrendered!"

"This is tremendous news, Cedric. Any word on the hostages?"

"Not yet, Bob, but we're going to see them. We've got a camera at the door."

"Fantastic, Cedric, what about the kidnappers?"

"Well, no word yet, but we think they'll be brought out too. There are all kind of rumours going about. There's been a lot of activity on the roof."

Here the camera wavered and then panned in on a long-focus shot of policemen walking in slow motion over the roof, stopping occasionally to look at things off camera.

"...It seems a hostage may have escaped."

"Escaped? A hostage, Cedric?"

"Well, Bob, there's been nothing said officially, I must make that clear, but it looks like it's been a big blow to the kidnappers. In the early hours a hostage disappeared and there's definitely a search in progress. Dogs have been brought in."

"Amazing."

More excitement, Cedric was looking to the left and so were all the bystanders.

"They're coming, the hostages are coming. And I think – yes! – There are only three of them."

With a vertigo-inducing sweep the camera focused on the doorway as we caught a glimpse of movement. First about twenty police filed out, then after a short pause the hostages appeared with minders around them. Cedric thought they looked well after their ordeal, but they looked disturbed to me. The salesman had a hangdog expression and the fat woman didn't look right, though the young boy seemed largely unfazed.

"A great moment," said Bob. "A great moment: and there's only three. Which one is missing?"

But Cedric was pushing his way forward into the ranks of the party. This would be shown all over the world and he was on the high of his life, shoving a microphone at the bewildered hostages.

"How are you, how are you? Have you got anything to say to our viewers?"

As it happened, they hadn't. The minders closed around them and they were ushered into a waiting limo which made off immediately with a police escort.

Cedric, breathless, turned to face the camera. "What a moment! I've never seen anything like it. The captives are free. Ah, I think there's going to be a police statement. Yes. We're going over to get it." Again the camera wobbled then focused on a senior policeman who made a statement about the Siege being over. Then he cleared his throat and said: "Four hostages were taken but only three have been identified. At present the fourth individual, a male of about thirty, has not been accounted for. There are reports of some violence. We are concerned about the safety of this person and are conducting a search of the building. So far we have nothing to report."

Sitting with my head down, I could hardly take any more. Yes, a hostage was missing, he was watching from his flat three miles away. The statement implied that the hostage may have been killed and ignored the fact that a terrorist was dead.

"Well it's all over, an absolute triumph for Scotland Yard. Wait, I think the kidnappers are coming. Can it be? Yes, I think something's happening. This is fantastic…"

A big police van had pulled up to the kerbside and the policemen began to look alert. A squad of armed soldiers, their guns pointing at the ground could just be seen in the background. Everybody was getting in on the act. More police filed out of the store, walking fast, followed by four groups each of which had a figure at the centre.

Four? There must be something wrong.

In the great British tradition, the hostages had blankets over their heads to preserve their identity until they appeared in court. First, despite the surrounding officers, there was no mistaking Madam Boss, her height giving her away and in no particular hurry. Then there was the tall man with his head down, followed by the brute who'd cleaned the guns. But what about the fourth? I gripped the seat for support as though I was seeing a ghost, and perhaps I was. He was shorter than his fellows, his shoulders were broad and even his walk was recognisable. It was the man I'd killed!

I had to leave the room and walk the corridor in an effort to come to terms with it. On that morning I had felled him with a terrible blow to the neck and heard him fall to the floor, stone dead. My hand was still swollen. Yet the anxious figure being escorted to the meat wagon was undoubtedly my victim. He must have faked his death.

In terrible relief, I switched the TV off and went to bed.

On the following morning I got up at five.

On their visit to Howardsons, the trio had invested their money in Ahmad's name on a long-term basis with the proviso that they might wish to go liquid at short notice. In response to this, I'd written a ten-share portfolio on a piece of paper from our office manager's notebook. He's a heavy handed fellow, our office manager, and I could see the depression of a word and an account number he'd written earlier. It was the details of Ahmad's account, including his security code which I'd copied into my notebook in the knowledge that it might come in useful. (At that time computer security was primitive.)

Then, I went to my secret store, a rented room, where I got my computer connected to Howardsons. Computers were slow in those days, the modem was nothing more than a device into which I inserted the handset and it took ages before there was contact. I had no screen: only an ancient IBM dot matrix printer that made faint impressions on the paper. Every line had to be checked and it was tedious, but that was a small price to pay for the joy of being on-line. Here the machine accepted the number and password for Ahmad's account but was reluctant to take instructions from me and I had to go through the whole routine several times. Finally it worked. All equities in Ahmad's account were to be sold and the proceeds, including cash in hand, would be credited to my account in Switzerland.

6

It being the first Monday in the month, the Pension Fund Committee – as big a collection of self-important oddballs as you could find in London – met in the boardroom to formulate business for the next thirty-one days. These were high-ranking managers who disliked each other, though they were united in a greater dislike for me their chairman and who can blame them? The whole thing was an exercise in futility that wasted half a morning. I was probably the worst chairman on earth, we all knew it and they never failed to oppose me. Most would agree that I'd a talent for investment but nobody rated me as a chairman, yet Howardsons refused to release me from the chore because they wanted me restrained by the dullards. For the seventh month, I failed to swing them in the right direction and failed to resolve any one of a dozen issues that should have been settled months ago. Since they controlled my buying strategy, I was prevented from making millions for the old firm. But it was not in their remit to worry about that, they were Guardians of Capital with a duty to repel Young Turks like me. And they were insufferably polite about it, too.

That over, I bumped into the office manager on the stairs who said:

"Those three men from the Middle East – remember?"

"…No."

"Yes, you do, the Middle Easterns…? Ahmad and two others."

"Oh, that was his name? Yes."

"Well they've gone liquid. We got a selling order from their bank this morning."

"Really? Everything okay?"

"Hunky-dory."

"Pity they sold. Mind you, the Market's going down."

"Yes, I'm afraid it is."

47

Next morning at five I went to check the figures. Again I had trouble with my computer and it took all of twenty minutes to connect. My head was so hazy I could barely focus on the printout. But the news was positive. Almost a million pounds had been credited to my account which now totalled two point nine million pounds.

This was my Donald fund. It had accrued over a period of nine years through a lot of shrewd dealing on my part. I might be a poor James Bond but I'd talent as an investor and had nursed it like an ailing child and someday it would be worth a staggering sum.

At that point, the money was in a South African bank, under the control of my Swiss account and would be transferred to Amsterdam at close of business. Next it would go to Lichtenstein and then to Barbados. No moss would grow on this rolling stone. Incidentally all of these accounts were my own, irrespective of the country they were in, and they were numbered with no mention of my name. I was relatively safe, though it was still possible for a diligent accountant to trace me, albeit he would need to get a court order in each of these countries to force that bank to reveal my details – no easy matter and by the time he'd obtained that information the money would have moved on.

Yet, I began to suspect I'd made a foolish gamble. Ahmad might be dead but surely his financial activities would be checked and only then did I realise my account number would appear on his bank statement.

Later in the morning, the accounts manager came to my desk with *The Times*, all excited. He wasn't known as 'Freddy the Fusspot' for nothing and my heart sank as I looked at his mournful face with its droopy moustache and heard him say:

"Did you notice? The three men lived at Fey Way."

"Fey Way?"

"Yes: that shooting on Sunday. It was our three men. We'd better report this."

"Let me see the paper."

A full spread was devoted to the incident. Now the police had identified the bodies and their names were listed with an appeal for information about their activities. One of them, incidentally, was described as a helicopter pilot. No doubt the cops would be fascinated to know that Ron Miles had transferred their money to his Swiss account for safe keeping. The manager's shaking finger pointed out the details while I gritted my teeth. If this were reported, they'd have me for dinner.

"I thought his surname was Ahmad. This is Ahmad Hammiel."

"All right, there's a difference, but look at other two blighters: Elias and Abdel. Hell of a co-incidence."

"Common names. The dead man has a different name to the account holder."

"Don't come that kind of stuff. That's our three men. No question."

"No it isn't. It's the account holder that matters."

"You're just playing with words."

"Be sensible, man. The account holder's name is different. There must be scores of men in town called Elias and Abdel."

"You think so?"

He was staring over his glasses at me and wondering why I was so dogmatic. I decided to cool it a little.

"London's full of rich foreigners. Forget it. Sir James is dead against anything that makes us look like police informers. And they'll take your office apart."

"I still think..."

"You don't have an argument. This man's surname is a terrorist's forename, a coincidence. The Market's down today, there'll be a slump for months and the whole company's going to be fighting for its life without you frightening our foreign clients."

He froze as my words sank into his thick skull.

"I hadn't thought about it that way..."

To my immense relief he shelved the idea.

Madam Boss and her sidekicks appeared in court, charged with terrorism, false imprisonment and possession of guns and weapons. There were many articles in the papers but that story was now superseded by a new one: The Phantom Hostage. Unbelievably the police hadn't realised how I'd escaped, the ladder was on another roof and I'd left no clues in my wake. A report described me as a natural with heights who had shinned down a drainpipe and somehow outwitted the cops on the ground. On TV, an 'expert' revealed that I'd pulled a drainpipe away in my descent – a close shave there – and how there were two scuff marks on the wall from my shoes.

There was also a muted mention of the forty-year-old man who had been shot on the previous night, though they were at pains to say his death was not connected to the Siege.

The bad news was that every paper had a sketch of me, drawn by an artist who must have taken descriptions from the hostages. It was surprisingly accurate, though the goatee beard might save the day. Even George, our commissionaire, jokingly pointed out the likeness, though I claimed to be better looking. But there was another worry. A few months ago I'd made three brief TV appearances on business programmes and though they were far from the multimillion category, I'd still been seen by a lot of people. Easy for me to give a prima facie rebuttal that I'd been at church that morning, but there were difficulties. Almost certainly 'John Smith' had been recorded when I identified myself over the phone and that could be linked to my real voice. Such matches are as accurate as fingerprints. Fortunately the cops are never keen to associate mystery persons with TV people since every newsreader has been 'identified' by an airhead at some time or other.

Some of the tabloids were speculating that the Phantom Hostage was a secret agent. He had been evasive about his identity, had given a false address and despite all the odds being against him, had made a dramatic escape which was near impossible to a layman though it was all in the day's work to a professional.

It was Thursday when I next checked my account. There was a fine drizzle and I almost decided not to go. After six tries I got a printout.

The information was devastating.

All money had been transferred from my account and my balance was zero.

Two point eight million had been stolen from me and a memo at the foot of the page said: *Kindly note, all dated Warrants will be called in ten days.*

7

I can pinpoint the moment when it all began, nine years ago on a Saturday afternoon as I made my way home, so irritated by the empty prattle of the shoppers who blocked my way, that I almost failed to notice something that would change my life.

Across the street a man was fuelling his car at a petrol station.

It was my boss, Donald, the grouch who made my job hell, but it was not the familiar figure I worked beside. There was no sign of his pinstripe or the silk tie, this man's clothes were rough, he was unshaven, and he looked like a convict on the run. I had never known he was a driver. Instinctively I moved into the background, well aware that the scowl on his face would ripen into outright anger if he saw me. This was something I might use to my advantage. His old battered Land Rover was loaded with cartons while two fierce men sat inside. Intuitively I knew this was the real Donald. The one at Howardsons was a tame version for domestic consumption only, while the man opposite lived in a lower universe. For sure he was up to something. Almost certainly it involved money and it was something he concealed from his colleagues, I could smell the villain in him. But what was going on? Suddenly I remembered overhearing some odd phone calls and I stepped into a bookshop to browse while watching from the window. Then, the car fuelled up, he drove out, cutting in front of a taxi to the blast of a horn.

The carload of cartons indicated some kind of trading activity and, like me, he had a contractual obligation to engage in no other business than Howardsons'. Since this was a sacking offence, there was likely to be a lot at stake and was probably illegal and of substantial interest to me.

Outside, I followed the slow-moving shoppers. Donald seldom missed the chance to insult me and he hated everyone in the firm, if not the entire world. I wasn't allowed to take a phone call or look at the mail and he blocked my attempts to study shares. For sure he had something to hide. He was travelling in my direction and a few minutes later I heard the same horn in the distance. Yes, there was a hold-up about half a mile ahead: he seemed to be reversing into a gap between two houses.

When I arrived, there was no sign of the ugly trio, though the Land Rover, now unladen and innocent, sat off-road on a fifty-foot strip between two blocks of flats. Somewhere at the back there was the shadow of a smaller building. As luck would have it, there was a coffee shop beside me and I went in for a coffee, taking a seat at the back where I could watch without being seen.

Hours went past and I didn't mind: I ordered more coffee, sandwiches and finally an omelette and chips. The waiter thought I'd been stood up by my girl (I was all dressed up, having played the organ at a wedding) and offered me his sympathies as he rang up yet another item. Eventually there was activity across the road. From a point beside the vehicle one of the men emerged, bearing a carton which he dumped onto the rear seat, a second man did the same and then they climbed into the front. Sixty seconds later a sullen Donald emerged and got into the driver's seat, his great paunch rubbing against the wheel. With a roar and lots of smoke, they moved off.

After a few moments I left to investigate and found a timber building, offset from the general thoroughfare, marked: *Boy's Athletic Club, secy. Donald Sherwood.* About fifty feet long, it looked secure with the windows boarded up and painted in dull grey, an unimaginative place, little more than a workman's shed, with an iron roof that had once been painted red. There were three mortise locks on the door and it seemed solid. But so what? A timber building was easy meat to a determined thief like me. First, to make sure there was no one about, I knocked on the door and when nothing happened, I stood back and thought about it. Then I went to a payphone on the main road and called, Frank. We hadn't been in touch recently but he never refused work.

"Listen, I've got something. Bring your keys. The usual arrangement, okay?"

The latter phrase meant I'd pay.

"Gimme quarter of an hour," he said with something approaching enthusiasm. In the background, the football was on and it sounded like his team was having a bad time.

Sure enough his battered van pulled up beside me and he was out with his case of keys cunningly disguised with the logo of a well-known insurance company. For this occasion, he'd changed into a suit and probably had a card in his pocket that identified him as a loss adjuster. Frank had all his wits about him and liked to have things looking right. He seldom missed a chance to relieve the rich of their surplus. He was no locksmith but had never failed with a lock. Shaking his head at the boy's athletic club, he said:

"What's going on here?"

"Some stuff went in earlier. I just want to see it."

"Hmm, three locks, looks like they believe in security. Needs time."

"Okay," I said, we're pros after all. "I'll stand guard in the street."

Fortunately the door was out of sight of both the street and the windows above, so I left him to it. Rather than make myself conspicuous at the coffee shop opposite, where the waiter might be a bad witness, I walked up and down, keeping my eyes open for an old Land Rover. This being early Saturday evening, it was likely Donald would be drinking whisky, but he was unpredictable. A confrontation would be unthinkable.

Silent as a ghost, Frank appeared beside me.

"It's open."

We both gave the area a quick shifty. There were still a few shoppers about, a group of youths in football colours were returning from a game, but no one was taking the slightest interest in us. In the coffee shop, the waiter was serving fish and chips to a family, it looked safe to proceed.

"Right, get a torch from the van and we'll have a gander."

Within seconds we were in the dark interior. This was the bad bit. Despite my gung-ho attitudes, I led a quiet life with little risk-taking. That said, it was sometimes necessary to live on the wild side and this was such an occasion. Entering the property was a criminal act. There was a lot to lose and I knew nothing of Donald's habits.

Once inside, we locked the door behind us. The trouble with a torch is that you get a narrow beam that never gives a complete view of a room. Even so, it was a dull place with fittings hanging loose and paper peeling from its walls. There was ancient gym equipment on the floor, everything was stale and smelly and clearly it hadn't been painted in years. Frank swung to the left where we found a utility room that housed bins, floor brushes and some old tools. Then there were a couple of dirty toilets and nothing else. Next he turned to the front of the building, moving slowly, to lessen the sounds of his feet.

"I thought there was stuff," he complained. He had a keen nose for swag. "Where? Oh, there's an office at the front – Uh, uh, it's locked. Three keys again."

This part of the building was more prosperous, with wood panelling done in such a way that you barely noticed the door. Frank made me hold the torch while he worked on the locks. But time was passing. The first rule of an illegal entry is to be as quick as possible and we were moving at a snail's pace. The danger of discovery was self-evident. Someone might have seen us at the door, Donald might return, or we could have tripped an alarm.

"I hate this," he muttered. "We could get trapped."

"There's a fire door on the opposite side."

"Use your eyes, it's chained. Ah, here we are."

The same three keys had been used in reverse order and the door creaked open to reveal the cartons in the murky darkness. Here the floor was concrete and to the left I saw the shape of an ancient safe in the shadows – that made sense, the key for a safe was taped to the lid of Donald's desk in Howardsons. There were empty boxes and sealing tape as well as suitcases lying under a table. Frank pushed past me to look at the cartons, one of which was open. He reached in to find a magazine.

Then I was subjected to a volley of expletives.

It showed a naked boy of about five hanging from a rope, his neck compressed to the size of a finger, his tongue completely distended.

So Donald was into snuff material.

"Pathetic! What the bloody hell are we doing here? Let's get out!"

Frank was all set to do a runner, blaming me for Donald's excesses, but I had to insist on the doors being locked again. The magazine was not to my taste, but there was no point in advertising our visit. If my boss realised there'd been a break-in, the security would be changed in a flash. And that would be bad because I intended to come back and look at the safe. There was an Opportunity here.

"If they catch us here *we'll* be on the end of a rope!"

At the outer door we encountered more trouble. By this time the keys had been mixed up, for once he had lost his cool and it took some time before he got it sealed again. Outside, we walked slowly to the van, Frank carrying his case like a bored insurance salesman. He had calmed down until we got in, then I got a tirade about my lack of judgement.

"Don't tell me you're into that stuff! What brought you here?"

In his present mood there was nothing to be gained by answering and it might be bad if he knew Donald was my boss. Besides, I was hardly to blame for his excesses.

I got the three keys from him, complaining that they were my only reward. I paid him and we parted.

8

Come lunchtime of the following day, the streets were deserted when I ran up the marble stairs to Howardsons Investment Corporation – one of the most prestigious firms in the City, whose policies affected most private pensions in the land and whose executives enjoyed unrivalled salaries and perks. Of course this largesse didn't apply to young lads like me who hailed from council homes. I was low in the pecking order and forever destined to be servile to people like Donald. It being Sunday, the main doors were closed and I rang the bell until George, our commissionaire, appeared. He does a spot of overtime every weekend.

"Well, it's Mr Ron Miles. What brings you here?"

"George, I forgot my notebook. D'you mind if I get it?"

"On you go."

In Donald's office, I took a spare key I'd filched from a rack and opened his desk to find a collection of notebooks and junk that had accrued over the years. The safe key was taped to the lid, geometrically parallel with the edge, its handle to the outside. To all appearances it was a duplicate to which he alone had access and it had never once been removed. I prised it off and left, trying to look as calm as possible.

There was going to be a robbery. I could smell money and that overrode all other considerations. Obviously he'd been trading for years and must have grossed a lot of moolah that would be useful to a rising executive like me.

Because I had every intention of being a rich man and no opportunity would ever be ignored. I hadn't been reared in a council home for nothing. Unlike many commentators, I knew what poverty really was and though my childhood had not been unhappy, I was determined to improve my living standards and that's difficult without the funds. For sure the safe had been installed to protect a trove, it could have no other purpose, and of course

Donald's would be a cash business, nobody issues cheques for that kind of rubbish.

And I didn't believe Donald was a killer. The picture of the dead child had probably come from the Far East. The victim's face had been distorted, but there had been something Chinese about the room's background.

Half an hour later I arrived, taking care to do an innocent walk past the club to ensure there was no Land Rover nearby. The street was deserted, the coffee shop opposite was empty and there was nobody on the pavement, the locals were having their Sunday rest and even the road traffic was sporadic.

At the boys' club I put on my gloves and knocked to make sure there was no one inside. Then I discovered the keys were ill-fitting and wouldn't turn. We hadn't marked them on the previous night and there was the problem of finding the right one. Eventually one clicked and the other two followed after a mind-boggling delay. By this time the hairs on my neck were bristling with fear. This was broad daylight and the entry had taken an age. Inside, I locked it behind me and spent a second age on the office door before getting it open.

Once in, I looked at the depressing room with its cartons piled on the table, all of them unchanged from my previous visit. The ancient safe lurked in the corner like the gateway to hell. An old *Daily Mirror* lay on the table, there was a smell of stale tobacco and two empty whisky bottles lay on the floor. At the safe, I turned the key and opened the door with a terrible screech that must have been audible in the street outside. There were notebooks on the top shelf and two shelves of transparent sheets which were probably graphics for previous issues. Then there was a great pile of magazines and assorted junk, including a set of false teeth. At the bottom, a big cardboard box was piled high with bank notes, some wrapped in thousands. others held by elastic bands while still more lay in untidy heaps where they'd fallen out of the box.

I paused for ten seconds to clear my head. It's at moments like this that we forget ourselves and do something stupid. But there were no footsteps outside, no keys in the lock and no alarms sounding, though there was something almost ominous about the silence.

Underneath the table there were several suitcases and I reached for the sturdiest, a wooden trunk that had been designed for sea voyages and emptied the money into it. But it wasn't big enough and a lot of cash spilled on to the floor with notes fluttering everywhere. It took time to retrieve them. Clearly some had been there for years. Of course Donald lived alone and was highly paid and wouldn't need the cash. This was probably his nest egg, something to gloat over, a handy trove that he'd use when it came time to retire.

Despite being scared out of my wits, I found myself smirking at his impending troubles as I packed the case. There were enough notebooks in the safe to keep the plods going for months. And they would soon be here. With the case full, I took one of his horrible magazines and put it on top. Then I sat on the lid and closed it.

My next problem was that it was almost too heavy to lift. Most of the weight was in the trunk itself, rather than the cash. But I am not strong, it was heavy, and it was now too late to transfer the contents to a lighter case. The time had come to go.

Taking a deep breath, I struggled to the door.

Outside, with the case down, it took more than two minutes before a key would turn in the door. My fingers were trembling with fear and rage – at any moment I could be trapped and the consequences of being caught were unthinkable. There was a temptation to leave the door unlocked, but that involved the risk of someone reporting it and it was best to delay discovery until the last moment.

Eventually, a lock clicked, the middle one, and I walked away with my fortune.

But my burden was too weighty. Any onlooker would notice a young chap carrying a case so heavy that he was almost overbalancing – the caricature of a spiv making off with the booty. The coffee shop had no one at its tables and no sign of the waiter; just as well, he would be a dangerous witness and would be able to describe me. Of course I could phone Frank for help but he was angry and might refuse to be involved. Also he might talk.

Essential to get away quickly, I walked for two hundred yards until I could go no further. The case was getting heavier, my back was sore and my fingers could scarcely grasp the handle. Out of breath and covered in perspiration, I put it down on the road as despair began to take a hold of me. What would happen if Donald arrived in his Land Rover? Surely I wasn't going to be defeated at this late stage?

It took all of ten minutes before a taxi appeared on the street and it looked like the driver wasn't going to stop, but after a moment's hesitation, it pulled up beside me. They say you should never hire a cab in a dicey situation, the drivers talk and they remember where you went, but there was now no option. I was wearing my Sunday suit, the picture of respectability, as I heaved the case into the back seat and gave my destination as the neighbouring street to my flat. The driver was a dull old man who took no interest in me. I said nothing to draw attention to myself.

The flat was a two-roomer that has now been demolished. My friend Wallace had the front room and I the other and despite its lowly status it had never been an unpleasant place. Unfortunately there were flats on the other side of the street and I was aware of several women watching me as they worked at their sinks. One of them, an ancient granny who seemed to be there every hour in the day, leaned forward to watch me return with my prize. She'd been there when I set off for church that morning. The case was so heavy that it was difficult to walk in a straight line and I had to put it down on two occasions. Eventually I reached the portals of my flat.

But nothing ever goes right, the door opened to reveal Wallace and his parents at the top of the stairs, talking. They stopped to stare at a sweaty Ron Miles struggling in with his case which banged against the portal with a loud thump that left its mark on the paintwork. I was blazing mad. Would nothing ever go right? Another three witnesses were three too many. But I was foxy enough to show a friendly grin.

"Hello," I said.

"Taking your case to court?" asked Wallace with shrewd eyes.

At this point I was climbing the stairs, out of breath and trying to make it seem light. I looked at it with a modest laugh.

"I bought some books from an old man."

"Really," said his mum, who can be a bit gushy: "You're a good reader, Ron – How was church today?"

"Oh there were about two hundred and fifty there; not too bad."

"Wallace, you should go sometimes."

"What, and listen to him play the organ?"

Both parents objected to this, but I said he showed sound musical judgement and we all laughed. After a few further remarks, I excused myself and went to my room where I flung the case on my bed. Having momentarily forgotten its weight, I nearly wrenched my arm off. Then, all innocent, I went to the kitchen to put a slice of bread in the toaster. In the background, his parents left with loud goodbyes and after a moment he came in. At first I wondered if I'd upset him, but he had something else on his mind.

"My uncle took a heart attack this morning."

Wallace worked in his uncle's private bank – a merchant, not a clearer, and little more than a loan office – that had been teetering on the edge of oblivion for years. Heavily made, he gave the impression of being older than he really was with a habit of looking on the black side. He was difficult to understand and often gave the impression that he was scheming against you. But he'd been a good friend to me and had masterminded my entry into Howardsons, previously I'd been a teller in Barclays Bank.

"Oh? How is he?"

"Sitting up, apparently. But he won't be back for ages, if at all. I'm his proxy."

"...This could be your big chance."

"Well, provided it doesn't fold first. Listen, I'm off to the office. Dad brought the keys. I want a look at the books... I've always been the junior till now."

"Dead right. By the way, could I borrow your typewriter?"

"Yes, I'll get it for you," he said, after the briefest hesitation. The word 'borrow' always makes him pause.

And he departed without having asked about the suitcase. It seemed that both our lives had made major changes on the same day.

I waited until he'd been gone for ten minutes, then I opened the typewriter and slipped an A4 into the slot. I typed:

To the senior officer
Vice Squad, Scotland Yard

This rubbish is published by Donald Sherwood. I wonder how long he will get away with it. It's been going on for years and you do nothing. Unless this is acted on I will go to my MP. He works at

Howardsons. His place of business is an alleged boys' club. Both
addresses are at the bottom of this letter.

I then addressed the envelope and posted it, aware that a lot of
things had happened in a few hours that would change my life
forever.

9

That night I slept badly, well aware that my problems were far from over. For a start Donald's cool mind would soon conclude that since I alone had access to his spare key, I was the probable thief. Tomorrow promised to be a difficult day.

I got to the office early, desperate to get the key in place, but my fingers wouldn't work and the sticky tape tangled. It took an age to get it fixed and he wouldn't be fooled for a moment. Every time I heard footsteps in the corridor, I panicked and closed the lid. To be caught at his desk would be all the proof he'd ever need. Finally I gave up, my nerves could take no more and I went to the canteen where I pretended to read a paper over my tea though I didn't know what I was reading. At eight I summoned the will to return and found him going over his mail. I was afraid to look at his face and my heart was beating too fast, but he didn't seem unduly angry and grunted in his usual fashion when I said, "Morning". So he didn't know. Or at least he didn't yet know it was me.

Keeping my head down, I took the Day Book and began to write. Outside, some staff went into the neighbouring offices with half-hearted greetings. Donald answered two phone calls about investment trusts, opened his desk and took out a book about statistics which he stared at for a long time, occasionally taking notes, apparently unaware that the key was dangling from the tape. Curiously, he didn't seem to be in a bad mood. Was it possible, that despite everything, he didn't know about the robbery?

There were no further comments in the next two hours and I was getting ready to fetch his tea, when the commissionaire's voice sounded in the corridor, escorting visitors. A bass voice grunted a reply and now I heard several footsteps. Out of the corner of my eye, I saw Donald raise his head. They could only be coming here and they were not on Howardsons' business otherwise the commissionaire wouldn't be with them. A tap on the door and George, immaculate in his uniform, said:

"'Scuse me, Donald. Two gentlemen for you."

I glanced at the visitors in some awe. Ultimately they represented the state and were near invincible: they were my real enemies and I had to hope they'd never come for me. Both were tall, in their forties, and wore tweed jackets over their black trousers. There was an air about them of being surprised at nothing, of having seen it all before. Certainly they were undaunted by Donald and the trappings of his office. The taller of the two held the envelope I had typed yesterday. "Mr Donald Sherwood?"

A grunt in assent.

"May we have a word?"

"You," said Donald to me. "Hop it."

Meekly, I left the room and went into Mr Browne's office next door, a nice man with a boring voice who gave me lessons on the Stock Market every Friday afternoon. He was sitting with his feet on the desk, doing *The Times* crossword.

"Anything I can do, Mr Browne?"

He put his feet on the floor and tried to look dignified.

"No there isn't. You were here on Friday. You should be with Donald today."

"I've been sent out. Two men came to see him... I think they're police."

"Police!" said Mr Browne nearly falling off his chair, revealing, I think, that he had some awareness of Donald's guilty secrets. He opened the door and we heard Donald say "No comment" in an aggressive tone as an unflappable voice asked another question which drew a similar response. He closed the door.

"This is terrible. I'd better phone the office."

But before he could reach for the telephone we heard the footsteps of Mr Fortescue, our general manager, hurrying towards us. The commissionaire would have notified him immediately. Clearly, this was an earthquake. Howardsons isn't the kind of place that welcomes policemen unless they've a fortune to invest. He pushed his way into the room, closed the door and we all looked at each other, saying nothing. To break the silence, I said:

"I think it's the CID, Mr Fortescue."

He wore a dark pin-stripe suit with a white handkerchief in his breast pocket and his trousers were neatly pressed, but such elegance was spoiled by his florid complexion. Putting his hand across his forehead he opened the door and listened to the interview for a moment. Then he turned to me, clearly alarmed.

"Do you know why they're here?"

"They just said they wanted a word."

At that moment voices outside grew louder and he opened the door again. Donald was standing between the two men and suddenly I felt sorry for him. He had donned his soft hat, his enormous paunch was protruding from his unbuttoned coat and there was resignation on his face.

"Can I help you?"

"Mr Sherwood is under police arrest. I want this room sealed till we come back with a warrant."

"A warrant won't be necessary, officer. I'm the general manager, you have my permission to search it."

But the big cop wasn't going to budge.

"I'm sorry, sir. Mr Sherwood has refused to co-operate. Lock the room."

Without a word, Fortescue produced a bundle of keys. The man's organisation never ceased to amaze me. He locked the door, they placed a seal over the keyhole and walked away with Donald waddling between them. I never saw him again.

Later in the morning, a group of cops arrived to search Donald's room. They brought cardboard boxes and removed a lot of material, including the key for the safe. The whole thing took less than thirty minutes. Apparently searches were also taking place at his flat and the boys' club.

"There's going to be some trouble over this," muttered Mr Browne.

Frank used to say something similar. He thought that in a fair world they should raid everyone, including His Honour the Judge, at some point in life's journey.

Here I have to confess to a colourful past. There had been a few minor thefts, before I lifted a bundle of notes from a very rich man who never even noticed. I'd used it to open a savings account in the Peckham Building Society under the name of E. M. Mertoun – at that time you didn't need to prove your identity when opening an account and it had funded many of my adventures.

"I've been in jail," Frank had said. "And I'll tell you one thing, you won't get nowhere being a boy scout. An' I'll bet you're earning no money in Barclays Bank, either. What we need is a proper burglary."

This was a good idea. Frank made a deal. I would pay him a fixed rate – equivalent to my month's salary at the bank and he would assist me without making any claim on the proceeds. He would also put me in touch with a good Receiver. We did two flats in central London for which I bought overalls and gloves, all of which were destroyed when the job was done. He had a jemmy that would have opened the Bank of England and we were in and out of the target houses in minutes. But there was one drawback. I made a substantial loss on both and wasn't slow to complain about it. All right we'll do a third, he sighed and I won't charge you. This was a first-floor apartment which we entered from an adjacent roof. I grabbed the only thing of value in the place, a gold brooch in a carved wooden box and we were out within two minutes.

On the following morning, one of the older girls came to my desk in the bank.

"Phone. It's your uncle. Tell him you are not allowed personal calls."

My uncle? It was Frank of course. "Meet you for lunch. Don't do *nothing*."

At half past twelve we met in a coffee shop.

"There's a right fuss. That was a gangster's flat last night an' he's gone bananas. You got his girlfriend's brooch an' he says there's three and a half thousand missing."

"Three and a...!"

"I know, baloney. But you can't sell that brooch. You'll get your throat cut."

"That means I've lost out again."

"Sometimes that happens."

That night in my room, I took the brooch from the box and examined it. Without doubt it was a tremendous piece of jewellery, the best I'd ever seen: one day I would give it to a beautiful girlfriend. When putting it away, I realised the box had a false bottom. It took a long time to find its secret but eventually I had it open and it was full of fifty-pound notes. I never told Frank.

We agreed that there would be no more robberies. I had noticed that all three were to a certain kind of client and even he admitted the third one was a gangster's flat: I suspected they were owned by his ex-colleagues and that sooner or later they would put their heads together and smash us. Yes, I would go straight in the future, yet here I was with a fortune under my bed.

As a matter of interest, I lived in the back bedroom, Wallace had the other and both doors had their own locks. If you moved my bed, which was on squeaky castors, and lifted the edge of the old carpet, you would find a loose floorboard which, if raised, revealed the wooden box. Inside, the brooch rested on the E. M. Mertoun passbook. One day I made a surprising discovery, the brooch was underneath the passbook. I hadn't left it that way. Someone – and that person could only be Wallace – had been going through my affairs. Probably he'd heard me move the bed and decided to investigate. I didn't know how he got a key for my door. Wallace was my best friend and I said nothing. Confrontation wasn't my style and he would only deny it. No harm had been done, though at that point I didn't want him to know about Donald's money. At lunch I bought a new lock and had it fitted before he got home that night. Maybe it didn't matter, shortly I'd have to use his bank to utilise the funds.

10

Within days Wallace was the boss of the bank, his uncle having been invalided out, though he was apparently furious to be replaced by so young a man. With the books in such a bad way, there was no chance of attracting a fancy banker to manage it. Clearly this was no picnic and Wallace was having a difficult time, though his attitude implied that things weren't as bad as he'd feared. Without doubt he would be rich one day: no penny would escape his grasp and there would be no careless loans. He had a good head for figures and would study ledgers all night, shaking his head at inaccuracies and making notes in his ledgers.

"I can put some business your way," I said light heartedly, though there was nothing casual about my remark. Ever since coming home with the suitcase, I'd endured a lot of worry as I mulled over Donald's fortune. The problem had to be resolved.

"Oh, how much?"

I told him, trying not to sound too guilty.

Wallace whistled and looked at me out of the corner of his eye. Business was slack, two men had been sacked and his solicitors had started to sue defaulters that his uncle had tolerated. Things were tight and he needed all the business he could get.

"This is legal?"

It was a desperate question, a stupid one, and of course he knew it couldn't be. Where would a boy from a council home get that kind of money?

"...Yes."

"Tell me where you got it."

"I can give you a covering letter."

There was a pause while he did some scheming. A banker's mindset is such that you should never tell him your money is hot. He might report you, or even – and there's nothing you can do about it – steal it, and you can't sue him without exposing your

67

own guilt. Frank would have to find a printer who would run off some stationery.

"...Well. Provided your covering note explains where you got it, something believable. Otherwise we'd have to report it. I mean, dammit, we get Inspectors in."

Problems galore: without doubt I would be arrested if I paid it into a bank on the high street. This might explain why Donald had left it untouched in his safe: he didn't need the money. But as a rising star on the Investment firmament I couldn't leave it in a suitcase – there was no alternative; it would have to be invested on the Stock Exchange where it would be undetected among the thousands of transactions that took place every day and where I could use it to hone my skills. For money-laundering reasons, stockbrokers are not allowed to accept cash; all transactions must be made through a bank and a bank will contact the police if the customer can't give a valid reason for having the cash. I recall my own manager doing that when a shifty-looking man arrived with twenty thousand pounds – as it happened he was legit and most indignant too. Meanwhile I was waiting in the wings with many times that money. And I was not a man of substance: I came from a council home.

Some airheads would have spent it, but my insanity didn't stretch that far. There are many old lags in jail who can tell you that it's unwise to be seen spending a fortune without a valid explanation for the largess. I had come from a frugal background that viewed expensive cars, fast women and fancy houses with some suspicion. Also I would be hauled in front of the management if I was deemed to be spending recklessly – they were touchy about these things in Howardsons – and that would have been the end of Ron Miles.

"How about inherited money, a lawyer's letter instructing you to invest it on behalf of a client? There are some good opportunities out there."

I could hear his mind clicking as he plotted the possibilities. Without doubt he wanted to do it. On his desk his typist had just deposited a bundle of mail for signing, the top one began 'Dear Sir, unless...' He was losing weight and looking desperate.

"Well, if you can do that. So long as it looks right. Better not a London lawyer, maybe one from the back of Wales."

"That can be done."

"Well, it's a deal then," he said without enthusiasm.

"Fine," I said with relief. "You'll be my broker – do the buying and selling."

"Right." Wallace stared at the floor for another minute and said: "I'll have to charge you for counting it, and I'll need to get a security firm to deliver it to our clearer, we're not used to cash here. It'll cost you." And he named a figure five times greater than Barclays' charge.

"Ouch." I hate losing money, even when I can afford it: but he had me over a barrel. "All right, I'll fetch a taxi and bring it in."

This was the work of a few minutes and shortly the case was taken to an empty room with several chairs and one table. Two of Wallace's men lifted the case on to the table and began to sort the notes into their denominations and then into their currencies which included Ulster, Isle of Man and Scotland – there were even big white fivers of ancient vintage. Then they started counting and they were slow, having no great experience at counting cash. Eventually it was totalled and they handed me a receipt.

Looking grave, Wallace reappeared in the room (he was far too important to watch the money actually being counted) where he supervised operations when they locked it in a vault. Then he took me to his office.

"Where did you get that money?"

"You're about to get a letter from a Welsh lawyer."

"Come on. The truth."

I looked at him in alarm. He was having second thoughts and I knew why; if this were to come to light he would be a sorry figure without a leg to stand on. There was no way I could have acquired such a sum legally.

"The owner's dead. No one's looking for it. No relatives."

"Obviously it's the proceeds of crime?"

For a moment I stared at the floor before deciding to be frank.

"To be honest, yes, on the dead man's part," I said, cursing myself for having to admit it, but there was clearly no alternative.

"I knew that. And you're going to tell me he gifted it to you."

"Well, not quite."

"So you stole it too?"

Wallace was frowning: I had never seen him so agitated. "I hate this. There are convicts doing time for one per cent of that. The cops should be told."

"They don't know about it and the man's dead."

"What kind of crime was he into? Don't answer! Best not to know... I can see it's accrued over the last thirty years. Some of these notes are out of date."

"But you can handle that."

"Agreed. What was the police involvement?"

"None, they're not involved. I told you, the man's dead."

"I'm worried about taking this."

I looked at his frowning face and almost admitted I was worried too. Without doubt the cops would know about the horde. They would assume the sender of the magazine had stolen the cash and shopped Donald by way of diversion. Clearly Donald had been trading in cash and the empty box at the bottom of his safe told its own tale. Since he had the main key, the thief must have used the spare one in his desk and I was the likely suspect. Elementary, my dear Watson.

"I tell you, it's one hundred per cent safe. I wouldn't touch it otherwise."

"That's exactly what I'd expect you to say."

"The cops don't know about it," I whined.

"You can't know that for certain."

"Look at the notes, man. They've never once been disturbed. They were flung into a box and left. There's never been one emergency."

"So he was rich then?"

"You could say that. Listen if you don't want it I can go elsewhere."

A bit of bluster there, but there are times when it's necessary.

He sagged a bit.

"Maybe it's all right then."

"Of course it is."

"But the lawyer's letter has got to be explicit. They are handling the money on behalf of a client and they must name you as the manager with full powers of authority – that's the only way I can accept it. If it's a limited company – and I think it needs to be – you'll have to produce the articles and memorandum before I can open the account. It's got to look right. Otherwise we'll both finish inside."

"Okay, I'll do that."

Wallace nodded while managing to look worried at the same time.

11

Phew! I had survived the whole business. A fortnight had passed, during which scores of things could have gone wrong – not least from Donald himself, who must have worked out the truth for himself and who was in a position to shop me – yet no enquiries had come my way. Undoubtedly the search of the boys' club must have revealed traces of the robbery, I'd been seen carrying the heavy case and of course I'd had access to the safe key, yet these things had come to nothing. During that time, I'd been a model citizen, working with my head down at Howardsons and even doing the occasional good deed. In fact I intended to make that my policy for the rest of my life. You can get too much excitement and Murphy's Law being what it is, something was sure to go wrong. There was a fortune at stake, yet I had never once been asked an inconvenient question, or indeed any question. Later, I was to learn that Donald had refused to cooperate with the police and though there were undoubtedly a lot of loose ends, these would be closed when they threw the book at him and I wasn't complaining.

I dined with Frank and told him I was going to go straight, but that we'd keep in touch and have the occasional dinner together. This was no great surprise to the man. I slipped him a hundred by way of consolation.

In Howardsons, Mr Browne went down with a heart attack and, much to my gratification, I was sent to mind his office where I'd the time of my life studying the Stock Market without Donald breathing down my neck. The management were pleased with me too. One day Sir James Howardson himself appeared at the door, looking around with an expert eye to see what I'd been doing. This was something he did from time to time and it was a worry to his managers. Behind his affable manner there was a shrewd observer, though he never seemed to blow his top and was usually a considerate visitor. He was in his late sixties, six feet tall with bushy eyebrows. The firm had been founded by his great-grandfather and had been relatively ordinary until he'd built it into one of the biggest investment corporations in Europe. He had also been a colonel in the army with a distinguished War record. I greatly admired him; he was the coolest old man I'd ever met and he was wealthy beyond belief.

"Pity about Donald, you heard, did you?"
This was about a month after his arrest.
"Donald...? Has something happened?"
"Oh, he gassed himself yesterday. There'll be an inquest of course. You'll have to go to the funeral: we'll keep it low profile. No senior staff. Of course, being a church organist you'll be well used to funerals."

In fact I wasn't. Most funerals took place on weekdays when I was not available, though I had managed a few on Saturdays. But what matter, I could hardly refuse to attend Donald's farewell.

"I'm sorry he's dead," said hypocritical me. "He was clever."
"Yes, wasn't he...? Do you like your work?"
"I do. I'm interested in trusts," I said, desperate to make a pitch for myself. "Mr Browne's Investment Trust doesn't do well. British Engineering needs pruning. I've worked on some suggestions." And here I produced a card that listed twelve shares to buy as well as seven I proposed to sell. He looked at it for a moment then handed it back.

Howardsons Corporation had a total of seventeen Investment Trusts of which British Engineering was clearly the worst.

"You're learning the trade, m'boy, I like that... But you're still a novice."

I put the card away, disappointed that he hadn't studied it, though I was well aware that as chairman he was miles above these petty considerations.

"To be fair to Browne, engineering's difficult," he said, realising he'd been rather brusque. "Things are changing and he can't adapt quickly. Show me that list again."

I handed it over and he put his glasses on to study it.
"Items eleven and twelve. Who or what are they?"
"Small firms that specialise in computers. They're profitable all right."

He frowned at it for a long time.

"Well I'll consider it. I like to think we've got talent in the firm, but I dunno, they're getting outa touch. There are times when a young chap's opinion is valuable."

On the following morning, Fortescue came in with a bundle of stationery.

"For you," he said. "The boss has taken up your recommendations. Now you've got a hundred forms to fill in. I just hope it works."

Attired in my dark suit, I went to Donald's funeral to find I was one of only five mourners, none of whom were the men I'd seen in his Land Rover, nor was there any sign of any familiar faces. In the obituary, the vicar said he had been awarded a First at Oxford and gained the rank of major in the army. In view of these talents it was difficult to fathom his descent into such a hate-filled personality. His brother, a short, thin man, shook my hand and thanked me for coming: he was ill at ease and nodded too quickly when I told him I'd worked in the same office and that Sir James sent his commiserations. He seemed a thoroughly decent man who was embarrassed by his brother's excesses. It was ironic that I'd played a part in his demise and was a mourner at his funeral: doubly ironic that I was investing his fortune in shares. When I got back I wrote a report to Sir James who sent me a nice note back, thanking me for representing the firm.

British Engineering's financial year ended with good results. Not all of my selections had worked, but that is the way of the world. The Trust had advanced eight per cent on the previous year, its first increase in a decade. But I received no acknowledgement, the whole thing was a non-event, and nobody even commented.

12

One day I glimpsed myself in a glass door, walking with my head down as though I had a lot of cares. Life wasn't going all that well for me. Clearly the management doubted my suitability for the higher echelons, regarding me as a backroom boy, a safe pair of hands, who would make a good manager's assistant. There were two cultures in Howardsons: Officers, and Rank & File and the former did much better than the latter. I had a talent for shares, the firm did well out of me, but I was Rank & File. Oddly, nobody doubted my qualities as an investor, there was universal acceptance that I was good and often I was summoned by a snooty manager to give an opinion, but they were not prepared to promote me. The smell of the council home still lingered.

Then I was moved to the Third Investment Trust, a big fund of about half a billion which had ten per cent of its capital invested in Hong Kong. There were five people in the office. I should have been manager, but was made 'joint acting assistant manager' with an old man called Norman who didn't like anybody and who was due to retire in two years. There were two typists, and a new manager, Mr Lionel Haize, the cousin of an earl who was said to have great experience, having returned from a stint in Hong Kong. Lionel was about thirty-five, tall, with broad shoulders and plenty of blond hair: the girls thought he was marvellous and so did he. On his first morning, we had been at our desks for three hours when he arrived with bloodshot eyes and the world-weary air of a drunk. The posh accent was there of course, but it was slurred. He shook Norman's hand, then mine, kissed the typists and after listening for a few minutes to our comments, adjourned for a three-hour lunch. When he returned he said we were doing an excellent job and saw no reason to disrupt our work.

"I'm not the kind of fella who fusses about detail, you know. Can't stand pettiness, and if you ask me it never does any good anyway. I want the big picture. Good investments in profitable companies, shares going up. That kind of thing…"

"Certainly, Mr Haize."

"Call me Lionel."

"…But we'll need a meeting to go over the Hong Kong stock. We don't know it so well and you're the expert."

"Nonsense, Norman. You're the experts. I was just saying to Fortescue what a good job you'd made of the Hong Kong shares. Mustn't underrate yourselves… Incidentally, I've arranged a reception for the Trust. We need all the publicity we can get. It's at the Connaught this Friday. We'll get some drinks and have a good time."

Then he went off to his club.

On Friday I arrived an hour early to the sounds of Lionel shouting and a fair amount of female giggling. Our publicity department had provided a linen-clad table which boasted a huge variety of drinks of which he was freely availing himself while chatting to two gorgeous models who were sporting a sash with the Howardsons logo. Also present was a photographer and his assistant. One wall was covered with a flattering graph of the Third's recent performance. Another table in the opposite corner was heaped with our literature and it was here I took my stand, my instructions being to answer financial questions. Annual general reports of all seventeen of our trusts were available as well as some leaflets which highlighted our pension plans. There was also a blurb about Lionel with a picture of him in front of a castle. It included a summary of his life and what a nice chap he was and how kind he was to animals – though not, presumably, game birds, since he was clutching a twelve bore.

While I was looking at the leaflet there was a call from Lionel, inviting me to join him and I went over, nodding to the two models who were both smiling at me. He was in an expansive mood and gave me a glass of red wine before offering a large whisky.

"No, I'll do something silly if I take that. I'm not a big drinker."

"Silly? You don't know what silly is," he boomed. "This is silly."

At this, he reached for the nearest model and pulled her skirt up to her waist revealing two magnificent legs as well as a nice pair of pink panties: all very fetching. The girl gave a shriek and righted her skirt in a second, while I, seizing the moment, made my way back to my post just as Norman arrived.

Soon guests were pouring in and we were busy answering their queries. It was surprising how much interest the reception had generated. Norman pointed out that most visitors were financial journalists of one kind or another who needed something to write about and something to drink. Since the City had few freebies at that time of the year, it was an oasis in the desert. At one point I looked up and saw Sir James and Fortescue chatting to visitors.

Across the floor, Lionel was being lyrical:

"...of course it's a big place and I wouldn't claim to be familiar with every bit of it. But I'll tell you this, there's money in Hong Kong and its shares. It's not as thrusting as it once was, but with good judgement there's a lot of opportunity."

"Listen to that. Judgement? All he's done is tour the brothels."

"Not too loud, Norman."

Come Monday, everything had returned to normal and we learned that the reception had been deemed a great success having been mentioned in the business columns of all the leading newspapers – including the Sundays – while one of the tabloids had a pic of Lionel laughing with the taller model: a head and shoulders, with no indication of anything untoward, though it was almost certainly taken when he pulled her skirt. They both looked rather well with the Howardsons logo in the background.

From my point of view it was a disaster. Despite all the odds against him, Lionel had firmly established himself. The reception had made him into a formidable figure, and, yes, that was a kind of talent too. So the eleven o'clock arrivals continued as did the three-hour lunches. Norman and I ran the whole thing from eight in the morning until five.

What was I going to do with my life? For sure, I wouldn't consider a career as a minor technical expert. Daily, I watched senior managers congratulating themselves when they didn't lose too much of their investments. Intuitively, I knew that this was the real world: to be technically excellent was no guarantee of a fair reward. I had talent, the Donald Fund had multiplied despite the FT100's dull performance. Of course I was taking no payment for managing it, all dividends were re-invested and it was paying no tax. There was a temptation to leave and live off its dividends but that would invite serious tax enquiries that would ultimately send me to jail.

"Tell you what I'm thinking," said Lionel to me after one of his long lunches. "I'd like to make myself useful."

Out of the corner of my eye, I saw Norman's head go up.

"I'll buy and sell the shares. Get a feel of the market."

"Yes, but there's a department for that, Lionel."

"'Course there is. But I can do it just as well."

"I don't know if they'll allow that," said Norman who had been listening open-mouthed. "It's quite a science."

"Oh, I've discussed it with Fortescue and it's okay."

Almost every day shares were bought and sold for which we would fill in a chitty and send it for action, but now Lionel would copy it in his bold script and pin it to a board behind his desk. He would then telephone the market makers after lunch, after which he would crush the notes and throw them into the bin. At a quiet moment I collected them and found that the wrinkles could be ironed out and they became as new. During the lunch hour, I pinned an order to buy 20,000 shares in ICI to his board. These had already been bought, but being disinterested in his work, Lionel remembered nothing. After lunch he bought them again. Five days later a vexed office manager came to complain. Buying shares is easy but they have to be paid for, which is why we usually sold something of similar value. Now there was a debit of fifty thousand pounds and we had to sell them at a loss to redress the shortfall.

The next incident was worse. It involved a second selling of fifty thousand shares in House of Fraser. Since you can't sell shares you don't own, we had to buy them back which meant we were losing again.

Next I planted a purchase of 20,000 shares in Barclays Bank. The resulting confusion was rewarding, and a grim Fortescue himself came to the office to rebuke Lionel and urge him to get a grip.

A week later I retrieved the sale of 20,000 Buggins and Co, a dreadful share that had been bought three years previously and had fallen by ninety per cent of its value. It had been rumoured to be a takeover target but that come to nothing.

This time the results were gratifying. First, the office manager came into the office, shouting. It amused me that he would harangue Norman for Lionel's incompetence. Then Fortescue himself arrived and spent some time talking to Norman while I dealt with the phone. Half an hour later Fortescue returned and began to examine things, shaking his head in dismay. Then he reached for Lionel's SAP book (sales and purchases) and found he had written nothing whatever on its pages. All of his transactions were therefore unrecorded. No wonder he kept buying and selling the same things, fumed Fortescue. His face became grimmer as the inspection progressed. Finally, with an angry sigh, he removed everything from the desk and took them away: a drastic step.

"What's going on?" I said to Norman when I was finished on the phone.

"They're clearing his desk."

"Does that mean...?"

Norman made a face and nodded.

When Lionel arrived at eleven, he was stopped at the door by George who took him to Fortescue's office where he was given his marching orders. It can't have come as a total surprise. Here was a man who had failed to run his own department who had no interest in its affairs and who couldn't be bothered to arrive on time. Nevertheless he came to bid us farewell. Norman said he was terribly sorry: I shook his hand and said I'd miss him, while the typists were kissed on the lips before he departed for lunch at his club.

Three days later, I was summoned by Sir James who made me the manager of the Third Investment Trust. I was given a good rise and the publicity department made a mild fuss about me, the youngest manager in the firm's history.

13

Thus began a good period. Norman and I argued about everything and sold thirty per cent of the stock, much to the consternation of the management. We then embarked on a buying spree of millions of shares. Sometimes it looked like the bosses would intervene but we were allowed to continue until even Norman declared it to be a good portfolio, the best in the stable. During this period the market made modest gains which accentuated our selections and soon the Third was flying. Within three months it was Howardsons' leading trust and by the end of the year it was declared the best in Britain and was awarded a gold medal which Norman and I accepted at a special dinner in one of London's grand hotels. We got a good bonus too, on which we paid 80% tax. In the meantime my Donald Fund was also doing well, having almost doubled during that year.

"I can sell you a flat," said Sir James.

He owned a new block, and probably others too, and he offered it to me as a goodwill gesture. The price was a perfect bargain, and I moved in, a little daunted by its empty rooms. A balcony gave a good view of London and when you turned to look inside you saw through a series of open doors to a boundary wall four rooms away and it was all mine. It was the first property I had ever owned. Sir James insisted that I use an expert to furnish it and an old man arrived who looked over the rooms and made a number of suggestions. I chose the style and gave him the keys. Walls were papered, carpets laid, and curtains fitted. Lavish amounts of paint were applied, suites of furniture arrived and shades were fixed to the light fittings. Suddenly it became a home that was nice to live in – I had never known such an environment before and I began to be more contented. There was only one problem and that was the price – it was expensive all right. I had to sell some shares through Wallace to pay the bill.

Shortly afterwards, at the age of twenty-nine, they raised me to Chief Investment Officer and I was in charge of the second biggest pension fund in the UK, worth many billions and much respected by financial advisers across the country. I say 'in charge' but that was a technicality. In fact I was merely the chairman of a governing committee, and that was a different thing entirely. The previous incumbent had left and there was such a dearth of talent in the firm that I was the only nominee. This was a different type of operation and it took a lot of adjusting on my part, the sums involved were so big that it required a new kind of discipline.

Much to my own surprise I had reached the upper echelons, mixing with top City people and working with some of Howardsons' high-flying committees, almost all of whose members were rich with private means. Without doubt I was a misfit in a world where they would sometimes spend an entire Monday morning discussing a shoot that had been attended by the Prince of Wales, who was always referred to in casual terms, as though he was an old friend of the speaker's family, the implication being that they mixed in that kind of Society every day of the week. I loathed this kind of thing and was more or less debarred from these conversations though they were always careful to be polite to me. In fact I seldom heard an uncivil word from one year to the next. That said, they didn't like me, and behind my back I was sometimes referred to as the 'cheap creep' while older members described me as 'psychologically flawed'. For all I knew their criticisms were correct. To be fair, I was frequently invited to shoots and hunt balls though I had the stock excuse of being a church organist and therefore unavailable. Once I saw one of the girls roll her eyes at this example of my social ineptitude. She may well have been right.

But I loved my work. It had just the right amount of mental challenge and there was something exciting every day in the Stock Exchange. Would it rise or fall, what would happen to Oils, and would X company be taken over?

There was little doubt that I was good, though that didn't mean all my selections worked. There were many failures. Such things are unavoidable, but in general I was more likely to be right than wrong. At best I might have averaged two or three per cent above my peers, nothing all that great, but over the years it made a lot of difference and of course that difference was accumulative. I believed in moving fast and it was amazing to see the difference of even one pence would make to a share if we got in quick enough.

Meanwhile the Donald Fund was flying. It was effectively my own money and I could do what I liked without having a dull committee to drag me down. I could buy and sell and go for the jugular at every turn and even Wallace was impressed by its advances. Earlier on, he'd been doubtful of me, but now I was on a winning streak and nothing was going to stop me. I knew every one of my shares from memory and could quote their prices and name all their chief executives. And I watched their directors like a hawk – you could learn an awful lot from that. When my peers in Howardsons were discussing last week's shoot, I would pore over the business press, much to their amusement, but I was determined to have the last laugh.

But maybe I should have been more cautious; it's when things are going well that the trouble always starts.

14

It was Friday afternoon and Howardsons was being visited by the Prime Minister. This had happened before, it being good politics to be seen in the City and there was no way he could ignore our firm. The building was bustling with security people, police and reporters. Business was interrupted for the entire day but the publicity was deemed to be worth it. The directors and their spouses were there to be seen with the great man and a lot of our staff lined the stairs for a photo backdrop.

On the previous occasion I had disagreed with one of his aides who knew nothing about the City and who had been aggressive to the extreme. I am not confrontational, but I had erred by responding to his wilder generalisations only to be rebuked by Fortescue when the entourage had gone: apparently guests are always correct and I should merely have agreed with his idiocy and smiled. This time, I elected to stay in my office and get some work done.

Then I looked up to see an old lady come into the room. She was expensively dressed and wore an enormous hat. At first I thought she was the Prime Minister's wife.

"So there you are," she said in her posh voice. "You *are* fond of your work."

Then I realised who she was.

"Ah, Lady Howardson, how nice to meet you."

She shook my hand and then held on to my wrist. This was surprising, bearing in mind she was at least seventy.

"Young man, I want you to be kind to James."

"James…? Oh, Sir James."

"He's been under a lot of strain recently, and, you know, he's getting older… As are we all. But he likes you so much and he's not under pressure with you. He's finding it awkward at the office these days. Everybody wants him to do something, and you know how impossible that can be."

"...I'll do what I can." I said, surprised. Lately I'd thought the old boy wasn't all that pleased to see me.

"You're young, and you don't know what it's like to be old, it's not easy, even if you're the Chairman... I'm so glad you're keen on your work."

"Oh, it keeps me off the streets."

"I'm sure you're not on the streets a lot."

"Actually I walk fifty miles a week. It's really only two hours of walking a day. That's when I do my worrying."

"Goodness, and what do you worry about?"

"Bad investments."

"Well James thinks you're good. Do you enjoy working for us?"

"Oh yes."

"As I said, James thinks you have natural talent. But I'm sure you won't mind me giving you some advice, some motherly advice?"

She tightened her grasp of my wrist.

"No, not at all."

"Young smart men go off the rails too easily. It's so important not to. Don't mix with the wrong types. Everything gets found out in the end, you know."

"...I see."

I left shortly afterwards to start worrying about her remarks. They were too apposite to be ignored. She had seemed a smart old bird, a kindly one at that, and was obviously referring to my private dealings. And she'd wondered what I was worrying about. Yes, there had been a breach in my security and it could only be the Donald Fund.

Phone calls were listened to, sometimes recorded, permission to do so was in my contract, I had always known about it, and had stupidly assumed it applied only to the buying or selling of stock. How much did they know? Over a period of time I had discussed every feature of the fund with Wallace, purchases, sales, total value, etc. Yes, it was a calamity. Obviously that kind of money was not legit, how could it be?

Running an alien fund in the firm's time was a sacking offence, not to mention the trifling question of where the money came from, but since they hadn't fallen on my neck the investigations must still be ongoing. In the meantime they wouldn't ask questions because that would stop the calls.

Presumably the warning had been authorised by Sir James himself who would never warn me personally. That was against his code.

15

I went to see Wallace.

"They're on to me. They've listened to our calls."

"What happened?" said Wallace looking up sharply.

"Lady Howardson warned me about going off the rails."

"That's all?"

By this time he was becoming prosperous, his bank was doing well and taking on more staff though I noticed he worked them hard and paid wages that erred on the low side. He'd also become less matey but perhaps that reflected the challenges of his business. Today I noticed he was dressed in a new pinstripe that must have come from a fancy tailor.

"It's enough."

Wallace asked some questions then sat down and thought about it. This was the kind of thing that brought out his cunning streak.

"How long have they known?"

"Dunno. Sir James hasn't been so friendly for the last three months."

"And he was all right up till then?"

"I think so... he's been distant ever since."

Wallace frowned:

"Your fund hasn't done much in the last three months. Likely they'd be listening before they told him. It'll go further back. This could be nasty. Better try and fade it out."

We agreed that the calls should continue as though nothing had happened but now no sensitive points would be aired. Nothing said on the phone was to be acted on. From now it was for the benefit of the listeners only. We should allow a bit of animosity to generate between us, but no ham acting.

"We've got to convince them. A change in attitude will be noticed."

"What about other non-Donald conversations?"

"Continue," he said. "Howardsons benefits from them."

Later that day we had an argument on the phone about a new share – the worst investment the Donald Fund had ever made. And wasn't it you that suggested it, I countered? Possibly, but he was merely the banker, I was the supposed expert. There was a possibility Mr Donald would close the fund. Wallace was a surprisingly good actor.

Meanwhile Norman left. We had decided to give him a dinner at the Savoy but he wouldn't hear of it and we all waited behind to give him two cartons of his favourite wine – except it wasn't: someone had erred and come up with a Claret that tasted – so he told me later – like dishwater.

"They couldn't run a bath."

Wallace phoned and announced in an indignant voice that the Donald Fund was being liquidated. This is all the thanks we get, he complained – looks like there'll be no more business: there's a dearth of money out there.

I said I was sorry.

It was never mentioned again and we must have convinced our listeners because I was never summoned to explain it. Perhaps they interpreted my actions as 'advising' rather than running. Also they didn't want to lose me.

Now I was in the ascendancy again. The publicity department decided to promote me on TV. At that time I was the youngest manager in the City and my looks could be improved by a good hairdresser and a better tailor. Nothing happened for months, then I was on twice in the same week and after a few weeks of inactivity this was followed by an appearance on *Panorama*.

Money from these was little more than peanuts and it took a lot of time. I was out of the office for most of the day to make a two-minute point. Also it generated interest from the public which I disliked: strangers pointed me out in the street.

"Why are you doing it?" said Wallace.

Since his marriage three years ago he had put on weight. I had played the organ at his wedding where his mother and father had treated me like an honorary son. Now he was the father of a year-old boy and had all the trappings of middle age.

"I sometimes wonder."

"Me too, I saw you last night. They made you look simple-minded... then you talked like a Smart Alex. You're never a TV man. How's the pension fund?"

"Down a bit."

He shook his head in bewilderment.

"That's what comes of your TV capers: you should be sweating blood instead of risking your career on the box. Nobody's sentimental about that kind of money: they'll shoot you down."

As a TV critic, Wallace could be dismissed as an amateur but his comments were basically sound. He had a dread of me losing my job, I was a source of business and the harder I worked the more he benefited. So I began to make changes to my life, refusing any further TV work and watching the pension fund like a hawk.

16

Despite its having reached two million, the Donald Fund brought me no pleasure. I earned a lot of money in Howardsons and could do what I liked without touching its capital. But if it were to come to light I would lose the lot and get five years for my pains. The bigger it got, the greater the risk of discovery. By this time the tax people had more powers and all it needed was one query from an inspector and the whole thing would explode.

"I want the Donald Fund moved to Switzerland," I said to Wallace.

"Oh it's still safe," he countered. He was making money while I took all the risks.

"It's got to be done. Move it to Switzerland."

He shifted uncomfortably, but didn't argue. Recently several prominent people had gone to jail on the discovery of untaxed funds. Only a month ago, government inspectors had spent a week in Wallace's bank, and though he said they hadn't even glanced at my account, a close study would have meant the high jump. There was little cash in hand, but any intelligent observer could calculate its size from the dividends it received.

"It'll continue as before," I told him, "except you'll use a Swiss cheque book. I'll transfer the existing shares with a simple change of address."

Frowning at his desk, he said:

"You'd need a hundred grand to open it. You've got it, of course."

"Yes, but how do I get it to Switzerland?"

Wallace made a face.

"It'll have to be bearer bonds drawn on one of the big banks."

"Yes but they'd be declared."

"Not necessarily," said Wallace with a cunning look. "I'm legal, I can't supply you without a declaration but I know a man who can. Mind you he's worth the watching."

"Who?"

"Oh he's big in the banking world. I've done business with him, good business. Mr D'Alfonso: they call him the Snake."

"How do we go about it?"

It seemed arrangements would have to be made through Wallace since the Snake had an unlisted number. First he'd have to approach him to see if he'd play ball.

"He's prepared to deal with you," Wallace told me a few days later. "But he won't meet you in an office. This thing's sensitive. It'll need to be a pub."

In theory a pub was safe for a meet since it avoided the possibility of a sting, though it presented other difficulties, not least being the host of witnesses who would see us doing business. Nothing's ever easy.

"Does he actually have a £20,000 bearer bond in hand?"

"Absolutely, more than you'll need."

I looked at Wallace to see if he was serious.

"Then he must be a rich man."

Since bearer bonds don't pay dividends, they are nothing more than custom banknotes. To have 'more than you'll need' is equivalent to having a fortune under the bed that can be lost, burnt or stolen – also it is depreciating by the day.

"I'd imagine so. For your part, you'll hand him a bank draft for the same amount made payable to 'bearer'."

For a few moments I considered this. Obviously he could be stealing the bonds and cashing my draft. But did that matter? So long as I got the bond I was safe, or was I?

"This is kosher?"

Wallace made an expression of impatience.

"Not strictly speaking, but you're hardly one to talk. I've done business with him before and had no trouble. It's *caveat emptor*, use your wits and you'll be all right. Make sure the bond has a watermark; I wouldn't expect him to do you."

"Okay, make a date. How will I recognise him?"

"He's six feet six and he wears a maroon waistcoat."

And so I was booked to meet him at The Robber Barron, a big pub with a lot of facilities, including a restaurant and a noisy bar where some colourful personalities, including Frank, are sometimes to be found. Appropriately enough, it had been named after a man called Barron who had been a noted robber of the eighteenth century.

I arrived in good time to find most of the tables taken. Some of the customers looked as if they were planning the destruction of civilisation. Of the Snake there was no sign. I ordered a drink and took a quiet table, becoming increasingly annoyed at the delay. A table away two fat men were having an argument: twice I thought they were coming to blows and some neighbouring diners insisted on being relocated. Apparently one had bought a shop from the other and was none too happy about it. Most people don't feel like eating when they get angry, but they were downing pints as though there was no tomorrow.

"Are you Ron Miles?" asked a big voice, and I turned to find the Snake looming over me, a huge man in a maroon waistcoat. He had been sussing the room before approaching me. Eyes watched from other tables and I thought I saw someone nod.

"That's me, what can I get you, Mr D'Alfonso?"

"Oh, a G and T will do."

This was procured and delivered without acknowledgement.

"I've had a trying day," he announced – and I noticed a foreign accent, "dealing with the chairman of one of our leading banks. The man is a total fool: I hope you don't have any shares in his bank."

He named it and I confirmed I was share-free.

"How the idiot rose above bank-manager level is a mystery. He doesn't understand the basics of banking."

I said there was a lot of that about, but it was unlikely he had ever been a bank manager: nowadays directors were almost always brought in from the City.

He raised his glass and drained it while giving me the once over. Cleary he had intended to make the same remark himself. I was a cheeky pup who had spoken out of turn: didn't I know that a man of six and a half feet deserved a certain amount of respect? He banged the glass down to indicate he could be persuaded to drain another.

I asked about his line of work, did I know his company?

"Oh I am freelance," he said. "I handle big stuff. Some people may want a billion pounds into dollars, or Swiss francs. Or perhaps they want it transferred to the Middle East. I do these things every day in the week, at least when I'm in London. Sometimes I'm abroad. I should imagine you don't do anything on that scale."

I agreed, but he had forgotten me and was looking at the angry men beside us. Tempers were deteriorating even further. One made a wide sweep of his fist which struck his glass and sent it flying through the air in a curve that just missed the Snake and struck my shoulder, showering me in spray. At that point I'd been wondering if the movers of billions delayed their transactions until the Snake was back in town.

"I think we should take a quieter table," said the Snake, standing up indignantly but this was no longer necessary, the efficient bouncers had the men ejected in seconds and one handed me a bundle of napkins to dry myself. Something like this happens every night.

"I could have done without the free beer," I complained, finding my collar and jacket soaked in the stuff.

But he was unconcerned with my discomfort, nothing was going to stop the flow. His voice was soft with a cunning streak that made you listen to him, there was also something that said he was used to talking and that he was seldom interrupted.

"A triviality. I can give you good terms on overseas transfers, to Switzerland or the like. Of course it would need to be a million or more."

On the table, I had a bundle of soaked napkins and was trying to dry my hair.

"I need more napkins."

"Ignore it. I don't have time to waste. Did you hear me: I can transfer a million to Switzerland at a day's notice?"

"Very good, if I ever have a million I'll consider it."

But why was he saying this, had Wallace been talking about my business? Or perhaps the devil knew everything.

"I can do bearer bonds drawn in US dollars or Japanese yen, and I have a discreet connection with Argentina that handles sums as low as a million, electronic transfer. Its official and the authorities have no record of it."

By this time I had my handkerchief out and was trying to dry my face.

"There'll be a computer record," I said, "surely."

"No: numbers only, no client identification. This is bona fides too."

"...I hadn't realised that was possible."

"It's a new thing. There's so much international traffic now. In Howardsons you could sell a million in Shell and I'd transfer it for you."

So Wallace had been talking, or perhaps the Snake read the business press.

"Yes, and I'd spend the rest of my life in jail."

"Of course you wouldn't. Go the right way about it and hackers – they're going to be the thing of the future, by the way – would get the blame, but I'm amusing myself, merely demonstrating the possibility."

"Interesting, but I'm just a minor figure."

"Well, you're a young man, but I'd advise you to avoid the mediocre. Have no truck with the ordinary: life's too short. Go for the bold, it's much more rewarding and, provided you use your brains, safer. You wouldn't be alone either, half the fortunes in London wouldn't bear looking at."

"That sounds true."

Yes I could see the Snake hated mediocrity: the very word brought a sneer to his lips, as did the mention of anybody's name. This was a man who didn't bother to hide his contempt for the human race. I looked at his long dark frame and wondered if he was the most villainous man I'd ever met, without a kind word to say for anyone and with no goal in life beyond his own interests. His face was merciless and he was so certain of his own superiority that his nose was forever in the air. That said, I had a strange feeling that he really did deal in billions: it takes a certain amount of financial weight to cultivate that level of arrogance.

"Of course it's true. Incidentally I can give you a good computer programme that's used by banks. You could use it to transfer money internationally."

"Oh, how much?"

"Nothing at all, fifty pounds, I think."

"I'll buy that. I'm getting a computer shortly. Is there a manual?"

"I think so. I imagine it will be another twenty pounds. I can find out."

"No, no, get them for me – I want another two bonds next week."

"I'll do that. Incidentally, for twenty thousand I can offer you a secure bank account in the Caymans that wouldn't be subject to government inspection."

And so it went on.

Eventually I bought a twenty thousand bond, after having to suffer his conceited conversation for half an hour. He could name every bank chairman and was – if you can believe it – on first names with all of them. The Snake's egotism was real but he had shrewd eyes. The big talk was a smokescreen.

The following day I took the bond to Wallace who confirmed it was genuine by phoning the bank. I met the Snake again and bought two further bonds as well as the programme. He told me he was going to Inverness for a fortnight's shooting with the Duke of Douglas.

"I can give you a reference to a merchant bank in Zurich," said Wallace. "You'll have to present the bonds personally. Of course you need another forty, better make it sixty; sixty thousand."

"What happens if the customs find them on me?"

"Don't let that happen. You're learning to fly, aren't you? Get your instructor to take you over: it should be fun."

Despite his avowed integrity, Wallace knew every trick in the book.

17

That was when I met John Masters. What interested me was a classified advert in *The Times* offering advice on self-defence on a one-to-one basis. This had always fascinated me and I booked a meeting, describing myself as a bank messenger who sometimes carried money and bonds. He was a well-made man of fifty without an inch of fat who claimed to have experience in the security services and had once been a lecturer at Sandhurst. There was no doubt he knew what he was talking about.

"How do I know if I'm being followed?"

"No easy answer, me boy, you can't be sure. If it's a trained team you might never know. Depends who's doing it. Amateurs are one thing, professionals another. If you watch the movies, the tail is a big guy that the women go for. In real life it's as likely to be somebody's granny – or a lame man, someone you wouldn't look at twice. I mean, can you imagine James Bond following you? You might just notice."

"Good point."

"If you think you're being followed there's an old trick. Swing on your heel and go back, as if you'd forgotten something, a 180 degree turn. That often throws 'em. And it lets you see who's coming behind. After a minute you do it again, this time you'll see if the same individual is behind you. He or she may be the most unlikely person. Tell you what: we've got an hour – go out for a thirty-minute walk. I'm not charging you for this. I'll follow. If you lose me you'll get a free lesson next week."

"...Okay."

"Now here's the small print. Act normal, usual walking pace. Don't look back unless you're crossing the road."

Can't say fairer than that so I walked to Piccadilly and lost him, I even doubled back for five minutes before turning into New Bond Street, quite pleased with myself. The thirty minutes were up when he seized my shoulder and laughed. He was wearing a black hat and a long coat that stretched to his ankles.

"Didn't you see me?"

I had to admit that I hadn't so much as glimpsed him. John Masters had made his case: I started taking lessons and learnt a lot. He wasn't impressed by my chances.

"You'll never be a fighter. Avoid violence every time, you'll get killed. You should have lessons in self-defence, mind; they'll make you fitter, but don't get in a fight."

"Not if I can help it. I don't want to be followed."

"Maybe you need a bodyguard." He was mocking me. "Ex-militaries are highly effective... Some can be a bit aggressive but they know how to survive. A crack team can steal cars and get you out of a bad situation. They do it in war and they're trained for it. Of course that's breaking the civil law."

"So they're the best?"

"Well, I'd say so. Suppose you rob a bank, how many gangsters would you need and how good would they be? Now envisage the same thing with a squad of soldiers. I mean it's a piece of cake to an organised squad. At the end of the day they're professional."

"I see. And I must avoid personal combat?"

He gave me a dry look.

"Avoid violence at all costs. There's never a guarantee you'll win, even if you're a prize fighter. But what's this about, thinking of robbing a bank?"

"I'm trying to guess how I might be attacked."

"Well don't live dangerously. Never get on the wrong side of the law. Am I learning you anything?"

"I think so."

"You're an odd bloke for a bank messenger. Never once asked for a receipt or questioned a price. You're a different animal. Maybe you're an investment manager."

"You've been following me?"

There was no response, but his shrewd eyes told me he knew who I was. John Masters was a cold man who could plainly be ruthless and who was neither for nor against me.

18

"Better get that Swiss account going," I said to Wallace. "Get me the Snake."

Wallace had an efficient phone directory on his desk that I could never work out. One stab of a finger always found the right number. The phone rang and rang.

"Nobody at home," he shrugged putting it down.

"Does he have a wife?"

"I don't know. Only he answers. I'll try later, what message?"

"Get me a draft for sixty thousand."

And so I met the Snake at The Robber Barron again and had to endure a long recital of his trip. Apparently he had been the best shot and had also done the six hundred miles in record time in his Lancia. At one point I saw Frank across the bar and we nodded to each other. Later he told me he'd seen the Snake several times and that he'd once been in the company of Mr Big, the well-known gangster.

"Do you need more bonds?"

"No: not in the meantime."

"Your shares must be doing badly," he said in a cunning tone. "There's going to be another slump. You should go liquid for a while."

Here I agreed with him. Having just emerged from a slump the economy was preparing to sink into another one that promised to be worse.

"I'm thinking about it."

It was the following morning before I suspected something. The bonds didn't feel right when compared to the earlier three. Then I noticed they were printed on different paper. In mounting panic, I got Wallace to check the serials and he told me the bad news.

"Duds. No watermark."

"He's nothing but a common thief!"

"I told you to check the watermark."

"How? Hold a bond to the light? It might just get noticed."

"It's still your fault. I'd have checked in a hurry."

Wallace phoned the Snake repeatedly and got no response.

"You'll ring that number a long time before he answers. Give it to me and I'll trace him." Or Frank would.

But Wallace refused point blank.

"He could sue me for breach. I can't pass on privileged information."

"But he's a crook."

"My point is well established in law. Ask the lawyers in your firm."

Wallace said he was sorry.

Sorry he might have been but I was sorrier. And the three bonds would still have to be bought. He offered to get them for me, it was the least he could do, buying them in the name of a client who had purchased some in the past. This was strictly against the law and could bring his bank into difficulties, but he felt he owed me.

A week later I booked Leonard, my flying instructor, to fly me to Zurich. He was delighted and didn't mind at all when I hid a hefty envelope at the bottom of the tools compartment.

"Love letters," I said. "I don't want them falling into the wrong hands."

"Your secrets are safe with me."

The Swiss bank was situated on a back street which my taxi had difficulty finding. It rejoiced in the title of Federal & Corporate Trade (1896) and was little bigger than the Barclays' branch I had once worked in. I presented myself to the front desk and passed the envelope to a decidedly cool official who looked as if he received something similar every day in the week. It included a letter of introduction from Wallace. The official seemed doubtful of me, perhaps I was too young, or maybe they wanted to avoid suspect personalities, and suddenly I was wary of them. This was a foreign country with different laws and practices and perhaps my money wasn't safe in this backstreet office. It took thirty minutes of fuss before the account was opened.

We flew back the following day. Leonard said I was doing well and we would shortly have to think about getting my air licence.

19

'...*all Warrants will be called in ten days.*'
I felt a pain in my gut every time I thought about it. Not that I had any warrants and I didn't dare to think ten days ahead.

There are consultants who can advise about computer problems. Some haven't a clue and others are as good as you can get. One such was Imran Sahid, who was deemed the best in the City. I called in sick, my first absence since joining Howardsons, and with all the printouts and floppies in a box phoned Imran at eight in the morning, describing myself as the security officer of a merchant bank that didn't want its name disclosed. It was essential to see him immediately: there had been a theft that threatened the firm. He didn't sound impressed: no doubt he hears these words all too often.

"I'm busy, is this an emergency?"

"Absolutely. Please see me."

"How are you going to pay me if your bank doesn't want its name disclosed?"

"By cash."

There was a long pause.

"All right, I'll give you two hours. Get here at nine."

You couldn't blame him for being prudent, a troubled bank is notorious at paying its bills. My taxi managed to get caught in a snarl-up while I sat in the back reflecting that my life's work had been squandered. I could hear the Snake sniggering I was lucky to be only ten minutes late.

Sahid looked like the original geek, not much older than me with straggly hair and a beard, badly dressed, and living in one of the most untidy flats I have ever seen. I had to pick my way over the floor after working out a path, putting the cardboard box into his hands, barely able to speak. A total failure, I sank into a chair after he had removed a pile of magazines and watched him read the printouts. Here was a man who wouldn't splash his money on luxury apartments. He'd stay at home and get on with his work. Unlikely he would lose the fortune either. For a start he wouldn't deal with the Snake.

"Hmm. Nearly three million," he muttered, as though it was a triviality. A full hour passed in a silence that was broken only by the phone which he declined to answer, studying the screen, occasionally making notes, while I sat in my chair, scarcely breathing, in case I disturbed his concentration. He was my only hope.

"This is an internal programme. It's handling only one piece of business."

"Um, correct, I think."

"Not recommended that. Easy meat for a thief. It's been altered, presumably by the thief. You know that, don't you?"

I said I wasn't into computers. My job was to catch the fraudster.

"Did he supply the programme?"

"I believe he did."

"Was this the computer manager?"

"No, he wasn't a computer man."

He held up the floppies.

"Bad copies of old software –"

"How did he do it?" I blurted, unable to take more implied criticism.

"They've been rigged. This programme's old... but competent enough – I know offices that still use it. It's been altered."

"...We wondered."

"There's an insert... it reports every transaction to a site elsewhere... he knows your every key stroke. There must have been trouble getting on-line."

"...I believe there was."

"It's gotta connect with the other line first. If that was engaged or unavailable, it wouldn't proceed. Almost certainly that other line was connected to a recorder. It's been badly written by an amateur, but it works. If he claimed to be a consultant, he was a fake."

I said the identity of the thief was known, all we wanted was information that would let us get our money back: if he would write out details, we were willing to act fast.

Sahid looked at me as though I was insane.

"But he'll be off... Oh, there's his phone, I can give you that."

"You can get it?" I said in sudden hope. "I tried, but it wouldn't come up."

"It's been hidden," he said, changing his tone as though I was an idiot. "But he won't be there now... He'll have scarpered."

"I'll move fast."

"Then good luck to you." He was studying a new screen. "Odd... A strange exchange... Auchenboggle 383, heard of it?"

"No."

"I'll check it."

There was a delay while he located a directory after moving a pile of books which fell over, blocking his way out.

"It's Inverness, far enough away."

I breathed a long sigh, the most northerly city in Scotland, and the Snake had been there for the shooting. Yes, this was a lead of sorts.

"It's a private number?"

He shook his head, anxious to get rid of me and my lost cause. It should be remembered that this was before Windows and the World Wide Web when communication between computers was a primitive business.

"I don't know... Unlikely it's his main number – that would identify him."

"And everything went there? To that number?"

"That is so."

"I'll look into it... Would he have an accomplice in Scotland?"

"Well... accomplices have to be paid and they're a risk. He didn't hire a professional to rewrite your programme. I can try the number and see if it's still extant."

"Don't. You'll blow the whistle. He's devious... leave the rest to me."

"I can scan the number without ringing it."

"You can?"

Nodding, he searched for a disk and loaded his computer.

"Auchenboggle 383" and he typed the number then said: "I'll be blowed: it's still on line... I wouldn't have believed that. Listen, it's active just now."

A small speaker played the familiar computer noise.

"Does that mean he's still there?"

"I don't know... it could be other business."

"Is it a professional site?"

"If it is I've never heard of it. Why use a village six hundred miles from London? There's enough trouble with bad lines without leaving town."

Imran started raking among a pile of books to produce an atlas and after some searching, located the village of Auchenboggle some five miles west of Inverness.

But time was up. He put everything in the box, including his notes. I asked for his bill and paid it, and his attitude changed immediately. Money can brighten up the dullest of days. Then he tried the number again:

"It's still on-line. I'd investigate that. Unlikely he'll be there. It's probably automatic."

"Surely he'd be there for the transfer?"

"Well, yes, if something went wrong he might lose the lot. Do you know if this has been set up purely to take your firm's money?"

How could I answer that? Was I the only sucker in his sights?

"I've no way of knowing."

"Would you describe him as dangerous?"

"Yes."

"Then get there as quickly as possible. I don't know how you can retrieve it, but you're a security man and you'll have your own agenda. Almost certainly he'll have relayed it somewhere. Perhaps you can negotiate with him… if he's there. But watch yourself. From what you say, you're dealing with an organised criminal… he'll have his own protection. I'd prefer a heavy team at my back before I confronted him… too easy to get killed. Presumably he's got money of his own?"

"Yes," I said, remembering the twenty thousand pound bearer bonds.

But his innocent description of me as a security man had made me feel like a fraud. I'd have to go alone since Frank would need notice and that would involve a delay. And how could I deal with the Snake without weapons or fighting ability?

"There are a number of possibilities. Auchenboggle 383 may be a line into an office, or a room in a big company, or he could be working for the local mafia from a pub. I've seen it all and nothing surprises me. Watch your back."

It was eleven thirty when I staggered into a taxi and drove home. I seized my travelling case as well as my crime bag which I'd collected earlier from my store. This contained a collection of tools as well as clothes, wigs and gadgets. My head was buzzing and I was desperate. But there were other problems.

What was the point of going to Auchenboggle if not to reclaim the money? Granted, that was unlikely, but should I achieve the impossible, what could I do with it? Plainly it couldn't be banked in my Swiss account since he would simply remove it again. Nor could I pay it into Barclays without a tax raid. It was essential to have a plan.

The answer lay in more bureaucracy. I needed another account. I'd spent weeks studying Swiss banks, so I phoned a bank in Zurich, Gill & Co. to propose opening an account with the two point eight million – the money to be paid by electronic transfer. By this time currency regulations had changed and the proposed transaction was legal, tax considerations aside. There followed a lengthy delay while they took my details after which a number was issued. I wrote it down, reread it, had it confirmed, and did the same with their clearing codes. When would the lodgement be made? asked the calm Swiss voice. Within seven days, I said, or not at all.

I copied the numbers on to a card and hid it in the lining of my jacket.

For fully two minutes I stood with my head in my hands and analysed the chaos of my life. This was probably an exercise in sheer futility that I couldn't afford. Why go north when the great bandit would be gone? Yet it was a lead that must be explored. Remaining in my flat over the weekend would be unendurable. This was the only address and telephone number I'd ever found for the Snake and though he'd never leave a forwarding address there was a small chance of tracing him and I'd have to take it.

Twenty minutes later I'd hired a car from my usual dealer and was heading north.

20

It promised to be the worst journey in the world and my head was spinning at the injustice of it all. The roads were a nightmare. The distance was long, there was severe congestion and it would take a lot more time than the guide books postulated. It was too late now, but ideally I should have chartered a flight and taken Frank with me.

My fortune had been stolen and that might only be the beginning of my troubles. So far I'd been too busy to think about it but now I had no alternative.

'...all Warrants will be called in ten days.'

Obviously this was not a threat to stop me reporting the theft; he knew I couldn't do that without admitting I'd stolen it in the first place. Almost certainly it meant he was going to expose me in ten days – probably by sending my file to the cops. From his point of view it made good sense and it would get me out of his way forever. But equally he didn't want me in custody in case I spilled the beans, so he was giving me a chance to run before the balloon went up.

But where could I go? You can't hide in the Western world any more: medical and tax records, to say nothing of the cops, would track me wherever I went. A new identity would have to last for the rest of my life and that was near impossible now that my money was gone. I was facing a future in which I couldn't get a job or even open a bank account.

Roadworks to the north of London caused more than an hour's delay. Then there was a long stretch of contra-flow at Birmingham where the M6 merged with weekend traffic from the M5 heading for the Lake District. I was uptight and ill-tempered, shaking my head at the incompetence around me, my face grim with intolerance, furious at every obstacle that the roads flung at me. At that time hundreds of miles of British roads were being rebuilt and the journey was interrupted by untold roadworks that involved endless queuing. My mood was as overcast as the sky. Many heavy vehicles were slow movers and as the journey progressed there were hordes of caravaners to add to the chaos.

Eventually I stopped at a service station near Manchester and found my hands shaking so badly that I could barely hold my cup. Without doubt I shouldn't have been driving in such a state and I wasn't even halfway. In the shop I bought a map of the Inverness district and located Auchenboggle. Returned to the car, I drove for a couple of hours before stopping at a hotel in Carlisle where I phoned the vicar to say I would miss the organ on Sunday. He wasn't pleased.

In bed, I tossed and turned for hours before nodding off: then I overslept.

My journey was pointless. This was the pursuit of an elusive man and too much time had been lost. Now the whole thing was a knee-jerk and I was unarmed. He had lifted nearly three million pounds and, on-line or not, he wouldn't be waiting for me to congratulate him. Almost certainly he had returned to London. Perhaps he'd passed me on the road – and, yes, he'd go in his Lancia.

Maybe that was to my advantage. On all the evidence, the Snake was more dangerous than the terrorists. The shooting at Great Square had to be his work. Madame Boss and her cohorts wouldn't have risked a death on the night before their operation. And though he was not involved in the Siege itself, he was implicated in its planning and his path must have crossed the dead officer. That meant I was dealing with an assassin.

It was ten on Saturday morning when I hit the road and now I made better progress, though the traffic was slow around Glasgow with a lot of roadworks. By three p.m. I had reached Perth, my eye blind to the beauties of the scenery around me. Inverness was still hours away and I was so tired I had to stop in Pitlochry to kill thirty minutes while I merged with tourists in a local shop. Here I bought a packet of biscuits and a nasty knife with a six-inch blade. John Master used to say a knife was better than a handgun at close range and it can terrify your opponent, (though he also said I was not an ideal knife man.)

Returned to the car I drove less aggressively and when the rain stopped I opened my window to get fresh air, eating a biscuit as I did so.

Without doubt my career was over. Monday was going to be bad. I would have to go to Sir James with a letter of resignation, pleading a nervous breakdown, saying I could no longer make executive decisions. Perhaps I would claim to have been in a private clinic over the weekend, where the consultant had identified a deep-seated aversion to the industry. But would that work? There would be an unholy row. I was his protégé, doing well for the firm, and there was no one to replace me. He'd turn into a colonel and order me to report to *his* physician. Nobody throws in the towel when he is in charge...

Alternatively I could run for it. First I could get a fortnight's leeway by saying something about bad headaches, the need for a rest and the doctor had advised a quiet holiday. They'd have to agree and provided I could get a visa I could be in Switzerland by lunchtime, where I'd arrange to sell the flat and get the money sent across.

But that wouldn't work either. When they realised I'd gone, Sir James would have a quiet word with the Chief Constable to have me traced: he wasn't a top man for nothing. He'd mutter something about security and of course he'd get full co-operation, particularly if the Snake had sent my files in. They'd trace my flights and have me in days. Then they'd start questioning me about the Siege as well as the Fund.

No, it would have to be the first option. Perhaps I could dig my heels in and refuse to see his physician. I could then sell the flat and move out of town, a total failure. But where would I go after that and what would I do? The prospect was a lonely one.

It was early evening when I drove through a dull Inverness and found the minor road that would lead to Auchenboggle. By this time I had become relaxed. All right, I had failed as had millions before me. Money had come easily and now it had gone forever. I would have to adjust my life to my limitations.

As I swung to the left I found myself looking at the entrance to a three-star hotel which sat at the top of a tree-lined avenue. Mentally exhausted, I was in no condition to face the Snake – assuming he was still there – and I needed time to get my wits together. I drove up to find a hotel that had fallen on hard times, with an empty car park and an air of neglect about it. At the reception desk I was greeted by a prim girl of thirty called Miss Prudence who didn't like the look of me. Her intuition had noted that I was uptight and not the typical Saturday-night guest I purported to be. But there was a room and, despite its being rather expensive, I nodded my acceptance.

Judging by the signs behind the desk, the hotel had a lot of negatives. No pets, no credit cards, no early morning calls, no food to be brought into the premises. All rooms to be vacated at ten thirty.

Miss Prudence's assessment of me was quite right. My hands were trembling and I could barely stand: the journey had been terrible and there was the possibility that my hated enemy was still around. I had violence in mind: there was a sharp knife in the car and I was almost too tense to breathe.

"Your name and address, please," she said, shoving a card across the desk. "Oh, and your car number too." But I wasn't listening. The telephone number on the card said 'Auchenboggle 381' – two digits short of my goal – and it wasn't easy to remain calm. Was this also 383? Perhaps there were other lines into the building.

'John Smith', I wrote with some confidence and then my hand trembled. It would have to be a false address that I could remember. In a moment of utter folly (I was fatigued and had been flung by the phone number) I gave the only one that came into my head – Bakevan Street, the same address I'd used as a hostage. I cursed myself silently, but could see no way of correcting it without raising the suspicions of Miss Prudence. Instead, I made an error of two letters in the entry for the car. I got the room nearest the front door.

"Dinner's at seven. And our chef is an award winner."

But dinner was the last thing on my mind. I threw my case into the room and went out to the car as though I'd forgotten something, looking up at the phone lines as I did so, noting that there was only one pair of wires into the building and they looked ancient.

Returned, I went to the lounge to find I was not alone. An old geezer of about seventy with a beetroot-red face and a whisky glass was glaring at me. I wondered, idly if he was schizophrenic then decided it was pure alcohol abuse: there's a lot of it about. He scowled at my greeting.

I wanted the address of Auchenboggle 383 and it was best to ask no questions of Miss Prudence who seemed suspicious of me and might be a bad witness if things went awry. In a shelf beside the window there was a telephone directory but it covered the shire, perhaps the whole north of Scotland. There were thousands of entries and, assuming it was listed, it would take an age to find the one I wanted. I ran an eye over a few pages without finding a single Auchenboggle number.

Then there was the most tremendous crash I have ever heard in a room.

Throwing myself to the floor, heart thumping, I rolled to the side in the best John Masters style. Never make a target of yourself, get down and plan your next move while you're still breathing. Obviously the Snake had found me. I hadn't seen a flash and there didn't seem to be any smoke, though the sound implied a bomb and there had been an air blast. My hearing had been distorted but footsteps were running. Then the receptionist was at the door, followed by two kitchen staff.

"It's all right. It's all right," they reassured me. "His Lordship takes these turns."

And sure enough, the chair on which the old fool had been sitting had fallen backwards to the floor. Its occupant, still in situ, was facing the ceiling with an equanimity that did him proud, his two ankles pointing heavenwards. He didn't deign to look at us. By this time I was off the floor and gave them a hand to right the chair: it was heavy.

"He does that when he gets angry. I hope you didn't get too much of a fright."

"No, no, barely noticed it."

"We've got a straight back on the chair in case he breaks his neck."

The kitchen staff escorted him out of the room. He walked like a military officer, looking neither to the right or the left, his stupid face pointing straight ahead.

"I'm terribly sorry," said Miss Prudence, bending down to retrieve the fallen whisky glass. "He hasn't done this for ages: he absolutely hates strangers in his house, you know. It's really too much. The Auchenboggles own the whole parish, they've been here for centuries, but Uncle Quintin – he's my uncle, actually – has got into the most awful debt and we've had to make his home a hotel. And he so hates it. This very seldom happens, you know, it's only when he takes a dislike to someone. Can I get you a sherry on the house?"

But I had other things on my mind: "Later."

21

The search for 383 had to go on. I left in the car. The hotel had two entrances and now I tried the other one which took me in the opposite direction where it joined a tree-lined road. Here I parked in a lay-by and opened my crime bag to don a donkey jacket that had a bullet-proof vest sewn into its lining. It was bulky and I hated it, but it might save my life. I strapped the knife around my waist and put on a workman's hat.

Then I checked the map and drove to Auchenboggle where I would commence my enquiries at the pub by asking if anyone had seen a six foot six maniac. This involved a triangular route that took me back onto the road I had used earlier. Past the first entrance, it became narrower and I drove on, noting a number of impoverished farms that were no doubt part of his Lordship's estate. A family car with two tall men, neither of them the Snake, passed me, the driver giving me a courteous nod when I pulled in to let them pass. Then the road came to a junction at which there were three houses. I couldn't believe it, this was the village of Auchenboggle. I learnt later that it had been of greater size but had croded over time. The house on the right had taken a lot of punishment from the weather and hadn't been painted for years. Two full grown trees in its garden hid most of its facia and the shrubbery had run amok. But it was the car that caught my eye.

A blue Lancia sat in its drive and it was a current model. He was there!

At the junction I turned slowly and, once out of sight, parked beside a gate.

One piece of stupidity would be the end of me, but that wasn't even in my subconscious as I jumped out and ran as close to the hedge as possible until I reached the house. So far as I could tell, no one had seen me. The two houses opposite seemed deserted, with their storm doors closed. There was no movement at the Snake's house, though there was a light in an upstairs room. I leapt the garden wall rather than risk the gate squeaking to find myself at the Lancia. Its driver's door was unlocked and his hat sat on the back window ledge. The engine was cold.

Everything about the house was drab, the garden was chaotic and several shrubs had overgrown the path. I had a surge of panic. This was too easy; the Snake should be hundreds of miles away. Perhaps I was making a huge mistake. For some minutes I put my ear to the letter box and heard nothing. Again I checked the houses across the road. No lights, no activity, probably deserted. Then I put my eye to the letter box to see an interior as dull as the exterior and it was completely silent. If he was here, he was alone, or so it seemed.

I am the man who doesn't believe in confrontation and this was going to be the mother and father of them all: but there was no alternative. It was either him or me.

I reached for my knife and pressed the button.

22

An old style bell reverberated through the house and for a few moments I wondered if there was anybody about. Then unhurried footsteps descended the stairs, the steps of a man who was in no great hurry and who had never once doubted his superiority. The door was of stout wood with a panel of frosted glass in the centre in which the image of the Snake gradually emerged with his maroon waistcoat clearly visible. I wondered if he would open the door. A man in his position would not expect many callers and he had good reason to be cautious. Then the lock turned and it began to open.

With the knife in my right hand, I put my left shoulder to the door and rammed it with all my force. He yelled and took a heavy fall. Then I was inside a dull hallway of brown varnish in which the long frame of the Snake was looking up at me from the floor. All was quiet, with no one rushing to the rescue. I slammed the door, waved the knife, and ordered him to his feet.

"You are a complete barbarian," he said.

"I am! Raise your hands! Don't try anything."

I surprised myself by sounding angrier than I was. It was a small hallway with an ancient carpet on the floor and several closed doors. He rose painfully, rubbing his knee. I made him lean against the wall while I frisked him to make sure there were no weapons. A difficult moment: he is a big man with long limbs that were capable of terrible blows.

"Are you alone?"

"You'll find out soon enough, I fancy."

The house seemed empty but there was no way of being certain, though it was unlikely he'd have answered the door if there'd been anyone else to do the chore. I kicked the door behind me and it opened on to a deserted room in which there was an untidy sleeping bag on the floor and an open suitcase. There was another door on his side of the hall but that was best ignored since it meant going dangerously close to him. Obviously this was part of

Auchenboggle Estate with its dilapidated airs and tired varnish. His overcoat hung beside the door and there were two suitcases beside it. Presumably he was getting ready to leave. There was a smell of petrol.

"Very slowly, walk up the stairs."

Like most houses in the Highlands it had been built to conserve heat, the hallway was too small, the stairwell too narrow and at a steeper angle than was comfortable. It was essential to get him up to the room he had left. Dicey, I couldn't get close without my face being near his heels and one kick could kill me. Currently I had the upper hand but this was a risky situation that would have John Masters frowning like mad. By this time I knew the whole thing was a mistake on my part, at the very least I should have brought Frank.

"Did you hear me? Get up those stairs, slowly."

The monster's brow was furrowed and he was scheming like mad. His hands had begun to tremble and sweat had appeared on his face. Reluctantly he began to ascend the stairs, a huge man, towering over me. I kept well back from his heels.

"I hope this is slow enough for you?"

"Watch it! And I can throw a knife," I bluffed.

On the top step he paused, his hands raised, while I was still only halfway up. There were two rooms on either side and he could rush into either and slam the door, but he hesitated and then sagged. My rage had frightened him. He was too aware of the knife and my alleged ability to throw it.

"Forward, against that wall," I bawled.

By now I was on the landing. On the right hand side there was an untidy bedroom with a great bed. So this was where he slept? Who used the sleeping bag downstairs? The opposite door revealed a computer that looked identical to Imran Sahid's.

"In there."

Yes, this was where he had been working: there was even a coal fire in the grate. The room was devoid of all furniture except for two wooden chairs and the table on which the computer rested beside two Revox tape recorders that were connected to the phone. I was in the Devil's lair: all his equipment was there and it was Spartan, without any human comforts. This was the man who hated mediocrity.

"Sit on the far chair."

A difficult moment, I had to find some way of tying him without putting the knife down. I took a plastic tie from my pocket and looped it.

"Put your right arm on the armrest."

Surprisingly he did it without protest and using one hand only I slipped the loop over his right wrist, enclosing it with the armrest, and pulled it tight. I could smell a fear from him that told me he was desperate. That didn't mean I'd won.

"We must talk," he said, clearing his throat nervously and changing his tune. By this time the swagger had gone. "I may have given you a bad time but that's the nature of the business. I concede all your monies. You may have them back."

I switched off both tape recorders, went over to the computer, and sat down. My hands were trembling so badly that I could barely hold the knife. But this was progress. The computer was a self-contained unit, all booted up with its integral screen glowing – a great improvement on the IBM printer of my own system. My eyes took a moment to adjust to its unearthly glow at which I found it was loaded with a programme similar to my own though there were some differences. Eleven million was there on the bottom right hand. Eleven million? Yes, and it was pounds, not dollars.

"Generous of you."

"That computer isn't working, the lines are down."

"It looks fine to me."

"No, try nothing. That's why I'm still here. I've had trouble – look, I'll transfer your money as soon as possible."

"I don't trust you."

"I mean it. Let's declare a truce."

"You can't expect me to trust you."

There was a minute's silence during which the only sound was his breathing.

"What were you doing at Great Square?" I asked, touching the controls, trying to get the feel of the thing while at the same time humouring my captive.

"Great Square? You were there?" His surprise seemed genuine.

"What were you trying to do?"

The Snake drew a breath and turned on the charm.

"Oh, I had to humour my companion. Surely you recognised him."

"No, can't say I did."

The keyboard was different and I couldn't understand some of its functions.

"Ahmad, without the face hair."

"Oh, Ahmad. What was he doing?"

Suddenly the room seemed to sway around me and I seized the table for support. My head couldn't cope with all the ramifications. I closed my eyes and took a deep breath. If I lost the screen now, it would be the end of everything, there being no likelihood of him rebooting it for me. There would be some kind of password, which presumably was already in place otherwise it wouldn't be displaying the account. His usage of the programme was entirely different to my own and my eyes ranged over the screen desperately trying to understand it. In the background the Snake said something that I couldn't hear. Perhaps he was trying to distract me. I was also troubled by the sleeping bag in the lower room. Undoubtedly there was someone else about though I had no doubt we were alone in the house at that point.

"He was trying to entice two Mossad agents into the Siege."

"Oh, was Mossad there?"

"Even he didn't know for sure."

Plainly the lines weren't down, so why was the computer still running when his bags were packed downstairs? The money should have been transferred as quickly as possible and the Snake knew that better than I did. There was a catch somewhere.

"A bloodbath."

"Exactly. But it would generate world publicity."

"Barmy."

"I thought so too."

"So who was bankrolling it, the Liberation Organisation?"

"Possibly... I don't know... Of course he's paid the price."

"What about the shooting on the previous night?"

"You're well informed," he said with a laugh, denying nothing. "It was... necessary. But we'll leave that for the moment. Now, Ron, you will have to be sensible. Not all of that money is yours. Take it all, and we'll both be in serious trouble."

"I am in trouble. And so, I think, are you."

"You can't take money that isn't yours. Not on such a scale."

"Oh, I don't know. In my shoes, I'm sure you'd take it."

"You can't do that. Loosen this tie and I'll transmit it to your account now."

"Yes, and transfer it back five minutes later."

From what I could see, he was using his own list of banks and his funds were not transmitted on a daily basis like mine. His transactions were manual rather than automatic, which meant they couldn't be intercepted electronically: it had been in a South African bank for three days and so far as I could see he was in the process of arranging a transfer to Beirut. But why hadn't it gone through?

"Why," I said, "were you involved in the...?"

On the edge of my vision I saw him go tense and I flung myself to the side, dropping the knife, narrowly avoiding a blow that would have felled a stallion. He was wielding an armrest from the chair which just missed my head and skimmed my shoulder leaving my arm numb. In so doing I had fallen to the floor and my enemy, his face twisted in rage, raised it to batter the life out of me, dragging the chair behind him. Apparently he was left handed and had dismantled the armrest while he talked. To save myself, I kicked my own chair in his direction, at which point he made a second terrible swipe that struck the light on the ceiling, shattering the lampshade into a thousand pieces before he fell over my chair and landed beside me. Meanwhile his right arm was still tied to his own chair which fell on top of him.

"You fool, you fool!" he roared, furious with himself for having missed. I kicked at him but there was no stopping this rabid monster. He was upright in a moment, coming at me with spittle running down his jaw, still dragging the chair behind him. I am no doctor, but it looked like berserker rage which makes its victim completely uncontrollable. Either that or it was some kind of fit. Ancient warriors were known to induce berserker rage in battle and I could see that it would rather daunt their foe.

I bolted from the room, leaving the knife under the table, there being no safe way of retrieving it and the Snake was now so unhinged that it was doubtful if it would affect his judgement. I would have to kill him to save myself and that was best avoided. On the other hand if he seized it I would be dead.

Here I found myself on the landing. There was a bit of trouble at the doorway when he fell over the chair for the second time, bawling like a baby. The armrest fell out of his hand and rolled down two steps of the stair.

He roared at me in a language I didn't recognise. He scrambled at me. My only possible refuge was the bedroom on the other side, but once trapped there I would never get out alive. He would merely fetch a gun and shoot me. Meanwhile I had neither weapon nor backup. I had been a fool. This should have been planned in advance. John Masters had warned me about violence.

The Snake threw back his head and roared again, and it was not a European tongue.

Grasping the chair like a lion tamer, he came at me with murder in his eyes. I deflected it into the wall causing it to rebound into his face with a satisfying 'thunk'. Then I rammed it at his head at which he fell back with a crash that shook the floor, shouting like a madman. At this point I might have overcome him if only I'd had a weapon.

"Stupid little man!"

Yes, when you are six feet six most of the human race is little and he was right about the stupidity too.

But the Snake was no fighter either. The bawling was a mark of incompetence, an attempt to cow me, a mask to hide his own incompetence. He didn't know what to do; at this point a trained man would have killed me.

Now his head was beginning to work again. Realising he needed a weapon his eyes darted in all directions until he saw the armrest on the second step. For the moment he'd forgotten about the knife. He charged at me, forcing me back, aiming the chair at my head. I seized it and tried to wrest it from his grasp but this time he had a madman's grip and he was surprisingly strong. Retreating to the stairway he kept his eyes on me while his hand felt for the armrest blindly.

My position was bad, I was trapped on a narrow landing with my only chance of escape blocked by my enemy who was reaching for a weapon to batter the life out of me. Not good, and if I didn't do something quickly there wouldn't be another day in my diary.

Desperately, I threw myself at his shoulder, bracing both feet against the wall for purchase. Everything happened slowly. His rage-filled face turned toward me as I struck him with all my weight, causing him to utter the most tremendous bellow I've ever heard, a near-inhuman sound as he overbalanced down the stairs.

But my momentum was too great and I couldn't save myself either. We were both carried down the steep stairs with the chair bumping behind us. At the edge of my vision I saw him go head over heels while he roared his protests. Then there was some confusion at the bottom when he fell on top of me. I was unhurt: my bulky jacket had absorbed the violence and I leapt away before he could grab at me. But here I was blocked from the front door by his long frame and the windows behind me were barred.

He was lying face down on the floor, seemingly semi-conscious. Of course he'd taken a lot of punishment but there was no certainty he was in any way impaired. His hands and feet were moving, implying no broken limbs, though he'd banged his head on the way down and the chair was lying on his shoulders. Was he shamming? If I made a dash for the door he might bring me down and strangle me with his hands.

Then I saw my chance. I grabbed a tie from my pocket and got it round his right wrist before he knew what I was doing. There was some half-hearted resistance when I pulled his left arm over and pulled it tight. Now his hands were tied and he seemed barely aware of it. Next, I tied his feet, narrowly avoiding a kick. Now he was powerless.

I cut the tie from the chair and lifted it away.

"Are you all right?" I said. "Do you need medication?"

No answer. He was staring into the carpet with spittle on his face.

I looked at his great six and a half foot frame blocking the entire entrance hall. By sheer accident I was the victor after stupidly intruding into a world beyond my control and but for his mistake on the landing I would probably have been dead.

Carrying the chair, I returned to the landing, unable to believe how drained I was. My hands were trembling, I could barely hold the chair or climb the steps and my head refused to function. Perhaps I should have retreated while I was still alive but I hadn't travelled six hundred miles merely to give the Snake a pasting. I went into the bedroom and sat with head in hands for five minutes until my mind began to function. The room was dreary enough to make a monk's cell seem luxurious, with dampness, peeling wallpaper, a rotting window frame and absolutely no comforts. Granted, this was only a temporary residence, but I wondered at his mentality, a rich man, perhaps a very rich one, living in a state of frugality that beggared belief. What's the point of money if you can't benefit from it?

But this was no time to be idle. I dragged myself to the other room where I sat again at the computer and studied it for a long time after retrieving the knife. This was taking too long, but my head was still fighting the Snake and I could barely read its screen. I produced my card with the Swiss account number.

Slowly, I erased the Beirut bank (the computer showed 'line unconnected' so it was the lines to the Middle East that were down) and typed my new account at Gill & Co. I must be cautious by nature, because my hand refused to press the Enter key. I went down to see the Snake.

"Are you all right?"

There was no answer. But he seemed to be breathing easier, though my knowledge of medical things is near zero and for all I knew he might have been at death's door. One thing I didn't need was a death.

"Do you hear me?"

His eyes closed in exasperation. Yes, he was conscious and possibly more alert than he seemed.

Returned to the computer, I checked the details again. Where had the Snake got such a mind-boggling sum? I flipped to the previous screen and saw the entry where my own fund had been added to the balance. Several pages back revealed a history of movement between various banks without any great alteration to its balance. His eight million went back a long way.

For a moment I considered altering the transfer to the exact sum he'd taken from me. I'd come to Auchenboggle to claim my fund, not to clean him out. My fingers hesitated over the keys, but it's not in my nature to refuse money.

I pressed the button.

There was a pause of a full minute, which seemed like a lifetime and then the screen displayed TRANSACTION COMPLETE. After a great sigh I took the cover off the computer and wrecked it with the armrest so that it would never work again, destroying the floppies by breaking them in two. Then I checked the rooms to make sure there was no spare computer. That done, I tidied myself as best I could, put on my workman's cap which was lying on the floor and went down stairs with the knife in my hand.

"I'm going now. Can I phone someone to release you?"

No answer.

"Did you hear me? I can get help."

He was staring into the carpet as if comatose, closing his eyes in rage as I spoke. Wariness crossed my mind, whatever the Snake's many faults, he is not stupid and his silence implied reserves I couldn't begin to guess. If he didn't want to starve to death while trussed like a chicken, he had a plan. But it was time for me to go when I was winning. I waved the knife and stepped over him, opening the door to the darkening evening.

Welcome fresh air touched my skin as I pulled the door behind me, unable to believe I'd survived. All was quiet. Opposite, the two houses were unlit and apparently unoccupied. The noise the Snake had made must have been audible over a wide area yet no one had heard him. Of course this was the north of Scotland, a country of wide spaces and sparse population.

It was difficult to walk: I was still fighting the Snake, wondering what would happen next and scarcely able to grasp the car key. I changed out of the donkey jacket, discovering I had wrenched all the buttons off in my fall down the stairs and left for the hotel where I would have a bath and wash my hair to remove all traces of the fracas.

23

At seven thirty I took my seat in the dining room on an oak chair that was centuries old and had never been designed with comfort in mind. This of course was the theme song of the entire hotel. It was cold and cheerless as well as far too big. In fact there were only two diners in the room, myself and the ludicrous Lord Auchenboggle who was sitting three tables away and occasionally looking up from his paper to glare at me.

I wasn't entirely happy. The Snake had been defeated but whether I liked it or not I would have to return and make sure he was all right. A blow to the head can cause serious problems and he'd taken several. If he died at the bottom of the stairs, there would be a murder enquiry and they'd soon trace me. Ideally I should have gone before dinner but I couldn't bear the thought of it. Of course I'd approach the house only if it was unlit. And I'd enter only if there were no other cars at the door.

I had scarcely been seated before Miss Prudence appeared with the sherry they owed me for the contretemps in the lounge and she had barely left before the chef arrived to say there were no menus but he would make anything within reason. Having twice been the winner of the 'Most Promising Young Chef' in the north of Scotland, his Sole Mornay was praised far and near and he insisted I have it as a starter. None of this sounded promising, but after some discussion we settled on a main course of Scottish venison. When he left I looked at the sherry and reminded myself that I'd eaten nothing all day and it might be best to keep a clear head. This may well have saved my life. I rose and took the glass to his Lordship who was pretending to read his paper and placed it on his table.

"My lord, a gift from a well-wisher."

Returned to my table I was seized by a spell of giddiness in which the room seemed to revolve around me. Such are the perils of a hectic lifestyle. In the distance a voice was talking and it sounded like Sir James. I couldn't believe it was coming from old Auchenboggle. Clearly he was an Etonian with a better voice than most newsreaders. However he spoiled the effect by speaking too loudly:

"Young man, I can see you're a fellow of good taste. And I can tell you there's not many of us left in this dastardly world. Your gift of fine sherry has been the act of a nobleman and I'll see that you're well rewarded."

His voice faded into welcome silence as the chef approached with the famous Sole Mornay. I thanked him but he wasn't listening. He had turned to see a party of two come into the dining room and I shared his surprise. One of them, clutching a handgun, was the Snake and he didn't look pleased. He was walking with a limp, his face bore several bruises and he had a black eye. Instinctively, I knew this was Getaway Day and he no longer cared about the aura of respectability he'd presumably built in the locality. Probably that was why he'd opened the door when I rang: he must have assumed I was the heavy who now accompanied him. Fortunate for me that he hadn't returned when I was dealing with his master.

"Hands up!"

I didn't move, but the chef did, dropping his tray with a crash.

The Snake's companion was relatively tall, dressed in a black leather suit with a bikers' helmet on his head and black gloves. He disappeared into the kitchen and ushered a young girl out: a moment later Miss Prudence, complaining loudly, was marched through. All three were lined against the wall and made to stand with their hands on their heads while the biker stood at the back and watched. He didn't seem to be armed. With a grim look, the Snake approached me, gun in hand.

"Mr D'Alfonso, what is the meaning of this? Put that gun away immediately," ordered Miss Prudence in her best headmistress's voice. It looked like the Snake was off the guest list for next year. But his eyes were fixed on me and there was a fanaticism on his face that I'd never seen before. My only option was to defy him – he could have stymied me two hours ago by doing the same thing. Now the boot was on the other foot and I had to hope the last thing he wanted was a corpse.

"You are a fool."

"So I've been told."

"You will come with us. Now."

"But I've ordered dinner."

"There is unfinished business."

"No there isn't."

In fact I didn't feel in the least defiant. The Snake's gun looked as if it was brand new and he couldn't miss at that distance. His whole frame was trembling but his gun seemed remarkably steady.

"Stand up or I'll shoot."

"I'd rather sit, thank you."

"Get up."

When it came, the crash was magnificent, far louder than the one in the lounge. Of course the dining room offered more in acoustical resonance and I could see that Lord Auchenboggle had taken a dislike to the visitor with a gun. The Snake, who prided himself in being surprised at nothing, found this a particularly difficult moment. There had been an enormous noise. A chair had been upset, a pair of feet in silk slippers was the only clue to its occupant, but perhaps there was a gamekeeper behind it with a twelve bore. Then he remembered to keep his eyes on me. But it was too late. My aim wasn't all it might have been and the Sole Mornay merely grazed his shoulder. But I could do better than that – the alternative was death – and before he could raise his gun my oak table battered into him with all the force I could muster. He went down with a crash that shook the room as it landed on top of him. Miss Prudence gave a decent scream. I leapt to the floor and seized his gun. With a clatter of feet, the heavy ran off.

The table shifted and the Snake, holding his arm – which seemed to be broken – sat up with an expression of utter disbelief on his long face.

"Phone the police!" I shouted at Miss Prudence. "This is one of the most dangerous men in Britain."

I handed the gun to the chef.

"You, keep him covered. I'm DS Smith from the Yard. Gotta go after that other fellow, he's a serial killer. Watch that gun now, it's got a sensitive trigger."

I went out, past the deserted reception desk and into my room. Difficult to know how much of my story they believed but I was taking no chances. Seizing my case, I opened the window and threw it out, before dropping onto the grass. In a moment I was driving at a fair clip down the back entrance, noting that there was not a trace of the biker. My last glimpse of Auchenboggle Hotel was of the telephone lines which had been cut and were lying on the driveway.

24

I drove fast, avoiding Inverness, keeping to country lanes I'd seen on the map. The road was quiet, though I had a heart-stopping moment when rounding a corner to find myself staring at blue flashing lights which fortunately belonged to a fire brigade.

Eventually I swung off the road into a forestry path.

The trees were magnificent in their millions. They stretched on every side towards a distant summit and there was no one within miles of me. I stopped at a bend and got out to stretch my shaky legs, noting the wail of distant police sirens as I did so.

Walking with my head down I analysed the last two hours and asked myself what I'd left behind that would identify me. Probably fingerprints on door handles, handwriting on the registration card, descriptions by the hotel staff. But this was six hundred miles from London and the cops had neither my prints nor my handwriting in their files. But there was one person who could shop me right down to my address and employment and that was the Snake. A pang in my gut told me I was finished. I might return to London tomorrow but they would come for me.

I went to a brook, its water as clear as crystal, and bent to slake my thirst. In the distance there was the sound of a helicopter and I cursed myself for a fool. Among that carpet of green my car would be easy to spot from the air. Fortunately the sound faded. It was unlikely that it had been within five miles of me and doubtful too that it was anything to do with the hotel. The police would only just be arriving. It was probably nothing more than a local tycoon on his way to the airport, but precautions had to be taken. I drove uphill to an abandoned farm where the roof of a shed would shield it from view.

Safe at last, I reached into the glove box and ate the remaining biscuits then I went to the stream for a second drink. Exhausted, and barely able to think, I locked the car, folded the passenger seat, wrapped myself in the donkey jacket and, despite repeated images of the Snake's hate-filled face, I fell asleep.

Strange sounds brought me awake. Rain was pouring on to the building and large drops were falling through its dilapidated roof on to the car. Outside it was pitch dark and the situation was as lonely as hell.

It was no longer possible to sleep and the likelihood of being caught when I returned to London was shattering. I had only made a bad situation worse. The millions in my account would soon be reclaimed, my promising career destroyed and all I could look forward to was a prison sentence for my stupidity. Events at Auchenboggle were nothing but a knee jerk from which there could be no recovery. I switched on the radio and, after fiddling with the controls, picked up a station which was playing Scottish dance music. Then it was the news and I listened to a litany of gloom before the local news featured a boring speech by the resident MP. Nothing seemed to happen in the North. Suddenly my mind focused,

"...described as a dangerous person. His local address, which was leased on the Auchenboggle estate, is ablaze with two fire tenders in attendance. Reports have not been confirmed, but it seems the injured man overpowered two policemen and escaped from the hospital where he was being treated after locking the policemen in an empty room. A manhunt is now in progress and extra officers have been drafted in. Meanwhile a plane has been reported stolen from a sporting estate three miles from the hospital and there are reports of a police car being dumped in Loch Ness."

Inside the car it was hot and clammy and I pushed the door open to get fresh air and was rewarded with a sprinkling of rainwater. How could the Snake escape! How did a man with a broken arm overpower two policemen? How could he drive a car? And how could he steal a plane? Nothing made the slightest sense, though there was one bright note and that was he wouldn't be making any statements about me. As past experience had demonstrated, news reports are often wide of the mark, but surely to hell they weren't making this up! There must be a stolen car, there must be a stolen airplane and there must be an escaped man. I stumbled about the shed and thought about it. No, it wasn't true; a man with a broken arm couldn't do it. Even if the Snake had a concealed gun on his person the police would surely have found it before they took him to hospital. And why have a concealed gun in the first place, surely it should be given to his companion for backup?

The companion. Now I began to wonder about that tall man in his biker's outfit. Almost certainly he was driving a car that had been parked on the opposite side of the hotel. There had been no sound of a motor bike. The outfit was a disguise. He had shown expertise by guarding the door. An amateur would have stood beside his master. And as soon as I'd got the gun he'd known the game was up and fled. What if he'd followed the police to the hospital and overpowered them? No doubt the plane was an easy option; the Snake would know everyone in the area.

In the background the music faded and a voice began to speak. I stumbled across in the dark and opened the door.

"...at Aberdeen airport. Apparently it made an ordinary landing at nine forty-four after giving false identification. Three men alighted and one may have had his arm in a sling. An airport policeman identified the missing plane at about ten thirty. Since then there has been no sighting of the men. All cars leaving the airport are being checked."

The local radio station seemed to be reading reports from a press association. There was no attempt to amplify any of the items. Three men... Where did the third one come from? And why three when only two went into the hotel? No, there had to be another explanation. Perhaps the third man had been standing guard outside. They wouldn't want the public wandering in and he may well have been armed. Possibly these were the two men I'd seen in the car on my way to Auchenboggle. The man who ran out of the dining hall probably met the third man at the door. We might all have met if I hadn't jumped out of the window. I'll never have a closer call.

I switched off the radio and blinked at the darkness. The rain had gone off, my head was buzzing and there was no likelihood of getting to sleep.

The car was hired and the mileage would be recorded when I returned to London. Already I'd done more than six hundred miles, but enough was enough. I took the torch from my crime bag and, after some difficulty, disconnected the cable from the milometer. I would reconnect it in London. With a bit of luck this might 'prove' I'd never been near Inverness.

The rain had petered out as I walked along the forestry path where I disturbed an owl that had been hooting. Even in the dark it was possible to see the shape of the trees from which rainwater was still dripping.

I stopped. Approaching me were several shadowy figures in the middle of the path. I leapt for the trees, sprinkling myself with rain water and causing a branch to break. When I looked up the path was clear, there were no odd shapes and everything was calm. It had been a small herd of deer which had scattered in fright. I walked back to the car and after locking the doors fell asleep eventually.

25

"And how are you my dear chap?"

"Still breathing."

"We thought it was an earthquake, you off sick."

"That's what it was."

"You've lost some weight. Been standing at too many street corners?"

"An old habit."

"Well, good to have you back. See you at committee."

"No, you'll get a memo shortly. It's off. Market's down and still falling."

"Eh? But we need to discuss next month's quota."

"All bets are off. No quota."

"No quota?"

"We're just not buying."

"But what's going to happen to us? Are we for the chop?"

"No, no. Some shares are for the chop. No redundancies, that's official."

When driving back from Inverness I had mulled the whole investment strategy. Recently I had driven things close to optimum, but now it was time for a new approach. There had been a rail strike, fuel had gone up and the market was looking bad. Shortly many firms would be in trouble, some would stop their dividend, others would go bust and there would be a serious loss for investors. Of course, Howardsons would survive but there would be a lot of unpleasantness.

Yesterday I'd bought Sunday papers on my journey back and found the incidents of the previous night were barely reported, and in a low key at that. Gun-related crimes are common enough and it had occurred when they were going to press. And this low-key element was echoed by the radio. Suddenly, last night's sensation was on the back burner and wasn't even mentioned after eleven in the morning.

The Snake's goose was well and truly cooked. The Auchenboggles would identify him and the charges would be serious.

But there were other problems. I had stupidly taken the contents of Ahmad's bank account without considering the consequences. The man was dead, but shortly a monthly statement would arrive showing nearly a million pounds had gone to my numbered account in Switzerland. Since this was a terror situation, the Swiss secrecy laws would be waived and they would name me as the account holder. Frank had to be summoned to get duplicate keys for Fey Way. This was a crime scene, still sectioned off, and it must have involved a lot of cunning on his part, yet such is his ability that he had the keys by that afternoon.

The Snake was an even bigger problem and though it was reasonable to assume he was out of the country that didn't mean he wouldn't act against me. You can seldom steal huge moneys without repercussions and I found myself worrying about his team. Judging by their activities they were perfectly capable of kidnapping me. I needed protection and since John Masters was the one person who could provide it, I met him in a pub that night.

"I want you to trail me in the morning."

"You're having me on."

"I think I'm being followed."

"Why would they do that?" he said, becoming an army officer and frowning at me as though I was a recruit who'd messed up.

"They have their reasons."

"Tell me about it."

"There's not much I can say, they're professionals"

"You've done something annoy them?"

"Maybe."

"Is there a lot at stake?"

"...you could say that."

"And you actually know you've been followed?"

"...Not in London, elsewhere. Not followed, confronted. They know my address. This is urgent."

"It'll cost you."

And he named an extortionate sum which I knocked back. We finally settled on a deal. It looked like he was glad of the work though he grumbled about getting out of bed.

"They won't kidnap you in front of the morning crowds. You know that?"

"We're dealing with dangerous men."

"I've got a whistle. If they move in I'll give it a blast. Usually that throws 'em."

"A warning."

"Yes, it blows my cover, of course. Last resort and all that."

"I leave at seven. I'll stand in front of my window before I go."

He shook his head and grimaced.

"No you won't. The other lot are going to wonder. Then they'll look over their shoulders."

"Oh...I see. Tomorrow I'm going to Fey Way first. Don't follow me into the building. Just see if anybody follows me back to my work. It might be the police."

He gave me a look.

No sign of Masters when I went to Fey Way in the morning. The place stank of smoke, the lights were off, but I had a torch and I searched Ahmad's postbox to find several business letters but none from the bank – there was an awful fear that it had already been collected or that the cops had intercepted it at the post office.

I met Frank at lunch.

"I want you to trace the Snake –"

"Eh!"

"– I'll pay you well. I think he's abroad but I need to know his background, his identity... where he worked. This isn't a joke, it's deadly serious. I'm wondering if D'Alfonso's an alias. The Snake is a walk-on part with one suit – he probably looks different in real life. Under pressure his accent changes."

"When did you see him under pressure?"

"This is critical. He tried to kill me."

"Eh?"

"Find out all you can. There's bound to be a lead somewhere."

Frank looked at me open-mouthed.

"What the hell's happened?"

"There's been trouble. I've gotta find out about him."

His mouth opened to ask questions, but seeing the determination on my face he closed it again and nodded.

"Okay, I'll do it. How about slipping me a hundred in advance? Thanks. I wouldn't mind finding out myself."

From my house I phoned the Swiss bank and spoke to a Mr Stefan Gill (yes, he was one of the original family) who was my co-ordinator and who confirmed the safe receipt of the money. I had hoped to see him on Friday of that week, but now Ahmad's bank statement would have to be intercepted. Pleading pressure of work I made an appointment for seven days' time, emphasising that the money mustn't be moved.

To my relief the statement arrived on Friday: it covered the entire month and there was no way the plods could have known about it. I shredded it with great pleasure

That evening I met John Masters and paid him.

"I saw nobody but can't say for certain you weren't followed. Guy with a beard waited across the road on Tuesday. He didn't seem aware of you and he never saw me, probably waiting for his girl, or something. Likely enough okay."

"Was he tall?"

"About six feet, but I'm fairly sure he wasn't after you."

"…I can't believe I've got away so easily."

"I wonder what you've done. Let me just say this: if they're going to snatch you, it will be at seven when you leave the house. Anything else is too unpredictable."

"I see… A hypothetical question: suppose a crook has to flee abroad… he's made a fool of the police. In theory he can get millions out of me and he has access to a professional team. He's short of money. Is he likely to kidnap me?"

I'd said too much and he gave me a curious look.

"No answer to that, me man. You're not looking at it right. Is he short of money or not? It takes money to flee the country, maybe a fortune if the cops are hopping mad. Why do you say he's short? Oh, perhaps you've taken it – speaking hypothetically."

"Well?"

"He's got a problem. No point in going to the continent, it's part of the EU. And a kidnap would need a team of at least three heavies, a safe house, an untraceable car, plus a wad of cash. And it's all got to be directed from abroad. Not easy."

"I've wondered."

"Look at it logistically. How does he contact his team to make plans? You say they're professionals, they'd want money in advance, they might trust him less than you do. There would have to be a meeting to thrash out the details and he'd have to pay them to meet him abroad: that means a lot of cash up front – and what's to stop them making off with the money and doing nothing?"

"But there might be loyalties."

"Oh, that's possible. Maybe he's got a hold on them. Yes, it's possible, but they're working men who need to be paid. What makes you think he's short of money?"

"Everything in his account's been lifted," I said, in blabbermouth mode.

But he was shaking his head violently.

"Means nothing. My old uncle was chauffeur to a lord. A week after the Wall Street Crash, he drove the old blighter to his stockbrokers and ten minutes later he comes back an' announces he's been wiped out. Now here's a question: what did he do?"

"Jumped out the sixth floor window?"

He gave me a dirty look.

"He took her ladyship and the six kids for dinner at the Savoy. My uncle was panicking, he'd worked there all his life and there was no chance of another job. And here's the crunch. He died twenty years later, still in his lordship's employ even though the old booby had been supposedly wiped out. That's the lesson, Mr Miles, and I've seen it among the officers at Sandhurst. Wipe them out and they've still got money."

"I'll think about that."

"But he's got a loyal team?"

"Oh, yes. They rescued him from the cops." I shouldn't have said this to a security man with shrewd eyes, but my head was spinning. "Very brave, very decisive."

John Masters was nodding his head.

"Professionals – they did it to save themselves. If their master went down, they were down too. That's the reason for the derring-do. I'll bet they never put a foot wrong."

"Yes. Mind you, I don't know if they got paid."

Masters through back his head and laughed.

"I'm almost sorry for them."

There was a weight like a mountain hanging over my head and I envied his easy laugh. Nobody in their senses lets eleven million go without a fight. But, now I came to think of it, possibly the Snake wasn't short of money. I hadn't been a bank teller for nothing. The computer had shown no small debit entries, therefore he must have had at least one other account to finance his daily expenses.

"Listen if I ever get in trouble. Rescue me and I'll pay you. That's a promise."

"If possible. I better shadow you next week again. Best be safe."

26

Among the many newspapers supplied to Howardsons is *The Inverness Journal* which had a photo on page five of a group of policemen watching a crane lift their patrol car out of the water. Obviously this was a difficult manoeuvre supervised by experts in hard hats with gallons of liquid spilling from the car. Underneath, the blurb said, *Yesterday a stolen patrol car was recovered from Loch Ness where it was dumped after an incident in which two police officers were locked in a hospital room. Shortly afterwards a plane was stolen (now recovered) and three men are being sought by the police. A spokesman said their enquiries were continuing.*

There was too much at stake. To lose a fortune for the second time in a month would be insane. I took two days off, not daring to wait until Friday. Bad weather or cancelled flights might stop me and who was to say what the Snake was doing in the meantime? So I packed my bags and caught a flight to Zurich where I clocked into a sedate hotel and studied my notes with care. At this point, I was walking a fine line and a mistake could bring disaster from which there was no recovery. After dinner, I strolled the streets for hours with my head down as I mused over my options. The unwelcome thought occurred to me that I might bump into the Snake at a corner.

On the following morning I presented myself to Gill & Co, to find an impressive building of four floors. Two young men who wouldn't even comment on the weather escorted me to an office that was every bit as grand as Sir James's where Stefan Gill sat at an oak desk that bore three telephones and a framed photograph of his wife and two kids. He was five years older than me with an inscrutable face and very shrewd eyes. I decided he was a born banker.

It wasn't entirely easy. The man was courteous at all times, but with big money involved I was under scrutiny and there were a lot of questions to be answered. First, I had to prove my identity, hand over my passport and answer queries about the original phone call that had opened the account. Obviously there was good reason for this: I might be an impostor trying to steal the millions. In a corner of the room sat a man of about sixty, ostensibly working at a desk, but undoubtedly the bank witness.

"Would you tell me where you obtained this money, Mr Miles?" Gill asked, looking at my file with a frown.

"It belongs to my client," I said with more confidence that I felt.

"I see, and who is this person?" said Stefan Gill, who had plainly heard that one before. On the positive side, he wasn't taking notes though the older man might be.

"I am not prepared to say."

"Is this client involved in crime?"

I looked at him with unease. If he refused my business I was in serious trouble; he might even refuse to release the money. He was a man of moderate height, with an honest-seeming face and he had good reason to be wary of me. How could a council home boy (and yes, they were certain to have run a check on me) acquire such a fortune? I did my honest Ron and even managed a self-assured smile.

"Mr Gill –"

"Call me Stefan."

"I can't answer that. As far as I'm concerned he has money to invest and that's good enough for me. I doubt if he's got a criminal record, he's associated with some of the big banks in London." This last bit was probably true, but it was a subject that was best avoided: Gill would know more about the London banks than I did and questions along these lines were dangerous. I switched to a mild attack. "Your question isn't fair. Even the Bishop of Zurich can't guarantee his Sunday offerings are all from impeccable sources."

Stefan gave a small smile – the Swiss don't laugh at money – and said: "What about terrorism? Is there anything of that in the background?"

What a singularly apt question! And it implied an awareness of the Snake. Only now did I see that it was all too likely my enemy had traced the transaction to Gill & Co and tried to reclaim the money. If he was already a client of the firm, I was finished!

"Terrorism? I've no reason to think so."

Stefan shuffled his papers.

"May I ask if you have a written contract with your client?"

"…Well, yes… an informal one."

"And it is available for inspection?"

"Yes," I bluffed. "But I haven't brought it with me."

"Oh I don't want to see it. But sometimes our authorities demand a sight of the paperwork if there is a possibility of contention."

Contention? Yes the Snake had been in touch. He'd certainly had plenty of time to claim ownership and I had to hope he'd be unable to prove it.

"There's no controversy associated with this."

Gill sighed at my whopper. "Do you confirm that your – um – client has given you this sum of his own free will for the purpose of investment and that you have legal power of authority over it?"

"I certainly do."

"Very well, then," and his demeanour softened. "What are your proposals?"

I didn't allow my relief to show. Speaking slowly, I told him my plans while his shrewd eyes watched me. The money would be invested under my supervision and if all was well it would stay in his bank for a lifetime: I could see that went down well.

"Where do you propose to invest it?"

"In the Stock Market when it picks up, I'm an investment manager."

Stefan almost smiled; perhaps I was singing his song at last.

"We're glad to be of service, Mr Miles –"

"Call me Ron, I've nothing to hide – though come to think of it, my client has had… trouble, an attempt to steal his fund… a man called, D'Alfonso, heard of him?"

"I can't say I have," said Stefan shuffling in his chair and looking away. There was some ambiguity here: he should have given a straight no.

"He's tall," I went on artlessly, "six feet six, ten years older than me."

"No, I can't say I've heard of him." Here the papers were given another great shuffle. "Anyway the money is secure and you can rely on us at all times."

"I appreciate that."

"Believe me. We welcome your business."

"Are you the president of the bank, Stefan?"

"No, no: a director. My father is the president." I spread the contents of my case on his desk and we checked figures against the computer and nodded our heads. There was a lot of work to be done and there must be no errors. I cleared my throat and said, "Stefan, we mustn't lose this money: my client insists on good security."

"And you shall have it. I know of you through your work at Howardsons. Here in Switzerland we are all too familiar with disagreeable parties who try to claim other people's assets. For peace of mind, we will impose extra security on your account."

This was music to my ears.

"I want an account that trades in shares, possibly some commodities and property too, mainly in the London market. You'll do the buying and selling. Better not to have my name too prominent. Howardsons might object to me managing this account, you know. If Miles appears at all, I want it understated."

"That is understood. It will be a business account?"

"Correct. I will be the chief executive."

We put our heads down and began to sort it out. A company would be formed called EQUITIES AND COMMODITIES (ZURICH), ECZ for short, into which the eleven million would be paid. There would be three shareholders. A; Myself with .02%. B; Artur Mann with 49.99%, and C; B. Friedland also with 49.99%. Since they didn't exist, Mr Mann and Mr Friedland would never appear at board meetings: they would be represented by proxy at the annual general meeting by lawyers acting in their interests. (These lawyers would be instructed by me, but not directly: instructions would come through independent lawyers who were unacquainted with the proxy bearers. Such a measure would ensure they were untraceable and protect them from curious eyes: it also gave the impression that I was working for two multimillionaires.)

"The shares for Mr Mann and Mr Friedland really belong to my client," I bluffed. "But he doesn't want to be named in the meantime."

"It will all be discreet," said Stefan, ignoring the fancy ethics of my plan, "and of course it will be legal." Strange that ten minutes ago he'd been worried about the fund being straight and now he was treating it like a gangster's trove, but that's a banker for you.

I would make all the business decisions and he would take instructions from me, and only me. A document would be signed to that effect today, otherwise there was a risk – unlikely with respectable lawyers – that they would outvote me, sell the company, and keep the money for themselves.

"These lawyers, how do I select them?"

He handed me a list of about twenty firms based in Zurich, established over many years and all of them reliable. I would select them and he would make the arrangements.

"Would I need to produce Artur Mann or B. Friedland?"

"No. They exist on paper only and their proxies cast their votes. That is all that is required by law. I imagine they would be deemed to be domiciled abroad."

"Very well, it's agreed. I'll select number seven."

"Acceptable, yes: decent people."

"I'll use lawyers in Dublin to instruct them, separate lawyers for each."

"Again acceptable, in the minutes of ECZ we will arrange to have the annual general meeting within six months of the close of its financial year. We have a suitable boardroom here. You must select accountants now. Here is a list of firms we know."

Anxious to avoid international accountants who would have London offices and might recognise me, I selected a local firm.

"Your money is currently in a numbered account," said Stefan. "When you're ready, we will transfer it to ECZ. But the numbered account remains: it is the master, it is strictly secret and you will deal through it."

I began to like the man: he gave the impression of being interested in my welfare and of being prepared to assist me. I could see he was dedicated to his job and was fluent in English – something that isn't true of all the Swiss. Lately I'd become wary of Wallace's mercenary attitudes and I hadn't liked the previous Swiss bank. Now I was in friendly hands. He had pictures on his walls and even a notice board with some cartoons.

"I want you to do the buying and selling for me. Previously I've used a friend in London, but that's stopped. No UK bankers will be involved. Everybody knows everybody else and there's a lot of gossip. Now only you and I will do transactions."

With business completed we went for lunch in a quiet restaurant where I found myself beginning to relax at last.

Lunch over, we returned to the bank where the typists had prepared documents for signing and we parted as good friends. I was in my home by nine o'clock that evening.

27

Frank came to see me the following day.

"I've had enough of the Snake to get me through the rest of my life."

"But you've traced him?"

"He doesn't exist! There's no substance. I've got nothing."

"Great Square."

"Great Square! You landed me in it. I goes walking into the store, as bold as brass, and asked the chief of security about the Snake. That was some business. Scotland Yard, the Home Office, the CIA, and even Mossad, would you believe, have been in on the same errand. I was only saved by some quick talking and my press card – and it's a forgery too. Here's the thing. The Snake wasn't authorised to be on stage. He walked on with a Middle Eastern man who was almost certainly one of the backup team. No one knows who they were: they had nothing to do with the Company –"

"Yes, yes I know some of that. But it's his identity I want. You're not going to tell me the cops don't have something on him. Who is he?"

"That's what I'm telling you. They don't have a clue."

"Listen, the other man was Ahmad Hammiel. The Snake was coerced by him to tempt Mossad. The cops must know that."

"…Yes, and they're not saying, an old trick."

"He must be on the cop files."

"Cop files I don't do. You need a bent copper for that."

"Are they in his pocket?"

"Aren't they always? How else could he get off with it? Anyway, I said I was only researching a story and knew nothing that wasn't in the public domain. Incidentally, I couldn't trace him at any of the banks either. I even stood outside their HQs and watched the hordes pouring in. No Snake."

My hands were clenched as he ranted on. Despite all my waywardness I had never once been the focus of police enquiries and this was a potential disaster of my own making. Had Frank's visit gone the wrong way he would have had to admit he was making enquiries on my behalf. And once they looked closely, those expert questioners would identify me as the fourth hostage and everything would come out, including the money.

"Think about this – Remember when the Snake used to come to The Robber Barron? Did he have bodyguards?"

Frank stared at the floor, frowning in concentration, he has a good memory and his judgement is reliable.

"He just might... something happened – can't remember when, exactly – Six foot man sitting by himself watching everybody, a bit like a cop, but not one, if you know what I mean. The Snake was there, I wondered if he was the driver."

"You think he had a driver?"

"I can't be sure. He'd a Lancia, or something. Yes, he'd a driver. You think he'd bodyguards as well?"

"I've wondered. Maybe he's richer than I thought."

"I was thinking that too... I'd forget him if I was you."

But he wasn't easy to forget.

The Snake had my entire dealings on computer. Granted I'd smashed his machine at Auchenboggle, but that data would be easy to retrieve and it could be sent to the authorities any day he felt like it and there was nothing I could do about it. When I remembered his berserker attack in Scotland, I knew he had all the malice to finish me.

28

It was eight o'clock in the evening and I was working in my flat, relieved that there had been a total silence from the Snake. Almost six weeks had passed and at long last my problems were fading into the sunset. My secret store had been vacated, the crime bag destroyed and from now on I would be going straight.

Then the phone rang and a smart woman with a breathy voice asked if I was Ron: she almost called me dear.

"Yes, that's me."

"Sorry to trouble you, Ron, it's the CID here. This is a lot of fuss about nothing, but could I see you for a few minutes?"

"Of course, come right over," I said, doing my honest Ron. Did I hear right, was that CID she'd said? The CID!

"– Perhaps in half an hour?"

"Of course, most welcome."

She arrived ten minutes later, no doubt to catch me on the hop. I had only just put my papers away and left two open hymn books in a prominent position on the table.

"Mr Miles?"

Slightly less than average height, she had close-cropped hair and wore a navy blue skirt and jacket. There was a sense of energy about her, though it was under serene control. I put her age at forty-five.

"That's me."

We shook hands at the door and she introduced himself as Robina Black. She looked too smart to be involved in a 'fuss about nothing'.

"Tea or coffee?" I said.

But she was giving the room a once over, walking away from me.

"Oh, excuse these hymn books, I'm a church organist."

"How fascinating, sir." Was she being sarcastic? "Some flat – I'm sure you won't mind me looking it over."

Here there was a dramatic change in her attitude: her voice had hardened, and she was no longer the polite guest. Before I could reply, she walked to the balcony, looked out, returned, walked back to the entrance hall and into the main lounge.

"Yes, quite impressive, if you like that kind of thing." She swung on her heel and went into my bedroom which was untidy to the extreme, with the bed unmade and clothes strewn on the floor. She looked under the bed, went into the walk-in wardrobe, and the en-suite toilet while I followed like a sheepdog. Then she did the same with the two spare bedrooms and the main bathroom, until she came to my study, which was locked.

"Key, please."

This was a command. Meekly I opened the door to reveal a reasonably tidy room with nothing too exciting in view. She headed straight for the safe.

"Come on, open it."

I did so and she leafed through the title deeds for a minute. Only a few weeks ago incriminating documents had been sitting on its shelves: I had even considered keeping the ECZ files there.

"The utility room." And here she checked that only my clothes were in the wash basket. Then it was the kitchen where she looked in the fridge and the freezer, presumably to see if I was buying food for more than one.

"Not everybody's cup of tea, but yes, quite a place."

Thank God my crime bag wasn't about.

"What were you looking for, bodies?"

"Oh, any little surprise would do. Do you need a flat this size?"

"I don't know, my chairman made me buy it."

"Oh, he did? I'll need to get a chairman, you live on your own?"

"I can't deny it."

"You've certainly got room for two or three girlfriends."

"Yes but they fight: I limit myself to one at a time."

We returned to the main room where she sat in an armchair, revealing two fine legs, to study me intently. I'd never met this kind of woman before: she was unpredictable, the mistress of the situation and she was no friend to me.

"What brings you here?" I said, wilting under her inspection and then getting up to make tea in the hope that it would afford a distraction.

"Oh, it's a piece of nonsense. Ever been to Inverness?"

I didn't allow any surprise to show.

"Can't say I have," I said, biting my tongue: I should merely have said 'no'. I handed her a cup and the biscuit tin, "Help yourself. What's wrong in Inverness?"

"It seems you hired a car that was seen there."

She'd come without a briefcase and there was no notebook.

"No, no, I do sometimes hire cars at the weekend, but I've never been to Inverness or had an accident."

"Oh, it's not an accident. The hire company says you did 625 miles, nothing like enough to get you there and back."

Her tone indicated she knew how to adjust a milometer too.

"625 miles? I must have been looking for a parking space."

"Your car went past a police camera in Inverness."

Damn. It had to be near Auchenboggle, the traffic had been light and a London registration would possibly get noticed.

"What happened?"

"It's a big enquiry. Two cops got locked up and their patrol car was stolen."

"Oh I read about that. My firm get papers for the whole country – but what connects with me?"

"Absolutely nothing, apart from the number – and it could be a false plate – though of course it's the same make and model."

"I remember now: there was a patrol car pulled out the water."

"We think there's a terror link. It's about the Great Square Siege."

I noticed shrewd eyes watching me when she mentioned it.

"But I thought the kidnappers were caught."

"This is the backup team."

Of course there had been a description of me from the hostages and there was an artist's drawing too. This woman would be familiar with these things.

"I see. Got anybody yet?" By this time my voice had lost its certainty. They would also have noted 'John Smith of Bakevan Drive' on my registration card at the hotel and that would identify me as the Fourth Hostage. Almost certainly she knew that.

"Not yet."

"Wasn't there a house burned down, who leased it?"

Here I was floundering, asking questions that implied prior knowledge and this was one lady who would notice. Yet I had to find out as much as possible.

"A tall man called D'Alfonso, you know him of course."

"No, no, I can't say I do."

Her voice became harder.

"Yes you do. You know him too well. Here's my card. I want you to phone me at the first sighting of him. If I'm out leave a message on the machine. You must phone me. Do you understand? This is a murder enquiry."

"Murder enquiry?"

"One of my colleagues was shot. D'Alfonso is the prime suspect."

Reluctantly I took the card.

"Thanks... Does that mean he's armed when he goes about London?"

"Probably. He's a very dangerous man."

"Robina, I know nothing. Surely you can trace him without me?"

"We don't know who he is, or his present location. He's disappeared... I know you've tried and failed to trace him. You must tell me if he contacts you."

"I honestly know nothing about him. I'm not sure D'Alfonso's his real name."

"It probably isn't."

"I think he's out of the country."

"Yes, but he flits in when it suits him. You'll phone if you hear anything?"

"I will."

She seemed to relax.

"Do you know John Masters?"

"Masters? I believe I've heard the name."

"He gives lessons in security."

Now she was telling me she knew a lot about my background, an old trick that can upset the coolest of customers

"Oh yes – I took some tuition in self-defence, nothing wrong with that surely?"

"It'll keep you fit for your girlfriends."

"Actually I didn't want to get mugged."

145

"Really? Anyway this is getting difficult. The leads have dried up. Would you be prepared to go on an identity parade if requested?"

"Of course, but why?"

"I was thinking you fitted the description of one of them – there was an incident in a hotel in Inverness, a bloke your age and size. It would let them see I'm trying."

Some mockery had crept into her voice again.

"Robina, I'm a busy man. You can't expect me to take a day off to go to Inverness. I mean, I'm running the biggest fund in the City."

Was this a blind stab, or the purpose of her visit?

"Yes, I suppose you are busy."

"I mean I've nothing to hide, but that's pushing things a bit."

"Perhaps we could arrange it in London?"

"…Always glad to help."

I awaited the uppercut: this is where she tells me they've got my fingerprints and twenty witnesses, including an archbishop, to identify me, but it never came. She stood up.

"Well, I'll put you down as never having been to Inverness."

"What about the stolen plane?"

"Oh they landed at Aberdeen airport. It's not every bunch of crooks that can produce an air pilot. Of course you can fly."

So they'd been doing a lot of research on me: this was not a casual enquiry. I remembered Masters' remark about my being an investment manager.

"I'm just a trainee. I don't steal planes, I lead a quiet life."

"Of course you do."

"But how did they get away – from Aberdeen?"

"There's nothing in the grapevine about that – Just for the record, where did *you* go in the hire car? 625 is a lot of miles."

"Um, I like to drive around the country, get some fresh air and do some walking. Seldom to the same place twice… I can't remember six weeks back."

"Think about it. Oh, is that the time? I must go."

I went to the balcony and waited until her car drove off but it was beyond my line of sight. After two minutes I left by the back door and took a footpath to the next street where I phoned Frank from a telephone kiosk and arranged to meet him at Oxford Circus.

My fists were clenched and I had difficulty walking in a straight line.

I was gutted by the mention of John Masters. He knew there had been an incident involving a team and I'd been stupid enough to let him follow me to Fey Way. Yes, he'd reported it and they would identify the incident in seconds. Robina knew enough to damn me. And Master wasn't the only one who had talked. She had known I'd 'tried and failed' to find the Snake and surely that involved Frank. Maybe he'd just happened to mention it to a plod and they'd surmised the rest.

Frank was already there. We went to a pub where I recited events.

"It's taken them – what? – six weeks? Did you see her identity?"

"Yes. The metal badge: genuine all right... nobody's fool: could have been a barrister, not your typical plod."

"I don't like it. What was her reason again?"

"I went past a camera."

"Only that? This in the back of beyond, hundreds of miles from London?"

I had been careful not to mention Inverness or even Scotland.

"Yes – I must say I never saw it."

"And you believe that?"

I looked at him in surprise.

"Why shouldn't I?"

"It doesn't take six weeks."

"What do you mean?"

"This is the Snake you're talking about, right?" said Frank, working it out as usual, "masquerading like a fool in front of thousands at Great Square. That's a terror situation. You're not going to tell me they didn't notice him: and they'll certainly take an interest. Now they're trying to root out the people around him."

"Oh, yes?"

"He's away, so they're going for you."

"She was looking for someone, she searched the flat."

Frank paused to stare at a man who'd just come in. He was about fifty and seemed desperate for a drink.

"You might have been hiding the team."

She'd said half an hour and arrived in ten minutes, hoping to catch me. So, yes, she'd be watching to see if anybody made a quick exit.

"She kept going on about it being a big flat."

Judging by his reception from the barman, the man was a regular and he hadn't even glanced at us.

"Okay, we've got to think this out. If it wasn't a camera, how did they get me?"

"You were in a hire car. They'd trace every hire in the country for that weekend, that's why it took six weeks. They'd have a description of it, right?"

"It's possible."

It had been the only one at the hotel though I'd entered a false number.

"She even knew I was a pilot."

"You're sure you weren't followed here?"

"Yes."

But of course I wasn't: if they were experts I'd never know.

"Very slowly tell me everything again."

I narrated it as Frank nodded silently.

"You've never been in the army. If you had, you'd have recognised your lady, she wasn't CID, she was an army officer, probably connected with the Home Office. A spy, call her what you will."

I looked at him.

"Army officers are a sight more dangerous. Okay, what crimes did you do?"

"…The Snake stole my money… I got it off him again. Well I took more than he took, if you know what I mean."

"Theft, except the Snake ain't gonna report it."

"I hope."

"But it wasn't his money. He'd stolen it too, eh?"

"Likely, and there's another thing. She said the Snake was behind that shooting at Great Square. You know, the CID man. She said the bloke was a colleague."

"So he was Home Office too… Did she say why he shot him?"

"No."

"…He must've been shadowing the Snake… Nothing gets worse than murder. I'd keep out his way. Can they trace what you did with it, the money, I mean?"

148

"It's in Switzerland, there's nothing in writing here."

But that wasn't accurate either. I had a file of papers in a safe deposit box in Wallace's bank but they wouldn't know about that, or would they?

"And that's all?"

"Yes, but there's a... difficulty. It was done by computer... They'll trace the last call to Switzerland. The bank can be identified. They could get my name."

"Swiss banks don't talk."

"Secrecy laws don't apply in a terrorist situation."

My hands were clenched, my world had been penetrated. Beyond doubt the Home Office knew I was the fourth hostage. Would they pass that information to the cops or was it a side issue to their enquiries?

"She knows enough to put me inside."

"You want to watch yourself. First you start following the Snake, now you've got the Home Office on your trail. I'd forget him for ever."

"Maybe he won't forget me."

He took a long puff at his cigarette.

"Keep your head down. The identity parade's a dodge to see how you'd react. Your woman was having a look at you and making sure you weren't hiding someone –"

"But she knows who I am."

"There's always someone that knows. Don't do nothin' daft. They might follow you, the phone might be tapped. Caution's the word."

29

If, like me, you can't cook, you have to find ways to sustain yourself and I was in the habit of going to Mario's restaurant near my flat. I liked the man a lot, he was courteous and the food was good. I was an early diner and the place was often deserted when I would take my table in a corner where I could read my papers (and sometimes do some work) in peace. Later in the night it would be mobbed but by then I would be gone.

A week had passed and I was reading a company report, with the screen in place, when I looked up to see a middle-aged woman of medium height push past it and approach me with a sly smile.

"Ron," she said. "We need to talk."

"Who...?" I blurted, noting her expensive get-up and her self-command. Her accent was educated-Londoner with a hint of fee-paying school.

"My name doesn't matter. I'm merely a spokesperson –"

"Is this lady annoying you, sir?" said Mario, with a waiter on either side.

"I think Mr Miles will want to hear from me," said the stranger smiling calmly. Then she looked at me and said: "I'm acquainted with your friend Mr D'Alfonso."

As she had doubtless expected, this had an effect, though she was only confirming my suspicions.

"It's all right, Mario. Bring a chair for the lady – and a refreshment."

"A glass of pure orange, thank you."

As a waiter hurried off, I could see Mario hanging around, just out of earshot, looking none too happy and occasionally glancing at me. The thought occurred to me that he had noticed a heavy team outside. Not unlikely: the lady looked confident enough to have some kind of backup. This might be the first stage of my kidnap. And there was always the possibility of a Home Office tail as well. My life was becoming quite crowded.

Still smiling, she removed her coat while I put away my report.

"What a splendid little restaurant – and I can see you get loyalty from the staff."

She wore a black suit and despite her age I could tell she lived dangerously.

"You mentioned Mr D'Alfonso?"

"I did."

Still smiling, she took a sip of orange that had just been placed on the table and nodded her head. It occurred to me that she could have a gun in her handbag.

"I want to contact him. I have some resources to refund."

"...Ron, Mr D'Alfonso doesn't want that, there's no need for refunds."

A terrible dread filled me.

"Then what does he want?"

Still smiling, she put a hand on her glass and looked thoughtful.

"That's best answered by simply maintaining the status quo."

"Which means?"

"Oh... Keep things as they are. I won't go so far as to say Mr D'Alfonso is happy, but he wants no changes... He's prepared to tolerate the account in Gill & Co. In your capable hands I'm sure it will accrue."

So the Snake was still in business with a computer running and meanwhile this smart lady had tracked me to my restaurant.

"I'd prefer to make a refund."

"Ah now, my dear young man, that would be unsuitable. Mr D'Alfonso is in a difficult position. A refund might create problems of a sensitive nature. You're a thoughtful fellow and I'm sure I won't need to spell it out..."

"So I keep it in the meantime?"

"Well, 'keep' is the wrong word. He wants it ring-fenced. He doesn't like you but he is not churlish and he has nothing but respect for your business skills."

"...Oh."

"What is the name of your fund?"

I looked up. Her tone had changed, it was a serious question. Of course they would only know it had gone to Stefan's bank: they wouldn't know the details.

"ECZ," I said, there being no point in hiding it. "Equities & Commodities (Zurich)."

"ECZ, yes," she said, memorising the name, or perhaps she had a recorder in her handbag, yes she had: it was sitting on the table and I could see perforations that hid the mike. "And it's overseen by Mr Stefan Gill, himself?"

So, yes, they had been in touch.

"That is correct."

"Then no changes will be tolerated. ECZ will run for the foreseeable future."

"...Future? For how long, months or years? I need to know."

She was smiling again, looking at her glass and seldom glancing at me.

"Oh, I wouldn't care to define the time lapse: years probably. You may not dispose of his... assets. Do you understand me?"

Aside from the staff there was no one in the restaurant, I began to relax. If I was to invest his money, then he was going to let me live.

"All right... But I was going to use power investing. It's a little risky... limited number of shares... maximised returns. Obviously that will need to be reconsidered."

She sipped her orange and stared at the table for a full minute.

"...Go ahead with your Power Investing. In your hands it's probably safe – if that's unsuitable I'll phone you."

So she was going to be in touch with him: well, that was expected.

"You'd better give me your card."

"No, I can't do that. I'm merely a spokesperson, not a representative."

"You're his lawyer?"

The stranger stared at the table and made no reply.

"I need an address for Mr D'Alfonso," I said, becoming businesslike. "Annual returns will have to be declared."

A shake of the head.

"Absolutely not."

"But surely he needs some kind of check on the fund?"

"He expects you to do your best... There must be no correspondence."

"But that's bad practice. Things aren't good on the Stock Exchange just now. What if he doesn't like my performance, can't I post the accounts to you?"

"Of course you can't," her voice disguised emotion, but I detected irritation. "I told you. I'm his spokesperson, not his representative. I wouldn't care to have his correspondence mailed to me. That could lead to... misunderstandings."

Yes, I could see that.

"So I don't even report to my principle investor. Very unorthodox."

"Oh come on now, I'm sure you're not so uninformed. ECZ will have to declare its annual results. Mr D'Alfonso's agents can inspect them in Switzerland."

So they'd got it worked out.

"Then certain arrangements have to be made," I said, suddenly becoming aware that there were a lifetime's problems ahead. "This has to be professional. I claim two point seven million of ECZ as my own. Mr D'Alfonso even offered it to me when we were... negotiating. "Yes, I'll invest it. All dividends will be re-invested, okay?"

"As far as the dividends are concerned, I agree."

"And I will charge a management fee of point five per cent per annum."

"No," she snapped. "There will be no fee. I won't hear of it."

Somehow I had anticipated this: she wanted to make a good impression. The Snake would no doubt get the tape.

"There must be a fee. You'll get no one to do it for less. What if I'm ill? Staff will have to be employed. There are costs involved as well as huge responsibilities."

"Mr D'Alfonso wants no costs."

"I'm sorry: I refuse to do unpaid work."

"Half of one per cent is an enormous amount of money."

"It's an enormous responsibility. I won't work for less."

"What you are proposing," she said, changing tone, "is one half per cent of the gross every year?"

"Exactly. If you don't like it I'll transfer his share to a safe deposit account and send you the passbook. That would be my preference."

There was a pause, while she stared at her glass. She would have to back down: her stance was nothing more than idle posturing.

"Very well, then. I'll accept that – provisionally."

"I've no problem with a refund," I said. "Twenty-four hours is all it takes. It needn't go to the UK: I can send it anywhere in the world. Mr D'Alfonso would at least get the use of his funds."

"No," the half smile was there again. "Mr D'Alfonso can live with ECZ. Elsewhere there are uncertainties. I shall phone you if there are... difficulties."

"When? I'll need to start soon."

"Within... ten days."

"I take it Mr D'Alfonso is abroad?"

The lady stood up and the sly smile appeared.

"I have no idea. Now I really must be going. I'm late."

A waiter fetched her coat and she was gone. I never saw her again.

30

A year drifted past, during which we were all unhappy, shares did badly and there was economic turmoil in the City. This didn't do me any good in Howardsons, there was a lot of bickering among the managers and although I tended to avoid any outright disasters, I was no longer the golden boy. Techniques that had worked in the past were no longer dependable and several big companies went bust, making a hole in our portfolios. There was even speculation by senior economists that the Stock Market was finished forever, with no place in the modern world. In Zurich, FCZ was still in bonds and had accrued by an unimpressive 1.7%. Madam Boss and her three henchmen stood trial, pleaded guilty, and received sentences ranging from nine to eighteen years. In Scotland, the Auchenboggle incident seemed to have petered out.

In church, I resigned as organist and this wasn't done lightly, in many ways I liked the old place. I was fond of the choir too and sometimes the services weren't too bad either. I liked the way rich and poor merged on a near equal footing and I liked its benevolent discipline. I also enjoyed playing the organ. What other organisation would give me an expensive instrument to play with? Church was the only place – apart from my work, and that was becoming tense – where I mixed with people. According to Freud, church is one's tribe and perhaps he was right. It was the only place I could relax. In my heart of hearts I didn't really like Howardsons. Sir James was all right, and George, the commissionaire was fine, but almost every other person in the firm wanted my job. I was no longer doing so well and the fact they'd no talent only made them jealous of me.

Yet I resigned from the organ. I worked five days in the week and I wanted to explore the country and that couldn't be done if I was tied to the organ, so I went. And maybe that was a mistake. I'd been there for fifteen years. They gave me a watch and thanked me for my 'years of faithful service' and now the weekends were my own.

In the spring, I got my pilot's licence, and after some research bought a twin-engined Cessna which would be stationed at Leonard's to the north of London.

In *Country Life*, I read about Dunglen Castle for sale in the South of Scotland, complete with sixty thousand hectares of land and several farms. I flew up to see it (provided I had nothing booked for the day, Howardsons let me do what I liked). Not exactly Balmoral, it had a central tower that rose three floors with a smaller, almost Disney-style tower, of two floors beside it. Its architect had bowed to a silly trend of its time and spoiled it by having no porch, the entrance looked like the kitchen door and there was an ugly fire escape attached to the main tower. It hadn't been painted for fifty years, the window frames were rotting and a lot of the masonry was covered in moss. As castles go, it was comparatively small and something of a failure. But I liked it.

I needed advice, human advice and my mind turned to Frank who was a kind of father figure to me and whose opinions were often helpful. He was nonplussed at the mention of a castle but agreed to come and we took off before lunch.

Sixty thousand hectares is a huge area of land, and it was of mixed quality. Essentially it was a grouse moor that had been turned into a coniferous forest, with some of the land too poor to support even forestry. There was arable land in the valley with a number of farms, but they erred on the side of mediocrity and, like the castle, were run down. A public road came to the entrance of the estate which was interconnected by private lanes that linked each of its four lochs and all the farms. The area itself was utterly delightful with some fine scenery.

"Not too bad," said Frank, looking around the place. "A bit dilapidated… you'll knock that off the price, of course. I'd say it had potential."

"You don't think it's a fool's buy?"

"Not if you've got the money."

"It's in place."

Frank looked at me: "Listen I've been thinking… that visit from the Home Office… It's not about you: it's anti-terror with the focus on the Snake. He's gone, but he's hardly safe. This ain't the

CID he's dealing with now, the Home Office can track him across the globe. He'll need to keep his head down."

"...Yes, that's what I thought."

"He could be out of it for good."

"Well I hope so."

"It ain't my business, but I'd keep out of his way if I was you. He killed that Home Office bloke on the night before the siege – probably because the guy was tailing him. That makes him a murderer."

He turned to study the buildings.

"You won't stay here permanently?"

"No, only at weekends."

"Selling your flat?"

"No, I need it for weekdays."

"A big step, but it's your life, though why a single bloke needs a castle beats me. What's the end game, just security?"

Security? Ms Spokesperson had given the impression that everything was safe under the Snake's benevolent care, but it wasn't quite that simple, nor was it believable that his 'respect for my business skills' was his real motive for leaving the fund in my hands. Almost certainly it was money stolen from the Liberation Organisation and he'd prefer to have it traced to my account rather than his. So I was a buffer, the money stopped with me, and so did the buck, I was red-handed and would have to deal with the terrorists myself. Yes, I could see his point.

But there was a business rationale in my attitude, too. The Stock Market was uncertain, so it made a certain amount of sense to invest some of ECZ's capital in Dunglen Estate. Ultimately the value of land would rise.

I returned in the following week to engage a firm of surveyors. Then I walked around the policies and climbed a big hill in the west in a few hours. It was a lot steeper than it had seemed and by the time I reached the top I was utterly exhausted. I came across a herd of wild goats, untidy animals with straggly coats who ignored me. Apparently they had lived on the hillside for thousands of years. At the summit I could see the Mountains of Mourne in Ireland, Scafell in the Lake District, and – it was a clear day, eighty miles to the north – Ben Lomond in Scotland.

A week later I met the surveyor, a tall, brooding Scot who was suspicious of everything, including me. He reached for a sheaf of documents marked 'Dunglen Estate' and said he wasn't happy with the asking price, he hated round numbers. The main buildings needed a lot of remedial work, as did the farms. It was all in the report. Offer them seventy per cent, he said, not any more.

This was a lot of money though it was better than I had anticipated and, after reading the survey, I decided it was a fair price and went to the lawyers and made the offer in the name of ECZ. It was accepted within seven days and Dunglen was mine.

31

Suddenly the castle became a grim reality. Obviously it was essential to keep it secret from Howardsons. It was all very well to say it was owned by landlords in Switzerland, but my bosses weren't exactly naïve and a quick glance at ECZ would invite queries that would do me no good.

But I had been silly. I'd had committed a fortune to a building four hundred miles away which blotted all other thoughts from my head and it was difficult to concentrate on my work. I didn't need a castle, I didn't entertain friends, I had no wife, yet I'd bought a mansion with enough rooms for several families. Once again I had made an impulsive move that could ruin me. And why had I done it? To this day, I have no answer to that. Perhaps I had a vision of living contentedly in the country without anyone breathing down my neck. Or perhaps an ego trip had made me buy something that probably couldn't be resold (my offer had been the only one in five years) and which would be expensive to run. I knew nothing about big houses, there was the welfare of the farm workers to consider and there being no urgent business for the day, I flew to Scotland in a very tense mood. Rather than land at an airport with its attendant expense, I opted for Dunglen itself, touching down on a field I had scouted on my last visit. This was slightly dodgy, but not all that dangerous. Unfortunately it created consternation among the locals who thought I'd crashed. Within minutes my plane was surrounded by a score of them.

But for once it was all right. The estate manager was known as Big Jimmy and he was a kind of tribal leader with more managerial qualities than the directors in Howardsons (though that wasn't saying a lot) and he could also run the estate at a profit. We respected each other from the start. By this time there were a lot of people round the plane, including wives, children, and three dogs. In the time-honoured fashion the boys were studying the plane and moving its flaps while their parents called them to order.

Meanwhile two Land Rovers arrived from other farms to see the 'crash'. I took off an hour later, after taking tea with Big Jimmy and his wife.

But I was unhappy: I'd lost my love of Dunglen Castle and got depressed every time I thought about the place. Why, oh why, had I done it? It was a series of great empty rooms that I could never fill and it was all being done with suspect money that might be reclaimed at any time. And it was too late to turn back.

I engaged Hamish, an architect from Dumfries, to sort out the buildings which started to eat money at a frightful rate. He was the clerk of works, supervising the tradesmen and approving all payments, doing a good job though it took almost two years to complete.

A beautiful set of stairs that was somehow both classical and modern, swept up to the first floor in a gentle curve. This had been constructed to Hamish's design for which specialist craftsmen had to be brought in. On the apex of the curve there was a small alcove no bigger than a telephone kiosk where an insignificant door opened on to a corridor that brought you to the small tower which was my bedroom. I preferred it to the master bedroom on the first floor which was big enough for Sir James's regiment. It occurred to me that a raiding party would have to look twice before they found me.

The castle was furnished by interior designers that Hamish had chosen and it was possible to lie on a couch in the small lounge and see through the main lounge into the garden (there was now a gardener) across the trees to a range of hills in the far distance and it wasn't bad. Unfortunately, once you'd seen it three times you didn't notice it again.

A hangar had been built with doors that could be opened from above and I could touch down and find them ready for me with the lights on. A runway had been constructed and now it was surrounded by a security fence – officially to prevent cattle straying on to the landing area – but its rationale was a lot deeper than that. A safe was installed and I put all the ECZ files in it. For too long they'd been lying in Wallace's bank.

We made a tunnel (specialist engineers had to be brought from Norway) that ran from the hangar to the castle, in effect a corridor that was covered with soil, which terminated inside Dunglen's basement. This meant I could touch down and taxi into the hangar and make my way home without being seen.

Before completion, a survey had been carried out by a security expert, the castle was frequently unoccupied and it must be burglar proof. Unobtrusive CCTV cameras were located at strategic positions. Infrared devices were installed that made an audible bleep if anybody approached the buildings: they also activated a recorder which gave me an opportunity to see who I had missed.

"You could sell it at a profit," the surveyor told me when I found Hamish showing him over the place one Saturday morning. "It's a choice residence now."

On Sundays I went to the village church which had a poor pipe organ that was played by an old lady who was far too laboured. They had a choir, and I elected to join it, I liked the camaraderie and it made me feel part of the community. In Scotland, vicars are called ministers and this particular one wasn't too bad: he may even have been my favourite cleric.

Meanwhile the market had rallied and there was a lot of hard work at Howardsons. For a long time we had been in the doldrums, but now the financial world was moving into top gear and we were making money again with Mr Fortescue rushing about and new people being employed. Sir James had become frailer and would sit in his office for hours, reading his paper, and drinking tea. Occasionally I dined with him.

During the week I stayed in my London flat. Sometimes I would dine with Frank who kept me informed of the many colourful people in his life.

32

One day Stefan Gill phoned from Switzerland on various points of business and concluded by asking:

"By the way, are you contemplating changes to ECZ?"

"No, why?"

"We've had an enquiry from an agency requesting the address of your two main shareholders. I wrote back offering to relay any mail to them. Nothing came of it."

"Is this a common thing?"

"No, it's the first enquiry I've ever had. Best ignore it."

I might have dismissed this as a triviality if the telephone hadn't rung an hour later with a query from a man with a big voice who wondered if I'd dealt with *Federal & Corporate Trade* in Switzerland about eight years ago. This was amazing, my number being an unlisted one. The caller, when I pressed him for his identity, said he was working on an accounting project for a well-known firm. He merely wished to eliminate my name from their enquiries, would I confirm it? No, I wouldn't, and who gave you my phone number? Oh, he said, your number was written on my enquiry sheet.

He didn't sound like an accountant to me.

Although ECZ is a Swiss based company, I also have two UK companies, Dunglen Estates & Co, and ECZ (UK) which links with the main fund. For these I have Scottish accountants and later they phoned to ask what I'd been doing.

"Living too quietly. Why?"

"Looks like you're going to have a tax probe into your affairs. I've got an advance note from the Inspector."

"Is this unusual?"

"I suppose it is… it's just a lot of work, that's all."

"But why me, why now?"

"I imagine something's happened to excite them. You've probably been moving some money around."

"I can't think of doing anything to disturb them."

I still remember Donald's arrest. It was a Monday morning and I'd been working on the day book when there were footsteps in the corridor and he raised his head, having realised that trouble was coming. It will be like that for me, I told myself.

It was Monday and I was working in my office on the top floor at Howardsons when Reception phoned.

"Ron, two gentlemen are here to see you on private business."

"Send them up," I said, and perhaps there was a wobble in my voice. In my time with Howardsons nobody had ever come to see me on private business and two meant trouble, particularly after the recent enquiries. They were tall, in their forties, with police shirts under their casual jackets and they were enjoying their visit. They bore me no ill will and were polite all times. I offered them a chair and one of them produced a black note book.

"Ever dealt with a bank called *Swiss Federal & Corporate Trade*, Mr Miles?"

"...No... never heard of them. You should make your enquiries to our Mr Fortescue. I'm in the share buying section: I don't deal with the banking side."

"Oh this isn't Howardsons' business...It's you personally. You're sure you haven't dealt with them?"

"When was this?"

A quick glance at the notebook.

"Eight years ago. A lot of money involved."

"How much?"

"About four million Swiss francs."

"I've never heard of them... or had that kind of money. What's the problem?"

"Well there are plenty problems... This is millionaire stuff... Where did you acquire the money? Is it the proceeds of crime? Has it been taxed? Did you have Treasury permission to move it out of the country? That's just the start."

"And you've got my signature on this?" I asked in an incredulous voice.

"I don't know about signatures, sir, but it's definitely your name and address."

"Eight years ago," I said, angry. "It's difficult to remember that far back."

"Surely you'd remember that kind of money."

"I buy a lot of shares. Why wait eight years?"

"The Swiss bank changed hands and some papers were sent to us. Four million francs in one calendar month. I'd remember that."

I gave them a look of baffled innocence.

"They're claiming this is my money?"

"Looks like it, sir."

"I've never had money like that."

"No? How did you buy an estate in Scotland then?"

"I didn't. I'm a tenant."

Obviously this was already known: the first one sat back then the other man took over. They were a professional team.

"It's the four million francs, Mr Miles. There may be a simple explanation. Perhaps you invested it for a friend or it's part of a trust? We need to have the details, that's all. Would you come and see our boss tomorrow, Inspector Hound? We gotta sort this out." He produced his black notebook and said: "Twelve thirty?"

I looked at their faces and knew they were going to run me down.

"...I'll be there."

I showed them out, aware that my status in the firm had changed forever. I left for Wallace immediately and found him busy with a group of businessmen. I had to wait forty minutes until he was free. Clearly he was annoyed at my unannounced arrival though he listened to me with an increasingly worried frown.

"Eight years ago? You only used Federal & Corporate for a few months."

"Yes, then I went liquid."

"And they've been taken over?"

"So they said. I've heard nothing."

"Oh you wouldn't, it's a tiddler. Four million francs. Is that right?"

"It's possible. We were selling shares at that time."

He put his hands in his pocket and walked across the room.

"Somebody's watching you. Don't make a statement. They're fairly sure of themselves, coming to see you. Doesn't mean they can't be stopped. Say nothing in the meantime."

"That's my intention."

"...Four million francs... This is going to take some sorting out."

"It is a lot."

He gave me a questioning look:

"Who would send them the papers?"

"The Snake knows a lot of things."

Wallace looked up.

"You're getting paranoid, the Snake. How could he know?"

I was silent, having no wish to tell him about the programme that had relayed a year's dealings to Auchenboggle. Without doubt the Snake knew every facet of my account: more than enough to damn me. Why he'd waited eight years was another matter.

"Have you got a lawyer? You need a good one."

"...It's early days. I want to keep it low key. A lawyer might presuppose a lot to hide... I'll try the innocent."

"Innocence has never been your strong point. It'll be well planned."

"I'm sure he's behind it."

"Well where is he? Nobody's seen him for years... Listen; would you keep our name out of this? It could be damaging."

For a minute we were silent as he stared at his desk.

"I'm seeing Hound tomorrow."

"Well, whatever you do, don't prattle." And Wallace began to read a letter on his desk. I was dismissed.

Walking back, I saw an empty kiosk and on the spur of the moment I phoned Frank and offered to buy his dinner at the pub. We met thirty minutes later and took a seat in the corner where I recounted events. His face was grave.

"It don't look good. Better get a lawyer, a good one."

"I'll do that later. Maybe I can settle it with Hound tomorrow."

"Settle it!" said Frank as though I was insane. He lit a cigarette and looked worried. "Anyone else involved?"

"No, only me."

He gave a sigh and shook his head

"Pity... you can't pass the buck... It ain't good when you're solo. I mean how can you argue with a bank? This needs a lotta thought, I'd get a fancy lawyer quick."

"Would you take a lawyer tomorrow?"

But Frank didn't know what to do. He was out of his depth.

"Dunno what I'd do. You need to shut 'em up. Got anything up your sleeve?"

"...Not at the moment.

33

The police station was a lot bigger than I had expected, several times the size of Howardsons, a modern building with a substantial car park at the back. Despite my wayward life, it was the first time I'd been in one. At twenty-five past twelve I presented myself at reception and asked for Inspector Jack Hound.

"I'll let him know you're here, sir, take a seat," said a young policeman and I sat in an uncomfortable chair for fully thirty-five minutes, watching some of life's misfits being escorted to and from their cells. The policemen formed a strong brotherhood that laughed at their own arcane jokes and seemed unconcerned with life's little difficulties. In some ways they resembled their prisoners.

At about one, I was escorted to an empty room on the second floor where I sat on another uncomfortable chair for twenty minutes before a big man of about fifty with a hook nose burst in. It seemed he was Jack Hound though he didn't identify himself. He was bulging out of his uniform and his double chin was almost choking his collar.

"You look like a weed to me."

I made no reply, though he wasn't exactly a Chelsea Beauty himself.

"If there's one thing I hate, its city slickers."

"I see."

"No, you don't see. I'll bet you're mad at missing your fancy lunch."

"Not at all."

"You're going to miss a lot of fancy meals. My heart bleeds for you."

At that moment two younger policemen brought in a box of files and I was shown the evidence which was nothing more than several sheets of papers. Each exhibit was enclosed in a transparent covering and was treated with great respect by the policemen who refused to let me actually touch any of them.

First was a bank statement for four million odd francs. Except it wasn't a statement as such. Obviously Federal & Corporate worked on a monthly basis and this was an internal document that would not normally leave the bank. It had been printed by an old-fashioned typewriter on a prepared form that bore my name and address and had a police evidence number attached in red. There were four entries:

Brought forward	Swiss francs	750,010
Lodged	4,121,427	
Bank charges	6,450	
Balance		4,864,987

Yes, it was a true report, I remembered it well. The money had come from the sale of Lonrho shares which was my first move when I went liquid. Had it continued into the following month, the balance would have been three times higher, thereafter it would have been zero since the computer would be moving it around the world's banks. This being a German-speaking bank, the form had technical instructions in six point font, in German. The title, *Swiss Federal & Corporate Trade Bank* differed from the bank's real name of *Federal & Corporate Trade (1896)* but that was not significant. Almost all banks have umpteen titles and no doubt this was the holding company's. The address was changed, too, but that was inconsequential.

I asked to see the reverse side which revealed a virgin surface that hadn't been pre-printed. This surprised me: most banks at that time would rather print on the reverse side to save money and also to reduce the risk of losing a vital document, but then every company has its own way of going about business.

"Have you anything to say about that?" said Hound, speaking with loaded contempt.

"No."

Second, was a letter, signed by the president of the bank, confirming that the document I had seen (account number given) was genuine and represented the business done by Mr Ron Miles in that particular month. The president regretted that he must decline Mr Hound's request for further details of Mr Mile's account as this was contrary to the Swiss Code of Banking and aside from confirming the previous document, no further details would or could be given. He also noted that the address of his bank was now altered, it having removed to a new address in the city centre.

"Show me the first document again."

One of the policemen placed it on the table. I leaned forward to read the serial number and nearly fainted. It was the number of my account with Stefan Gill, now worth many millions. So the documents on the table were bigger than they seemed. They were a compilation of my Swiss dealings: someone was telling me a bigger secret.

They passed other files to me.

These were letters confirming the previous evidence, as well as a bill for one thousand Swiss francs for services rendered. The final exhibit was a declaration by Inspector Hound that he had telephoned the Swiss bank and confirmed all of the above. All in all it was difficult to argue with the evidence.

"The case is proven," sneered Hound. "No question."

"I reserve my defence."

Now I was subjected to an ugly twenty minutes. The young policemen sat and took notes without comment. I could see the Inspector was on shaky ground at times and understood nothing about banking, but he was determined to get me. I answered all his questions though I had no rejoinder to the Swiss account and I was put on a police charge which demanded I present myself to the station in seven days' time.

Once formally charged I was finished at Howardsons – I suspect that was the sole reason for the charge, apparently it was unnecessary from a legal point of view. I remember the Snake's cryptic note: He wanted me finished in the City and although it had taken time, his objective had now been achieved.

I went to my flat and wrote a letter of resignation to Fortescue in which – there being no point in embroidery – I stated the facts and formally resigned from the company. After posting the letter, I went to my plane and flew to Scotland where I donned old clothes and helped move sheep to a fresh field, glad to feel the cool wind in my face.

Several articles appeared in the business press under the heading *'Ron Miles Resigns'*. Howardsons released a statement saying they'd received my resignation with regret. Their shares started to slide downwards.

Ninety days were to pass before I was formally charged with eighteen offences relating to the Swiss account. It should be remembered that on the date of the bank statement it was illegal to move money out of the UK without the authority of the Treasury, which gave them the opportunity to throw the book at me. By this time I had a defence team which took up a lot time and accomplished little, perhaps they were influenced by my sense of impending disaster.

34

Unwelcome distractions from better days kept coming back to haunt me. One was a letter in poor handwriting from Sir James, inviting me to visit him in the near future. He was said to be suffering from advanced prostate cancer and hadn't been seen in public for months. Not having seen the great man for a year and now with my resignation and disgrace, I felt doubly guilty and though I was tempted to ignore it, I could hardly disregard a request from my principle benefactor. After two days of indecision, I phoned Lady Howardson who told me he was very poorly but anxious to see me. There was just a hint of rebuke in her voice that said I'd let the side down.

They stayed at an old manor some seventy minutes from London and I arrived with a heavy heart, noticing subconsciously how mundane it seemed beside my own flash castle, but that didn't matter anymore. It was sited in a hollow, surrounded by trees, without a view and it seemed to be crumbling under its own weight. I had brought neither flowers nor a gift and I was well aware that this was bad form, but what do you give a man as rich as Sir James?

Several cars were at the front. I parked at the side and walked self-consciously to the door, which boasted a new ramp for his wheelchair.

The bell was answered by his son, Martin, whom I have always despised. A wastrel and a no-gooder, today he was warm and welcoming, looking healthier than I had ever seen him. He shook my hand expressing sympathy with my problems. In his time he too had dealt with the Law and had a history of offences involving drugs. Now I was the failure and it irked me to receive his sympathy. Lady Howardson came into the hall and gave me a kiss on the cheek as well as a maternal cuddle. It seemed I was not entirely condemned or perhaps this was nothing more than olde worlde courtesy.

For a moment there was an awkward silence as we looked at each other on this my first (and only) visit to the manor, yet I felt I'd been there before. It was the brown varnish that did it. The Auchenboggle's weren't the only gentry to be sold on dullness.

"He's very ill," she told me. "Don't tire him."

"Yes, but he's been looking forward to you coming," said Martin.

I looked up at the sound of squeaking wheels and wondered at the old man in the wheelchair. He was totally bald, his head little more than a skull, and his frame reduced to a shadow of its past self. There was an anxious expression in his face, his eyes seemed fanatical and his hands had a constant twitch. He had always been smartly dressed and now he looked like an inmate from Belsen. A man in a white coat guided the wheelchair.

"So you've come at last m'boy."

His voice had become high pitched, the piping sound of an unhealthy twelve-year-old and his face was thin with suffering. For a brief second his eyes rested on me, then wandered over the place as though he was no longer sure of his location or of his own stability

"Nice to see you, Sir James," I said, wincing at the lie, and shaking his hand which was utterly limp.

"And you, m'boy. Let's get out to the back garden, my favourite place."

"Not too far now," warned Lady Howardson.

"Garden's not far. Open that door, Martin, there's a big world out there."

"It's cold in the wind."

Wordlessly, the white-coated man held up a rug and wrapped it around the patient; then he placed a knitted cap on his head. This was done without consulting him. Martin held the door while we went out at the pace of the wheelchair, swinging to the left of the house, and following a path that had been gouged in recent times.

"How are you feeling, Sir James?" I asked in subdued tones.

"Oh, I can cope. Never been poorly in my life before, you know: taken a knock or two in the army, but this is the first time I've really been ill." I had to lower my head to catch his words which were too feeble to carry. "Everybody's been kind to me, and, you know, it's not too bad…"

We followed the path to the east of the house which seemed to go on forever.

"What a big house," I said, looking for something to fill the silence. "It's huge."

"Far too big: been here, on an off, for sixty years and there are rooms I've never been in. How's your own... castle?"

Normally I would have protested that I was a mere tenant, but that didn't matter now. It was embarrassing to have a castle when I didn't have the gravitas to carry it off.

"...Not too bad... It's the surroundings I like, the walking. There's a herd of wild goats on the hill... and plenty of deer."

"Yes, I can see you doing your walks... I used to like that too, but we all need people an' I like the family about me now."

How many times have I listened to such sentiments at funerals? At the end of the day we all finish in a box with a clergyman bleating about how we loved our family. But it was easy for me, a lone man, to mock him, Sir James was speaking of the wisdom of family life and I knew he was right.

By this time the wheelchair was at the rear of the house and we turned to the right where the garden extended upwards in a gentle slope. The chair was battery powered and the white-coated attendant guided it on its way, studiously ignoring us.

"If I can, I come here every day, y'know... means a lot to me."

Eventually we arrived at the head of the garden where a section was encircled with meshed wire. The man opened a door and the wheelchair was reversed into the section which gave a view of the area and the house.

"All right," he said turning to the silent man in the white coat. "Go and have your smoke. First thing they did was stop my cigars, first thing they do is light up." The man gave a mirthless laugh and walked away.

"Sit down and talk to me, m'boy," and now his voice became animated. There was a wooden stool and I sat on it. "This is a terrible business you're in. What happened?"

"I don't know."

"Who shopped you?"

"I don't know. Somebody sent papers to Inspector Hound."

"Yes, yes. But you're not entirely daft, you must have suspicions."

"Well... a man called D'Alfonso. They call him the Snake."

"My God, that swine!" he shouted. "How did you get mixed up with *him*?"

"You know him!" I blurted in amazement.

"Never mind that. How did he get into your life?"

"...A transaction years ago. What can you tell me about him?"

Having overexerted himself, Sir James was silent. He reached over and scattered what looked like birdseed on the ground. After a few moments a pheasant, then another, came scuttling in to eat. They were quite tame.

"I love feeding 'em. They wait there for me every day."

"I wondered why the alcove had the mesh."

"Yes, gotta keep them out of the garden. He knew about your Swiss account, this D'Alfonso?"

"...Not as such. Well maybe, perhaps he was tapping my computer."

"I hate that," said the old man, exploding into an impotent rage, spittle running down his chin. "What a mess you've made of your life, a complete mess! Yet you were once so good... What's gone wrong, why make such a mess of things? Dammit, you're a walking failure. If you used the same attitude with the Prosecutor as you did with Howardsons you could send them to hell and back. Now you're dithering on the bridge while the ship goes down."

From his position fifty feet away the white-coated attendant looked at me reproachfully: no doubt a man of Sir James's fragile health should be kept as calm as possible: the spasm of rage had reddened his face and frightened the pheasants.

But my skin was tingling with excitement. For the first time in a year a lucky chance had come my way, the world was a smaller place than I'd supposed. Who would have believed that Sir James knew the Snake! Perhaps it would be possible to trace the rogue and negotiate some kind of deal. If he were to withdraw the evidence the case would collapse. Or would it?

"Sir James, you can help me," I said, too aware that after his outburst I sounded like a schemer trying to sell him a used car. "What do you know about D'Alfonso? I need to get in touch with him."

Yes, it was the wrong question. His old head swung at me with a puzzled frown, momentarily unable to follow my line of thought, then his eyes narrowed and I knew there would be no support.

"The man's a rogue. I know nothing."

Now he was wary of me.

"But he's associated with big banks," I said, sensing knowledge somewhere.

"Is he hell!" his high-pitched voice had turned to exasperation again. "He works on his own, an' he's rich, I dunno, I think he's based in the Middle East."

"You think so?" I said, aware that some of the Middle East states would be an excellent cover for the old rogue. "How can I contact him?"

He looked at me in consternation and snorted.

"I don't know! Its years since I was in banking. I've never met him."

But he'd been too quick to call him a rogue: without doubt he knew more and I looked at his old face in desperation, hoping he might have information to save me. His eyebrows were gone, there were a few wisps of hair on his head and his eyes seemed bloodshot. How are the mighty fallen.

"Have you any idea how I could get in touch with him?" I repeated.

"Absolutely none. Are you asking me to believe he engineered the whole thing and hasn't contacted you?"

"...He's the only person I can think of."

"And that's all you know?" said Sir James, suddenly sharper than I'd anticipated. "Has he been in touch?"

"...No."

"Then how do you know it's him? That kind of man never does anything for nothing. Forget him an' concentrate on your problems. An' you've got plenty. Your lawyers are useless."

"You think so? They were recommended."

"If they'd been investment managers you'd have sent them packing. All they're doing is collecting fees while they send you down."

Strangely moved by this I found myself unable to speak.

"By the way," said Sir James calming down. "I'm not faulting you for having a secret fund. Nearly everybody has one, including, to my knowledge, most judges. We've all had to do it: socialist politicians too. The trick is not to get caught... I suppose you did Donald in? That's what the Donald Fund was?"

"I can't go into that."

Wrong answer: and it enraged him again, but there are times when confession isn't good for the soul and I was in enough trouble without acknowledging further crimes.

"What's happened to you? Where's your leadership, you're a weakling!"

We were silent while the white-coated attendant blew smoke from his nose and shook his head at me.

Then he uttered a sigh: "Sorry – it's the pills... I didn't mean to be offensive."

"None taken..." I said, though I was annoyed at his outburst.

We were silent, with nothing to say. The sky was overcast, the manor was set low with no view and there weren't even birds singing in the garden.

"...I'm in Court shortly," I said to break the silence. "What do I do?"

He raised his thin hands to his face and rubbed his nose.

"Sack your lawyers and get good ones."

But was it that easy? In reality no lawyer could save me. How do you defend yourself when the evidence is signed by the president of a bank? Of course there were two funds – the Donald Fund and its successor, ECZ, now worth many millions with its master account quoted on the statement. Get rid of the first and I might have far bigger problems with the second. My only hope was to discredit the evidence and I couldn't see how fancy lawyers would be any better than the current ones.

"I'll think about it, Sir James. You've been kind to me, more than I deserve."

Uttering a sigh, the old man sank into his chair. I could see our meeting had brought him no joy. Without doubt he'd been looking forward to seeing me, we were old colleagues with much to reminisce about and now the whole thing had turned ugly, a pity, because we would never meet again. I began to see that he'd a paternal attitude to me: his own son, Martin, was a loser and now I too was a disappointment.

"Oh you've been good to us," he said, though he sounded displeased. "The only talent for ages – it's folly not to encourage the young and that's all I've done... although I've spoken sharply, I'm still on your side. Now our firm's in a bad way, there's nobody to replace you and the management don't seem to be trying. I hear a lot of pension business has been taken elsewhere, someone's buying up the shares, too."

"Oh, who?"

"Not known. It's being done through a bank. We'll find out soon enough. Have you given up the organ?"

I shifted in discomfort, his tone indicated that I'd done wrong there too.

"Yes, I'm afraid so. Years ago."

"Pity... I thought you did well. You should never have left London. I wish you'd stayed, you were doing some good."

The man in the white coat threw his cigarette away and began to walk towards us. My time was up.

"Sir James, you've been a good man to me, and I'm glad to have met you."

"All of that's meaningless at the end."

"No, no."

"Yes, yes. But none of us can avoid it. Take me back in, it's cold out here."

35

Nothing was going right and the deadline was nearing by the hour. I could neither sleep nor think properly: my luck had turned bad, outdoing all the breaks of the past and shortly I would be exposed to the world for the fraud I was. Every meeting with my lawyers was another blow to my confidence: I felt nauseated when I walked into their building and the outcome of every meeting was another nail in my coffin. Sir James was right: I was dithering on the bridge while the ship went down. What had happened to me? Once I had been full of ideas and capable of executive action but now I had nothing to celebrate but my own incompetence. In truth I had no aptitude for the law, I didn't understand it and my mindset couldn't abide its attitudes. I've met people who thrive on that kind of thing but we belonged to different worlds.

For a year I'd avoided Wallace who was busy in his bank. By this time he was a fat man in Saville Row suits who smoked Havana cigars and was jealous of his time with no wish to listen to failures awaiting their turn at court. Now a rising figure in the City, his services were much in demand and everybody said he was good. It took days before I could even get him on the phone. Earlier he had asked to be excused from my pre-trial difficulties on the simple grounds that he was a banker who knew nothing about the law and might misadvise me. That seemed fair enough.

Being realistic, I doubted if he could help me. In recent years my business with him had trickled to zero and he would certainly resent that. Eventually his secretary phoned with an appointment and I went to find his bank enlarged and bustling with activity. He was busy and I had to wait for five minutes before being ushered into the Presence where his office had been revamped to reflect his new stature. He was seated behind a magnificent desk that looked as if it was a hundred years old though it was only a reproduction. There was also a fine oil on the wall.

As it happened, he greeted me like a lost brother, shaking my hand and rebuking me for looking so down. What's happened to the old Ron Miles?

"They've got a copy of one month's trade," I told him, "the month we sold Lonrho and there's a letter from Switzerland confirming it. What can I do?"

Wallace was sympathetic to the extreme and I found that galling. A year had passed since we'd last met and I could see his bedside manner had been cultivated in a serious way. Now he let me do the talking while nodding his head occasionally. We were sitting on leather chairs with our heads down while the rain battered against the window.

"Ron, tell them it's somebody else's money."

I'd heard this before, everybody said something similar, but perhaps he had an original slant that might work.

"Yes, but whose?"

"Ah that's the hard bit. Not easy to produce a living person... maybe someone who died after you handed it over."

"That's crazy! They'd have to be named and we'd need details."

Wallace adopted his cunning look.

"You forget. This is Switzerland. They can't order the bank to give evidence in a UK court. You could say that a Mr Somebody, who already had money in Switzerland, asked you to invest it for him."

I looked at his fat face to see if he was serious.

"Where did I meet this Mr Somebody? And if he's dead shouldn't his relatives be yelling for their dough?"

"You aren't thinking this through. You refunded his money."

"All right, where are his relatives to confirm it?"

Wallace closed his mouth and looked at me.

"How am I going to prove it?" I persisted.

"It doesn't need proof. It just needs to be convincing – You could say you've known him for years... he admired your investment strategy. You met him at church."

"There were two hundred people in church every Sunday. Odd that nobody saw him. Isn't that a bit chancy?"

"You're being too negative, Ron. Your nerves are bad. Helpful suggestions shouldn't be shouted down."

"My lawyers have looked at these things. They say I need a believable name and address and some convincing documents before that will work. Unless the defence is solid it's pointless and it'll mean a bigger sentence."

"Ron, listen," said Wallace pulling his chair towards me and dropping his voice. "You've got the money: you can splash out. What about getting an actress to say she invested her cash with you. For a hundred grand she'd be brilliant."

"They're going to ask for proof."

"Oh but you'd get her from the Continent, maybe Switzerland. There are plenty actresses that could do it. Get some documents forged to make her look rich. It's easy. She gave you the money eight years ago and you returned it when requested."

"Where would I find her?"

"Well, there's bound to be a theatre agent somewhere. Trouble is I –"

"– don't know any. I've been there before. My lawyers say an actress is fine so long as she sticks to the script. But the prosecutor won't, he'll flatten her in court, then where would I be? Jack Hound's going to investigate her like the devil. And if she's rich she won't take risks to save me. That's a dead end."

All over the world people are influenced by the Hollywood court with its kindly old judge and comfy characters. The hero is on a serious charge and the jury is getting ready to send him down for a hundred years when in walks the Believable Stranger whose testimony demolishes the case and our hero walks free to the congratulations of all. But is it that easy? In real life the case would be stopped, the Believable Stranger's evidence would be examined only to re-start if it's found to be suspect, possibly with a second charge in the wings for the Believable Stranger if he's shown to be lying. Take the actress scenario. She has given me four million francs to invest. How does she know me? Where did she get my address? Did she phone me? (M'Lud we can't trace the calls.) Is she in the habit of handing fortunes to strangers? Where did her wealth come from in the first place? How did she pass it to Ron Miles, where is the evidence in her bank statement? Where did she put the money when Ron Miles refunded it? In fact her evidence would be nothing more than hot air that would be discredited in ten minutes.

"I've got a friend who knows a theatre agent. Maybe I could try –"

I wondered what had happened to Wallace's sharp mind. Was he seriously suggesting I approach this 'friend who knows a theatre agent' with instructions to find a suitable actress to give false evidence in court? That would be a gift to a blackmailer: it could be the talk of every pub in the land.

"I need something a jury can believe."

"From the sound of things you're virtually admitting guilt."

My legal team had explored this subject with some energy. Being good upright lawyers they couldn't possibly approach an actress themselves. But I could do it and they'd work with her to produce a convincing case.

But there were insurmountable problems. The movement of the money would have to be proved. Usually it would be paid by cheque and it would appear in the actress's bank statement and my own. So where is the evidence? Nor could I forge it since a forensic lab can now establish the exact time a document was printed. The document would have to have been printed eight years ago, not last month. And of course photocopies are unacceptable.

There were business difficulties too. Why had I invested it in a current account that bore no interest? Since equities were bad at that time, I could have opted for bonds or a hundred other things, but no, it had gone to a non-interest-bearing account which was startlingly bad practice. My rationale was clear enough: I was going to move it around the world to keep it safe from prying eyes. But that was a song I couldn't sing in court.

"Is there any way *you* can cover it," I said.

"Oh, heavens, I can't do that, dear man! Where would I say the money had come from? Whose account? Oh, no. I'm just a small bank and that's a big whack of money. I'd be in the dock beside you. Sorry, old man, I'd love to. But that's a no-no."

"It's the only chance I've got."

"If it was possible I'd have offered months ago."

"What about something involving the Snake, he's not around to argue?"

"He never did business with me on that scale."

36

It must encourage thoughtfulness to know that one is to be shot in, say, a fortnight. Every day would seem like an age. You can make no plans, do nothing, go nowhere, and all the time the deadline is getting closer. No doubt major surgery and a few other things have a similar aspect, though in my case I was likely to survive the trial which meant that my worries were less than life or death.

Come D-Day I was collected by one of the legal team at eight in the morning. As instructed, I had packed a few possessions in a suitcase, on the unhappy assumption that I would be a guest of Her Majesty for the immediate future. Some of my neighbours' curtains twitched when I exited the flat and that too was predictable, but I didn't care: I would never be there again. By this time I was resigned to disaster but even so it was disheartening to note that my legal companion wasn't even interested in the trial. Perhaps he was quite right: the accused was resigned, so why should he be concerned? One thing about arriving early was that I avoided the press.

Later in the waiting room I met the QC, clad in an immaculate suit and red bow tie, who told me it would go well. He was no favourite of mine, a media personality and one of the biggest snobs I have ever met. A moment later he was briefing my team of five (how's that for over manning?) with a lot of muttering and head shaking, like doctors diagnosing an obnoxious cancer.

Then I heard the clerk call my name, an usher repeated it, the QC nodded and all seven of us filed into the courtroom. There had been a bit of talking in court which faded into silence as we took our places. Then we stood for the judge's entry, I was struck by her self-importance and couldn't help remembering Frank's comment:

"That's Mrs Jemima So-And-So: her man's a regular at the Shimmering Moondust Massage Parlour. Tell her Nina the Knocker is asking very kindly for him." How Frank was aware of that little snippet remains a mystery.

Jemima gave us a dignified nod and we sank to our chairs and listened as the clerk took an age to read all eighteen charges. The whole thing was like church without the music, the judge acting as vicar, and the public gallery as the restless congregation. Obviously this bit of the service was the Bible reading and my team had their own copies of the charges which they perused with many a sigh as the clerk rambled on. They had even brought a spare copy for me, but it wasn't good reading. I noticed that the press gallery was full and there wasn't a spare seat in the place. Now I was on my hind legs confirming my name and stating that I understood the charges. At this I looked up to find Jemima staring at me over her glasses. Perhaps she was disappointed by my East End accent. She had an impatient look, as though someone had jumped her in the queue.

I won't touch on the case, but half the submissions seemed to have little to do with the charges. There was too much money in the City and it was high time something was done about it. Out of all the profligacy I stood out as the leader and they were out to put me in my place. Who does he think he is: a QC?

"How could this man, a product of a Council-run home, have acquired four million Swiss Francs in less than fifteen years? So far he has not enlightened us: the acquisition of this trivial sum appears to have slipped his mind. But I believe he remembers very well, he doesn't look forgetful to me, it is my contention, M'Lud, that this cash is dishonestly obtained. I submit that its history wouldn't bear the light of day. And he denies nothing, nor will he explain its purpose in a Swiss bank or where it is now. He has made no attempt to assist the Crown enquiries."

Rather than leave for lunch, I elected to have a cup of tea and a biscuit in the waiting room. When court resumed, my QC asked for time to consult his client and I went to council's chambers with all my lawyers.

"Going badly," he grunted, his breath smelling of good wine. "How do you feel about guilty to the first two charges? They'll withdraw the rest. It's not going well."

After much muttering they nodded. Even a super optimist would have had second thoughts about my chances; nobody thought we were winning. Then the defence and prosecution teams went to chambers and reached an agreement. Before sentencing, my QC made a good speech in which he said I had done a lot for the City and often handled substantial sums and it was all too easy to misunderstand a transaction especially after an interval of several years.

The judge gave me two years. This was a first offence and the Crown case was not all it should have been, though Jemima didn't quite say that. I had expected five. An order was made to seize my assets so that they could recover the tax. I was taken below, handcuffed, and marched to the meat wagon where I sat with a police escort for half an hour before being driven away. I had made a request to be spared the press photographers and somehow it was granted. They never got a shot of me.

37

According to Dante there are various levels in hell. Court may have been the first but now things took a turn for the worse as I sank deeper into the pit. Some of the warders made an effort to make life bearable but it didn't work for me. I am not the kind to take to prison. I couldn't take the confinement, I couldn't stand the convicts (and, yes, they didn't like me either) and I couldn't endure the aura of the place.

First I shared a cell with a young burglar who was plainly insane, who talked and shouted in his sleep and was incapable of stringing a sentence together. He hated me, wouldn't speak, and twice lashed at me with his fists without warning. At an interview with my social worker I broached the subject and pointed to contusions on my face, but he merely shrugged: this was prison after all and you can't expect civilised behaviour from everybody. Nevertheless the burglar was escorted away one morning and I never saw him again. Next there were two fat men, old timers who had seen it all. They were cheery and sometimes good fun, but I was an object of their contempt and got the worst of every deal. Their jokes and tastes were violent and I hated them.

I never shaved in prison. Once the door had slammed I had reached my ultimate destination. Even as a schoolboy there had been a premonition that one day I would be on the wrong side of the wall, perhaps that was why I had taken so many risks. Somewhere at the back of my mind I imagined it as a cathartic experience that would change my life, that everything would be plain sailing thereafter. But that was a false hope. There is never a situation that can't get worse.

Frank came to see me: he had his head down and was looking wary. He hated the place, his sympathies were with me entirely and he wouldn't be waiting long.

"You're a bit white, but that's usual innit? Not missing much outside, I can tell you that. Things are duller than ever. Don't look so down, you'll be out soon."

And he scuttled off.

In the canteen two of the boys took me to a table where the big boss sat. A huge man with the look of an oversized Winston Churchill who inspired fear in everybody from the warders down, not because he was violent in himself (though he was doing life for murder) but because he controlled the entire underworld of the prison. Taking a seat, with some reluctance, I had a paper thrust in my face, a mediocre selection of shares that even Mr Browne could have bettered.

"Any good?"

I looked at the array of companies in bewilderment.

"Well, not really, I'm afraid."

"What's wrong with it?"

"The selection's... uninspired."

"Gimme new ones."

At this point I was out of touch, only occasionally seeing a newspaper, and seldom so much as looking at a business column, but it would be folly to offend a man like that, so I wrote a list of suggestions on the reverse side and handed it over. Wordlessly he put it in his pocket and I never heard from him again.

The minister came down from Scotland. He told me everything was going well at Dunglen and Big Jimmy was running things fine. Everybody sent their good wishes and hoped I would be out soon, etc., etc. I said little, there being nothing to say. It was nice of him to come even if he was on expenses and getting a nice break out of it.

"All right you," said a warden coming to my door on a dull Monday when I was lying on my bunk staring at the ceiling. "Come on."

"What is it?"

"Visitor."

It was Wallace, clad in an immaculate three-piece suit and he seemed agitated when they brought me to the grill. As I sat down, there was an outburst of swearing from the person on his left who was speaking to another inmate and he glared at the man.

"That's some beard you've got." (Wallace isn't into beards.) "How are you?"

I could only nod.

"Listen, I haven't got long," he leaned over the grill and speaking softly so that he wouldn't be overheard. "You're not going to believe this. I've looked at the Swiss bank that sent you down. It doesn't exist. It used a name similar to *Federal & Corporate* but it has nothing to do with them. There's no bank at that address and there never was; there's not even a street with that name. You've been sent to prison on a forged ticket. Are you all right, did you get that?"

I nodded.

"It's Hound, he's been accused of doctoring evidence before. Wait till you hear this. I did a survey among some banking friends and he was paid twenty thousand pounds one week after the trial by a firm owned by Lord Madden. D'you get it?"

"Yes I get it."

"Are you following me? You've been jailed on a false ticket."

"I've always known. How did Hound find out about *Federal & Corporate* in the first place?"

"We'll never know."

Fumbling in his brief case, he produced a letter which he thrust at my grill. This brought a roar from the warder who rushed up and seized it, shouting that nothing can be passed to prisoners. Wallace, suddenly furious, shouted back so loudly that three warders came hurrying in. The man sitting next to him even stopped swearing for a moment. Eventually the letter was returned to his case and he resumed his seat, speaking softly:

"I want to pass this file to good lawyers. I've gotta do it anonymously. Bankers aren't allowed to reveal information. Do you agree?"

"What lawyers?"

"My own, they're brilliant – better than your last lot."

"Well they couldn't be worse," I said, though a lot of the incompetence was my own. I had more or less admitted guilt.

A few days later a team of lawyers, two men and a woman arrived to interview me for what seemed an age. They brought books of files and fussed away about a lot of petty details, much of it seemingly irrelevant – but that's lawyers all over. The case against Hound was utterly damning and he'd been stupid enough to sign a statement claiming to have confirmed the documents with the bank president. He didn't have a leg to stand on and now he was well and truly finished.

When they'd gone, I saw a doctor and complained of headaches, making such a good job of it that they moved me to hospital for tests. Shortly there was going to be another fuss about Ron Miles and this time I wouldn't be the greedy bastard but the poor innocent. If there's one thing I can't stomach it's a fuss and this one promised to be incandescent. I like my privacy and once exposed to the baying paparazzi I'd have none for the rest of my life.

The lawyers came again and, clad in a house coat, I met them in a room at the hospital. I wouldn't be going back to prison: the case would be repealed. A judge had already granted an interim release order. In the near future there would be an official court hearing at which the facts would be laid bare and I would be declared Not Guilty. There was now a question of compensation. Having lost my job, and being one of the highest earners in the City, I was entitled to be reimbursed for all my potential earnings for the rest of my life, which would amount to millions and it would be tax-free, too. Also the Customs Revenue having sold my flat and furniture would have to repay all the proceeds in full, with interest.

"What happened to Inspector Hound?"

By this time Inspector Hound's world had collapsed and he was dead of an overdose. How he had hoped to get off with such audacious behaviour boggled the mind. (Though there had been an element of natural justice about the whole thing). That said, I couldn't begin to guess how he knew about *Federal & Corporate* or the number of my Swiss account with Gill & Co. My original defence team should have uncovered his deceit in the first days, but I had more or less conceded the charges were true.

Sir James was dead and though I had ignored him in the last year, I was aware that there was no longer a benevolent figure in the background; a good friend had gone for ever. It was a pity that our last meeting had been unhappy. But with hindsight, I suspected he was as angry at his own impending death as he was about my incompetence. He had given me my one break in life and but for him I would never have got anywhere. Perhaps it was just as well he wasn't there to see the present debacle. I had failed to defend myself though I was technically innocent and now I was a walking has-been. He had been absolutely right: the whole thing could have been avoided with a decent defence.

"I want no publicity," I told the lawyers, "no court appearances or TV."

"But you must meet the press," they said in shocked tones, as though I was mad. "This has been the leading item on the news, they're looking for interviews and there's a TV programme in the offing. You must meet them."

"No." These expensive lawyers wanted all the publicity they could get from my exposure but I wasn't going to be pressured into a media circus. Fame was the last thing I needed, thank you very much. I'd dealt with too many pop stars and actors to be in any doubt of that. It would be sheer hell to be recognised wherever I went and it would last for a lifetime. "You do the talking. Say I'm unwell."

Yes there had been a lot of TV comment about the affair, questions had been asked in the House and there'd been yet another shake-up in court procedure. Thousands of emails had arrived which I would never read. At least two journalists were said to be writing books about me and a coterie of reporters waited at the hospital gates, several of whom had tried to sneak inside. All of which was an excellent reason for avoiding further publicity.

Then there was the question of the instigator of the whole affair, not Jack Hound, but the figure at the back of it all, the one who had supplied the information for the forged documents and who had quoted my numbered account on the stationary. Who was that person? For sure it wasn't the Snake, now I came to think of it, he didn't know the number of my Swiss Account.

For that reason I decided that the only sane course for me was to fade into obscurity as quickly as possible and hope that the world would forget me.

Shortly afterwards a court pronounced me 'not guilty' though I didn't make an appearance. My lawyers had me excused on the grounds of ill health and the judge sent his best wishes, hoping I'd be better soon. The Press were disappointed by my absence.

"Why did Jack Hound do it?" wondered the lawyers.

They shuffled about and said there was no clear lead, though there was a rumour – well, someone had sent a photocopy to their office though that was hardly legal evidence – that he'd been paid twenty thousand pounds by a subsidiary of the Madden Group which had now bought Howardsons. Unfortunately that couldn't be confirmed. Even though the inspector was now dead and presumably a lawyer was collating his affairs which must, if Wallace was right, include a cheque for twenty thousand somewhere in his assets. Was this another cover-up? I phoned Wallace and asked about the Madden connection.

"Madden paid him all right... I've sent photocopies... but it can't be proved."

Some of these things would come back to haunt me in twenty years' time.

38

In many respects hospital was worse than prison with its mind-numbing routines. I hated its discipline, I hated the way they ordered me about and I hated the very smell of the place. And some of the younger doctors were becoming quite adamant that there was nothing wrong with me, though I came up with some very convincing symptoms, having read every available book on the subject, I knew a lot about sore heads. But it was time to forget them, the headaches had fulfilled their purpose and it was time to return to the real world.

"Do you mind if I go now?"

"Yes, you can go," grunted the consultant. "Let me know if you get any more of these headaches... Personally I think they're psychosomatic – and I'm not blaming you. We can all get these things at some time or other. You've gone through a difficult time. So, yes you can go – you've been a good patient."

He shook my hand. Of course I was a celebrity of sorts and I'd also given him some help with his shares and he in turn had been resolute in keeping the press at bay. I knew he could recognise a malingerer with his eyes shut and he was trying to leave me out of that category.

I packed my case and donned the clothes I'd worn at the trial. The peace and quiet of the castle was never more inviting. The nurses all came to say goodbye, the young doctors wished me all the best and my fellow patients sent their good wishes. Then Leonard collected me in an old van and I hid in the back as he drove to the plane, laughing at the doughty reporters still camped at the gates.

Within two hours of leaving the hospital I'd touched down at Dunglen.

Big Jimmy, all eagerness, came hurrying to see me, with a case of papers. I signed some cheques and transferred money from the Swiss account. He wasn't keen on my beard and, being a farmer, he shook his head at my lost weight. To be too slim is an alien concept to a man who can tell if a flock of sheep is undernourished or if the Highland cattle are getting scraggy. On a farm everything revolves around the supply of food.

"And what are you going to do?"

"Nothing much, I'll have a walk. Relax a bit."

"Aye, but what are ye going to eat? There'll be no food here."

This turned out to be true. Except for bread and some odds and ends in the freezer, there was nothing. Nobody had lived in Dunglen for months. The upshot was that he was going to the bank and would collect sandwiches from the village shop.

An hour later, with both Labradors in tow, I left for one of the lochs, having changed into old clothes. There was the chance of the odd photographer about, though Jimmy had seen no one in the car park. Perhaps they wouldn't recognise me with my beard.

With the dogs running twenty paces ahead, I walked a footpath to emerge on to a road that fed the west loch. Both sides were lined with coniferous trees that stretched as far as the eye could see. A new peace settled on me, perhaps the oxygen from the forest was having an effect; I began to think this was the happiest moment in my life and my eyes filled with tears at the beauty of nature and the singing of birds. At long last I was free of the prison and its horrible aura, perhaps now I could get on with the rest of my life.

I turned a corner to find the dogs, who had run ahead, waiting expectantly by the water. This loch is more than a mile wide and completely enclosed by trees. On the far side two mountainous hills dominated the skyline – one of which had been home to a pair of golden eagles as recently as twenty years ago. The dogs wanted a swim but since that would result in two wet animals I ignored them and found a glade among the trees where I could eat my sandwiches in comfort. At the sight of food they were around me in seconds. The glade was comfortable and I sat for an hour admiring the view, with the dogs sleeping at my feet.

I was disturbed by a spot of rain and looked up to see a rare mauve-coloured deer watching me from a distance of twenty paces. Since it was a windless day, the deer hadn't smelt the dogs and for sure the dogs hadn't scented the deer otherwise there would have been pandemonium. I gave a light cough and it flitted silently into the forest. The dogs awoke and were stretching themselves when they found the deer's spoor and I had to call them back with a few shouts. Overhead the sky was promising a downpour and there was dampness in the air as I began the return journey. At a corner I found a Land Rover driving towards me. It stopped and Big Jimmy got out.

"So you're here," he grimaced. "This is the fourth loch I've tried. They're lookin' for you. Road's full of cars back there. Television van as well."

"Damn."

This is what comes of being in the news. Somebody must have telephoned when the plane came in.

"I've tried to shift them, but they won't move, cheeky prats the lot. What happens now?"

"Won't they have followed you?"

"Naw – Well they'd need to walk – I locked the gate."

We settled on a plan. I lay flat in the covered boot, the dogs sat on the back seat and the Land Rover made a circuitous return via several fields to emerge on to the public road three minutes below the castle. Then we went through the gates to the landing strip where I entered Dunglen without being seen. Outside the road was now blocked by cars and there was some horn blowing as Jimmy tried to get home.

I went up to the top floor in the tower and shook my head at the paparazzi. Clearly it was going to be difficult to escape from the real world. Groups of reporters watched the gardens while several enterprising photographers had gone into the fields to get new angles of Dunglen Castle, but Arthur, our prize bull, didn't like that and they made a hasty exit when he approached.

But this was prison all over again, shut up in a room with the paparazzi baying at the gates. I packed a case and went to the hanger and flew away. As I rose above the trees I could see the faces of a hundred reporters watching me.

39

It was the following day, the rain was heavy in Zurich and everybody seemed to have black umbrellas except me. Rather than run the risk of meeting the press, I had avoided fancy hotels and was staying in a small hotel on the outskirts of the city where no one would look at me twice in my old clothes.

Arriving at the bank, there was some difficulty with the receptionist who was not impressed with me. Dishevelled figures were unwelcome in those hallowed precincts and Stefan himself had to come to the desk to identify me: his face was grave.

"We have urgent business."

"Later. Fund first."

The Fund had done all right in my absence with one notable exception which we sold immediately.

"I have to tell you," said Gill. "Attempts were made to capture your fund when you were out of circulation."

He produced a file of earmarked papers.

"We received this order about two weeks after you were sentenced. It instructed us to liquidate your equities and transfer the proceeds to an account in Lichtenstein. You will note your signature."

"It's not mine."

"Exactly, a forgery: no, not a forgery, a reproduction of your signature. It has been printed by litho and embossed. Cunning."

I ran my finger over the paper and felt the depression the 'pen' had made.

"Did you realise it was false right away?"

"In fact I didn't." At least Stefan was honest, not many bankers would have made such an admission. "But I would not do anything so drastic on the strength of a few sheets of paper. I could sell only at your verbal confirmation – that was our original agreement and I was honour-bound to stick to it. For that reason I proposed to fly to your prison and speak to you. Then we noticed the signature hadn't been written by pen –"

"They're all different!"

Yes, there were several documents, some instructing the sale of equities, one getting rid of Dunglen, others authorising the transfer of all proceeds and still another instructing the closure of the Swiss account. They were covered by a letter ostensibly from me with a handwritten 'Dear Stefan' apologising for the closure, thanking him for his good work and promising to restart the Fund on my release. All bore convincing signatures, and here was the astonishing thing: they differed slightly from each other; they were not identical though they were all facsimiles of my various signings. Who knew enough to do this and where had the signatures come from?

Of course I had signed scores of papers every day at Howardsons, but these were internal documents that never left the building. Difficult to be sure, but I doubted if anyone in the old firm was capable of that subterfuge. Besides it was some time since I'd resigned. Also no document in Howardsons would start with a handwritten 'Dear Stefan' at the top. I pointed this out.

"I am the only person you are likely to address as 'Dear Stefan'. But there has been no leak from this end. Over the years you have written several such letters to me. Here is a copy of them all."

He spread papers across his desk and I saw that none of the genuine letters had been used. In fact the letter's heading was not in my handwriting though someone had gone to great lengths to ape it.

"This is alarming."

Stefan Gill took off his glasses to polish them with a terrible energy.

"Begging your pardon, I have studied the notes of your trial. Effectively, the case against you was built on litho printing – the bankers' draft, various letters purporting to come from Swiss banks, all very convincing – now this. It has been done with cunning and the inference is that the person who triggered the case is the one who attempted to steal your account, no doubt that was the objective in the first place."

"It's the Snake: D'Alfonso, possibly a false name."

I uttered these words and doubted them immediately. This didn't look like the Snake's work: it was the action of a trickster who was afraid to reveal himself. And besides, the Snake wanted me to invest his money.

"But where would he get your account number, or the signatures? You mentioned him before."

"Well... I don't know... he's got a lot of banking contacts and he's resourceful. Did you know that Inspector Hound received twenty thousand from The Madden Corporation? And now they've bought Howardsons."

By way of response, Gill started walking around the room with his lips pursed.

"We must make security changes. New account numbers... alter a lot of the details. Anybody that can do this is a serious enemy. I have prepared documents... Yes, I knew about Inspector Hound. I don't believe Madden is your enemy."

"No?"

"I doubt if he, or his firm, would be so witless. It is hardly his style and it would be an enormous risk to take. Perhaps he has been used as a decoy. You'll note your lawyers have now abandoned all enquiries in that direction."

This rang true. I was surprised he knew so much about it. But by this time I was one of his best customers and he would take a serious interest in my affairs.

"Well it's persons unknown, then."

"We'll say that for the moment, but we must review all your procedures. There is a tremendous leak in your security which you of all people cannot afford. Sooner or later they may try again."

———

Arrived back at Dunglen, I found a letter instructing me to telephone a number in London and speak to 'Ms Spokesperson': I held it to the light, wondering if it was connected to the original letter, now long destroyed, that had started it all. So far as I could see, it was entirely different. The phone was answered at the first stroke.

"Ron, our friend is concerned about his account," it was the same lady all right, though there was a cutting edge to her voice that I hadn't noticed before. "Has it suffered during recent events?"

"Isn't your friend responsible for the recent events?"

"You can discount that immediately, what about the account?"

"Oh, I wouldn't worry too much."

"Please answer my question."

"...ECZ is fine: there has been an increase of one point three per cent when I was inside. But what do you mean by 'his account'? Surely part of that is mine?"

"I don't want to get involved in that either. To return to the question, the account hasn't suffered because of recent events?"

"That's correct. I'm comfortable with it. Would it be possible to refund his share? I want rid of it."

"That is not an option."

"I want rid of it. I'm no longer with Howardsons. I don't have their research at my disposal. It's unlikely I'll do so well in the future."

"I shall report that. But in the meantime the status quo remains."

At that the phone went dead and I never heard from her again.

All in all, it looked as if the Snake had nothing to do with recent events.

When putting the phone down, I glared in disbelief at two photographers setting themselves up on the public road with long tom lenses on tripods: then I stepped back from the window in case they got a shot of me. Would the intrusions never end? Apparently a current picture of me was worth money. The media was complaining of my reclusiveness, I had never given a press conference, appeared on the box, or even allowed them the opportunity of a photo shoot. How could I be so inconsiderate? A hundred journalists wanted interviews, some were writing books. Then there were the TV producers rooting for an 'in depth' interview that would show the human side of Ron Miles.

I lifted the phone and told Jimmy that I was flying to Switzerland again and that it might be some time before I returned, though I'd phone him at regular intervals.

This time I rented an apartment near Zurich and used it as a base while I toured my way through the Continent. It would be a year before I returned to Dunglen and by that time the press had largely forgotten about Ron Miles.

40

Exactly twenty years had passed since my release from prison. Overhead a light aircraft crossed the valley at two thousand feet, a relatively unusual event, but I wasn't interested, having given up flying some years ago, there being no need to commute to London and I'd formed a hatred of airports.

On the human side, the years had not been successful, I was an oddball in the community, a loner with few friends who accomplished nothing of note. It has been said that the rich make their own hell and maybe I was doing that very thing. Somewhere in that double decade, I should have done the decent thing and married a nice girl and raised a family. I almost did it too. At that point I was still troubled that the Snake was creeping up on me so I remained single, remembering wryly that a philosopher had once said there are few things more useless to human society than an old bachelor.

Financially, things had been all right. ECZ had grown to one point two billion. All dividends had been reinvested and latterly I'd reduced my management fee to a mere point two per cent. In fact I hadn't done all that well: there were at least five investment trusts that had beaten me, though there were several hundred that hadn't.

It was a fine autumn morning and I decided to walk to Loch Skerrow, a nice little ramble, much loved by the cognoscenti, some of whom came from overseas to walk its length. I collected a Land Rover and set out with my current Labrador, Ben, calling first at the village shop for a sandwich and a newspaper. Then I parked in the village of Mossdale (you can find these things on the map) and walked miles along an old railway track through some interesting scenery with red deer, big foxes and hares, as well as a lot of wild flowers, some of them quite rare. The loch was as pleasant as ever, with ducks swimming and a couple of swans watching from an outcrop. I threw a stick into the water and the dog dived in for a swim, snorting with delight and causing a great commotion.

In the paper I found little of interest. The Stock Market was slightly down, a politician was 'setting the record straight' about some financial matters and yet another footballer had been caught with his trousers down.

Oh, and Totho, an African president, had yesterday attended his successor's inaugural banquet. At least his head was there on a pole behind the new president's throne: an interesting case that would have had John Masters shaking his old head in dismay. Two days ago, when the rebels were twenty miles from his palace with a superior army, he had refused to flee, despite having a rumoured two billion in a Swiss account. Pouring himself a glass of good malt, he had mocked the rebel army and declared himself president for life. No doubt he had been of the opinion that your troubles vanish if you ignore them.

I opened my sandwich box and Ben joined me for lunch. Overhead I watched buzzards and a kestrel: to my right, an owl swooped silently among the trees.

I didn't know that my stay in Scotland had come to an end.

Lunch over, I walked back to the Land Rover and though it was not a warm day, the dog's coat had dried when we reached the car. When driving through the village I reflected that in my years at Dunglen Castle there hadn't been a change to a single house in that time. I waved to the minister, now an old man, but still fit, and nodded at the postman who was digging his garden. In passing the hotel, I saw a black car in its grounds with an antenna on its roof. Ten minutes later I pulled up at Dunglen.

"Two men lookin' for you," grunted Jimmy, who was getting older, and too fat. "Big fellas in a black car, sounded like Londoners. They're coming back later."

In the castle I touched the recorder to see a video of the callers. Both were in their fifties and wore ties, the older one clutched an official-looking envelope and they had the stern look of officials fulfilling a duty. They approached the porch purposefully, their eyes flickering over the windows and then they leaned forward to read the screen which declared me absent. Nodding, they left to intercept Jimmy whose Land Rover was slowly drifting into the background.

But this was ominous – the hand delivery of an envelope by two men who had presumably driven from London on a Saturday.

Saturday didn't sound like good news. Then I saw the red light on the phone that said Stefan had called. I phoned him.

The news was dire. An action had been raised against me in Zurich in which it was alleged that my company ECZ was using assets belonging to the pursuers.

"They want full redress," said Stefan, "including interest for the past twenty years. The amount sued is greater than ECZ itself and they are pursuing you, personally, for the balance. The court order prohibits us from managing the Fund."

"Who are they?"

"A well-known firm of lawyers. I don't know who they're acting for. Have you been served with a writ?"

"No. But two men called when I was out."

"Don't accept it. Keep out of their way. If they can't serve the writ the case collapses in seven days." (A hand-delivered writ must be given to the defender in front of a witness.) "If it's served you may not be allowed to leave the UK. And you must come here to institute a defence. It covers events far in the past, I am no lawyer, but I imagine a strong defence could be mustered."

"Strong defence? Stefan, read it to me… slowly."

And it was the end. I recognised phrases and references to distant events that were known only to the Snake, with a lot of detail about Auchenboggle – and it was well done. At long last Nemesis had arrived. The writ alleged that money had been stolen electronically after I had assaulted a computer operator. I was accused of purloining assets to which I had no title, of failing to negotiate with its rightful owner and of taking measures that denied the pursuers of their rights to trace their money. This time the fist of justice wouldn't miss. And to make things worse, since this was now under contention, details of my contract with Mann and Friedland would have to be shown to the Swiss authorities. No easy matter since they didn't exist.

Beyond doubt it was the Snake. Only he knew these things and his case was watertight. Of course he'd never be able to prove I'd assaulted 'a computer operator'. That was his word against mine, but he'd be able to show that ECZ was founded on 'his' money and there was no easy answer to that.

But why had he gone to court when he could merely have contacted me and asked for his share? Many years ago I had agreed with his 'spokesperson' to ring-fence his assets and had done so. Why change it now?

The answer was that he was demanding every last penny in ECZ, my share as well as his own. The Snake wouldn't trust me to cede anything. In my shoes, he'd never do it and the minor cost of a case would only strengthen his arm.

"Stefan, I missed that bit," I said, my mind in a whirl as I tried to see a way out.

"... 'and in pursuit of their legitimate aims, the plaintiffs have supplied a computer file to the UK authorities which lists all transactions relevant to Mr Miles which reveal he was handling large sums of money when he was ostensibly a minor executive in Howardsons'. – Oh dear, that's not so good, is it?"

So this was not merely about money, this was about revenge and he's good at that kind of thing. He'd sent the file to the UK – and even after twenty years it would be easy to cross check the entries – and that would prove the existence of the Donald Fund. It was also prove I'd lifted a million from Ahmed's account – I was done for. Once the UK press found out, they'd go incandescent.

There was a bitter taste in my mouth. I am no lawyer, but it seemed that if I capitulated it would be an admission of theft and assault. At the very least, the case would be very damaging.

"This is the end, Stefan. I don't want to do a Totho. I have to go."

"But the Fund!"

"Not mine anymore. I'll spend the rest of my life inside. This is the end."

"But you must fight it! They're going to take everything from you, including your Dunglen Castle. They can't prove you assaulted a computer operator twenty years ago."

"This is the Snake we're dealing with. He's been plotting for years. He wants blood, and he'll get it – I have to go."

Stefan didn't sound pleased; he was looking forward to a case. In his view I was a winner with a good record in court, who had never once been defeated. But this was a different kettle of fish and now all the advantage was to my enemy. Ron Miles would be a sorry figure in court: the whole thing would be pored over by the UK authorities who'd never forgiven me for my earlier victory and the files he'd sent would give them plenty of meat for a new case and this time it would be watertight. I put the phone down.

Even so, I sat for a long time and ran the whole scenario through my head. But there was no defence. The money wasn't mine and even if I won in court, the outcome was certain to lead to other cases. The Snake had planned this well.

Of course it would be possible to send a lawyer to negotiate with his legal team. But was that realistic? He had once sent his spokesperson to me and was patently ignoring the deal.

He wanted recompense.

Ultimately it could only lead to prison again. I'd made a fool of the law once – twice was too much to expect.

It was time to go forever.

My safe was a comprehensive one with an autodestruct facility which I activated to destroy all my records. I sealed the windows of the castle and phoned for an urgent courier, hoping it wouldn't clash with the two men. I made several packages that contained parts of my Will which had been prepared in Zurich some years ago, one containing instructions to liquidate ECZ, the others with orders to Stefan and various banks. Then I started at the top of the castle and removed everything that applied to me including all photographs (except a twenty-year-old portrait which I left in the main lounge) and shredded the lot, including my passport. I took the master manual for the tunnel, the instructions for the security system, the key to the safe and left them on the hall table. I destroyed several mobile phones and formatted each computer. At that point the monitors pinged to announce the arrival of the courier. He signed a receipt, we cracked a joke about the weather and he was gone. I locked the gate behind him. Now I no longer owned Dunglen Castle or anything else. In the UK 250,000 people go missing every year and Ron Miles was going to be one of them. Then I got my Emergency Kit – I'd had one since my first day in the castle – and changed into old clothes, donned a rucksack that contained my remaining documents, including the E. M. Mertoun passbook – ironically a relic of my first crooked act, some clothes and a handful of emergency cash. There was also a bag of money in the study for which I had no room in my rucksack. Anyway, cash is nothing but an embarrassment to a tramp. Outside, Jimmy was driving past with a bale of hay to feed the cattle in the Low Pasture and I stopped him. He looked at my destitute appearance with open mouth.

"Jimmy, something's happened, there's going to be changes."

He was sitting in an untidy Land Rover that was strewn with hay, a curiously big man who gave the impression of being bigger than he really was. His farmer's cap was pulled over his forehead and his hands were covered with honest calluses. This was a man who never panics.

"Eh?"

"Jimmy, listen carefully. It's come to an end, the party's over, I'm leaving... You haven't seen me and you'll tell nobody about this conversation, do you understand?"

He nodded his head, mouth open, and made no comment. I walked to the other side of the Land Rover so that I could see the public road where oncoming lights would warn me of the men's approach.

"I've been here for a long time and we've got on well, but this is finito. I've got enemies and I'm leaving. This is for you."

He looked into the bag.

"What's this for?"

"You."

"I can't take that."

"If you don't others will, I'm going."

"What, permanently?" he was incredulous. He put the money in the glove box.

"'Fraid so. I think you'll still be employed from Switzerland... Just carry on as normal: the only difference is I'll be gone."

I looked at the darkening sky and was disappointed to see heavy clouds. Soon it would be dark and soon it would be raining.

"But ye canny up sticks and leave all this," he waved his hand at the castle.

"No option."

"Think it over for another day, man."

"That'll be a day too late. These men are looking for me. You saw them: I've gotta go. You'll look after the dog for me?"

Jimmy nodded while looking indignant

"Of course, but what am I supposed to say? There'll be questions asked."

"You last saw me at four when I came back from my walk. I told you I was leaving and that I might sell the place. You didn't see me leave and you haven't heard from me since, okay?"

"Are you really going?"

"Yes. Don't give them any modern photos of me. No matter who asks – police or press. I don't want my pic aired – give them the old one in the lounge, right?"

"Police? Are they involved?"

"Only because I'll be a missing person."

Jimmy's face darkened and he shook his great head.

"You're happy about going?"

"I'm not happy, but needs must."

His big face looked at me with an anxious expression.

"You're no' gonna do anything drastic, are you?"

"I intend to live, if that's what you mean. Tell no one you saw me. Wait there: I'll get the keys."

In a black mood I went back and walked through the castle for the last time and locked every door. There were ten keys on the fob which I handed to Jimmy.

"Are you sure you're doing the right thing?"

"I'm sure of nothing. Go and feed the cattle, Jimmy. I'm leaving forever."

But he didn't budge. "I'm sorry about this. Phone me if ye need help. Anytime, day or night. You're the best boss I've ever had."

A rare moment, the only compliment I've ever heard him utter.

"Bye."

We weren't going to get emotional, we're not that kind. We shook hands and agreed everything would be fine. Then he drove off and I never saw him again.

41

I had often mulled the options, but there was really only one escape route, and frightful though it was in the dark, that was over the big hill. No one must see me: otherwise the whole thing was pointless. If I took a car it would have to be abandoned and if I walked to the main road I would be seen, and anyway what would I do when I got there? A lift from Jimmy wasn't viable either: his car would be recognised and remembered. Forty people lived in the valley and they noticed passers-by and their cars. The flight was costing a billion and it would have to be done right. So it was the big hill.

I started walking.

By now it was dark but, even so, a part of the night that was blacker than black moved towards me and I stopped to pat Ben who was wagging his great tail, ready for another walk, but it was forever too late. He sat when ordered and when I turned after fifty paces, my eyes having adjusted to the dark, he was still watching me with a sad mien, hoping I'd change my mind. Farewell forever you faithful friend we will never meet again.

After a mile I came to the west gate and crossed into the dark forestry road where the trees were so high that visibility was near zero: a mere detail, the dog and I had walked it so often that I was sure-footed. Drops of rain began to fall. There was a crash on my left as a deer that had been grazing with its back to me ran off. Two miles on, I passed the first loch, slightly luminous even in this darkest of nights and began a gradual ascent that would take me to the base of the big hill. Many years ago when my heart was bursting with ambition, I had walked along this same road. What would I have made of myself now? Maddeningly, the rain became heavier. I had hoped it was nothing more than a sporadic shower, of which we get hundreds every year, but now it was adopting the pattern of a steady downfall. That would mean trouble when I started to climb the hill itself. And I was wearing domestic shoes too. At this point the trees had thinned out, revealing the faint shape of the hill on my left and it looked so forbidding that I stopped to think for a long minute. Already I had covered three miles: perhaps I should return to the castle and wait for better weather? But no, that would mean a delay of twenty-four hours. Tomorrow being Sunday there would be walkers on the hills and I would have to wait for darkness and anyway it might still be raining. I couldn't go back; I no longer had keys for the castle.

An old signpost, erected by the Ramblers, indicated the long distance path and I turned to the left. For three hundred yards this is lined on either side by deep ditches – no great hazard on a clear day, but perilous in the rain and now swollen with fast flowing water. Over that catchment area the ditches fill fast. Thereafter the path reaches a rickety style which almost broke when I crossed it. Here I was at the base of the big hill which towered in front of me though I could no longer see it for the rain. Tramping slowly I covered about five hundred paces to find myself facing a rocky outcrop. Already I was off course but that was no problem, I recognised the place and climbed for ten minutes to sit out of breath for a brief rest. The rain abated slightly and now the shape of the hill reappeared, looking steep and forbidding in the gloom. Usually I take three rests to reach the summit but today the ground was so sodden that every step was difficult and I was carrying a rucksack. The trick is to relax and not overexert yourself: unfortunately I was walking on wet ground, continually falling, with my shoes coming off when they stuck in the mud. Turning to look back, I could see the shape of the valley and the dull glow of the loch: it was dispiriting to see how short a distance I'd covered. Onward I creaked towards the steepest part of the climb. Then I found a rock to rest on, but the rain began again and I moved on, putting one foot in front of the other until I found a sheltered place where I could sit for ten minutes. But here the cold wind was worse than my fatigue and I got up and walked on. After an age I was at the top of the section where I found the path again which was now largely stony and therefore easier to follow.

Suddenly a face looked at me in surprise. It was a wild goat, last year's alpha male, with water dripping from his nose as he grudgingly moved off into the night. His species had survived this weather, and worse, for thousands of years. An age had passed when I next looked back to see that I had made progress, the rain had lessened and it was possible to make out the shape of the valley again. On an ordinary climb I would have assumed that the worst was now behind me: usually I could reach the summit from this point without a stop since the route makes a more gradual ascent for the final mile, but this was no ordinary climb. Now the bitter wind was biting into my clothes and it was getting worse. Nothing for it, I put my head down and walked with eyes glued to the path which was strewn with hard stones that made walking difficult: it was no place to sprain an ankle. Half a mile from the summit, there are a series of giant boulders where the path comes to a junction. Ahead, the path would bring me to a great curved cliff that sloped down to the north valley – the wrong one – while the left one led to the summit of the big hill. Exhausted, I wedged myself between the boulders to take a few minutes rest, my head resting against the biggest, I wasn't looking, scarcely able to think, when a herd of bedraggled deer walked past me in single file, completely unaware that I was less than a few feet away. Before continuing, I emptied water out of my shoes and tried to shake my clothes dry. Not a healthy situation. Onward again, I reached the summit ten minutes later.

Presumably the top of the hill has been honed by the wind and ice over millions of years resulting in an almost flat surface on which, but for the scraggy heather, it would be possible to land a fixed-wing aircraft. Today the pilot would have been in trouble with the wind, or more accurately, gale that was sweeping its surface. It was no longer possible to see beyond twenty feet and here I had to be cautious since I was unfamiliar with this side of the hill. I walked without pausing, keeping my eyes on the path, now no longer clearly defined, since only one in twenty climbers would approach from this side. After a few minutes the descent began in earnest and this masked some of the gale though at that point the rain began again and I had difficulty finding the path – if there was one – but at least I was going in the right direction. After a mile, I became aware of another problem. This valley was covered by a forest that was fed by a single road. Since it is difficult to walk through a coniferous forest it would be best to approach that road through one of its firebreaks. Unfortunately I could see nothing beyond fifty feet and would never find a break. Already there were occasional trees around me.

By this time I was stumbling with fatigue and it was some time before I twigged the loud noise in the background. It was the sound of a river in spate and it intersected my route. Too weak to be angry, I sank to the ground and watched the white waters cascade downwards. No hope of surviving such a crossing, I would have to re-climb part of the hill and it was ten minutes – it could have been much worse – before I found a way over and restarted my descent. Inevitably, I reached the edge of the forest with no firebreak in sight and since I doubted if I would survive any further delays I had to go through it. To prevent being blinded by pine needles, it is necessary to walk backwards between trees and it is a pained process made all the worse by the darkness. This went on for ages until I found myself sliding face down into a steep gully with another – or was it the same? – river rushing downwards. I lay face down for some time, spitting mud out of my mouth when I became aware of a bridge only twenty feet away. There was a danger of losing my footing and sliding into the water but I made it, clambering over the fence to find myself on a forestry road that led in the right direction, I followed it for thirty minutes until I saw the glow of a big loch on my right. Then I crossed a gate to find myself on a public road where, not fifty yards away, was a modern house overlooking the water. I banged the door as loudly as I could and shouted through the letterbox. "Frank, it's me."

42

I grew aware that someone was watching me. Frightful things had happened and at first I couldn't remember the details. To my left, the door had opened by a few inches and Frank, who is nearing seventy, his head white, was looking in with a worried expression, then seeing I was awake, he came in.

"Okay?"

"Yes, six?"

"No, nine."

"...I said six."

"You didn't look up to it. I let you sleep."

"The whole point was to get away at six."

Frank looked out the window for a minute: the rain had stopped though the clouds were still heavy.

"Where were you going, Carlisle?"

"...Yes."

"What happened?"

I was lying under rugs on Frank's leather couch, hands and face covered in dried mud, with my shoes falling apart. There were aches in every muscle, I could hardly move my arms and could sit up only with difficulty. The couch was covered in mud.

I narrated a summary of events.

"Who's behind it?"

"The Snake."

"The Snake...? Are you soft in the head or what? Carlisle's the first place he'll look. I'll bet he's there now. Or his men."

That had occurred to me too. The whole thing could be a trap, with the writ and court case as mere side props. If he's nothing else, the Snake is subtle. However I had never intended to blunder into Carlisle, there was a plan of sorts in my head.

"Let me get this right," said Frank his voice sharpening. "You've given up Dunglen Castle and ECZ on the strength of a writ in Switzerland?"

"That's right."

"But, hell man, that must be – what? – a hundred million!"

"One point two billion."

"One point two billion!"

Frank began to cough. "You should have fought it."

"And what's the defence? The money's stolen... The writ gives dates and details. Jail would kill me."

He walked across the room and said:

"That's ECZ. What about your personal money? You must have loads."

"I'll be discovered if I collect it."

"How much?" He sounded like an angry bank manager.

I said nothing. Now that money was irrelevant, it was pointless to brood on the fifty million or so that I'd saved over the years.

Frank got up and looked out the window for a long time.

"What's he up to? Two men driving up from London on a Saturday: and they let you get away."

"Court officials – they're not actually in the Snake's employ."

"...and he didn't second guess that...? I wonder if – Oh."

He seized a pair of battered binoculars and focussed on something.

"What is it, man?"

Still holding the binoculars, he turned around.

"Four deer, haven't seen them for a week... just grazing... There's no one about. If a car comes they'll scarper."

"What were you saying?"

He peered down the valley for a minute before replying.

"With a billion at stake, the big git's gonna be dangerous."

"I didn't need you to tell me that."

"Stay till tomorrow. They won't come here, this house ain't on the map yet and we can see a car coming for miles. It's the safest place in the county."

"He'll work it out. I must go."

"Where?"

"Never mind."

"You can't hide, you know. They're gonna trace you wherever you go."

"I'll take the chance."

"Almost all missing persons are found, even the dead ones. You can't hide from the State. An' you're a prominent person... They'll take it seriously."

There was a pause while he stared out the window.

"Does anybody at Dunglen know about me?"

"I've told no one."

He took a long drag at his cigar and looked out the window.

"Then he's scuppered. He can only find you when you break cover. It's the moving that's dangerous."

"I don't want caught."

"...You're hyper. Sixty million people in this country –"

"Only a hundred here."

"...Avoid old haunts then..." I admired Frank's way of looking at things, and he was nearly always right. "He's acting blind. Who'll get your fortune?"

"The Red Cross, I sent the documents to Switzerland."

Frank gave a laugh that ended in a cough.

"I like it. All good things come to an end."

Some seven years had passed since he built his house to a modern design on the site of an old ruined cottage. It had been a troublesome construction in which he had disappeared for six months. There had been times when he couldn't find money (he refused a loan from me) and times when he couldn't get tradesmen, but now it was fine, though he rather spoiled it with poor furniture. His wife, who had left him many years ago, would have had the place looking well but that was no longer an option. Outside, the building was marred by an old caravan where he'd lived during the construction. He claimed to have been going straight for years, but I'd noticed the lorry that delivered his roof timbers had come from a firm that had reported a theft of materials: perhaps it was a co-incidence.

"I'm leaving too, getting old: and this wild country ain't ideal anymore."

"Oh."

"Well it's lonely. I've been all right, mind, but it's time to get back to London town, can't spend my remaining days fishing, though I'll miss it. I'll get good money for this house, y'know. I'll be richer than you, imagine that."

"More power to your arm."

Frank picked up the binoculars and surveyed the valley for an age.

"Did I hear you right, his case stops if they fail to serve the writ?"

"That's right."

"But, hell, man he's stymied. And you've given the money to the Red Cross."

"He won't know that – yet."

Frank turned to look out the window again.

"If you ask me he used the writ to flush you out... I'll bet he'd a team in place down your road. They'd see you coming for a mile. But you went over the hill. Anything odd happened recently?"

"The two court officials. Oh, there was a plane overhead yesterday."

"That's unusual?"

"I didn't recognise it."

"Has he put a team together?"

"What d'you think?"

He took the binoculars and scanned the valley again.

"I'd assume the worst – sussing the place from the air. That would take money."

"He's got money. But he's a wanted man... The cops were looking for him."

Frank was staring out the window.

"That's – what? – thirty years ago... The trail will have gone cold. And he'll keep his head down. Is there any way he knows your plans?"

In fact I didn't really have any plans, though I wasn't going to tell him that.

"No point speculating."

"Well you're right there. Are you worried about the future?"

"A little."

Frank shook his old head and coughed.

"All this had to happen when you're old. It wouldn't have mattered if you'd been young. Blokes our ages don't recover so easily."

"Got to live within our limits."

"As long as we're still breathing."

43

The following morning was cold with a bitter wind sweeping the valley. Frank and I had a gloomy breakfast, not speaking, and occasionally looking out the window at the loch which could just be seen in the darkness. Today, the heavy clouds meant dawn was going to be late, no unusual thing in that part of the world and it added to the sense of menace that we were trying to overlook. In reality we were watching for car lights in the distance, something that would herald the end of it all. During the night I'd barely slept. I'd been in a back room beside an open window, ready to jump at the first sign of violence. Now morning had come and neither of us wanted to leave: there was trouble a-plenty waiting in the big world outside and in token of this Frank was as subdued as me, sighing, repeatedly and shaking his head. But we left at seven. We have our own kind of discipline and nothing would alter our schedule. He took his old van, a fishing rod in its long case strapped to the roof, looking more like a fisherman than most fishermen with his soft hat and green jacket. I lay in the back under a travel rug.

"D'you remember?" he said, clearing his throat as we pulled on to the rough road, "our first visit?"

"In the plane, yes."

"I thought that was tremendous. You flew here in your own plane an' bought a castle. I couldn't believe it. Ten years earlier you'd been a teller in Barclays."

"Now look at me."

"I thought you were gonna be the emperor of the world."

"Well I wasn't."

"You're down but you're not out."

"Oh, I'm out all right."

By this time it was beginning to get light, we were passing trees and the shape of the hills was becoming clear to the eye. I should have been immensely sad to be changing this for an uncertain future, but there was a far greater fear. I didn't want to die.

"What happens if we meet another car?"

"I'll pull on to the verge," said Frank, taking care to misunderstand me. "Never had trouble yet."

"If it's the Snake?"

"Forget it. He won't come here."

"How do you know?" I said with some bitterness. "Better have a plan."

"It's okay," he said, but he sounded tense. "Keep your head under that rug. A face in the back gets noticed."

The car moved up a gear and Frank gave a dry laugh.

"Well it's over. The boy wonder's made his billion an' it wasn't enough."

"Don't rub it in."

"Once you got your castle, you'd the same problems. What's it all about, eh?"

"Ask a philosopher," I muttered in irritation and he clammed up in annoyance. But I was being ungrateful to my sole surviving friend and I should have known better. "He won't know either."

We were silent for ten minutes until we joined the main trunk route, the A75, which carries ferry traffic to Stranraer and ten minutes later had passed the road that led to Dunglen. It was now becoming light and there was a lot of traffic about.

Suddenly Frank shouted:

"Lie low!"

I pulled the rug over my head.

"What?"

He continued driving in his relaxed style, smoking one of his cigars, untroubled about a queue of traffic behind us.

"Car in the lay-by at the back under the trees… barely saw it. Two big men watching the traffic, London registration. They've got binoculars an' they look alert."

"Looking at us?"

"Just a glance."

"Are they coming?"

"Nope, stay there for now."

"If they're the Snake's men, they're red hot."

"Where does he get men like that?"

"He's rich, he can afford them."

"You never told me he was rich. Who said that?"

"Sir James Howardson. Are they coming?"

"They're still in the lay-by. They ain't playing games, two smart men watching the traffic at this time in the morning. An' it's a good place, they can see the hill and the river too. The Snake's rich?"

"Old Howardson would know."

Then we reached a dual carriageway where a dozen vehicles passed us. We drove for a mile along a tree-lined section which I would never see again.

Again Frank shouted: "Down!"

"What now?"

"Another car, off road – Damn it, another two men. They've got binoculars too."

For twenty seconds he was silent as we drove past.

"Maybe they're cops?"

"No way, the car's dirty... it's had a long journey. That's the Snake's mob. They'd need that. If the first lot spotted you they'd radio ahead to tail you."

"Are they following?"

"Nope. You're in trouble. They ain't doing that for your good."

"We got past them, we're all right."

"Are we what! There's bound to be others. What say we abort?"

I looked at the back of his head in alarm.

"No way. I've got plans."

In fact I hadn't. My future was in a poor state, but one thing was certain: Frank's house was a potential trap. Sooner or later the Snake would realise I'd gone over the big hill – it was really quite obvious – and it was absurd to suppose they didn't know about the house, particularly when there was a team   or was it teams? – in the area, not to mention a plane. It was a wonder they hadn't called yesterday.

"Two cars," I said, my heart sinking. "They think I'm still here."

"Looks like it. There'd be a big lot of them in Carlisle yesterday."

"You can't be certain."

"They guessed correctly. You're still here… probably hiding in someone's house, an' they're right. Only they didn't know about me. It's the moving that's dangerous. That's why you should abort."

"I've gotta go."

"Go?" said Frank in sudden anger. "I dunno what you're thinking about, you're deranged. This is the Snake we're dealing with an' he's damn near got you. What happens when the cops start looking for you too? An' they'll be doin' that soon. You're too prominent to disappear. No matter what you do they're gonna have you in days. You can't leave the country an' you can't live anywhere in Britain without payin' poll tax. An' that means you gotta be registered. They'll have you in minutes if you need medical attention."

"And you think I should stay and face the music?"

"Well, I dunno," said Frank, losing his anger. "I just don't think this is right."

"It's all right," I said, trying to sound wise. "I know what I'm doing."

"You've given away a castle," he said, a little embarrassed by his outburst. "I'd go easy if I was you."

"Get me to the rail station, I'll be okay."

"You ain't going to the station. I know it and they know it. It's full of cameras. You're taking a bus. That's the out-guard back there: the bus station will be swarming."

"You think so?" I said, taken aback that he'd outguessed me so easily.

"You should abort."

"… No way."

"…Well it's your funeral. The Snake's gonna be dangerous. He's a wanted man. Once he's got you, he can't let you go again. An' he's got form – the dead man at Great Square for a start. I could drive you to Glasgow."

"More delay. Is there anything following us?"

"Twenty cars: all angry at my driving but none of 'em the Snake. I hope."

Forty minutes later we joined the motorway, crossed the border into England, and shortly the signs indicated Carlisle. Frank had started to whistle tunelessly.

"Listen, we'll both go to the bus station. They won't expect two."

"I'd rather go alone, please."

"Nope – you gotta have support."

I gritted my teeth. The whole point of the thing was to be incognito at every stage and Frank would add a complication to my getaway. If he was caught (which wasn't unlikely) they'd get information out of him. But there was no point in arguing.

"Now listen, I'll park three streets away. I'll carry your haversack an' you'll do your lame walk. Keep your eyes down and don't look around. I'll do the watching."

"Okay." This being Monday, the traffic was heavy and there was a delay from the inevitable roadworks. Eventually we swung off the busy road into a back street that I didn't know existed – trust Frank to discover it – and shortly we were walking to the buses.

"Heavy odds," he muttered, looking round. "This could be the biggest robbery in Britain. Well, if you hadn't given your money away."

The bus station was a hive of activity with lots of people milling around, some smoking, some eating doubtful fare from a fast food kiosk, while still more were rushing about trying to find their bus. There was a group of cyclists drinking coffee while two motorbikes purred on the far side. Buses were revving and contributing to the smell of diesel.

"Head down. Stop at that timetable."

A group of tourists, who were probably exploring the Lake District, were arguing in a foreign language beside an empty bus bay. Frank put my haversack down and stopped to light a cigar.

"There's your London bus," he muttered through his teeth.

A smart single-decker was being boarded by a number of travellers while the driver talked to an old man. Everything was reassuringly normal with not a sign of the enemy: only an old woman waited to greet somebody among the crowd.

"I didn't say I was going to London."

But he wasn't listening

"Don't move," said Frank, in an undertone. "Abort – abort!"

I was careful not to look up or make a sudden movement.

"The old woman – Come on, not too fast. Back to the van."

She was greeting nobody, the passengers were boarding, not exiting, and she was leaning forward to study each face. I remembered John Masters: a good tail is the person you least expect.

As we ambled away, a tall man looked up from the crowd to look at my face for a brief second, while two security guards, who were probably collecting a parcel, gave us a bored glance. Frank stopped to shake ash from his cigar as though we had all the time in the world. We paused to let a couple and their three fat kids on to a bus.

"Motorbikes, too.... They're organised."

"Nothing to do with the Snake, they're eating."

"No...? They're browned off: they've been there for ages. Listen, they'll be watching the London depot too – the Snake's gonna be thorough for that kinda money."

My spirits were low enough without Frank pointing out the bleeding obvious. Back at the van, I took the passenger seat.

"I told you there'd be a presence."

"Listen," I said, improvising. "I'm heading for Newcastle. There's a country bus due at the riverside, a mile away."

"...Oh... Well I'll get you there."

"What would they have done?" I said as we drove off. "It's a free country... they aren't police, they can't use violence – I could have walked away."

"I'll bet you wouldn't get far..."

Because of the morning traffic it took some time before we reached the main road and I wondered if we'd be too late. Eventually we turned a corner to find a small queue waiting for the bus which had been delayed by the roadworks: none of them glanced at us. Frank stopped to study them for a minute.

"They're okay. Genuine travellers, I'd say."

Then the bus turned into the street, an old wreck with black smoke in its wake.

"So it's all systems go?"

"Yes."

"Will we meet again?"

"How, if you sell the house?"

"Not easy. Wait six months. Phone The Robber Barron, Thursday nights."

"Okay. Thanks, old man."

"All the best," said Frank in an optimistic tone, as though we would meet next week. "Out you go, I'll drive round the block an' make sure all's well. If something happens just run into that street. I'll be there in a minute."

I got out of the van feeling like a lost soul. Now that he was gone, I had no friends left in the world.

Shortly I boarded the bus and sat at the back, hoping no one would give me a second glance. It would make many detours into villages and hamlets but at least it was taking me away from the enemy. Three hours later in Newcastle, I boarded a London bus that would take an age to arrive, during which I sat beside a fat man who talked about horses until I never wanted to hear the word again. That said, I had assumed the role of a Polish immigrant of the name of Klutza and I got an opportunity to practise my accent.

44

It was evening when the bus made its entry into London – the longest journey time to the city I'd ever known, there had been moments when I'd wondered if the driver had fallen asleep. I was bored out of my head and aching from hours on an uncomfortable seat. As we neared our destination my worries began to soar. The Snake could predict both the bus and its destination and though I was approaching from Newcastle rather than Carlisle, as luck would have it, both routes finished at the same terminal and he would certainly have people there. Two miles short of Victoria Cross Station, the bus stopped for roadworks and I leapt up with my rucksack.

"Me go now, plis," I said in my best Polish.

Wordlessly, the driver opened the door and I struggled out to a street that was moderately busy with pedestrians and even a couple of joggers. With a bit of luck no one would give me a second glance though I was careful to keep my head down and walk with a limp in case Sod's Law sent someone who knew me. Here I had two options, one was a budget guesthouse of a hundred rooms which was often filled with working men and that meant many witnesses. The other was a safer option, a semi-permanent location, a charity I had supported in the past and it was within ten minute's walking.

To explain: although ECZ is a Swiss company, it had a British counterpart ECZ (UK) which handled links with the banks and also received my management fee. Since it paid British tax I made a point of supporting a different charity every year. To be honest, I hate many of the charities for their inefficiency, greed, and sometimes outright fraud and always made a point of donating to an organisation that would do some good. This was one such. Haven House, which owned a block of flats for the homeless, run by a bloke called Wilson who seemed to be doing a good job. Prior to making the donation, which was for two hundred thousand, I had visited him to make sure it was kosher and had been impressed with his work. That was years ago and it was unlikely he would recognise me in my present garb, but I could use it to my advantage if he did.

Haven House was a council tower, an old one, a dull building of unimaginative architecture that spoke of the sixties. Entrance was by a swing door and I went to the reception desk where an old lady of Asian appearance was arguing with the receptionist, a middle-aged woman I'd seen before and who was being quite rude. There might be good reasons for that, the meeting point between charity and the real world is often a hard one. Then it was my turn.

"I vish Mr Wilson, please."

"He's not here."

"I haf letter for him. You give me room."

"There's no room!"

Reeling, I handed over the letter, which had been written in Frank's house and she read it with a frown then swung on her heel and went into a backroom where there was some muttering. Suddenly Wilson appeared, sporting a ponytail, holding a can of lager and frowning at my letter.

"You know this man?"

"I haf tea with him in his castle."

He took a long sip at the lager.

"Will you be seeing him again?"

"Yus. I wuss bank manager in Poland. Him got me to work in office."

Another long stare at the letter.

"Actually, we don't have any spare rooms, Mr Klutza. But I'll give you a temporary one. You'll have to pay four weeks in advance. Cash."

"Four weeks?"

"The rules of the house, sir. It's a nice room on the tenth floor but there's no lift."

He named a price which wasn't bad, considering.

"I take it."

There then followed a lot of form-filling, some of which included questions about my previous abode. Obviously this was for Council Tax purposes and I gave an address in Warsaw, saying I'd just returned from visiting my family in Poland. In my rucksack there was a forged passport in the name of Klutza with several convincing customs stamps and with the pages crushed and dog-eared. Ideally I should have presented that and claimed social security but sooner or later the forgery would be discovered and that would be fatal. In due course there'd be inspectors at my door to arrange my tax and I'd have to move to pastures new. My future promised to be an unsettling one.

Wilson named his price and I produced crumpled banknotes that had survived the flight over the big hill.

Money was going to be a problem, medical and dental treatment would have to be paid by cash, there being no way I could collect a pension in my present status. Nor could I take a proper job. In my new persona I had no National Insurance number and to use my own one would identify me in seconds.

He gave me a key for the door, linen for the bed and I made the long haul to floor ten where I found a tidy flat of two rooms with a cooker, kettle, fridge and TV: the balcony gave a view of the site of my old council home, now demolished to make way for a vast housing estate. In the middle distance there was a huge supermarket that had been built in recent years. Further to the left, the streets and houses were unchanged since I last saw them forty years ago. For twenty minutes I lay on the bed and relaxed, it had seemed that I'd never get this far. Now I wondered why I'd come.

But I hadn't eaten and tomorrow was a working day – assuming I could find work. On my way to the supermarket I passed a builder's yard that bore a handwritten advert for painters. After buying some food, I got a pair of white overalls and returned to Haven House where I found the hall mobbed by a crowd of East Europeans in the company of a social worker who was having difficulty getting them to write their names. As I hurried past with my head down, I wondered if I had been given one of their rooms. Also there might be Poles among them who would spot me for the fraud I was.

London has always been a place where fortunes are made and pittances are paid. I had experienced fortunes and now it was my turn for the pittances. Monday was a dull overcast morning with a sense of impending rain, when, in sullen silence, seven of us waited at the builder's door, each of us afraid to look at the other in case he got the job we wanted. All were foreigners except me, and I was a pretend one, and each of us, I suspect, had something to hide. Most were family men with moaning wives and complaining children.

Fifty feet away there was a group of regular workers, professionals, who disdained us as they complained about their day's rota.

Then a Jaguar arrived and the boss jumped out, a plump man of thirty with shrewd eyes who spoke only rarely and then only if necessary; he was smart enough to know that it's best not to talk. To my relief, he asked no questions about our NI numbers. This was casual labour and we were hired at a low rate – but that was net, he said, after tax had been deducted and though the taxman probably knew nothing about it, I wasn't complaining. It was a job. Then we got into a van (a good thing for me, the open street held no attractions) and we were driven to an empty tower that was being renovated where we were instructed to paint the walls, each to his assigned room. Everything was rough and ready, he noted my name, spelling it Klute, and nodded when I said my bad arm meant I couldn't hang wallpaper. I am a rotten painter too, but I thought it best not to mention this.

"Don't use so much paint," he complained, when I started. "That's money."

Nodding, I applied less and when I next looked he had gone. We worked in desperate silence for four hours, not even seeing one another, until one of the experienced hands indicated a lunch stop. As casually as possibly, I looked at the other men's work and saw it was no better than my own. I had the room finished by the time the boss got back.

"No' good paint," I whined. "Needs second coat."

But he wasn't the kind of man who worried about fine details. He shrugged and said. "See you tomorrow at the yard."

And so it went on. None of us was making a good job and I couldn't see how his client would tolerate such poor workmanship. Nor was there any complaint that the floors were splashed with white paint which was so mediocre that it dripped from the ceiling onto our heads. On Friday he arrived with our wages. At least there was no quibbling about our workmanship and he paid for the full duration, including lunch breaks.

"See you next week," and he was gone. On the way back in the van, the driver stopped to talk to us, a shifty character who could barely speak English and he offered us extra work over the weekend.

"Same rate. Cash, don't tell boss."

Most of us agreed and this time we met at a car park and were driven to a new housing development where we worked for twelve hours, with better paint and did a better job. But try as I might I couldn't bring myself to like it, though I began to acquire something of a painter's skills. But at least I was earning money.

Several weeks went past.

At Haven House, I paid more rent and was moved to the third floor where I was now deemed to be a permanent resident. In order to qualify, I had to declare myself disabled, suffering from a bad left arm, the result of a childhood injury. This was a mere formality, the receptionist took my word for it and filled in the appropriate form, warning me that rent must be paid in advance, otherwise I would have to leave immediately. As ever, the important part of the deal was the money. What's new?

It will be remembered that as a youth I had opened an account in the Peckham Building Society under the name of E. M. Mertoun: an easy thing to do in those days since no proof of identity was required. That account still existed with a good cash balance, having been serviced every year and I had the passbook with me. On my first free Saturday and wearing my one presentable jacket, I called at the branch and paid in my spare cash. Astonishingly, one of the women who had worked there when I first opened the account recognised me. In my best Welsh accent I explained that I was in the oil business and was often away for months, if not years.

In an effort to maintain my Polish image I grew a beard which I cut with scissors to a half-inch length which made me look older.

There was a serious risk of discovery when I walked the streets and I went to a lot of lengths to disguise myself. On a two-mile walk I might pass several hundred pedestrians and possibly a thousand vehicles and the latter were my real worries. In the past, thousands of Londoners had known me, and of course there had been a media fuss, and all it takes is one vigilant driver, a passenger in a bus, or even a cop in a patrol car. And there were CCTV cameras all over the place too. Even when you're heavily disguised you can be recognised from your walk or the way you hold your shoulders and once spotted, the damage can't be undone.

All in all, I did seven weeks as a painter and found it increasingly unpleasant. The smell of paint is sickly and since we were working indoors it made me nauseous. Also I was developing pains in my back and once narrowly avoided injury when I fell off a stepladder. It wasn't a good time, but it was a lot better than jail.

During a lunch break I was reading a day-old newspaper when I found a short reference to myself at the foot of a column.

MISSING MILLIONAIRE

Police have expressed concern about the absence of estate-owner, Mr Ron Miles, 59, who has been missing for nearly two months. Mr Miles, who was jailed twenty years ago after a police inspector forged evidence against him, received record compensation from the Metropolitan Police. He owns Dunglen Castle in Scotland. Sergeant McGinty of the local force said there had been no sightings of Mr Miles and his friends were worried. He urged the public to keep him informed.

Reading between the lines, this was a low priority issue that would do me no harm. In the past I had been away for much longer periods. I wondered who had instigated the enquiries: surely by this time it would be known that the Red Cross had acquired the estate?

On the Friday of that week, after the boss had paid me he produced a letter.

"You're Polish? Translate this," and he handed me an official-looking letter of which the only words I could recognise was the city name of Gdansk and the figure 20,000. It looked like a quotation for something. I blinked at the paper for a moment.

"No read. No' got glasses. You bring letter on Monday an' I read it. Yuss?"

He was none too pleased and neither was I: Ron Miles would have to find another job, there being no way I could risk him discovering I was a fraud. This was a pity, I'm no tradesman but at least he tolerated my poor work. Where would I be on Monday?

The answer was Glassford Electronics. I had passed their workshop when walking home, and having once, forty years ago, constructed a valve radio with circuits from *Wireless World* I could at least use a soldering iron. This was an Indian management, owned by a middle-aged man called Singh who imported goods from Hong Kong which were supplied without transformers and mains leads. These were fitted in his workshop and the goods thereafter could be marketed legally as *made in the UK*. There were ten employees, and at seven thirty on Monday morning he didn't seem keen on taking me on, telling me to come back later. Then he changed his mind and soon I was behind a desk.

They monitored my work for the first hour, after which I was part of the family. He had a son and a daughter at other desks as well as several Nigerian women and we all worked hard. It seemed to take ages but we got through a lot of boxes in the day. Sometimes there was a great fuss when a truck collected a thousand cartons for a warehouse in Luton. Pay was slightly better, though it varied according to the workload, some weeks I worked for four days, and others seven.

Another eight weeks went past.

Again it was lunch break when I saw a reference to myself, or more accurately a photograph of Dunglen Castle in the TV pages of one of the tabloids.

8.30 Tonight. Bob Bitter investigates the mysterious disappearance of Ron Miles from his castle in Scotland. Interesting, with details of his earlier life from council home to Senior Fund Manager and false jail term for which he was awarded millions. He was last seen four months ago and his friends are worried about his wellbeing.

I forced myself to look away and passed a box I hadn't worked on, only to fall over a chair when I tried to seize it back. Why this? Surely there was nothing about my life to excite a TV producer? For twenty years I'd been careful to do nothing that was remotely newsworthy and surely there was no mystery about my disappearance from the castle if it was known that the Red Cross had acquired it. Plainly something had gone wrong: a television programme could blow my cover sky high. In my early days at Howardsons I had been stopped in the streets by goggle box addicts who wanted my signature – and that from a two-minute appearance on a minor business programme. A half-hour feature was likely to go into a lot of detail and though they would have difficulty finding up-to-date pictures of me, it was a fair bet they'd have something.

45

Nothing in history can match the influence of TV. It can make or break politicians, demonise manufacturers and sway the public's attitude to a thousand things. Its influence is endemic and it had the capacity to expose my folly to the entire country. I was sick with worry when I switched it on and it lumbered to life, an idiot who had given away a fortune for the dubious pleasure of anonymity and hadn't even been able to hide in a city the size of London. The set was old and barely functional, with a flickering screen and faulty switches, but I got it going and stared in suspense at its garish colours. I hadn't eaten, my hands were clenched, I was covered in perspiration and I watched with the volume low in case the neighbours noticed a change in my habits. My rucksack was packed and I was ready to run, though there was nowhere to go.

This was *The Bob Bitter Show*, a sorry programme that had outlived its usefulness if it ever had any. What would he say if he'd known I was the fourth hostage at the Great Square Siege? The years hadn't been kind to his waistline, his face had the look of a drunk and his voice was more pompous than ever.

Predictably the programme opened by zooming in on the castle where its main tower was half covered by morning shadow. Then it panned on the locked front door while Bob told us everything was looking well but there was no one at home.

"Nobody on the farm wants to speak about it, but the Laird of Dunglen has gone missing." At that point the camera swung round to Jimmy's Land Rover as it drove past. Jimmy and Bob Bitter would not be natural buddies.

Bob's pronunciation of 'Laird' was less than authentic and he wasn't going to be impressed with my castle. But Ron Miles was treated respectfully, I'll say that: there was nothing hostile about me in the whole show, though that was predictable.

As he spoke the camera zoomed in on a herd of deer grazing beside the forest before panning into a long shot of the big hill which was majestic in the morning light.

Then it was my photo, the one I'd left in the castle lounge – not a good likeness – and it was all of twenty years old, taken when I had a head of hair rather than my present baldy tonsure. Slowly, this merged into an artist's impression of a typical sixty-year-old, with reduced hairline and an ageing face that was, to my eyes anyway, not a recognisable Ron Miles. If this was the best they could do, I still had a chance.

A voice-over declared that Ron Miles had vanished several months ago – it did not say who had claimed I was missing and nobody from the estate appeared to support this contention, though at the end of the programme, Big Jimmy, leaning out of his Land Rover window, said Mr Miles had disappeared before, though not for so long. Here he had failed: I'd told him to say he'd last seen me at four when I said I was leaving.

Apparently I'd last been seen on a Saturday when walking the dog. Cue Ben, who appeared with much tail-wagging. No one could remember seeing me afterwards and a full month was to pass before some concern was expressed. It didn't say who had expressed this concern.

"A 'Walk for Ron' was organised," said Bob, "to search the hills. And there's a lot to be searched."

Here the camera gave another view of the big hill which gradually faded to a crowd of people who had climbed it from all angles and walked through miles of forest in a vain attempt to find me. I couldn't believe I was so popular. They were pictured with the castle in the background: sixty of them were women, some of them young and beautiful. Big Jimmy's glum face could be seen at the back: of course he would have no alternative but to join the fun. Despite this activity, which must have annoyed the wild goats no end, nothing of interest had been found.

"But people don't just disappear into thin air," said Bob coming on-screen and attempting to look wise. "What do you say, Sergeant?"

Now the camera focussed on a big policeman.

"We're concerned for Mr Miles. We'd just like to know he's all right."

"You don't think he's had an accident on the hills?"

His jowls wobbled in a negative.

"We're reasonably sure of that... a fit man, and familiar with the terrain. And it's been thoroughly searched. It looks like he's gone away."

"But his cars are all accounted for."

"That's correct. We don't know what happened, and we know he didn't walk down the valley to the main road."

"Perhaps he was picked up by a plane?"

"No, we know from Air Traffic Control there was no plane – fixed-wing or helicopter – in the area at that time. It's a mystery."

"Yes, a mystery," said Bob. "But that's Ron Miles. There's much about the man that is a mystery. Who was he?"

Now there was a flashback to the old council home where I was reared and where I was apparently the star turn.

An oafish character, his voice slurred with drink, said he remembered me well: Ron Miles was a goody-goody who never did nothin' of note and never once joined him for a drink. Only now did I recognise him as one of my fellow inmates – not bad, I had assumed they'd all succumbed to alcoholic poisoning.

Next the camera panned in on Barclays bank where I'd worked for four years: my old manager, now retired, said I was good at counting and he was sorry when I'd left.

Then there was a shot of the Howardsons building, now part of Madden Corporation, which was followed by an old man sitting in his garden who told the camera he'd worked with Ron Miles.

"He was as interested in eliminating losers as picking winners, and he didn't like big spreads. That's what made his portfolios strong. Most investors tolerate the odd doubtful share because the rest are doing fine – or so they hope. But Ron would fuss away until he'd sussed out the loser before it could do any harm. He wasn't sentimental."

"Would you rate him highly?"

"Oh I don't know about highly. He was competent, and he was no gambler – unlike today's lot who shouldn't be near a piggy bank."

The old man was Norman and he must have been ninety odds.

"We had many an argument," he laughed. "He could be pig-headed."

Then a seventy-year-old head appeared with a white ponytail. Martin Howardson, still a hippy and no doubt living off his family's fortune. He was in the back garden where I'd my last sad meeting with Sir James.

"Yes, I remember Ron," the posh accent was still there though he had adopted the air of an old bishop. "They always distrusted him, you know. They watched him in case he brought the firm down. And for a time he was the best in the City, not bad for a council home boy, ho, ho. The finance world's a damn funny place."

Now the scene changed:

"Ron Miles was the ruination of Howardsons," said a voice so thick with accent that it sounded like an actor playing a crusty squire. The camera focused on an old square figure with the face of an eighty-year-old. Mean, bleary eyes stared over a bibulous nose. Who? There was something familiar about the face but years of drinking had rendered it unrecognisable. He was sitting in a great room that was resplendent in brown varnish. "We were a patrician company until Ron Miles arrived with his cheap shoes." (At one time the upper crust had a thing about shoes. What he meant was I didn't have bespoke ones).

"He wasn't popular?"

"The concept of being popular didn't exist. Personally I found his attitude repugnant. We didn't need his get-rich-quick mentality: we were the best of our kind in London, possibly the world. Now look at it – all gone."

"But you can hardly blame him for that: it was doing well when he left."

"Possibly, but we were brought up to have some respect. Ron Miles didn't even address the Chair when he was in committee, much of the finer points of life had passed him by, and he didn't know his wine."

A caption appeared on the screen. He was one of my old colleagues, a fellow manager. It seemed the passing years had boosted his self-esteem rather than his intelligence. But he could slag me as much as he wanted, I didn't mind.

"He was a bit of an upstart?"

"…Just workaday. I suppose he was never impolite, but he was discourteous in other ways. He never attended a hunt ball or a shoot, despite many invitations. For a senior figure he was curiously aloof from the rest of us."

So my weakness in blood sports had damned me forever, no wonder the firm had gone. But keep up the good work Percy; you're doing well.

"And he didn't fit in?"

"Exactly. I've frequently been alone with him and there was nothing to talk about except business. He had no interest in our social life, and he had none of his own."

Next the voice-over said that I was the leading stock picker in the City, and then through no fault of mine, things went belly up. Cue to a photo of Inspector Jack Hound. Bob Bitter perked up at this, he likes a villain in every show.

Now there was a lot of waffle about the case and the jail sentence. Several lawyers did a valuable job in time wasting. Procedure for court had been completely revised following the debacle. 'Lines had been drawn' 'Lessons learned' and they had 'moved on'. The lawyer, now in his eighties, who had got me released, said the trial should never have taken place, the judge should have stopped it, though of course Miles had pleaded guilty to two charges.

Then the minister from the village appeared to say I was a church member who sometimes played the organ.

Next the camera zoomed in on a rose bush where, after a brief commotion, the hospital doctor's face appeared among the leaves, blinking at the camera in his bewildered manner.

"Yes, I remember him," though he sounded very doubtful. "He didn't have a good time inside, some people just can't take to prison."

"But he shouldn't have been there!" exclaimed Bob.

"Quite so, but nearly every prisoner claims to be innocent."

Now the camera showed a hill, partly tree-covered, and zoomed in on a castle with a deserted appearance. The door opened and a man of about seventy-five approached, smiling, holding a wine glass. Lionel! How he had survived on a diet of alcohol was amazing. As always, he was in good voice.

"Yes I remember Ron well. I used to be in the industry myself, y'know. He took business too seriously, far too seriously. A bit of an ascetic if you know what I mean, he didn't go out for lunch, that kind of thing. He enjoyed work a lot more than I did, haw, haw: but mustn't fault him for that, eh? I'm sorry he's gone."

"Any ideas why?"

Lionel took a swig at his glass, and frowned on finding it empty.

"I could never work him out, you know. What did he stand for, what was his goal? All right, he was climbing high: but when you're top of the heap at thirty where do you go after that? I dunno. Now he's been living alone for years and life must have lost its challenge. Mind you, haw, haw, I shouldn't be talking: I live alone in Dracula's Den here. Maybe I've lost my challenge too, haw, haw."

He pointed at the castle where the camera focussed on a broken window.

"Do you think he's gone abroad?"

"You know he never struck me as a great traveller. Maybe he's hiding in my castle, I've heard funny sounds at night. Or maybe it's just the death-watch beetle, haw, haw."

"Thank you, Lord Haize."

Then the surprise.

A stout man of my age, dressed in casual clothes, sitting on an oak desk in a room that looked familiar. Wallace! I had never seen him like this before, I didn't even know he wore casual clothes and – even more unlikely – he was smiling at the camera like an old pro. It was a wonder the lens didn't crack.

"Yes I knew him well. We were mates when we hadn't two pennies to rub together. We both worked in banks at that time."

"And what do you think of his disappearance?"

"To be honest, I'm worried. This kind of man doesn't go in for drama."

"Is it about money? He wouldn't be the first rich man to have debts?"

But Wallace was giving a wise shake of the head.

"I'm a merchant banker… I didn't handle his personal business, but he was never short. I doubt if there are any debts at all."

"Why has he gone missing then, have you any theories?"

"Well, yes. I'm concerned he's been kidnapped."

"But surely there have been no ransom notes?"

"Perhaps hijacked is a better term, I don't know, I'm just concerned." He looked at the camera with confidence and said: "Ron if you're out there, please get in touch with me, you know my hotline. You have no problems, business or personal, and we're concerned about you. I just want to know you're all right."

"Thank you, thank you," gushed Bob. "Wallace is one of our leading City bankers. Now the question arises about Mr Miles's possible whereabouts. Here is Mr Simon Snook, an expert on survival. Assuming he has run away, for reasons unknown, what would you expect him to do?"

You could see Simon was glad to be on the box, he took a deep breath that almost burst his shirt:

"Well this is a rich man with expensive tastes. Look at his character: he didn't spend a lifetime making a fortune just to throw it away. I'd look for him in a five star hotel on the other side of the world. It'll be an exclusive one, he won't mix with British people and he'll have changed his name. You could argue he's been preparing for this for years."

"What makes you say that?"

"Photographs: he was camera shy. The only one available is twenty years old."

"Interesting point."

"He's living abroad, in style, without drawing attention to himself."

"But why?" wondered Bob. "Why throw everything away?"

"Not known," said the know-all. "Maybe he's making huge money somewhere and doesn't want to pay tax. Maybe he got fed up with Scotland's weather – he wouldn't be the first – or a kind of mid-life crisis, it happens a lot."

"Well that's it," said Bob to the camera, "the story of a man from London who became the Laird of Dunglen and then vanished. There's another chapter waiting to be written and some of you may help us write it. If you know anything, phone this number."

One of the good things about appealing to the public is that any number of airheads will muddy the tracks. It was a near certainty there would be a few allegations of my having been abducted by aliens or running a pub in Dublin.

The programme closed with the camera panning on to the locked door of the castle with Jimmy's Land Rover disappearing into the distance.

I had to get outside to think. When going through the hall I noticed that the TV in the back room was tuned to the same station: they had been watching too.

No word of the Red Cross or change of ownership. Since any form of impartial reportage would have to mention it, the assumption had to be made that the deal had fallen through. Plainly the Swiss case against me was irrelevant since it hadn't been touched on and Wallace had said there were 'no problems'.

There had been a lot of research in the programme. How they had known who to contact and where to find them was a mystery to me.

46

At Glassford Electronics the following day there was no mention of the programme. Usually the women talked about the box incessantly but none of them had noticed anything, perhaps a popular soap on another channel had claimed their attention. At that time we were working on audio amplifiers with our heads down, the scale was smaller and we were finding it difficult.

On Saturday, under the alias of E. M. Mertoun I went to the building society where there was a typical Saturday queue. I was at the back and got the fright of my life when a heavy hand fell on my shoulder. It was the manager, a young chap of about thirty who would make a good rugby player.

"Mr Mertoun, we've had an enquiry about you yesterday."

"Eh?"

"One of your relatives is looking for you."

The room was going around in circles and I felt weak at the knees. After the television programme this was all I needed. I don't have a surfeit of relatives.

"Relatives?"

People in the queue were looking round and I forgot my Welsh accent. My head had gone blank.

"Yes, a man of about seventy: tall chap. What was his name again?"

In a desperate effort I calmed down, took a deep breath and to give a confident impression said without thinking:

"A thin fellow... six feet six... foreign accent?"

"That's him, yes. You've to look him up, there's a lot to catch up on."

The Snake, but how could it be the Snake? How the hell had he found me under the name of Mertoun in London's myriad building societies? The room became smaller, the manager was looking at me closely. My beard didn't fit the E. M. Mertoun image. How could the Snake do this?

"Ah, that'll be old Dennis, I hope you didn't loan him any money."

With a laugh he went away. I would like to have gone too, being ready to collapse, but in the circumstances that would have been a mistake. I withdrew five hundred pounds, and left as casually as possible.

Peckham Building Society is next to the tube, which is why I chose it so long ago. I hurried down its steps to board the first train that came. After three stations I changed, caught the next one back and exited at the one beyond where I scurried up the steps, along two side streets and into a small public park that I'd known as a boy. Taking a seat I watched for pursuit. There was none, but had they been watching with a camera to note my current disguise? London's full of photographers and I recalled seeing someone watching from across the street. He was probably innocent or was he? One pic would give the Snake an insight into my current lifestyle. He's not the kind to move without first weighing the details

But why had the manager told me? It's against the law to speak of any client's affairs without written permission. Probably it was a damage-limitation exercise to cover an indiscretion by one of his tellers. The Snake has a lot of charm when he chooses to use it. I reached for my passbook. Yes, someone had paid twenty pounds into the account. So that's how it had been done: "Excuse me, I've to pay this money into my relative's account, E. M. Mertoun, Oh good, you know him? Yes, that's the man. Splendid. Tell me, has he been in recently? Oh, a month ago, he must be keeping better. Thank you." And in these few words he had established that I'm in London.

But how had he known my alias of E. M. Mertoun? That was one piece of information that couldn't be gleaned from a computer. Aside from myself there was only one other person in the whole world who knew my secret, and that was Wallace and that made him my enemy: a secret colleague of the Snake's who had passed on potentially fatal information. I recalled his sick-making appeal on TV, a bit too groomed for a banker: "You know my hotline, and I'm a friend…"

And it was Wallace who had first introduced me to the Snake, and had been unhelpful about his background.

So that gave an eloquent answer to the original question, the one that started it all: who wrote the letter? It wasn't the Snake, it wasn't Frank, it was Wallace. I'd often mulled the possibility and now the truth was unmistakeable. Perhaps his motives will never be known, but it was likely that the Snake, in his time-honoured manner, had reneged on a deal and he'd sent the letter as some kind of comeuppance. What a blind fool I'd been! For two years the original papers for ECZ had languished in his bank from which he would obtain all the necessary facts to send me to prison.

I started walking to Haven House. Wallace had been the force behind the programme. The 'concern' came from London and, come to think of it, almost everybody that had been on the show had been Londoners. The appeal had the smell of TV grooming and in order to exert such influence he must have paid for the whole thing. Bob Bitter had even described him as 'one of our leading bankers' a nice little advert that would do no harm. This meant there was a fortune at stake, over a billion in fact, and there was no mention of the Red Cross – that side of the plan had plainly failed, the money was still up for grabs, hence the present interest.

What was it Sir James said about the Snake?

"He works on his own, an' he's rich... I think he's based in the Middle East."

Sir James had once been a director of Barclays Bank. Quite possibly they had been swindled by the Snake which would explain both his exasperation and his refusal to discuss the matter. That must have been before I joined Howardsons, therefore the Snake was a rich man even then – who else would have a stock of twenty thousand pound bearer bonds in hand? But rich men don't go on agent-duty, usually they have assistants, therefore he was taking a serious interest in my affairs.

On a long street on the way back, the traffic was hammering along in both directions when I did a John Masters and retraced my steps to make sure no one was following me. Then I turned and went home: unable to guess what he'd do next.

47

Two days had passed and after a busy time at Glassford Electrics I elected to sit on the veranda and read my paper, something the weather seldom lets me do. The veranda offered a good view of the forecourt which gave me the chance of noting a follower and I watched for lone walkers and solitary faces in parked cars. So far as I could see, there were none, but I was not particularly happy. Eyestrain had given me a headache and there were a lot of aches and pains from staring too long at circuit boards. On a neighbouring site, the kids were playing a game and their shouts were annoying. I tried to do the big crossword and failed. Then I heard the lift stop at my floor. The lift is for the exclusive use of the management and mere residents use the stairs. In all my time at Haven House, I had never heard it stop there before. Suddenly everything seemed uncertain.

The doorbell rang.

I opened it to find myself looking at two cops, a man of thirty-five and a girl of about twenty-five.

"Mr Klutza?" said the girl.

"Yuss? My papers they in order. I get them for you, yuss?"

"We're not here about your papers, sir. Can we come in?"

I stood back making a mental note to say as little as possible: my accent wasn't quite right and she had looked at me with shrewd eyes. But this was where an English inflection would never work, I had to do the Polish bit and make it convincing, or I was sunk. The man was standing back, not too bothered, I had the impression they weren't getting on, not an ideal situation.

We went inside and she took out a black notebook.

"What is your age, Mr Klutza?"

"Sixty-five," I lied

"And your address is Haven House?"

She had jet black hair and a rather plain face, the kind of girl who would avoid the superficial at every turn. Her earnest attitude was that of someone who had recently taken the job and no question would go unasked and she was not easily deceived. Dangerous.

"Yuss."

"How long have you been here?"

"Um – fourteen weeks."

"Do you know Mr Ron Miles?"

"...Mr Miles...? Oh, Miles – Yuss... I haf tea with him in castle."

"When was that?"

"Um... Him see me five months ago... no six."

"Have you seen him since?"

"...No."

"Heard from him... phone call... letter?"

"No."

During this time the man was walking about, peering under the newspaper and looking at my only jacket in the wardrobe, my bed was untidy and a pair of trousers was strewn on the floor. There was plenty of poverty about and it was the real thing. He went out to the veranda and returned with hands in his pockets. He was dangerous too: he considered the questions a waste of time and he was in a position to note my phoney accent. I'd noticed him glancing at my shoes and hands. He opened the fridge and freezer to see how low my supplies were.

"Did you know Mr Miles well?"

"I haf worked for him."

"For how long?"

"Um... one day."

"What kind of work?"

"Clerical." But this was too improbable. My voice had lost its certainty. Why would I let this half-baked idiot near my books? "I haf been bank manager in Poland."

"He never let you near his books," said the man coming over. "Everything would be on computer."

"He gets me to list Treasury bonds in book," I said with some indignation. "Great bundle. Then he checks with computer."

"I'll bet that came to a pretty penny."

"I no' say. Confidential."

I don't know if he knew what a Treasury bond was, but I'd never disclose a client's financial information if I really was an ex-bank manager.

"How come he employed you for one day?"

She was looking at me with narrowed eyes. This was the impossibility of it all. No castle owner is going to trust a near-vagrant in his home.

"I know him from past. Yuss, I meet him five – no six – six years ago."

The girl returned her attention back to the black book.

"Did Mr Miles say if he was going anywhere?"

"Him no say."

"Was he in good spirits?"

"Yuss, he was laughing at me."

Behind me, the man chuckled and she closed her notebook.

"Mr Miles has disappeared."

"Whoa, not me…"

"Nobody's accusing you, granddad," said the man, anxious to get away.

"If you hear anything will you phone the station?" said the girl, handing me her card. She had an impersonal air about her which made it impossible to judge her real attitude, certainly she was playing by the rules and if I had made a mistake she wouldn't disclose it at this stage, whereas the man would have flung it in my face.

"Yuss."

In a moment they were gone and I went out to the balcony to watch them drive off. This took five minutes: obviously they'd stopped to speak to Wilson or his receptionist who had no doubt reported me.

First the Snake, and now this. I had thought I was safe from even the most casual questioning: now the police had me on their books. Something in the big picture had gone wonky and I'd been too obtuse to avoid it. The more I thought about it, the more I became aware that the edifice was crumbling around me. For all I knew the Snake might have access to the cop files. In fact there was nothing to stop him (or one of his sidekicks) phoning the station and asking how the enquiries were going. There was nothing secret about this and the girl would possibly say they'd called on a Mr Klutza. Not necessarily a disaster, but there was always the risk of him following up on that lead. He was cute enough to know that I didn't let Polish vagrants into Dunglen Castle.

To move to another part of London would be risky but it might be necessary to reconnoitre a few possibilities.

48

Two days later, I awoke to find myself staring at the cracked ceiling and asking some searching questions about my life. My bed was uncomfortable, the environment wasn't great and I had a foreboding that things would get worse (though forebodings can come in a castle as well as a doss house). Yet in many ways I was not unhappy. Provided there was no calamity, I could live in Haven House for years, the lifestyle wasn't all that bad and it was infinitely better than jail. My health was reasonably good, I'd lost twenty pounds in weight and aside from an uncertainty about the future there were no immediate problems. Despite being disturbed by a TV programme, a police visit and the incident at the building society, my flight to London had been all right so far.

I rose at six, switched on the kettle and went to the newsagent for a paper. Returned, I had tea and toast while flicking the pages, shaking my head at the sensationalism that even the quality papers have now adopted. Then it was time to go to work, a distance of two miles that would take about forty minutes and which was relatively pleasant. I locked the door and went down the stairs.

Two weeks ago I had to pause in the vestibule while two undertakers carried a coffin – which had been placed vertically – out of the lift to their white van on the forecourt. The leader was able to open the door while supporting it with his other hand. Someone had died in the night and the undertakers had been summoned before the place got too busy. The coffin seemed to be of cardboard and was tastefully marked 'size: medium': no doubt funerals at Haven House were low budget affairs with Social Security picking up the tabs.

By this time I was one of the family, having paid my rent and caused no trouble. Today Wilson, who works a long day, was checking something in his book and looked up to nod as I went to the front door where a white van sat – I'd started to notice white vans, wondering if they were collecting more coffins and remembering, too, that ultimately they'd come for me. I almost cracked a joke about it and stopped myself in time when I saw the insensitivity of such a remark: and also that it would be out of character with my Polish role. And there was a risk that Wilson remembered something of Ron Miles, twice I'd caught him staring after me with a frown.

My journey went through a park that reminded me of the garden at Dunglen – provided I ignored the broken bottles and the hundred other people hurrying to their work. By this time I had begun to recognise the regulars. There was the Cheery Whistler who would overtake me half way, the dog walker with two poodles, a man in pin-stripes moving in the opposite direction, two nurses who seemed exhausted by their night's stint and several newspaper boys on bikes.

But all was not well.

Footsteps approached from behind, new ones that I didn't recognise, and I slowed to let the walker pass but they slowed too. Without looking back I walked faster and cursed when he – I knew it was a man – did the same. This didn't sound good. I swung to the right on to a deserted path only to be followed. Then I did a John Masters and spun on my heel, walking in the opposite direction to pass an ordinary-looking guy of about fifty who had the look of a security guard, though he was shorter than average. At least he wasn't the Snake and he seemed to be alone, which didn't mean he wasn't an agent.

"We must talk, Ron," came a voice from behind with a foreign inflection.

I walked faster, experiencing a lurch at the mention of my name. It had been months since anyone had called me Ron and it was strangely moving to hear it.

"I'm the Red Cross. There has been a failure: we can't access LCZ without you."

If I was the Snake I'd certainly open negotiations that way, in fact, bearing in mind the man was a stranger, there was no other feasible approach. I swung to the left to join the main body of people who were ambling towards the exit with dull faces, not looking forward to their day's work: there might be safety in crowds, but for how long? I would soon be out of the park.

"We must talk."

Famous words which mean the speaker wants you to listen. Almost certainly he was the Snake's man and so far he'd said nothing to contradict it. How could the Red Cross locate me in my present role? I was quite prepared to believe there was a legal difficulty, that much was obvious. But there was no future in co-operating with the Snake. There had to be teamwork here, my follower was the sheepdog and I was being guided towards a trap, but where was it? I was out of practice, my reflexes were slower and it was years since John Masters had tried to hammer the basics into my head. There seemed to be nobody watching me, but could that be right? Perhaps they were serious experts, though I could have sworn I'd seen every other person in the park in my morning walks. Nobody waited at the park gates and no vans (you need a meat wagon for your victim) were revving up in the street outside. I recalled the presence at Carlisle and was unable to relate it to this casual scenario.

Ahead a crowd of workers entered the park, coming in my direction, unsmiling men and women who looked like City people and I spun on my heel again, passing my follower in an instant, and joining the crowd. About average height, he wore a suit and dark tie and didn't seem to be a threat. He had the open-faced, almost innocent, look of a social worker and there was nothing in his mannerism to suggest violence. That might once have put my mind to rest but I'd seen too many such faces in prison. By this time I was walking too fast for an older man and getting some curious looks. There was still no sign of the team, but they must be there. For sure the Snake would never send one single man to intercept me – he'd used twenty at Carlisle, possibly more and I'd seen this man before, I couldn't remember where, but without a doubt he'd been tailing me, the white van came to mind.

"I am employed by the Red Cross."

Yes, you said that before.

John Masters had been good at describing the issues of the tail and his quarry. Admittedly, there were times when it's nearly impossible to know you were being followed, but sometimes you found out. Then a stalemate occurred, what do you do next? At the end of the day Masters, despite his fighting talk, was a mediocrity without a solution to the problem. How do you shake a tenacious follower? He didn't know.

"The Case against you has been dropped."

Yes, that's why I'm on the run. You need someone in the dock to get a case going, otherwise the judge has no one to glare at. I've been there before, remember?

For a minute silence reigned. He was six feet behind me.

"All right, I am going. Phone Stefan Gill today. I'll be here in the evening."

When I looked two minutes later he was gone, though I think he shadowed me in case I did a runner. There was no indication of other followers. By this time I was ready to drop, finding it difficult to walk in a straight line. At Glassford Electronics I apologised to Mr Singh for being late. I said it was a family matter and that I'd need to take a thirty minute break in the middle of the day. He nodded, none too pleased.

That evening, I approached the park with great care, hoping to hell there were no suspicious persons lurking in the background. Long before I'd entered I'd seen my follower sitting on a bench and so far as I could see he was alone. But that didn't mean a lot, he'd had a full day to prepare a trap and the Snake is subtle. If I'd planned it I too would have had my man sitting alone on a bench. And I was wary of this open-faced man and his smug expression. All right he was a foreigner, but something about his voice put my nerves on edge. He was the kind of person I'd tend to avoid.

"Hello Ron."

"What's your name?" I said, wincing, because I sounded brusquer than intended.

"Jack Baurr," he said, and yes he sounded like a social worker with his calm-you-down tones. "I'm Swiss. Let's go to a pub and talk."

I didn't move. My eyes went around the entire park and located no suspicious persons. My flight had cost a billion and I was reluctant to surrender another inch of my freedom.

"Are you alone?"

"Have you contacted Stefan Gill? Yes, I'm alone."

Well he would say that anyway. Wordlessly, we turned to the nearest pub, I was aware of the uncertainty but so far as I could see there was no evidence of a team. Then we crossed the street and went into a pub where I insisted on sitting in a corner beside the fire exit where I could watch the door. He ordered a toasted sandwich for me.

"Are you all right?"

"Not particularly," I said, finding it difficult to speak in straight English. The Polish role had taken over my life. "You don't sound Swiss."

"I spent twenty years in the States."

The pub was sparsely filled though there was a group of drinkers making a lot of noise at the bar itself. So far nobody had followed us in. But just because this man knew of Stefan Gill, didn't mean he wasn't on the Snake's payroll.

"You've been following me?"

"…Yes… I located you three days ago… It's been six weeks now."

"What's the problem?"

His eyes wouldn't quite meet mine. There was something I didn't trust about Mr Jack Baurr, though perhaps I was being unkind, at that point in my life I didn't trust anyone.

"I've to make you an offer," he said. "I represent the Red Cross. The lawyers have messed up. ECZ still belongs to you: the document you signed is invalid."

Having spoken to Stefan, I knew this to be true and so would the Snake.

"I see."

"We'll have to get you to Switzerland to sign an affidavit before witnesses."

I shook my head. Maybe this was the trap. For the moment I would commit myself to nothing. If the Snake was involved, he'd want me out the country too.

"No, there'd be trouble at customs. Cops are looking… so are my enemies."

"The cops are only interested in your welfare."

Not if the Snake has sent my file in.

"If they find me, so will the others."

"All right, I can see your point, but let me finish. You'd go via the Swiss Embassy, under diplomatic cover, not through customs as such. If you're still prepared to make the entire Fund over to the Red Cross, they'll grant you Swiss citizenship, a new identity, a retainer, and a permanent residence for the rest of your life."

My head went up. This was the stuff of which dreams are made. After the recent upheavals it was too good to be true. But I was plagued with uncertainty.

"Have you proof of identity?" I asked, only now realising I should have seen it before going to the pub. He produced a letter, more or less saying the same thing. Of course it proved nothing: I'd gone to jail on forged documents.

I began to fire questions at him: who does he answer to? Does he know such and such? Describe him, when did he meet Stefan Gill? Why did he meet him? Does he work alone, or is he the front of a team? Etc., etc.

His answers seemed honest, he hesitated on nothing and even volunteered some facts though his eyes still refused to meet mine. Perhaps it was a personal characteristic.

"How did you find me?"

"That was the hard bit... weeks of work. Then I heard the police had interviewed an old man, Klutza, who had worked for you at Dunglen. It sounded interesting so I started following you."

"You've been very thorough."

"All part of the spadework."

But I was not convinced. Perhaps this man was connected with the building society line of enquiry. The Snake had a tendency to be ahead of the pack and he didn't want me to bolt.

"Were you followed at any time?"

He squirmed in surprise.

"Not that I'm aware of."

I told him about the Snake, without mentioning name or details, how he had even found my emergency account and how I thought the original fund belonged to terrorists. He listened without displaying any signs of agitation, nodding sometimes.

"You're a Swiss agent. He might have you followed."

"No, no. You're overstating. There are millions of people in London. He's not that good. You've been on the run too long. I'll take you to a safe house. Your enemy may be dangerous, but he's low life."

Possibly no one hates the Snake more than me, but this was too glib.

"He's a very dangerous man."

"Forget it, you'll be safe."

I looked at him. That assumed I wanted to go, but, yes, I did. My present persona was crumbling. If Jack Baurr could find me, so could the Snake. My whole life would have to be re-organised. The prospect of the safe house had swung me.

"I want things out of Haven House first." Money and papers, including the E. M. Mertoun pass book which I daren't lose.

"All right, but don't hand over your key. Collect your things and leave the building as though you're going for fish and chips. Don't draw any attention to yourself."

"I'll do that."

"Things happen when you make a change. No point in inviting trouble."

"Okay – Where are we going afterwards?"

"Not far. A safe house on the outskirts – you'll find it comfortable."

I grimaced at the mention of comfort. All I wanted was security, it wasn't a lot to ask for but it might prove to be elusive. That said, I wanted to survive and it was essential to be ahead of the pack, a new address, however temporary, would be preferable to the upheavals of late.

"All right, let's go."

We left the pub and drove to Haven House where I removed money, personal papers, and left my rucksack behind forever. When closing the door I realised how sorry I was to be leaving, my stay had been a relatively happy one and it was to be hoped my next venue would be as satisfactory. Wilson nodded to me as I left; we would never meet again.

Two minutes later we pulled into the rush hour traffic. I hadn't been in a car for months, and possibly that made it worse, but Jack Baurr was a poor driver who veered about the lanes and all but struck a taxi.

"I was thinking about your enemy... He could get someone to email him if my name appears on a flight – I do all the Red Cross work, by the way. He may know I'm here. We'll keep our heads down. He would need a team to monitor all the aspects."

"There's more than a billion at stake and he has a very good team."

"I'll bear that in mind."

Ten minutes later he pulled into a car park that was nowhere near a safe house or indeed any house. He was a somewhat clumsy man who couldn't seem to work out the consequences of his actions and stared at me in surprise when I said in some alarm: "What's going on?"

"Shopping," he said. "You need clothes."

I looked around the park to see if a heavy team was closing in and saw nothing.

"Well, I suppose I do. How am I going to pay for them?"

There was still money in my wallet but it was essential to have something to spare. If Mr Baurr was all he claimed to be my troubles were over, but in an emergency, money is often more useful than a gun and I'd taken too many risks to be complacent. Never be penniless when disaster strikes.

"Oh, I will pay. You need two changes of clothes – A suit for the Embassy, and something casual, shoes too."

Ten minutes later I was kitted out in a mens' outfitters. Here Jack Baurr was impressive, acting the part of a social worker whose client urgently needed clothes. Neither he nor the salesman even spoke to me. Sensible things were chosen and I changed into new clothes and shoes. I was even given a smart suitcase. My old clothes were packed in a plastic bag which Baurr took to a refuse site. He knew his way about this part of London.

Then we drove to the safe house. Two centuries ago it must have been built for an important person on its own substantial grounds. The original owner may well have had ten children and twenty servants, and he wasn't short of money either, because the rooms were big as were the doors and windows. Now it was divided into several flats with a substantial car park at the back. He took me to a ground floor apartment that was kitted out with good bed-linen and even some food in the fridge. Here I was given a phone with his number already entered and a hundred pounds for expenses. He was organised after all.

"Nod to the neighbours, be polite, but don't converse," he told me. "These people may have seen you in the past. And there was that TV programme. Best be careful."

"I surely will."

"Well I'm going now but I'll be back tomorrow evening. I'll be at the Embassy. Gotta get papers for you – that's going to take time, you've no passport. We'll need to get your photo taken. But it should be okay. Maybe we could make the flight on the following day – I'll certainly aim for that."

"Oh, that would be good."

"Just to confirm: you are still prepared to assign ECZ to the Red Cross?"

"Yes, absolutely."

"Well that's fine then. If you have a problem, phone me right away."

"I'll do that."

Then he was gone. I made myself a cup of tea and went for a long walk and enjoyed it very much.

49

Come the following morning, I looked out to find it raining. The sky was dark with the promise of several hours of drizzle which meant I'd have to stay indoors, but that was fine, the house was comfortable, the radio was playing softly and apart from the occasional closing of a door, there wasn't a sound in the place. Altogether it seemed that my lifestyle had made a major improvement and I was sorry to have been so suspicious of Mr Baurr. The thought of moving to Switzerland filled me with hope. I could live in anonymity for the rest of my life without having to worry about the Snake or anybody else.

This was the first safe house I'd ever been in and it was of high quality. On an impulse, I searched it and discovered nothing of its previous tenants. Everything was so immaculate that it must have been professionally swept. But who did it belong to? It was rather grand for the Red Cross and I couldn't see it being the property of the Swiss Government either, though there is no limit to the way civil servants can spend money. I explored the main stairway where the back windows gave a good view of the car park and all was well. My neighbours had Audis and BMWs and all of them had been there on the previous night. There was no one about. Yes, it was a peaceful refuge.

For lunch, I made myself beans on toast and then, noticing the clouds were thinning and the rain was off, I went outside to walk through a rather ordinary park on a rain-sodden path with water dripping off the trees. Fed up with wet shoes and dampness I headed for the shops and looked around for a couple of hours. My phone buzzed. It was Jack Baurr speaking against the noise of traffic, telling me he'd arrive at eight in the evening. By this time it was almost five o'clock and I went to the cafeteria in a supermarket and ordered scampi and chips which may well have been the worst dish I've ever eaten. I returned to the flat just as the sun came out. Since it would be silly to lose the chance of a walk on my penultimate night in London, I left for a riverside path that was signposted from the main road.

This was a small river, a tributary of the Thames, where a footpath had been constructed along its bank and it was largely deserted of walkers. There were many ducks, several of whom scuttled towards me in the hope of food. I walked with my hands in my pockets, utterly content, speaking to a granny who was exercising four terriers and nodding to a jogger of about fifty who looked dead beat. At this point I had covered about a mile when I observed a tall man three hundred yards behind me. Nothing unusual about that, there are plenty of tall men about and I have nothing against them. It was not until twenty minutes later, when a cheeky pup ran up to me and put some paw marks on my clothes that I noticed he was still the same distance behind me – and I had been walking slowly too. The owner of the pup arrived, apologising and I patted the animal to show there was no hard feelings. But I'd covered two miles and it was time to go back. I'd been careful not to look around and now when I started back, the man was nowhere in sight. Unhurriedly, I walked for thirty minutes without raising my head. Then I paused to admire a family of ducks that were being fed by two little girls. I glanced behind and he was there again, staring into the river as though he expected a sea serpent to appear.

With hands in pockets, I sauntered back to the flat. Once inside, I threw my things into the suitcase and left by the other door. In leaving, my eye caught a car, sitting on the verge at the back with its door open. My follower was speaking on the phone, nodding his head and making gestures. Outside, I ran down the street where by sheer luck I found a taxi that took me to the supermarket. I'd been quick, it was doubtful if he knew I'd scarpered.

But who was he? Clearly he was a lone operator and almost certainly one of the Snake's gang. It was reasonable to assume there were several such operators checking other venues. Had they known I was there, I'd have been swamped in seconds. He'd been unsure of me and had followed to see what I was going to do. I was relaxed and wasn't acting like a fugitive and of course he would have no current description of me. My white beard would also raise some difficulties.

Reading between the lines, the Snake must have known I was on the move. Perhaps he'd got to Haven House just after I'd left and now he'd sent agents to my possible ports of call. But his organisation was mind boggling. Perhaps they'd followed Jack Baurr at some point in yesterday's events and lost him. Or perhaps someone had seen me in the van and pressed the button. For sure, it was not a tip-off otherwise the whole team would have got me.

Trying to keep my voice neutral, I phoned him: "Jack, don't go near the flat. Something's happened. Get me at Tesco's car park at eight."

"Will do," he said without emphasis, acting like a professional and uttering no unnecessary words. The call had taken less than ten seconds. I went to the cafeteria and got a tea and a biscuit, watching the main door which was milling with people. There were many tall men, but I saw no follower. I was waiting outside when he arrived five minutes early and I climbed into his van with some relief.

"You are sure?" he was saying, his open face making him seem stupid. "He could have been an innocent walker."

"He's as innocent as hell."

"But how could he have traced you?"

"I dunno. They could be checking all the safe houses. This was a one-off. He went straight to the phone in his car. I'll bet there's a team there now."

"I don't know."

"Well, I do. I won't be staying there tonight."

"But I have no other houses."

"I tell you I'm not staying there again."

"I understand that, I've had trouble too. I need to go back to Switzerland for papers. Bureaucracy, I'm fed up with it!"

"Why, what's happened?"

"Oh, it's petty. You have no passport and we need papers from the Red Cross. We've pencilled your flight for six days' time. I'll only be away for two days."

I thought it through: this wasn't much of a problem.

"Okay. I'll go back to Haven House."

"No, you won't. You've left, there's no going back."

"Come on, man. They don't even know I wasn't in last night."

"How do you know? You've broken your pattern."

I was beginning dislike his attitude.

"Well I know of a budget guesthouse," I said. "I can go there. It should be safe enough: scores of people use it every week. They'll never notice me."

"Let's look at it."

It took an hour to drive over and we gave it a once-over. I'd never stayed there but some of our farm workers booked it every time they went to London. There were jokes about its dirty toilets and small bedrooms – they said Ben, the dog, had better facilities – but it was cheap and cheerful even if you didn't get breakfast in the morning.

"It's all right," said Jack peering at it. "Obviously lots of people pass through it."

"I doubt if the Snake's ever heard of it."

"True."

"Well, do I book in for six days?"

"Yes, I'd say so. You have money? Good. Phone if anything goes wrong."

50

Apparently the guesthouse was run by an East European family and had the disadvantage of having a group of men hanging around the entrance all day. If Baurr hadn't already driven off, I'd have tried another one in the next street, but in case anything went wrong, it seemed best to keep to the agreed venue. As it happened, no one paid me the slightest attention. I signed my name as James Jones and spoke in a Welsh accent that was lost on the sullen youth at the desk, paying for six days and waiting for an age while he wrote a receipt.

Next morning, I breakfasted in a nearby coffee shop and left to explore the city where I mixed with tourists, drank coffee and walked through Hyde Park. By way of disguise, I had a hat pulled across my forehead and I did my lame walk, leaning forward with a slight stoop, well aware that I could be recognised from passing cars and busses, never mind the myriad of pedestrians around me. Perhaps I shouldn't have bothered, nobody looked at me twice. For lunch, I'd a cheese sandwich after which I walked along the Thames until the sky darkened. Then it began to rain and I browsed in Foyles for an hour, before taking a longer walk that culminated in a supermarket where I ate fish and chips. Altogether, the whole thing was depressing. London was lonelier than I had ever known it. At seven o'clock I returned to find more people in the hall, making a lot of noise. Seemingly they had just arrived and were getting familiar with their relatives. This went on through the night and I slept badly. When I left at eight in the following morning several of them were sleeping in the hall. This time I tried to vary my routine but it was largely a repeat of the previous day with more boredom flung in. Returned at seven, the hubbub fell quiet when I entered the hall. After hours of tedium I was tired and bored out of my head and none too alert. For someone who had been near paranoid a few days ago, this was a curious lapse on my part. Next morning it was raining and I delayed my departure until nine. This time I noticed them watching me go through the hall and I almost seized up.

Outside, I turned in the opposite direction, walking fast along a pavement that had a fair number of innocent pedestrians. But I wasn't going to get away. After two hundred yards, two tall security guards appeared beside me, clad in smart uniforms with shining shoes and reinforced helmets.

"Sorry, Mr Miles. You'll have to come with us," said the older one. He had a London accent and a policeman's way of giving orders.

At that moment a security van pulled on to the pavement beside us. I'd been aware of its engine somewhere in the background. Ordinary people were walking past me, hurrying to their work and taking no interest in my little problems.

"There must be some mistake," I said with a quiver. "My name isn't Miles." We were all being very polite.

"In that case we're sorry to trouble you, sir."

During this, the driver's mate had run out and opened the back doors, at which I was lifted into the van where two minders, who had been waiting inside, grabbed me as the door was slammed and locked. It drove off immediately, leaving the men on the pavement – presumably they had their own transport. Their professionalism was impressive. The whole thing was over in seconds without one member of the public noticing. Meanwhile my guards went through my pockets, taking my phone, keys, pass book, money and all my papers which they placed in a metal box. There were no windows and it was impossible to see out. One of the guards looked familiar.

"Where are you taking me?" I said, trying to keep a whine out of my voice.

"You'll be there in a few minutes."

Both were alert, one on either side, not taking their eyes off me. I was in trouble.

"Who are you working for?"

"I'm not at liberty to say sir. But you will be well treated and released shortly."

So he was speaking in the language of officialdom rather than the street, something I hadn't expected and though it might mean I was less likely to get beaten up, it inferred I was up against a serious player. But I'd always known that.

"I object to this." A futile point, they didn't expect me to complain to my MP.

As near as I could estimate it, the journey took forty minutes, revving and turning corners that sometimes sent us sprawling about the floor, there being nothing to hold on to. It stopped frequently, no doubt for traffic lights and road junctions: plainly the driver was an expert with London's roads. There was a final stop of about a minute and then we moved for ten seconds in first gear, during which my guards dusted their clothes. The journey was over, footsteps approached and the door opened to reveal the backyard of an old manor house. A high stone wall around the yard was breached by a solid door which was slowly closing. It was not unlike the yard at prison and it looked escape-proof.

"Come out slowly and don't try anything," said the driver, who was clearly the boss and who was no longer pretending to be polite.

Effortlessly, they lifted me down and held my arms as we went to the big house which the boss unlocked with a group of keys, each with a label attached. An alarm started to bleep a low warning that was deactivated in seconds.

"This way," he barked, bitterly unhappy, glancing at me with a frown and uttering several great sighs. It took me a moment to realise he wasn't actually angry with me: it was my status as a prisoner that annoyed him. This man was just as unhappy with my kidnap as I was: he wanted nothing to do with it, he belonged to the world of law and order and had no wish to be involved in the darker side of things. Yet he had to obey orders.

"Wipe your feet."

Meekly we rubbed our shoes on a mat before entering a room with a lot of expensive furniture and flowers. It looked too pristine to be lived in and it made my own furnishings in Dunglen Castle look like a sale lot. Then we were in a panelled lounge which must have been hundreds of years old with expensive tapestries and some big oil paintings on its walls: one, a modern oil by a world-class artist, was a full length portrait of a robed man who might have been a sheik, standing in the desert beside a black horse. Would I be safe in his tender care? There were a lot of cushions on the floor. Was this the Liberation Organisation?

"Stand there."

Behind me, the driver and his mate were doing something with a control panel. There was a loud click from the wood panelling, a motor hummed, and a whole section moved aside to reveal a rubber door. Another click and it opened on to a tunnel that looked as if it sloped all the way to hell. The door was steel with a rubber surface, presumably to avoid a hollow sound on the panels.

"Follow me," said the boss with an angry sigh, walking into the tunnel, his head pointing straight ahead and paying us no attention.

With guards gripping both arms, I watched the boss's heels for at least sixty yards as we descended into the depths. Then he stopped to unlock a horrible metal door that I knew was the entrance to my cell. This was no jerry-built extension, it was more solid than the doors of the prisons I'd served in and there was no chance of escape. Clearly we were no longer under the house. I noticed one guard was carrying two small containers.

"Get in," said the boss, turning to me. It was a concrete cell with a toilet and wash basin in the far corner: the ceiling was out of sight and there were no lights, the sole illumination came from the tunnel behind me. On the floor lay two sleeping bags.

"Listen carefully," said the boss, speaking from the doorway. "We'll come every day at twelve with food. It'll be in two containers, one for lunch and one for dinner. Here's today's," and the assistant handed them over. "Have you any questions?"

"Yes, why am I here?"

He closed his eyes in exasperation at my stupid question.

"You'll find out soon enough."

At that, the door was closed leaving me in total darkness. I'd never experienced such blackness before. Few people have. Even in the darkest of nights there is a small measure of light, but here it was absolute. The lock turned, to be followed by retreating footsteps and then the slam of the steel door. Now I was utterly isolated from all parts of civilised life, without anyone to speak to, with no access to a telephone and absolutely no chance of escape. I had to hand it to them: this was a secure room.

Despite that, I had a walk. First I kicked the sleeping bags to one side and put the containers on top as I walked across the room in six paces, turned back, and repeated the procedure one hundred times. In all I covered about quarter of a mile and I was dizzy. Not much fun.

Now I tried feeling my way around the cell. Three sides were of painted brickwork and the fourth was solid concrete and all of them smelt of fire. I went to the steel door to discover that it curved outward. Curvature was less than the thickness of a finger but it was unmistakeable. How odd: I couldn't see the point of that. The floor was cold and composed of poured concrete. On a sudden impulse I put my nose down and smelt fire again though it was less pronounced. Then I got the sleeping bags and sniffed them. No fire, but somebody had slept there recently. No doubt the two bags were to insulate the sleeper from the fierce cold of the floor. There were no tables, chairs or beds, which meant no potential weapons. Not a very promising situation.

In the distance, the sound of London's traffic rumbled on: the movement of heavy vehicles could be felt across the room and they were not immediately above me.

So why was I here?

Beyond doubt it was the Snake. I now recalled seeing one of my guards at Carlisle bus station. Clearly the staff had been well trained and none had uttered a remark that would be useful to me if I were to escape. On the previous evening they must have known I was in the guesthouse and had shown good judgement by making no attempt to seize me until I left on my own volition.

Yes, it was the Snake all right. At the end of the day the best man had won. He'd taken an objective view of the situation and now the victory was his while I had given a fortune away and been unable to hide. As always, Frank had been right: you can't hide in the modern world; they'll trace you whatever you do. My collapse was total. Throughout my life, I'd privately mocked people who'd become destitute after losing fortunes and now I had joined their ranks.

I felt for the smaller container and opened it, smelling the contents cautiously. Two cheese sandwiches in brown bread. Presumably I would have to drink cold water from the tap. Too early for lunch, I put them back. Then I took off a shoe and flung it at the ceiling to find it was about twenty feet high. What a weird room.

Nose to the wall again, was it fire? No it was something else and it explained the curve on the door. Cordite. There had been an explosion strong enough to bend the steel door and it had doubtless removed all traces of the previous occupant's DNA. Possibly they'd carried him out in a nice box beforehand. They must have forgotten to replace the sleeping bags.

Total darkness has a peculiar effect on time and it isn't good for the health either, though I don't suppose my captors were troubled about that. About a hundred years had passed after I'd eaten my dinner and I was in the sleeping bag when bright lights in the ceiling flooded the room. Dazzled, I couldn't see for a bit and then when my eyes adjusted, I went to the door and waited for an age for something to happen. I tried knocking on its surface: I tried shouting, but there was no one there. It seemed the lights had come on remotely.

Then I paced the floor again, this time diagonally. What time? Obviously early morning, say five, the traffic above was reduced to a few rumbles a minute. I counted two hundred journeys, about half a mile, before stopping, dizzy and dazzled. Latterly I'd walked with my eyes closed to shield them from the glare. I noticed that the toilet suite was new, a replacement of the previous one which would undoubtedly have been destroyed by the explosion. Possibly there would have been a leakage of water that would remove some of the cordite from the floor. On the edge of my vision I knew that high above me were four lights of about 250 watts each and beside them was the shape of a trapdoor or service hatch built in to the ceiling, but what good was that? How do you climb a twenty foot sheer wall? I'd cursed the darkness, now I began to wonder if this was worse. An age passed then the lights suddenly faded into darkness. Above me, the traffic had grown quieter and at first it didn't make sense. Then I knew it wasn't morning, it was late night. It took a long time to get back to sleep.

Awake again, I noted an increase in the traffic, apparently it was morning but what difference did it make? Rush hour came and rush hour passed: the traffic went about its business while time had come to a standstill. It was well into afternoon: possibly evening and no food had arrived. There was the question if they'd starve me.

Eventually there were sounds: clicks of locks, a thump, more clicks then the steps of three men coming down the tunnel at a smartish pace. A key turned in the door, a small movement and then dazzling light filtered in from the corridor. My eyes closed, I couldn't see them. After the total darkness the light was blinding.

"There's your food. Come on!"

Containers were pressed into my hands. They weren't all that interested in me and were making no attempt to be kind.

"Give us the empties. Oh, all right, I'll get 'em."

And he brushed past to collect the containers of yesterday's food. I could barely see him though I was aware of two guards watching me from the tunnel. They were taking no chances.

"What time is it?"

A voice from the door said: "Half past eleven."

"Did you miss a day?"

A laugh: "Did we hell!"

Then they were gone.

In the darkness I sank on to the sleeping bags and asked myself how they'd caught me. When I'd first booked into the guesthouse no one had looked at me twice and it wasn't until the evening of the second day that there had been a change in attitude. Something had happened in the interval and that could only have been a tip-off from Jack Baurr – the only person who knew where I was. I'd been suspicious of him from several angles and cursed myself for a fool in allowing myself to be moved to the guesthouse. Haven House was far superior and at least there was some kind of security in the place. Also the claim that the flat was the only safe house in town was risible: there must have been other options. For a start, where was *he* staying? Baurr had also pretended the Snake was low life and that he was no threat. The excuse for a six day delay wasn't credible either. Clearly he'd done a deal. And the deal, like every one the Snake has ever made, had been a double-cross. That was why they'd nearly caught me at the safe house. The Snake wouldn't trust Baurr. Every available agent would be despatched to likely safe houses to look for me. And they'd nearly got me too.

How they knew about each other was another thing altogether – for sure I couldn't have contacted Mr D'Alfonso to save my life. So how would a Swiss resident know? When talking in the pub he'd given the impression of being unaware of any opposition though his eyes had been shifty and his attitude had been peculiar. I got up and started doing exercises on the cold floor. In a sudden temper I went to the door and kicked it, cursing myself for failing to note the obvious.

There was also the question of the previous occupant. Who was he? This posed another question altogether. Who was the owner of this stately pile? This was billionaire stuff and though the

Snake was well off it seemed unlikely he was that rich: also he had been out of the country for twenty years, or seemed to have been. In any event, why would the owner need a cell/dungeon under his palace? Clearly this was an illegal room that would fascinate the police and its discovery would probably result in a jail sentence for someone, the courts have little sympathy with illegal detentions.

I did more exercises on the cold floor.

51

Many days passed, perhaps fifteen, perhaps twenty, I'd lost count after five, there being no pencil to mark the wall. The lights came on for ninety minutes in the middle of every night, possibly to prevent the prisoner becoming permanently blind, the guards came with food at lunchtime and nothing else happened or could happen, except that my beard grew longer. Then one morning there were new sounds when I was still in the sleeping bag, I scrambled out and waited while the door was flung open with its blinding light. Lately I had found it best to face the wall at the opposite end of the room, thus reducing its impact. Gradually my eyes focused on the guard at the door.

"Come on!"

I walked forward to the door and being swamped by the light, sat down. There were three of them and they seemed to be the same team that delivered my food. This was likely, my detention was illegal and the Snake wouldn't want to share his secrets with too many security guards.

"I can't see."

"Move: This isn't bright." Then, exasperated: "Midge, give him your shades."

Someone put dark glasses on me and I rose to advance up the tunnel with unsteady steps. Opening my eyes, however briefly, caused flashes of pain and the glasses weren't much help. In the top room we waited while the tunnel was closed and the panelling returned to normal. There was some whispering among my guards. One man was watching the door. There must have been house staff about and presumably they didn't want them to see the tunnel.

"Wait here," ordered the leader, who was looking tense and uttering great sighs. I sat down on the floor and tried opening my eyes which were gradually coming back to normal. The guards had well-polished shoes. I looked at the sheik standing beside his black horse and noted the cruel lines of his mouth. Someone entered and said:

"About five minutes."

A minute later an attractive woman of about thirty, who looked like a secretary, came in and frowned at me sitting on the floor with my unkempt beard, old clothes, and sunglasses. She looked questioningly at the leader who said:

"It's all right."

Five minutes later they took me through a magnificent entrance hall to a room that was big enough for fifty people and was lined with scores of collector's items. Beside the window sat a big desk covered in papers at which sat two men, one of them the Snake, and he didn't seem to have aged since I'd last seen him: he was on the phone and gave me a cheerful nod as they led me in. He sported a delicate beard that changed the whole balance of his face which was tanned by years of sunshine. Despite my hatred of him I had to concede that he looked well in his mohair suit and silk shirt. Yes, Sir James had been right; I could see he was a rich man. Didn't make a lot of difference, I had once been rich too.

"Sit there, sir," said the leader to me, clearly ill at ease in the grandeur of the room and addressing me in civil tones for the first time. He coughed nervously as he spoke and one of his men put me on to a solid chair in front of the desk.

In the corridor outside, two men went past with a filing cabinet, followed by a number of smart girls who were carrying an array of files. Meanwhile the Snake was having a detailed conversation on the phone. It was a busy place.

In a relaxed manner, the Snake finished his call and exchanged some words with his colleague, who nodded, picked his papers from the desk and left.

"Well it's been a long time," he said with a laugh. But was this the Snake? There were no supercilious airs, he seemed to bear me no ill will for the tremendous beating I'd given him and he was acting like my best friend. Perhaps he'd taken Holy Orders.

I probably agreed.

"Looks like you've had a hard time. Not my doing, at all. I've only just flown in." (I didn't quite believe that.) "How are you?"

"My eyes are bad."

The Snake peered at me considerately: "If you need medical attention…?"

"No, no," I said in some alarm, having no wish to find out if the guards were good with hypodermic needles.

"Try taking the glasses off."

I did: the room seemed far too bright and I put them on again.

"I'm all right."

"Well, if you say so... Something to eat, biscuits and tea, perhaps?"

"No, no." Was this to be my last breakfast?

"Have a sherry then." He poured a glassful and handed it over.

Things were swimming in front of me, I couldn't quite follow his drift and this was my enemy...

"Let's get down to business." He leaned back in his leather chair and looked at me in his kindest mode. "My boss, the Prince, is getting old and frankly won't last beyond the year. I have to tidy up his affairs. As you've no doubt guessed our interest is in the ECZ fund which is founded entirely on his money. Are you prepared to cede it to us?"

Once I would have refused to discuss it, but my will had been worn down and I was not in a good negotiating position.

"...Yes, I've wanted to do that for years. I left a message with your spokesperson." A slight exaggeration, I had only intended to cede his share. Twenty per cent was my own, or at least it wasn't his, I'd stolen it myself, but what's a few million?

"I know, I know. But there were difficulties... Well there's no problem then... You're doing the right thing. Incidentally I'll give you a cash package of twenty thousand pounds for expenses. And your effects –"

He opened an old cash box that contained my money, the Klutza passport and the E. M. Mertoun passbook – I was moved to see them again.

"– Have you any objections to signing the deeds today?"

Everything was moving too fast.

"...No... no objections."

"Good. We'll have to get you some decent clothes. I'm glad you're co-operating: this whole thing's been troubling me for years. The Prince said not to worry: you were managing the fund so well. But there will be trouble when he dies. He has two sons who hate their father as well as each other. I don't want to leave outstanding business."

"And they're brothers, too?"

"Well step brothers. So I'll prepare a document that gives us one hundred per cent of ECZ?"

"Yes. That's what I was going to give the Red Cross."

"I have little sympathy for the Red Cross," smiled the Snake, writing something on his pad. "Dear me, imagine putting you into a budget guesthouse after all your generosity," he shook his head in wonderment. "Well, we're agreed. Sometime this afternoon we will go to my lawyers and finalise it." He lifted a small case on to his desk. "Yours," it was bulging with cash. "If you don't mind, we'll use some of this to get you into shape. New suit, shoes and a hairdresser for a quick trim."

I said that would be all right.

Then the minders took me to another part of the house – it was some place – where they made a note of my shoe size and measured me for a suit. Later I had a leisurely bath while two of them stood guard, facing the other way. In due course someone came with clothes and I found myself dressed in a business suit with matching shirt and tie. Then they took me to the Snake, passing another group of secretaries who were carrying sheaves of files. This time he was sitting with *The Times* on his knee in a splendid room that overlooked some fine gardens. He looked me over and said:

"Fine, Ron, there's a stylist coming to do your hair. Better shave off that beard."

"No," I said, suddenly sullen. "Ron Miles doesn't exist anymore."

The Snake frowned and spoke with some authority.

"I think you should remove it."

"No," I said, forgetting that he was a very dangerous man.

He shrugged.

"Well trim it, make it smart."

In due course a hairstylist arrived and they took me to another room where my beard was trimmed and haircut. This took a long time, the man was nervous of the place and he wasn't happy with the two minders who had crowded into the room to make sure I didn't do a runner. Eventually he held up a mirror and I looked in dismay at the old man's face that stared back at me.

"Is it all right, sir?" he said, rubbing his hands anxiously.

"Sit still," said one of the minders, producing a camera. "We need a picture."

He seemed to be an expert and took several head and shoulders shots of me while the hairstylist watched with a worried frown.

Returned to the first room with minders in tow, we found the Snake on the phone, having a long conversation in a foreign language. They placed me on the chair in front of his desk and brought a tray of sandwiches and tea which made me feel better, though I was tense in the Snake's company. After a few moments, he ended the conversation at which his phone rang again. This time he spoke in English, mentioning something about files and making a remark about title deeds. Altogether he seemed very relaxed and capable. I could see that old Howardson had been right about the Middle East. There was something Arabic about his features and his skin had been burnt by years of sunshine. He put the phone down.

"Ah, you're looking well, Ron. That beard suits you after all."

It was difficult not to squirm every time he looked at me.

"Despite all the years, I recognised you immediately," he said as he sank back into his chair with a half-smile. "And it's a long time since our last... meeting. I tend not to travel nowadays, though I'll have to go to the States next week. It's rather tiresome."

On his desk there were a lot of printouts and several ledgers that had been written in hand. One piece of paper, partly covered by the phone, showed an inventory of numbers that seemed to total three billion.

"You live in the Middle East?"

"I do. I'm the Chancellor and have been for forty years, would you believe."

"I see – And the Prince... is he in oil?"

"Oh yes. It's a small country but we have oceans of the stuff. Though I say it myself, I have been a good Chancellor – the best in the Middle East. I've dealt with British prime ministers and met all the US presidents several times. I've also been the Prince's envoy to OPEC. You've probably seen me in the news and failed to recognise me – the beard helps. Now I'm getting ready to retire and I'll put my mind to banking again. I have a lot of ideas."

"You'll stay in the Middle East?"

"No, no, it's not safe now... To tell you the truth, the Prince has bought me a big ranch in Texas. I take possession of it in a few days. It belonged to a previous vice president of the States and it has brilliant security. I'm looking forward to it."

There was a silence while I considered this. Though my head was spinning, I knew he shouldn't be telling me his secrets.

"What do you think of the house?" he said looking round.

"It's yours?" I said, uncomfortable under his searching eyes.

"This house? Oh no, I own nothing here. It belongs to the Prince. And he has never stayed in it, though it's used as his UK headquarters with its own staff."

"Surely your country has an embassy in London?"

"Oh yes, but it looks after our national affairs. We handle his personal business from here – such a fine building. You should have had a place like this, Ron – living like a hermit in Scotland, such a waste of talent!"

"I liked it."

"Possibly, but you should have gone for the bold. I told you that. By this time you could have been a great tycoon, adviser to the government, a figure to be reckoned with: why, you could have been a lord – but you blew it."

"It was jail that blew it," I said, mentally rejecting his assessment.

"Oh, I'd forgotten that, who shopped you?"

"Wallace."

"Wallace…! Even he should have known better. A greedy slob. I've never respected him…" He shook his head at the preposterousness of it all: I was tempted to remind him he was once in cahoots with Wallace but I let the moment pass. "So he got you jailed and still failed to grab your fortune? Ha, ha. Well that's poetic justice for you. But you needn't have gone down. The whole thing could have been avoided."

"Sir James said so."

"And he was absolutely right. The terrible thing, Ron, is that you have rarely used your abilities. Had you been a big shot you could have stymied the opposition with ease. A quiet word with MI6, and you'd have had me licking my wounds. Good heavens you could have had the SAS after me – particularly after the Great Square Siege."

"I'd almost forgotten about that. What happened, remember a man was shot?"

The Snake shifted in a moment's discomfort.

"Ah, an unhappy moment: Ahmad was never blessed with subtlety and had attracted the attention of the Home Office. The man was tailing him and I'm afraid Ahmad shot him. I'd nothing to do with that."

There was a moment's silence. Mention of the death had taken the wind out of his sails and now his mouth had closed like a trap.

"Who was in the cell before me?" I said. "Someone has used the sleeping bags and the room's been cleansed."

"Dear me," he said, with a phoney laugh. "You ask the most awkward questions – I don't know the man's identity, but I think they got their hands on a potential assassin, not a nice fellow at all... Never plot against a powerful monarch, Ron. It's bad for the health. You're not only fighting the Prince, you're taking on the whole state. And the world's a small place now. You can't hide."

"No, you can't."

"All of these things are in the past. Put them out of your mind... But enough, we have business."

The Snake dropped his eyes to the desk. His little talk had been a warm-up to keep me sweet – it was unnecessary, I'd lost all my fighting spirit.

"I've got papers for you to sign," he said, producing a file and putting on his glasses to read it, looking like a wise old grandfather as he did so. "Yes, this is a declaration about the ECZ Fund. Read it over and see what you think."

It was a beautiful piece of vellum which declared that I was *de facto* the beneficial owner of ECZ, and that the other shareholders, Artur Mann, and, B. Friedland, were fictitious characters of my own invention. I also acknowledged that the original money had been stolen from Mr D'Alfonso at Auchenboggle in Scotland, date given, and transferred by me to Gill & Co in Switzerland and as a consequence and by way of making amends, I now ceded everything including accrued interest and other considerations, to Mr D'Alfonso.

"I'll sign it," I said, there being no alternative.

But this was no easy matter, it having been some time since I last signed the name of Ron Miles and he made me practice several signatures on blank paper before indicating that I should go ahead. Afterwards, two girls came in and signed as witnesses.

"Splendid," said the Snake, returning his pen to its pocket, as his voice became fiercer. "We're leaving in a few minutes and I just want to remind you that this is a formality: you are signing ECZ over to me. I don't want any trouble in front of those expensive lawyers."

"Neither do I."

He had a good look at me and then he relaxed.

"Then it will be a pleasant visit and I'll make sure you get your tea. After that you'll come back here to collect your money." He held up the case. "Then you may go. One of our lads will drive you to a hotel – or wherever."

Yes, 'wherever'. I noted that with some misgivings: it didn't set my mind to rest.

52

At two we left for the meeting. My minders led me out to the backyard where several cars were waiting. We arrived just as the Snake got into a chauffeur-driven Bentley, with smoked windows at the back, rendering him invisible to onlookers. It bore CD plates and though he was a wanted man, they would render the plods powerless. An attendant of about sixty, carrying a bulging briefcase, held the door for him and I recognised him as the companion in the hotel at Auchenboggle. It's a small world.

"This way, sir," said my minder, ushering me into the back seat of a Range Rover then getting in beside me. Another man sat at the wheel with a chauffeur's cap on his head.

Behind, there was a third car with several men, driven by the security boss who was obviously the road manager and who seemed rattled by the size of the occasion. I wondered if he knew the Snake was a wanted man. Two red lights on the wall began to flash, then the outer door opened and the Bentley purred out, followed by the Ranger Rover, with the security team taking up the rear. I looked back and saw the big door begin to close behind us; yes, it was remote controlled, but who was pressing the button?

I began to focus on the CD plate. Never once had it occurred to me that he had diplomatic immunity, it explained his getaway from Auchenboggle and the ease with which he could flit into the country. No doubt there had been a jet with CD status waiting at Aberdeen Airport to whisk him off to the Middle East. Had the incident at the hotel gone awry, I might well have found myself there too, never to be heard of again.

This was a back street in a select part of London with minimal traffic and few pedestrians. The house and its grounds took up its entire length and it ran parallel with a busier road that I'd often heard in my cell. I asked my minder the name of the street, but he refused to answer questions.

The lawyers owned a very smart building too. We followed his Bentley into their car park, which also had high walls and was attended by a man who checked our car numbers and then sealed the gate.

"Out you get," said my minder becoming alert.

In front of us the Snake was being given a hero's welcome by two partners who had come rushing out to welcome him. Both were dressed in what looked like Saville Row suits and looked very important. The senior one asking about the Prince.

"Not well, not well at all," muttered the Snake, not too bothered. "I fear the end is near."

Then he turned to me, waving a long arm:

"Mr Miles."

I was given a hero's welcome too, though I was gobsmacked at being identified so openly. I was, after all, a Missing Man. In the corner of my eye, I saw the security team, in dark suits, standing beside their car and watching events.

"Ron and I have come to an agreement," the Snake explained. "He is co-operating with us entirely and he's happy about it."

I nodded. The partners thought this was a good thing.

"Incidentally, Mr Miles takes occasional seizures, nothing serious, I'm glad to say, but he's accompanied by a medical orderly as a precaution."

The partners thought this was very wise too: one said his nephew also took seizures and had refused to have an orderly much to the dismay of his family.

"Yes, well," said the Snake turning away. We followed him into a board room where he was greeted by a group of lesser partners. A great table dominated the centre of the room, furnished with all kinds of drinks and stacked high with legal papers. I knew this wasn't for me and took a seat against the back wall to be joined by my orderly with his first aid case. A lovely girl brought a tray with tea and a huge selection of biscuits for me. In the madness of the moment I pocketed half the biscuits. This must have been a reaction to my imprisonment and I wasn't even hungry. No doubt they were being charged to the Snake anyway. The room was too hot, the talk at the table was boring and after two sips of tea I fell asleep, why, I'm not sure, perhaps the unusual nature of the day had tired me, or perhaps my recent food had been doctored.

I was awakened by angry voices, and the frightening thing was that one was the Snake's – something I could never ignore. My minder was sitting in his chair reading a newspaper, oblivious to the drama, while the Snake's acid tongue dispensed criticism against a background of growls. Difficult not to admire the way he could command his side of the table.

"All of this for nothing!"

Unbelievably, the deal was off. Having been asleep, it took time to get my bearings, but it seemed a fatal flaw had been found in his proposals and it centred on my fellow shareholders, Artur Mann, and B. Friedland. Apparently the document I'd signed an hour ago was invalid, it was nothing more than a personal statement which had no effect on corporate law. In fact these two gentlemen had tremendous legal implications that no lawyer could ignore. To say they didn't exist was ludicrous, hadn't they voted at every board meeting in the firm's history? Their non-existence couldn't be established by a mere slip of paper. Nothing less than a High Court judgement could do that and it would involve a six-month delay to allow adverts to be placed in the papers so that Messrs Mann and Friedland (if they existed, and yes, for that kind of money there would surely be some) would have an opportunity to put their case. There was of course a way out of the mess and that was for me to visit my Dublin lawyers and have them issue instructions for the sale but that would take time – something the Snake didn't seem to have and no doubt he wouldn't trust me to do it. The chairman, who had taken no part in the dialogue, held up a paper he'd been reading and made a remark that brought instant silence.

"More incompetence," said the Snake.

"These are your papers, not ours."

A lot of hands reached for papers and silence reigned momentarily. From what I could gather, ECZ was to be registered in another country (he wasn't even pretending it was the old Prince's now) and something in The articles and memorandum of his own company wouldn't allow it. More angry comments followed and then the meeting broke up. Towering above them he spat abuse. Plainly he wasn't cowed by expensive lawyers.

Sensing it was over, my minder rose and we made our way to the car park and into the Range Rover. A grim-looking Snake appeared at the door followed by the chairman who stood back to watch him talk to my driver. Then it was over and he turned to the chairman, while we drove out to the street. Nobody in the car spoke but we all sensed something momentous had occurred. When we reached the manor house, the driver turned to me and said:

"Sorry about this, sir, but you'll have to go back into detention."

"For how long?"

"I don't know sir."

"This is outrageous – kidnap – false imprisonment – you could get years for this."

"I know sir."

53

They put me back into the cell, assuring me my stay would be short and that they'd bring food at lunchtime. I told myself it would be all right: the Snake would need me when the paperwork was ready, nobody, least of all my enemy lets a billion go that easily, but that was to ignore the failure I'd read on his face – something I'd seen before and something that might spell the end of it all. Shortly, he was due in the States. Perhaps he would travel in the robes of a sheik, under diplomatic cover. But would there be a return journey? If the old Prince had died, the Snake's status would be altered immediately, he was likely to be *persona non grata* with the new regime and would no longer have diplomatic immunity and that made travel hazardous. Our police have long memories, there were charges of terrorism, murder and gun crime in the air and they don't close their files. An ugly feeling in my gut said he'd go to his ranch and leave me to rot.

The curious thing was that there was no need for the drama. There were, or had been, several ways of resolving the impasse though they would have involved a few days' delay. One, was to force me to sell all the ECZ's shares to Mr D'Alfonso (or whatever name he went under) for the grand total of, say, a pound, thus gaining more than a billion pounds and surely that was better than zero? So why wasn't he doing it?

Perhaps it had all happened at zero hour and now it was too late. (Though that begged the question of why they'd left me in the cell for so long. Clearly, the Snake been in London for weeks and had even had the time to visit the Peckham Building Society). I recalled that he'd always been unpunctual for appointments and at Auchenboggle he'd been late in remitting his money to Beirut, perhaps tardiness was a weakness in his psyche. When you're as important as the Snake, there's no need to hurry. Only little people do that.

And there was also the question of his ultimate motive, the real reason for the pursuit of Ron Miles. Why was he doing it? Obviously he was wealthy enough to afford at least twenty security guards, with their attendant costs. I'd once been rich too and I knew that the second million was less exciting than the first and by the time you get to a billion, you get a bit jaded with it all. I suspected that despite his recent affability, he loathed me for the drubbing I'd given him at Auchenboggle, perhaps the end result would have been the same whether he'd won or not: he'd never let me go, I would still be in the cell with the same problems.

As I walked about in the darkness, occasionally stumbling over the sleeping bags, I remembered the chocolate biscuits in my pocket, each in its wrapper and they were too much of a temptation. Uncertainty had made me hungry: I ate one and it was good. Then I put the remainder in the far corner.

Yes, the situation was worse than bad. He had nothing to gain by releasing me. My head had been spinning all day, but I'd seen and heard too much and I was his enemy. In fact he'd be a fool to release me: I knew enough to damn him twice over. Even the existence of this underground cell was dangerous knowledge. The unpalatable truth was that he would never release me. I would have to be isolated from the world for the rest of my life and that was likely to be a short one.

And so the days went past, just as they had always done. The strong light came on at midnight: the rush hour traffic came and went. The only difference was that my food didn't come. Nothing came. There were no footsteps in the tunnel, no guards, and most certainly no food. The unbroken silence said I was forgotten forever. Using the heel of my shoe I battered the door and yelled at the top of my voice, but the silence was absolute. The cell was isolated from the real world and there was no one to hear me. I drank from the tap, which by some oversight hadn't been turned off and ate two biscuits every day.

I wondered at the security guards, those quasi-legal officials who had rushed into my life at his bidding. Clearly they knew I was locked in the cell and had a responsibility to ensure I didn't starve. Perhaps they no longer had keys and had been sent elsewhere on business. For sure he couldn't allow them to talk. Then I remembered the secretaries carrying files in the big house above.

Were they moving out? Had the old Prince died and was the great mansion unoccupied, with its prisoner in the basement forgotten?

Anger had driven me for the first few days, some of it directed at myself, but now a terrible weakness began to eat at my bones as it changed to something I had never known before. Now that there was no chance of escape I began to see death waiting in the wings. There was no other interpretation of my chances. I compared myself to a wild animal that becomes old, ill, or injured and realising that death is imminent, goes to its place of death and dies. I've seen that with some of the dogs at Dunglen. Several times a collie that was due to make its one-way trip to the vet would disappear never to be seen again. Where did it go? Perhaps the other dogs knew, but we humans didn't have a clue and no trace of the deceased was ever found. The deer and the wild goats were exactly similar, I never saw a dead one. Somewhere at the back of their minds, their final destination was known and when that time came, they went there on their single-minded journey. A naturalist once told me the dying animal seemed to find solace when it reached its resting place. To say it was happy might be an overstatement, but it was able to tolerate its condition.

It was at that point I realised I'd moved the sleeping bags into the corner and was lying in a foetal position staring into the wall. Not exactly a healthy sign. Was this my place of death? All my anger was gone, all hope for the future was gone and now I was staring into eternity.

When the lights blazed at midnight it was a moment of pure violence. This was no gentle illumination but an assault on my vision in which the four glaring orbs seemed to burn through my eyelids. I also saw the shape of the trapdoor in the ceiling. Had it been put there to torment the prisoner?

They say there's always a way out, but that's nonsense, how could anybody climb a sheer wall of twenty feet? Yet there was a way, I'd known it for some time, the snag was that it was beyond my abilities. Three of the walls were brick, but the fourth wasn't concrete, it was plaster. Already I'd kicked several holes in it and had broken the toes of both shoes. For sure it wasn't ordinary plaster, perhaps it was an exotic import or maybe there was an additive in its mix. It was solid and it took a lot of force to penetrate its surface, but it could be done.

Then I remembered there were hard heels on my shoes.

Why hadn't I thought of it before? I took my shoes and belaboured the wall until I'd battered down the first five feet. A fair amount of plaster had been skimmed onto plasterboard that was mounted on a standard wooden frame, I was working in darkness but could feel the heads of the nails. By this time the cell was in chaos, there was plaster in my eyes, my hair, and the sleeping bags. Every time I hammered another piece, the fragments would release a cloud of dust. Of course this was merely the first five feet, barely one quarter of the height and the difficulties would increase as it went higher. And I'm not good with heights.

However idleness was not an attractive option. I'd been despondent for days and I didn't fancy my place of death. It seemed best to do something, however futile it might be.

At midnight, the lights revealed an ugly room that was grey with particles and plaster dust. Back at the wall, I made two new holes six feet up, making sure they were supported by the wooden frame. Then I put my left hand in one and stepped up. Now I was a foot above the floor and shoeless though my socks absorbed some of the harder edges. Then I stepped up to the next level and hammered out a new section above me. Only one hand could be used to batter the wall since the other was supporting me and it was exhausting work. My shoe was a poor substitute for a hammer. But when the lights went out I was well above the floor though my hands and arms were so tired that it was difficult to hold on. That's the problem with enfeeblement: there is a gradual loss of energy on all sides. Down on the floor I washed my face and hair, glad of the cold shock of the water now that I was perspiring. I shook the sleeping bags free of dust and slept for a long time, almost in a fever, sometimes half-awake, dreaming I was still suspended on the wall.

Awake, I lay in my sleeping bag in the dark and thought about it. It was best to make cautious progress and avoid any form of over-exertion. The higher I got, the greater the risk of falling on to the hard floor and broken limbs would be fatal. Twice I'd nearly fallen during the previous stint and maybe the third time would be the bad one. I felt for my shoes and was dismayed to discover the heels on both were nearly broken.

And what if it wasn't a trapdoor, what if it was a mere decoration?

After half an hour of wakefulness, I rose and climbed the wall with a shoe in my pocket. The darkness was total but by that time I knew the wall so well that it was possible to work in the dark. In a few minutes I got to the next level and then I almost fell when a lump of plaster struck me in the face, I dropped the shoe and had to climb down, my feet searching for each foothold in the darkness. Clearly it was best to wait for the light.

But I couldn't wait. The trapdoor might be a false hope but it was the only one I had and an hour later I was up there again to make another step. By this time the ceiling was little more than a yard above my head. Two pairs of incisions and the trapdoor would be within reach.

Of course there was the question of whether I'd be able to reach it. My feet would be in holes on the wall and I would be facing in the wrong direction. One hand would have to support me while the other searched behind to open the catch over a twenty-foot drop. I would then have to bring my left hand over, twist round, since I was facing the wrong direction and lift myself by sheer arm power into the section above. Was that possible? I went to the wall and put my hands into two holes and couldn't raise myself. Therefore it couldn't be done, the whole thing was a failure and the situation was hopeless.

I washed my face and lay on the sleeping bag, refusing to think about it.

But now that I had work to do, it wasn't easy to relax, and an hour later I was back on the top rung knocking out the final holes. At this point it would have been possible to reach for the trapdoor, my hand brushed against its edges, but the room was in darkness and rather than risk a fall, I made a descent. In fact, about five feet from the floor I missed my footing and fell. No damage was done but I was demoralised and I crept into a sleeping bag, weak with hunger and frustration. Eventually I fell asleep.

Blinding light awoke me. I'd been asleep for a long time.

Again I climbed the wall, holding on grimly, and reached for the trapdoor. The heat from the lights was in the one kilowatt region and it was uncomfortably hot. I grabbed the handle and almost fell to my death. The whole thing was loose, there was no hasp, it must have been damaged in the cordite explosion and it fell to the floor with a great crash that reverberated across the room.

Grimly, I held on to the wall, suddenly aware that all was not lost. For the first time in days, I was breathing fresh air that flowed in liberal quantity from the open aperture.

Above me, the ceiling was mere plasterboard and that wasn't going to stop me. I went down to the floor and returned with a shoe and battered it away, ignoring the plaster that fell on my face. Soon I'd made a hole into the service tunnel which I saw was little more than three feet high – I'd been in narrower ones in Dunglen. Clearly workmen had used it when the cell was being constructed. There was a serious drop below me, but that didn't stop me either. Remaining in the cell was certain death and this time I was facing the right direction. I gripped the wooden support, put my feet into the uppermost holes and pulled myself into the tunnel. I had to lie for a long minute in the three-foot space until my breath came back to normal.

54

It must have been twelve thirty in the morning when I clambered out of the tunnel, through a floor hatch, into a dark utility room that smelt of mustiness. I was covered in plaster and cobwebs and barely able to believe I'd done it. The light from distant street lamps said this was an old storeroom that contained a lot of tools and ancient gardening equipment. There was complete silence. After some fumbling I found the light switch and risked a quick flash to see that nobody had been there for years. The whole room was covered in dust and cobwebs with nothing modern on view, the tools might well have been a century old and the walls were of wood with paint peeling off them. No surprise, there are similar rooms in all the great houses in the land. Inevitably the door was locked, but it had been designed to keep people out, not in, and I grabbed some tools from the workbench and unscrewed the hasp in two minutes. The door swung open. Sounds carry in the night and I stood in silence for all of five minutes, dreading investigating footsteps or the wail of alarms, but all was still. Outside, there was a dusty corridor with bare boards that made me wonder if it really was the Prince's magnificent mansion. Cautiously, I moved forward, cursing the creaking boards and hoping against hope that I hadn't made a bad situation worse. Then in twenty paces I was through a smarter door and on to a carpeted corridor that took me to the splendid entrance hall. Warm air brushed my face. As was to be expected, the heating was on (the temperature would have to be stable to preserve the furnishings and oil paintings) and the house was in darkness, though there was ambient lighting from the street and there wasn't the slightest sound in the place.

At that point I was interested only in food, it had haunted my every thought and if the Snake had appeared with a gun I'd have pushed past him to reach the kitchen. It was essential to eat or die. My feet touched the carpets without making a sound, the floor didn't squeak and there was nothing to stop me. Aside from eating I had no other plans. It didn't matter if they shot me later – there was nothing else to lose – but one must eat. Hunger had made me climb out of the cell, had blunted my caution and made me take risks I'd never take again. The kitchens were easy to find.

At the back of my mind an alarm bell was ringing. You don't gorge yourself after a period of starvation. Everybody says you have to eat in moderation, yet my psyche was urging otherwise. There is a risk of guzzling everything in sight, the urge can be uncontrollable and you can rupture your gut. Certainly this was not the time to become ill. But there was a question of how poor my health really was. I was not dehydrated and had eaten two chocolate biscuits every day, therefore I was not exactly unfed though I was undoubtedly underfed. The loss of weight wasn't necessarily all that unhealthy.

There was only one window in the kitchens, they were gloomy but tidy though the tabletops surprised me by being dusty in places. Off the main tiled section I found a store resplendent with everything from cereals to tins of soups. I grabbed a packet of muesli, and a fruit juice, closed my eyes to other temptations and hurried off before I succumbed. On an impulse, I went upstairs to a room on the first floor that had a view of the entrance hall where I ate everything without being aware of my actions. There was a terrible urge to go back for a second helping but I resisted it. The room was big with black wallpaper, white trimmings and an intricate cornice that must have cost a fortune. Outside, the window gave a view of the yard with its great wall and closed door. Everything was deserted. I forced myself to lie on the fancy couch beside me. My gut felt queasy, my head was spinning and I wasn't sure what I was doing. Slowly I began to relax.

The dawn was breaking when I awoke, feeling not too bad, though, if anything, my hunger was worse than ever. Before moving I listened for fully five minutes, well aware that it was too early for the pampered guests – if there were any – though the servants might be active. But I heard nothing. It seemed to be deserted and what I remembered of the kitchens seemed to confirm this. It looked like the old Prince had died, the mansion had been closed down and his sons had decided to ignore their London venue. That didn't mean I was alone.

At the door, I stopped in consternation. None of the lights were on, but I could see my footsteps in white plaster dust stretching across the hall and up to my door. They'd find me in seconds. I took my socks off and in bare feet went down to the kitchen where eventually I found a damp cloth with which I tried to erase every mark, chewing a cereal bar as I did so. Even so, an observant onlooker would see traces.

Back in the kitchen, I took more fruit juice and something else to eat. The food disappeared without my being aware of eating and I couldn't even taste it – an after-effect of starvation. A few minutes later I felt queasy again. Outside, the yard was deserted of all life and this confirmed my view that the house was empty though that didn't mean there would be no security visits. With millions of pounds of trimmings, it would have to be supervised, though that might be nothing more than an external inspection of the doors and windows. I couldn't see the Snake coming. He had attempted to starve me and by implication had washed his hands of ECZ.

Then I decided to explore the house. I started with the next room, the biggest bedroom I'd ever seen, with a fancy four-poster and a white carpet. The cornicing looked like gold leaf and the bed also had liberal trimmings in gold. Very sumptuous, and this being the back of the house, it was not the master bedroom. Presumably there was an even more elaborate one at the front. There was a fine layer of dust on the fittings.

I paused to look at the terrible figure I presented to the mirror. My clothes were ragged and covered with white plaster as was my hair and beard and I had bare feet. There was a fanatical expression on my face that made me look like a lunatic and I had lost a lot of weight. What matter, I was still alive and with a little bit of planning I might be able to get on with my life again. I washed myself, rinsed my socks and left them to dry.

Then, as I was about to go to the next room, a door slammed.

It was like a gunshot in a distant part of the building, reverberating throughout the place with a lot of violence, bringing me out in a sweat and destroying my sense of security. I was not alone after all. Presumably the morning shift had slammed the door while entering the mansion.

For ten minutes I didn't so much as move, cursing myself for not making a better job of the plaster trail that led up the stairs – and it would be more pronounced when the lights came on. It would certainly lead to my discovery.

The geography of the place was unknown to me, but the building was big and the new arrivals might not approach the entrance hall, the slight layer of dust around me suggested it had been neglected recently and I would have to hope that they would stay away. I went to the window to find it sealed like a jail cell. There could be no escape, nor was there anything I could use for a weapon.

But there was no activity, no voices, no footsteps and no more slamming doors. The time was seven o'clock. For sure, I was trapped in the building. Clearly there was no way out, everything was sealed and even if I got outside, the yard offered no escape with its high walls and strong door. In fact the whole place was a prison though there might be accessible doors in other parts of the building, unreachable with servants about, but offering possibilities if I survived to the end of their shift. I listened very carefully. There were no human sounds, nobody seemed to be working and there were no radios playing. Of course the place was well carpeted, footsteps, even in adjoining rooms, would be close to inaudible. Only now did I remember the offices and their workers. Clearly it was too early for the officials, but this was when the cleaners would come to tidy things up. Yes, that was likely and maybe my predicament wasn't so bad. after all. Usually cleaners stick to their own routine and ignore everything else. They wouldn't be looking for extra work and would probably ignore the plaster trail on the stairs if this part of the house was outwith their agenda. Or would they?

Then I shook my head at the obvious. There were no workers in the house − all the evidence pointed that way. The slamming door had been the work of security guards on an early morning inspection. They would fire a code into the system and proceed to their next call. Naturally they wouldn't inspect the whole house, no security-minded manager would tolerate that idea. The guards would merely ensure the integrity of the building and go on their way and of course I would have to avoid them otherwise I'd be returned to the cell in short order. Yes, that's what had happened − but why had I heard no sounds of their van? Surely they'd have parked in the yard behind me?

Of course, the mansion rejoiced in triple glazing and thick carpets. Sounds don't carry well and I had not been all that attentive before I'd heard the door, but I'd listened very carefully afterwards and would certainly have heard a van leaving even if it had been at the other side of the house.

Did that mean the door-slammer was still in the house and had been all the time?

Thirty minutes later, I flitted down the stairs, keeping to the extreme left to avoid creaks, turning to the rear of the building, going through the panelled room with the painting of the sheik and into the back where I found the door – which was reinforced by metal – was triple locked, with a lot of connecting cables that would need a major talent to negotiate. Clearly it couldn't be bypassed without a set of keys or security codes. Undoubtedly alarms would explode if the hasps were to be unfastened – and that would almost certainly bring the security guards who had imprisoned me in the first place. For sure I was trapped in the building. And if I knew anything about security that meant all the exterior doors would be similarly sealed. I went back up the stairs to the first room.

Perhaps, that person was a caretaker who would shortly go to the kitchen for food. I left the door open by a handbreadth, pulled a chair over and sat down to watch.

It was nine thirty when I moved away. No one had crossed the hall in two and a half hours, nor had there been sounds from the kitchen or audible activity elsewhere. At the very least, a caretaker should have made an early morning inspection. In the far distance, a phone began to ring. I went downstairs, collected another cleaning cloth, and used it to erase my trail which in daylight was more obvious than ever. When I went back to the room, eating a biscuit, the phone was still ringing. The office was unattended.

Suddenly I was very tired, my gut was sore, the couch was inviting and I lay on its expensive surface, weak and queasy and thought about things. Eventually I fell asleep to wake up about one o'clock. Hungry, I went downstairs for more food. In the distance, another phone rang for a long minute.

But there was a presence in the house, there had to be. From the beginning I'd been vaguely disturbed when the alarms didn't explode at my exit from the tunnel. Clearly the interior security had been switched off.

And it was very unlikely that there really was a caretaker. In so grand a place, there would surely be a rota and a caretaker would be obliged to patrol the building at regular intervals, punching a code into various points along the way. It was unthinkable that there had been no security consultant involved and such people are very strict on the issues of rotas – that's if they'll tolerate the idea of a caretaker at all – in fact they hate the uncertainty of human beings, with their attendant false alarms and lockouts and what can they do that electronics can't do better? What's to stop the caretaker making off with the goodies, or doing a deal with the robbers? No, with such competent electronics built into the system, the human element is redundant. The caretaker is a liability.

So who was I sharing the house with? Who was hiding in the other wing? Clearly that person was not a guest. There were no servants to prepare food, the kitchens were covered in dust. It had to be an insider, someone with clout and someone who could use their weight to use the Prince's facilities.

But why stay in the prison-like environment of a deserted house? Was it possible that he – because it was almost certainly a man – was trapped in the building, unable to breach its formidable security and in as much trouble as I was? Presumably that person didn't like the main kitchen with its Western foods and had a cooking arrangement of his own. I remembered the house in Auchenboggle where my enemy had lived in apparent privation, and I thought I knew who the door slammer was.

It could only be the Snake.

So things had fallen apart. As Lord Jenkins had once pointed out, all politics end in failure and he was no longer with the winning team. With the demise of the old regime he was now of lesser rank than his own servants, possibly deemed to be a criminal by the new administration, with a price on his head. It happens a lot. Certainly he'd been using the Prince's facilities on an epic scale and that would be recorded in a hundred files for all to see. No doubt the ranch in the States had been rescinded – was it possible that it was the real reason for the urgency? He needed the resources of ECZ to pay for its purchase and that opportunity had now passed for ever. No doubt, too, his hyper-efficient security guards were the Prince's. The procession of three cars to the lawyers was a conman's dream and he didn't have the personal facilities to do anything. The whole thing had been a con that didn't work. Now he was isolated from his native land and no longer had diplomatic immunity in the UK, a Wanted Man who couldn't venture into London's streets.

And he was hiding in the same house as me.

In the slow realisation that I was finished, I stared out at the prison-yard below. There had been a certain exhilaration in escaping from the cell and in eating again, even if I'd been unable to taste the food. But that only masked an enormous problem which would now have to be faced. I had no money and no shoes on my feet. For the first time in my life I had no reserves, I had absolutely nothing. Once outside I'd be unable to make a phone call, buy food or shelter and there were no friends to approach. Maybe that was fair enough, I'd had a good life and shouldn't complain. The road, as all roads do, had come to an end, I should be stoical and accept my status without complaint. Different if I'd been young but there were no dependents in my life.

I'd just have to accept my fate. Not much else I could do, trapped in a mansion with my enemy.

55

Two days had passed and despite some aches and pains my health had almost returned to normal and I was beginning to plan for the future, though the uncertainty promised to drive me mad. Several times doors had slammed in the distance though there had been no other signs of my enemy. Perhaps he had a window open, or maybe he was in a fury and, yes, that sounded likely. Undoubtedly no one had approached my part of the building, I'd placed small markers against each of the doors in the entrance hall and none had been moved.

Then I put an eight-inch knife from the kitchen in my belt and went to find him.

This involved a lot of searching.

Over the centuries, the mansion had been extended many times and was now so convoluted that it was a wonder anybody could find their way without a map, though there were discreet signs (in Arabic) in the main parts of the house. It abounded with over-the-top opulence that began to jade my eyes. There were several big rooms with bars in their corners and a ballroom that looked like it had hosted no dances in recent times though it had been well furnished. On the grounds outside, I saw a tennis court and a fair-sized lake. The big rooms were nerve-wracking to enter, most of their doors squeaked, he would hear me coming and it would be easy to overlook him. I climbed stairs to fancy landings that fed bedrooms, games rooms and in one case a twenty seat cinema. One stairway took me to a group of bedrooms that were distinctly less lavish which I approached with caution, well aware that they were a possible danger zone. But their doors were open and there was no sign that anybody had been there for weeks. There was a strange place that might have been a massage room with two Jacuzzis nearby and a convalescent room beside an operating theatre. One stair led to four floors of an ancient tower with several big, empty rooms that hadn't been used by the present management. In another wing I found a swimming pool that had been drained. There was also a sauna and a lot of changing rooms. Then I found a corridor on the ground floor that led to a suite of offices in which a phone was ringing. Beside it there was a room of men's clothes, dark suits in a wide range of sizes, presumably for guests who needed western outfits. On an impulse I threw my rags away – they were caked with plaster – and donned a jacket and trousers after finding a fine shirt. It took a long time to get something that fitted me now that I was a near-skeletal shape. I also got a pair of shoes.

Then I went on with my search.

But I was looking in the wrong places, the slamming door had been further away, loud noises that came from a distant wing. Elsewhere, stairs descended to basements, corridors went off at tangents, but I ignored them. Eventually I found a smaller hallway that was discreetly hidden from the main part of the house and which, after twenty paces, terminated at narrow stairs of bare boards that were well worn and which rose at too steep an angle. For sure it led to the servants' quarters and there would be no opulence there. It was where I'd expect him to be.

The ancient boards promised to squeak like the devil. At one time the US army had recommended their agents to climb narrow stairs backwards, getting each foot as far into the corner as possible for a silent ascent. If the stair is going to creak it's most likely to do so from the middle, not the edge. Unfortunately that also meant they couldn't see their enemy and that wasn't a good idea either. But I adopted it in the hope that the Snake was not on the alert. Unbelievably, I got to the top without a sound.

This was the mean part of the mansion, an uncarpeted landing with cheap doors and worn linoleum. It was in the upper reaches of the house, immediately inside the roof, with a low ceiling that meant the Snake would have to bow his head when he was upright. To my right, there was an ancient bathroom and a sorry kitchen with an old kettle resting on a worktop. Opposite, there were doors to the bedrooms, one closed, the others open. After the wealth, this was poverty and quite possible more people had lived in this small area than in the rest of the house, though for once I couldn't blame the Prince. That accolade would have to go to the English gentry who'd owned it for centuries.

Not moving, I stood for a full two minutes to take stock of the situation.

There wasn't a sound but I could smell a human and surely that meant the Snake was nearby. Slowly, with the blade in hand, I moved across the open doors to see dull rooms that were bereft of all comfort and absolutely empty. Every third room had a small window, the rest were in near darkness. Therefore he was behind the closed door. Several times the floor had squeaked and once a loose board had creaked so loudly that it must have been audible on the floor below.

On the door, some of the panels were loose, it had once been varnished but centuries of neglect had exposed the wood and the poor carpentry. On the floor there were specks of paint that might indicate it had been slammed recently. Ominously, there was a big gap at the bottom that meant he might have heard me.

In silence, I stood for all of five minutes with no stomach for a fight, aware that the immediate future was going to be decisive. I'd nearly starved in the cell and I'd no wish to risk my life again and for sure there was little to be gained from a confrontation with the most untrustworthy man in town. It was tempting to go back and forget him, but that too raised difficulties. Soon he'd come for *me* with a nasty surprise. All the old concepts were redundant. Killing the Snake – and I'd no intention of going that far – would merely reduce one negative while increasing my problems.

Yet the Snake would *have* to be addressed. There could be no cooperation between us, but it was essential to know what was going on. Were we still at war, or was this the time for a truce? I wasn't thinking about forgiving and forgetting, that just wasn't on, but surely the present deadlock altered the ballgame?

Yes something would have to be done, the devil would have to be confronted.

I grabbed the door handle and flung it open to find an unlit room, with one window and a lot of clutter. The bed was nothing more than an unsightly mattress with no linen and no headboard and the Snake was lying on it aiming a handgun at me. He seemed utterly calm and was clothed in the same suit he'd worn to the lawyers though now it was crumpled and unsightly with his trouser legs around his knees and the jacket almost corrugated. His face had an unhealthy pallor, his eyes were bloodshot and his beard had gone ape. It looked like he hadn't eaten for days.

"Get back against that wall," he ordered and his voice was slurred but confident. He was prepared for my visit. "Put your hands on your head."

I did it, letting the knife fall with a bang. The gun – an old one with signs of wear – was one thing I hadn't expected and now I saw how badly I'd miscalculated. Again, he'd been one step ahead of me: the fire power was all on his side.

So this was how it would end – I'd been doomed from the start, but at least the uncertainty was over. I sat down on a rickety chair.

"So you've hit the depths," he said with curled lip.

And what about you? I might have asked. But since it's best to be respectful to the armed man, I said nothing.

"What's going on, why come at me?" he demanded.

There was still a swagger in his voice, a denial of failure and a certainty – despite the epic failure around him – that he was better than everybody else.

"You're a bumpkin," he said, annoyed. "By sheer luck, you've touched the top and made nothing of it. You don't know how to live, your whole life is a mess and now look at you! Back where you belong, an unlamented nobody."

In fact I did feel like lamenting, but I said nothing.

He looked at me, angry at my silence then he glanced at the floor.

"You're a barbarian," he shouted when he spotted the knife, repeating a remark from Auchenboggle when I'd also confronted him with a blade.

"So are you... putting me in a cell without food."

"You look fit for a man who hasn't eaten."

Now the Snake was staring at the knife, a serious weapon with a long serrated edge and a strong handle. His head was almost touching the ceiling, he was too big for the bed and too big for the room. He would have liked to reach down and seize it but that would need an acrobatic sweep that was plainly beyond him and he was wary of me.

"No thanks to you."

"You are a pure mediocrity," he said, flaring up, unable to take any form of criticism. "Why come at me with a knife?"

This was best left unanswered, so I stared at the floor.

"You're a fool, a failure from every angle."

Coming from the Snake, this was rich, but I'm very tolerant of personal criticism.

"You could be right."

During this, he'd been lying on the bed with his feet projecting over the base. His shins were brown and there were sores on his feet which boasted a pair of wooden sandals. Now, with a lot of effort, he raised himself to an upright position, his head touching the ceiling and the gun pointing in all directions as he moved. His hands had a kind of tremor and his eyes seemed unfocussed. Had I been younger I might have rushed him, but that was no longer an option.

"How did you get out the cell?"

The pallor of his face matched the cruelty of his voice and he didn't bother to look at me when he talked. The gun must have belonged to his security team, it looked like it had a history and the safety was off.

"Why, you aren't interested in my well-being?"

"I'm not, but how did you get out?"

"That's my secret."

A spasm of rage crossed his face. He raised the gun and aimed it at my head. Goodbye, I said to myself, but the end didn't come. He lowered it again, his eyes wandering for a moment as he collected his thoughts. Somewhere at the back of his mind he had an agenda, his eyes flickered and a frown crossed his face.

"How did you know I was here?"

About to mention the slamming doors, I hesitated and said nothing. Why deal in trivialities when you reach the end?

He looked down at me, waiting for an answer and then turned away. The gun was still clasped in his right hand but it was no longer aimed in my direction.

"Are you alone?" he said, looking over, and this time there was an anxious wobble. So that was his real worry. Possibly someone had released me and was waiting in the wings to deliver justice. Well, let him worry. I shrugged and said nothing.

"I knew you were free. You have been out of the cell for days – I've been aware of you. I have all my faculties."

Yes that was possible. Maybe he'd heard water running in a cistern or noticed a change in the draught when I opened a door. It also indicated that he'd made no attempt to approach me. A big man like the Snake would have difficulty moving silently and anyway it was beneath his dignity to follow me.

"Why this charade?" I said with curled lip. "Hidden in an attic waiting for your deserts – what's it all about? You're finished."

The Snake put the gun down and stared at the wall for a moment.

"I've been here before and survived." His voice was still defiant, the ego was still there but there was also a recognition that he'd had a setback. "Recovery is a few simple steps away."

I gave a dry laugh.

"Don't mock! I'm abler than you realise."

"What, hiding in a housemaid's room?"

"This is temporary."

"I say its failure."

Outside, a shower of rain began to batter against the window which was rattling in the wind. The room was unheated and I wondered how he, with his Middle Eastern background, could tolerate the cold. Perhaps his anger kept him warm.

"What will happen to the ECZ money now?" he said, his tone changing and his eyes focussing on me.

What a mind-boggling question! Now that we were both destitute it seemed irrelevant beyond words.

"You are still the Chief Executive," he persisted, when I didn't reply.

I shrugged, tempted to tell him to pull the trigger.

"We will go to Zurich and collect it."

On the other side of the bed sat an old bookcase that held his personal effects, including small boxes and notebooks that had lost their binding and were held together by elastic bands – all of it old man's stuff, trivia of the past, remnants of his life and all contained on two shelves. Unsurprisingly there were no photographs of wives, children or friends, possibly there were none, but who am I to talk? His life was summed in these dusty ledgers (though, come to think of it, I didn't even have that solace). On the far left sat a small CCTV screen that revealed the stairs I'd climbed. So he'd seen me coming.

"Zurich?"

The man was deranged.

"I mean it. We could halve the proceeds."

After a few seconds I said with some irony: "You've got the air fare?"

He pointed to the bookcase.

"There's twenty thousand in that case," he said.

Now I recognised it on a lower shelf beside a cash box that probably contained my things. With a bit of luck my E. M. Mertoun passbook would be inside it too, but that seemed irrelevant at this late day. "It is a simple matter."

Simple wasn't the right word, but my head went up. For the first time, I began to see a possibility of survival. Clearly the Snake had been doing a lot of scheming, though I'd no faith in his ability to carry anything out. This was a man who'd spent his entire life in pursuit of money and had failed every time it came within his grasp. His share of ECZ had been available for the asking, but no, he'd gone for the lot and lost everything. He'd no idea how ridiculous he was.

"Simple – you think it's simple?"

"Yes simple." His voice hardened. With his unkempt beard he looked like an old prophet who'd exceeded his forty days in the wilderness. "We'll do it."

I wondered if his head had gone. Did he really believe he could take me to another country at gun point? The gun was almost certainly unlicensed and Customs can be a bit awkward at the best of times. But I wanted to hear more.

"How would you do it?"

Slowly, he raised himself from the bed, towering over me, his head touching a shabby ceiling that looked about to collapse. Again the gun was aimed in my direction, though it did a lot of wavering. At the bookcase, he bent and lifted the case that held the money, putting it on the mattress while he turned to get the cash box. I took my hands from my head, fed up with the stupid posturing and he swung the gun at me, turning slowly like an arthritic old man.

"Don't move! Put your hands back on your head."

I didn't bother; then seeing I was still against the wall, he turned away, opened the cash box and emptied it into the case. I glimpsed my keys and passbook with the Klutza papers attached and regretted how much my life had deteriorated since even Haven House.

"This won't work," I muttered. "It's not possible."

"It isn't possible for a mediocrity like you," he spat, and there was no disguising his contempt. "But *I* can do it."

In the dark shadows, his hand moved as he sealed the case. Yes, the old idiot was going to go ahead.

56

"Now we'll go downstairs," he said, gesturing with the handgun. At that point his voice broke into a falsetto: "Come on – move!"

But I didn't bother. The door was open, it would have been possible to rush out and slide down the stairs, but what's the point? I would still be trapped in the house. And anyway, I wanted to know his plans. Blindly obeying the Snake wasn't a good career move.

"Did you hear me? We will go to Switzerland and collect a fortune. You will be rich again – Move!"

"Really?" I said. "Is it that easy?"

But he was impervious to scorn. His eyes were flashing, his head was higher and he was beginning to look dangerous.

"It's utterly possible. I have a plan. We will both survive. Now rise!"

I looked up. He was his old self again and suddenly I was in awe of him: the Chancellor issuing orders and it was almost impressive. I stood up.

"Carry this."

With his foot, he pushed a case towards me that had been resting on the floor. This one did not contain the money: he'd carry that himself.

"Now go."

So he was as devious as ever, too cunning to give me any insight into his plans and ready to be ruthless in their execution. With a sigh, I made my way out to the landing while his sandals clacked behind me. Then we went down the narrow stairs, on through the hallway and swung to the left, to the office suite. At the door, he paused to produce a hob of keys which he stared at like a myopic pensioner, before selecting one and turning the lock. The door creaked open.

"Get in."

This was the reception area and it had been completely denuded of all the trapping of power which had presumably gone to the Embassy. There was dust and debris on the floor. Then I was ushered into an office that was dominated by a big desk with two phones on its surface. In a corner sat a filing cabinet with all drawers open and empty.

"Give me that case," he said, "and stand against that wall – No sit."

Meekly, I pulled a chair against the wall and sat down. At the desk, he put his glasses on, produced a file from the case and started to read it, looking like a perfect madman in his crumpled suit and unruly beard. His glasses were so strong that he would probably be unable to see much of me. The gun was now lying on the desk beside the keys and he was utterly absorbed in his reading, sometimes holding a paper up to the light and scrutinising it with narrowed eyes, occasionally taking notes. Of course he was a professional civil servant with a lot of experience. He seemed to have forgotten about me. Half an hour drifted past, perhaps more, during which I did a lot of thinking.

When I'd approached him in the attic I'd had little hope for the future. At that point I'd been penniless, locked in a great building, with no prospect of escape. But now there were thousands of pounds and a set of keys resting on the desk within ten feet of me and that was enough to make me raise my head. And for sure my enemy was clearly beatable.

Suddenly the Snake finished reading his papers and swallowed a pill. Next he produced a telephone directory and reached for one of the phones, making slow deliberate movements with his long fingers which trembled as he punched a number. He looked at me for a moment but I was pretending to be asleep, though I was concentrating on him as though my life depended on it. And it did.

"Ah, good morning," he said. "Central Logistics, please..." His voice had become brisk and he spoke like a manager who was rather bored with his work. Certainly he didn't sound like a seventy year old madman. Account numbers were quoted and he was referred to the General Manager, a Mr Smith.

It seemed he'd a consignment for Zurich, an old master, that he wanted over as soon as possible. It was already in a security carton and, for insurance purposes, it would have to be escorted by two men. The hairs on my neck stirred. He'd a plan after all and it might work.

"We'll supply the two escorts," he said. "I wouldn't mind getting it over tomorrow. This house will be empty shortly and we don't want to take any risks. How are you placed? A chartered flight? Well yes I think it needs to be, it's an important oil. How much? Oh that's in order. The account will be settled by our treasury. It's all part of the Prince's estate."

So he was his old self again and it was working a treat with Mr Smith who seemed glad of the business. Even across the room I could detect his enthusiasm. His voice had risen by semitones at the prospect of a chartered flight. No doubt the wheels of commerce always turned for the Prince. Snippets of the conversation drifted over to me.

Mr Smith said there was a plane available and once the flight had been slotted with the aviation people, he'd come back with a departure time.

"Anything between eight in the morning and noon will do," said the Snake, all consideration. "You'll need to send a van to collect it, of course, but no doubt we can arrange these details later."

With my eyes closed, I tried to work it out. My life depended on the fine detail and so far there was none. Clearly, the Snake couldn't force me on to the plane at gun point. Nobody in their senses takes weapons near a modern airport, they'll have you in cuffs in five seconds. Therefore he expected me to board the flight voluntarily and to do that he must have believed he could coerce me. But how?

That's what he'd been scheming about. Getting two men and a painting over to Zurich was comparatively easy. Forcing me into the caboodle was something else and I'd have to be a willing participant.

Then the call over, he put the phone down and stared at me with shrewd eyes. I pretended to come awake when he spoke.

"I've a carton in one of the basements that contains an oil painting. You'll have to carry it up the stairs."

"Why, what's happening?"

For the second time, I listened to his plans which this time differed slightly from the first. We would trim our beards, get smart clothes, and travel in style, he as an art curator and I as a security man. In Zurich we would claim ECZ from Stefan Gill and be rich.

I shook my head in exasperation.

"Won't work, Stefan Gill will smell a rat. He'll refuse to discuss business with you in the room."

But the Snake had an answer to this objection.

"Oh, but we will use some subtlety. You will introduce me as the new owner of ECZ. You will tell him that we have come to a financial arrangement."

"Stefan Gill's too shrewd to believe that –"

"What matter? You are the chief executive. He will have to obey you –"

For sure I'd been desperate to get away from the mansion, but the Snake's companionship was one thing I didn't need. Once ECZ had been dealt with, he'd certainly forget about my half share and Ron Miles would never be heard of again. Yet I had to admire his audacity. Despite certain difficulties, it might actually work.

"How would we get through Customs without passports?"

"Unnecessary – We're part of the crew."

This sounded like blatant nonsense, but I'd an ugly feeling he might be right. Rules get bent all the time and the Swiss would want to accommodate the Prince. Quite possibly consignments got nodded through every day in the week. As an art curator the Snake would probably avoid detection, though modern Customs Officers are sometimes very efficient, and he was a dead ringer for an art curator – so, come to think of it, was I.

He was sitting in his chair, thinking hard and gazing into the far distance, with the gun forgotten, probably wondering how to deal with a wayward lad like me. I noticed that his nose had risen by a few inches. He intended to do it.

"Then how do we get back to the UK?" I persisted. "We *do* need passports."

"We're part of the security detail – the Company looks after that." This was said so convincingly that I almost believed him. "Anyway, you should remain in Switzerland. It's perfectly agreeable. And you'll have plenty of money."

"This is nonsense," I said, though there was a lot to be said for going along with him for the moment. "We must have passports."

For a moment he ruffled in the attaché case before producing a booklet – a passport – which he opened and held up. Even from across the room I could recognise myself, though the details were unreadable at that distance and clearly he didn't want me to see them. I was struck dumb, remembering that the minder had taken my photo before the trip to the lawyers.

"All eventualities are under control," he said. "I am a supreme organiser."

"I'll grant you that."

Then the phone rang. For a moment it looked as if he wouldn't answer it, then an uncertainty crossed his face and he lifted the receiver.

"Mr D'Alfonso, speaking. Ah, hello, Mr Smith. The account's closed! What do you mean closed? We've dealt with you for years without a problem. Yes, yes, the old Prince is dead, but this is part of his estate, the exchequer will honour his commitments. You're being ridiculous! But that will take time, I want it over to Zurich tomorrow. Of course arrangements will be made with the new regime, but I want it there tomorrow."

As stealthily as possible, I slid off the chair. He was engrossed on the phone, white with rage, and completely unaware of me. On all fours I got over to his desk and when he started shouting I rose and grabbed the gun. He slammed the phone down.

"Don't try anything," I said. "I'm making the decisions now."

The Snake seemed to slump in his chair as he stared at me. The balance of power had shifted again and now he was no longer calling the shots.

"And what have you decided to do?"

"For a start I'm not going to Switzerland with you."

He looked at me with monumental contempt.

"You're an idiot. You could have stayed there for the rest of your life. Now you've opted for the mediocre again. You're a fool. And you always will be."

This was a bit of humour from the old booby. It was possible to survive his contempt, but his partnership was another thing altogether.

"You won't be going to Switzerland either. The old Prince is dead and the new one's singing from a different hymn book."

He considered this for a long time and then he looked up.

"I almost agree with that. Now tell me what your plans are."

But that was something I didn't care to disclose: they were vague. For the present, I was locked in a secure mansion with a madman and there was a limit to my options though my mind was buzzing with ideas.

"Get up," I said, but he remained seated. By this time we both knew the routine. Since a corpse was the last thing I wanted, I wouldn't shoot him, and perhaps he was near death anyway. Certainly, he could defy me and there was little I could do about it, though there was the possibility he might have another weapon on his person.

The Snake put his hand to his chin and ruffled his untidy beard, thinking furiously. His long fingers were skinny and unhealthy and his finger nails were long.

"Listen to me carefully," he said, lowering his voice and sounding like a wise old councillor. "We may not be the best of buddies but we have to cooperate. We must both go to Switzerland. We need the money to survive and neither of us can stay in London. I have access to a forty room mansion outside Zurich where we will be out of the way until this business is done."

"Didn't you hear the man?" I mocked. "Your account is closed."

This he dismissed with a wave of his hand. He was ahead of me.

"There's a case full of cash. We may be unable to charter a plane but there's more than enough for one of the regular flights and Mr Smith will be most cooperative, I assure you. Let's do it."

It's at moments like this when a hasty decision can ruin the rest of your life. Of course I didn't trust him for a moment. This was the man who had attempted to starve me to death and there was the question of why he'd waited to this late day to make his proposition. He could have come to my cell any day and I'd have jumped at the chance and now I had other options. And his plan was too facile to be believable, I couldn't pinpoint the flaw, but the whole thing was surely about vengeance. I would certainly be the loser.

"Not on your life," I said. "I don't trust you."

"You are a fool!"

"You're repeating yourself."

He gave a sorrowful sigh at my pitiful insight and said: "You are lost without me. We can be picked up in that backyard and taken straight to the airport. I have documentation that will take us to Zurich."

"I prefer to be lost."

The Snake seemed to think this was unbelievable. Then he went on the huff:

"Then we can't co-exist here. One of us will have to go."

"That's what I'll do," I said.

"You are making a foolish mistake."

"Thank you for your concern," I said, lifting the keys. "I'll go now. I'll take the money with me."

No chance of that of course. This is where it gets nasty. Mr D'Alfonso doesn't part with money lightly, though he'd lost billions in his time.

"No you won't."

"I have the gun."

"So what? I'm keeping the money."

"Some of that is mine."

"It's mine now."

I lunged at the case, grabbing the handle. At that moment he struck me a fierce blow to the head. I don't know with what, perhaps it was a metal ruler or a stick and it was enough to disorientate me for a moment. Even so, I held on, pulling back without letting go as he came at me like a madman, ready to knock my head off with a greater blow. There was only one thing to do, I head-butted him in the belly, forcing him back and over his chair while he roared like a madman, a sound I'd never wanted to hear again. When I looked up, he was lying on the floor, in foetal position, groaning. The room was well-carpeted and I doubted if he was injured, though he was seventy odds and in ill-health.

"Get up," I said.

But he remained on the floor, unmoving.

My head was still stinging from the blow, but my mind was working. I put the gun in my pocket and looked at the keys which had small labels attached. My other hand grasped the case with the money. I was clothed in a new suit and though my beard was unruly, it would attract little attention on the city streets. I'd go to a small hotel in the outskirts and phone Stefan Gill. Arrangements would soon be made and I could spend the rest of my life in Switzerland without having to look over my shoulder. In my gut, I wanted to live and now there was a chance to do it. I walked to the door and paused.

"You've had it now," I declared, suddenly aware that for the first time in years I didn't have to worry about him anymore. "I'm clearing off, I'll leave the keys in the door."